Praise for NICCI FRENCH and the Frieda Klein novels

"**Fabulous**, unsettling, and riveting."
LOUISE PENNY

"Complex . . . Intriguing . . . **Truly unique**."
TAMI HOAG

"Searing . . . In the rich vein of **Kate Atkinson**."
JOSEPH FINDER

"**Unforgettable.** Psychological dynamite."
ALAN BRADLEY

BLUE MONDAY

"Terrific."
New York Times Book Review

TUESDAY'S GONE

"Psychological suspense at its best."
Booklist (starred review)

WAITING FOR WEDNESDAY

"Richly detailed and intricate."
Library Journal (starred review)

FRIDAY ON MY MIND

"Deliciously surprising."
Independent (U.K.)

Sunday Silence

Sunday Silence

NICCI FRENCH

WILLIAM MORROW

An Imprint of HarperCollins*Publishers*

SUNDAY SILENCE. Copyright © 2018 by Joined-Up Writing. All rights reserved.
Printed in the United States of America. No part of this book may be used
or reproduced in any manner whatsoever without written permission except
in the case of brief quotations embodied in critical articles and reviews.
For information, address HarperCollins Publishers,
195 Broadway, New York, NY 10007.

HarperCollins books may be purchased for educational, business, or sales
promotional use. For information, please e-mail the Special Markets Department
at SPsales@harpercollins.com.

Originally published as *Sunday Morning Coming Down* in 2017
by Penguin Random House UK.

FIRST WILLIAM MORROW PAPERBACK PUBLISHED 2018.

Library of Congress Cataloging-in-Publication Data has been applied for.

ISBN 978-0-06-267668-9 (paperback)
ISBN 978-0-06-281984-0 (library edition)

18 19 20 21 22   LSC   10 9 8 7 6 5 4 3 2 1

Glendower. I can call spirits from the vasty deep.
Hotspur. Why, so can I, or so can any man,
But will they come when you do call for them?

William Shakespeare,
Henry IV Part One (Act III, Scene I)

PART ONE

The Body Under the Floor

I

All at once the flat was full of noises. The phone rang, stopped, then rang again. The mobile rattled on the table. The doorbell sounded once, twice, and at the same time there was a thumping sound on the door itself. Detective Chief Inspector Karlsson lifted himself from his chair onto his crutches, moved to the door and opened it.

A very short, very thin woman was looking at him with a frown. Her gingery-brown hair was cut almost to a bristle at the back, but with a long fringe that fell over one eye. She had a narrow, pale face, slightly asymmetrical, with colorless brows and eyes the brown of cinnamon. She was dressed in a black anorak, baggy gray jumper, dark trousers and orange trainers. Behind her the rain was falling. Her face was wet with it. The branches of a plane tree creaked above her.

"I'm Chief Inspector Petra Burge."

She looked too young, Karlsson thought. But then he saw the fine lines around her eyes. And she had a scar on the left side of her head, running from her ear down her neck. "I've heard of you."

Burge didn't seem surprised by that, or flattered. "I've got to take you to a crime scene."

Karlsson gestured at his crutches. "I'm on sick leave."

"It was the commissioner."

"Crawford sent you?"

"He said to tell you that there's a body in Saffron Mews."

"Saffron Mews?"

It was like he'd been punched in the gut. He put out a hand to steady himself. "What's happened?"

"We're going there now. I've got a car."

Burge turned to go but Karlsson reached out and grabbed her sleeve. "Is she dead?"

She shook her head. "It's a man."

A man, Karlsson thought. What man? As if he was observing himself from a distance, he heard himself tell Burge that he would come at once and felt himself turn in the doorway to take up his coat, checking his own ID was in the pocket, sliding his crutches under his armpits, pulling the door closed and smelling the potato in the oven as he did so. It would burn away to nothing. Let it.

He slid into the back of the car, pulling his crutches after him, and saw that someone else was there.

"I'm so, so sorry."

In the darkness, it took him a few moments to recognize Detective Constable Yvette Long. She leaned toward him as if to take his hands. Her hair, usually tied back, was loose, and she was wearing a shapeless jumper and old jeans. There was a sob in her voice.

He held up a hand to stop her talking. His leg hurt and his eyes were sore. He sat quite still and straight and looked at the road streaming toward them out of the wet darkness. "She's alive," he said.

Burge got into the front seat. Beside her a driver was staring straight forward. From behind Karlsson could make out only his cropped hair, his neatly trimmed beard.

Burge twisted around so that she was facing the passengers in the back.

"Aren't we going?" said Karlsson.

"Not yet. What's all this about?"

"I don't know what you mean."

"Commissioner Crawford rings me at home. The commissioner. I've never met him, never even seen him. And he rings me at home, tells me to drop everything, go to a crime scene and head an investigation I've not even heard of. Not only that. On the way I've got to collect a DC I've never met and a DCI who's on sick leave. 'It's Frieda Klein,' he said. 'You've got to watch yourself,' he said. 'It's Frieda Klein.'"

There was a pause.

"So what's your question?" said Karlsson, who was in an agony of impatience.

"What am I getting myself into?"

"If Crawford appointed you personally, then that must show he's heard good things about you. So shouldn't we get to this crime scene?"

"Who's Frieda Klein?"

Karlsson and Yvette Long looked at each other.

"Is that a difficult question?" said Burge.

"She's a psychotherapist," said Karlsson.

"And what's your connection to her?"

Karlsson took a deep breath. "She's been involved in various police investigations."

"As an investigator or a suspect?"

"A bit of both actually," said Yvette.

"That's not fair," said Karlsson.

"Well, it's true. I mean look at—"

"Stop," said Burge. "What I'm asking is: why is the commissioner getting personally involved? That's not how things are done. And then why is he warning me?"

Karlsson and Yvette looked at each other again.

"I've worked with Frieda before," he began.

"We both have," said Yvette.

"Yes, we both have. She's got abilities. Very particular abilities. But some people find her . . ." He paused. What was the right word?

"Incredibly difficult," said Yvette.

"That's putting it a bit strongly."

"She gets people's backs up."

"It's not her fault," said Karlsson. "Not entirely. Is that enough for you?"

Burge nodded at the driver and the car moved forward. "When did you last see her?" she asked.

Karlsson glanced at his watch. "About three hours ago."

Burge looked around sharply. "What?"

"She'd been involved in an investigation."

"What sort of investigation?"

"She was trying to get an innocent person out of a hospital for the criminally insane."

"Which innocent person?"

"It was the Hannah Docherty case."

"The Docherty case? That was Frieda Klein?"

"Yes."

"It didn't go well."

"No."

There was silence for a moment. Karlsson's mind was racing. There were so many questions to ask. "This body," he said. "Is it someone Frieda knows?"

"Why do you ask?" said Burge. "Do you suspect something?"

"Nothing in particular."

No more was said until the car turned away from the traffic of Euston Road and then they saw a haze of flashing blue lights. As the car pulled to the curb, Burge twisted around once more. "Are the two of you here to help her or to help me?"

"Can't we do both?"

"We'll see. At some point maybe you can explain to me why you're employing a psychotherapist on criminal investigations."

"I'm not exactly employing her."

"Don't judge her by your first impression," said Yvette. "Or your second impression, in fact."

Burge shook her head in irritation, then opened her door and walked quickly forward. It took longer for Karlsson to edge his way out of the car and raise himself onto his crutches. Yvette followed him. He could hear her breathing heavily. A crowd of people had already gathered on the pavement, held back by the tapes and by several uniformed police officers. So it was true. All at once, he felt himself growing calm and detached. This was his world. He steadied himself on his crutches and swung rapidly toward the scene. There were flashes of light. The media had already arrived. How did they know? One of them had climbed up onto a wall and was crouched with his camera at the ready.

A young officer was controlling access behind the perimeter. Burge moved quickly past him, flashing her ID. Karlsson felt like an old, sick man, fumbling for his own ID while leaning on one of his crutches. The man took it and began laboriously copying Karlsson's name into his logbook.

"Why didn't you stop *her*?" he said, pointing at Burge.

"She's in charge," the man said. "We were expecting her." Then he looked at his watch and added the time before handing back the ID, then did the same with Yvette's. Karlsson suddenly felt that he was back but not really back.

He was into the mews now, his crutches sliding on the wet cobbles. An ambulance was parked outside the lock-ups, its doors open and a paramedic inside, bending over something. As they made their way toward the house, another ambulance drove into the mews, its lights making the narrow space unfamiliar, pooled with blue, then fading back into darkness. Around him were figures, purposeful but silent. He could see faces at the opposite windows, staring down.

A man stood by the side of the door, leaning against the wall. He was dressed in white overalls, but his hood was pulled back and his face mask hung from his neck. He was smoking, dragging on the cigarette urgently, exhaling, dragging again.

"Where's the SOCO?" asked Burge.

"That's me," said the man.

"What are you doing out here?"

"I needed a minute."

"You're meant to be in there."

The man looked up at Burge and then at her two companions. Even in the light from the cars and the street lamps, they could see that his face was a gray color, sweaty. He looked as if he was going to be sick. "I do robberies mainly," he said. "Crashes. I've never seen anything like this."

Burge looked round at Karlsson and Yvette and grimaced.

"We need to go in," said Yvette, sharply.

The officer led them to the open door of a police van.

Karlsson felt frantic with impatience and dread; he needed the help of Yvette and a crime-scene officer to pull the overalls over his suit and get the plastic shoes on, then the mask and the latex gloves. Yvette tried to support him as he walked toward the door but he pushed her away. He rang the bell, as he had done many times before, and the door was pulled open.

2

Karlsson took a deep breath and stepped inside. He was blinded by the tungsten lights arranged on stands and hit by the smell, like a blow in the face. He had a sudden sense memory. A hot summer, lifting the lid of a plastic rubbish bin where scraps of fish and meat had been left for days, a sweet, rotting gasp of air that made you lurch and gag.

He could see human shapes, white-suited. Burge approached one. She was speaking to the shape but Karlsson couldn't make out the words. The other held a bulky camera. It flashed and flashed again, leaving blue floating swirls in Karlsson's visual field. He had been in this room many times but the walls and ceiling seemed unfamiliar in this laboratory light, every ripple, every line and flaw exposed.

The shapes weren't looking at the walls. They were looking down and Karlsson followed their gaze. This didn't make sense: why were the boards up? Why was the smell so strong, so terrible? Karlsson felt a ripple of dread and then, as he glimpsed what lay in the gash in the floor, a rush of relief that ran through his body, like a pulse of electricity. He leaned on his crutches, utterly confused.

Burge had already told him that it wasn't Frieda, that Frieda Klein wasn't dead. But, still, it felt different to see it for himself. He could hear Yvette saying something next to him, calling him by his name, but he couldn't make out the words. He couldn't think or even feel. He simply stood and let the world come back into focus. Then he made himself examine the scene.

It was all askew and strange. There was no floor. The boards in the center of the room had been removed and piled on one side, haphazardly, not neatly in a pile. Karlsson leaned across and peered down. He could see the beams. Or were they joists? His brain seemed to be working slowly. Keep calm, he told himself. Breathe. Think. This is when your training kicks in. He could see the improbable London soil underneath. Houses are such thin, fragile things, keeping the world out.

There it was, crammed into one of the rectangular spaces. It was the body of a man, but it was somehow all wrong. The eyes were yellow and opaque, staring upwards. The skin on the face was waxy, off-white, stained with patches of blue. The torso was inflated, bulging against the blue shirt, which had dark, oozing patches. There were traces of movement, bloated fat flies, and on the soil around the body, maggots, some coiling in on themselves, some still. Dead, probably. Karlsson didn't want to, but he looked more closely. There was something in one of the hands. It was dried and damaged and it had lost its color. But it was a flower. A daffodil, he thought. Seasonal. It was March. He stared at the terrible face: it was missing both ears. Someone had cut them off.

A figure in a suit was kneeling by the gap, rummaging in a medium-sized white box. Karlsson recognized it. It contained evidence bags, containers for wet and dry evidence. He started to speak and quickly realized that his voice would be nothing more than a mumble. He pulled the mask away from his mouth and suddenly there were more

smells, sicklier, sweeter. Karlsson thought he might vomit.
You're a chief inspector, he told himself. Don't be the one
to throw up over a crime scene. He took a breath and re-
gretted it. "How long has this been here?" he said.

The figure looked up and said something he couldn't
make out. He gestured helplessly.

"Pathologist on his way," said the voice, which sounded
like it might be female.

Karlsson was aware that Burge was beside him. "Where's
Klein?" she said.

The figure pointed away from the room, toward the
back of the house. Karlsson pulled his mask back on against
the terrible smell. He and Burge went through the door
into the kitchen. Frieda Klein was sitting at the table, her
back quite straight. It seemed strange to step from that
scene of destruction and decay and crime into this space of
order, where a pot of basil stood on the windowsill, a cat
was delicately lapping water from a bowl on the floor and
there were orange tulips, not yet fully opened, in an earth-
enware jug. For a moment it felt to Karlsson like a stage set
and behind him was the awfulness of reality. Quite slowly
Frieda turned and looked at the two of them with the alert
dark eyes that had always unnerved him, even when they
were smiling, and now they weren't. Her skin was even
paler than usual. There was something different about her
expression, Karlsson thought. And then he understood:
she didn't recognize him even though he was on his
crutches. He pulled back his hood and tugged off the mask
that was covering his nose and mouth. She gave the faintest smile but said nothing. Burge stepped forward. She introduced herself and then she sat at the kitchen table facing
Frieda.

"Are you able to talk?" she said.

"Yes," said Frieda.

"You'll need to give a full statement but first I need to ask you a few questions. Can you manage that?"

"Can I talk to my friends first?"

"You need to talk to me first."

"All right."

"You seem rather calm," said Burge.

Frieda's eyes seemed to darken. "Is that a problem?"

"A body has been found in your house. Most people would find that distressing, shocking."

"I'm sorry," said Frieda, in a low voice. "I'm not good at putting on a show."

There was a sound from outside and Burge, turning her head, saw that a figure was standing in Frieda's small back-yard in the heavy rain. The end of the cigarette glowed and faded.

"Who's that?"

"A friend of mine. He's called Josef Morozov. He found the body and is a bit shaken."

"How did he come to find it?"

Frieda lifted her hands and gently rubbed her temples. Burge saw that she was just about holding herself together.

"I came back a few hours ago after a difficult day. There was a smell. I didn't know where it was coming from. Josef is a builder. He helps me out sometimes. He came around and took up a floorboard. I thought it would be a rat."

"Do you know who he is?"

"Yes. He's an ex-policeman called Bruce Stringer."

Burge paused for a moment. She barely knew where to start. "Have you any idea who did this? And why they would put the body of an ex-policeman in your house?"

Now it was Frieda's turn to hesitate. Burge saw her look around at Karlsson. He gave her a small nod. "I'm sorry," said Burge. "Am I missing something?"

"All right," said Frieda. "I'll tell you my opinion. I strongly believe that Stringer was killed by a man called Dean Reeve. Have you heard of him?"

"Is this for real?" said Burge.

"It's what I really think, if that's what you mean."

"Everyone has heard of Dean Reeve," said Burge. "He was responsible for a series of abductions and a murder. The problem is that he killed himself more than seven years ago."

Frieda shook her head. "When you go back to your office, you'll find that there's a fat file on me. And one of the things in that file is that I keep trying to tell people that Dean Reeve is still alive and that he's committed other murders."

Burge looked at Karlsson. "Do you believe this?"

"I do," said Karlsson.

"If this is true, then why would he kill this man and why would he go to the trouble of putting the body in your house?"

Frieda wiped her eyes with a hand and took a deep breath, as if she were trying to collect herself. When she spoke it was with a composure that seemed to take an immense effort. "Bruce Stringer was helping me look for Dean Reeve and I think he must have succeeded. And I think Dean Reeve put the body here as a message."

"What message?"

"This is what you get if you look for me."

Burge stood up. "I'll send a car for you. You'll need to make a proper statement. Be careful what you say to anyone. Even your friends. Don't go anywhere. Don't talk to the press. Now I'd better go and look at that file of yours."

She nodded at Karlsson and left the room. He stood his crutches against a work surface and sat at the table, whose surface was clear apart from a glass of water in front of Frieda and another with a finger of whisky in it and the whisky bottle it had come from. He leaned slightly toward her but neither of them spoke. Then she held out a hand and Karlsson took it between both of his. She closed her eyes briefly.

"Why can't you be in charge of the investigation?"

"It wouldn't be right."

The door leading into the backyard opened and Josef came in. His face was dazed with shock. His clothes were sodden and his hair flat against his skull. Karlsson gestured to a chair. Josef looked blindly at him, sat down heavily, then lifted the bottle and filled the glass almost to the brim. He drained it and then tipped more whisky into it.

"I take up the boards." His voice was slightly thick, his brown eyes glowed.

"That must have been . . ." Karlsson stopped. He couldn't think of anything to say that wasn't obvious.

"I have three of the whisky," said Josef. "And now I have three more."

"Is that your van outside?" said Karlsson.

"I bring my tools."

"Maybe take the bus home."

"What happens now?" Frieda asked.

"Someone will come to take swabs. With your permission. They might want your clothes." He looked at Josef. "Yours as well."

Josef emptied his glass again. "Mine?"

"They'll get you some others. And they'll fingerprint you. And take hair samples. And they'll want statements from both of you. It'll take some time."

The door opened and Yvette came in. She pulled off her mask and crossed to Frieda. Her face was blotchy. Karlsson saw there was sweat on her forehead and her upper lip.

When she spoke, her voice was loud with awkwardness and distress. "If you need anyone to talk to about this," she said.

"Thanks."

"I'm probably the last person you'd choose. I'm not good with this sort of thing, but if you . . ."

Yvette was unable to say anything else. Frieda patted her hand as if to comfort her.

Josef held out the glass of whisky to Yvette and she took a large swallow, then coughed violently. Her eyes were watering.

"More?" asked Josef, encouragingly.

She shook her head. "I hate whisky. It gives me a rash." She looked at Karlsson. "The commissioner wants you."

He sighed and pulled his crutches toward him. "I'll see you soon."

Frieda made no reply. Her pale face was blank; she stared at him with her dark, unnerving eyes. He didn't know if she even saw him.

3

"You know what this means, Mal?" Commissioner Crawford's face was florid. He tugged at his collar to loosen it.

Karlsson nodded.

"I was called out of dinner at the Guildhall. Halfway through the bloody salmon *en croûte*."

He took a coffee from the desk and contemplated it. "Could someone get me a fresh coffee?" he shouted, at a person Karlsson couldn't see. "You want one?"

"No, thank you."

"I know what you're thinking."

"Really?"

"And I know what *she*'s thinking."

"Who?"

"Your Frieda Klein must be thinking that she's won. You were right and your beloved Dr. Klein was right."

"I don't believe that's what she's thinking at the moment."

Crawford got up from his desk and looked out of the window. Karlsson swung himself across and stood next to him. There wasn't much to see. Just a police station car park whose high wall was topped with coiled razor wire.

"Did you see the body?"

"Yes."

"It really was under the floorboards?"

"It really was."

"It'll be a big story. The press loves that sort of thing. The corpse under the floor. What do you think Dr. Klein will say?"

"About what?"

Crawford turned his face and frowned. "About *it*. About the case. About me."

"About you?" said Karlsson. "In what sense?"

"I'm the one who stopped the Dean Reeve investigation. I didn't believe her. Now Frieda Klein has me where she wants me. I bet she's laughing about this."

"Commissioner, I can honestly tell you that she's not laughing and that you are not at the forefront of her mind."

Crawford continued speaking as if he hadn't heard what Karlsson had said. "You know the woman. We need to work out how to handle this."

"The way to handle it is to solve the crime."

"Yes, that's right." Crawford took a large white handkerchief out of his pocket, unfolded it, wiped his forehead and replaced it. When he spoke, it was in a mutter, as if he were talking to himself. "I've got someone good on this. Properly good. Did you meet her?"

"Yes, I did."

"A woman. That might balance things up a bit."

"We just need her to be good."

"We do," said Crawford. "I'm fighting for my life here."

Leaving the station half an hour later, Karlsson saw Frieda getting out of the back of a police car. She walked up the steps, an officer beside her. When she stopped beside him, he laid a hand on her arm and it felt as rigid as a piece of wood. She looked at him as if she barely knew who he was.

"I need someone to take care of my cat," she said.

"I'll sort it out."

Frieda was shown into a small room. There was a ficus tree in a pot in the corner. She saw that it needed watering. The window blinds were pulled down, and there was a box of tissues on the table. Like a therapy session, she thought. All those tears. Someone came in with a jug of water and two tumblers. She was asked if she wanted tea, but she didn't. Or coffee? No. Biscuits? She didn't want biscuits either. There was a clock on the wall: the time was ten minutes to twelve.

She took off her long coat and someone hung it on the hook on the door. She sat down on one of the chairs and poured herself a glass of water. Her hands were quite steady, her heartbeat was normal. She could hear the rain outside. The minute hand on the clock jumped forward.

At four minutes to midnight, the door opened and a tall young man stood there. He had broad shoulders, thick dark eyebrows and a nose that looked as if it had been broken sometime in the past and not properly reset. He came further into the room holding three disposable cups of coffee on a tray. Petra Burge was behind him. She slipped a leather backpack off her shoulders and dropped it to the floor.

"This is my colleague, Don Kaminsky. One of these coffees is for you. I can get you milk if you need it."

"I'm all right."

Petra Burge took a sip of her own coffee. "Even burglaries are traumatic," she said. "People feel invaded, violated."

"I've read that."

"And this is a body. Of someone you know."

"That's right."

Petra Burge looked at her through narrowed eyes, then gave a nod. "Are you all right to give an initial statement? I want to get going at once, unless . . ."

"I feel the same," said Frieda.

"Good." She sat opposite Frieda and drew a notepad from her backpack. "Don will take down what you say properly but I might make a few notes as well. Is that OK? At the end, you'll be asked to sign your statement."

"I understand." Frieda took one of the coffees. She was cold to her bones, and its warmth was comforting. "I'll have this after all."

More than two hours later, DCI Burge sat back in her chair. "We're done. You must be exhausted."

"Not really." In fact Frieda's mind felt hard and clear.

"You've had a bad day. You need to sleep."

"I need to walk."

"I think it's still raining. And it's nearly half past two."

"I know."

Petra Burge gazed at her for a few seconds, then looked at her colleague. "Don, go and see who's available."

"Available for what?" asked Frieda, as Don Kaminsky left the room. But Petra Burge didn't answer, just stared intently at the few words she'd written on her notepad, among a succession of doodles. There was a fierce frown on her thin face.

Kaminsky returned with a young female police officer. She had dirty-blond hair, flushed cheeks, a nervous expression. Petra Burge introduced her as PC Fran Bolton. Frieda shook her hand, which was limp, with bitten fingernails.

Even though she was presumably on the night shift, Fran Bolton looked tired and pale, as if she had been kept up past her bedtime.

"Go and change into street clothes, please," the DCI said to her.

The young officer left the room.

"Fran Bolton will be accompanying you."

"I don't need someone accompanying me."

"A body was found under your floor and you believe that it was put there by the murderer Dean Reeve. She will accompany you. If you walk around with a uniformed police officer, you'll attract attention. People will wonder what's up. They'll think you're under arrest or that something's going to happen. Of course, it's a trade-off."

"Dean Reeve wouldn't be put off by a uniform."

The officer returned in dark trousers and a brown corduroy jacket. Frieda had thought of walking down to the river and along the embankment toward the east, then back along the canal. But she didn't think she could subject the young officer to the wind and the rain and hours of walking. And it was difficult to see that she would be much use as protection. She was small and slightly built as well as looking like a schoolgirl on work experience. She had a radio. Perhaps she could call for help. Anyway, the point about walking was to walk alone.

"It's all right. I won't go for a walk."

"I'm going to arrange somewhere for you to stay, just for tonight," said Petra Burge.

"So I can go home tomorrow?"

"Absolutely not. Tomorrow, or perhaps the day after, we'll have something more permanent for you."

"I don't like the sound of that."

Petra Burge put her head to one side, as if she was examining Frieda. "That's how it is going to be."

"I don't need anywhere tonight. I've already arranged that."

"Give me the address. We'll put two officers outside the house."

"Really?"

Petra Burge paused for a moment. "I spend a lot of time like this," she said finally. "Talking to people after there's been a crime, a body found, a house burned down, that sort of thing. Sometimes they're crying or they're angry or scared, or sometimes they just shut down. But you're just . . ." She searched for the word. "Normal. Calm."

Frieda looked at her for a few seconds. "How do *you* react when something terrible happens?"

She raised her eyebrows, considering. "I get fired up."

"I become very calm," said Frieda. "That's what I've found."

"You sound like you're talking about someone else."

"No, I really am talking about me."

In the car, Bolton asked where they were going.

"To a man called Reuben McGill," said Frieda. "He's an old friend. And another friend of mine, Josef Morozov."

"The one who found the body?"

"Yes. He lives with Reuben."

"Oh," said Bolton. "So it's like that."

"No, it's not like that. But I need to explain to you about Reuben. Maybe even warn you." Then she noticed Bolton's apprehensive expression. "He's not dangerous or anything like that. You know that when you train to be a psychoanalyst you have to be in therapy yourself. For three years I was in therapy with Reuben, five days a week. He was important to me and we became friends. Deep down, he's an intelligent, sensitive man. But when you meet him, it's not always immediately obvious. That's all."

4

Although it was three in the morning when the car arrived at Reuben's house, the lights were all on downstairs. Before Frieda could knock at the door, Reuben opened it.

"For fuck's sake, come inside. Come on."

He stepped forward and embraced her. She could smell his scent, the same he had used for decades, the cigarettes he'd been smoking, the wine he'd been drinking, and for a moment she closed her eyes and let herself be hugged.

"It's so late," said Frieda. "You shouldn't have stayed up."

Reuben stared at her. "You're kidding me, right? A dead body under your floorboards and I shouldn't have stayed up?"

"I don't want..." began Frieda, then stopped. She didn't know how the sentence should end.

"Are you all right? Frieda?"

"Yes."

He put his arm around her to lead her into the house, then looked with curiosity at Fran Bolton, who was standing behind her, holding out her ID. "Are you under arrest?"

"My protection," said Frieda. "Are you going to come in?"

"Whatever suits you," she replied. "I can stay in the car."

"Look at her sad little face," said Reuben. "You can't leave her in the cold."

He took his arm away from Frieda and wound it around

the shoulders of an alarmed Fran Bolton and almost pulled her inside. Josef was sitting at the table. Judging from the bottles and glasses scattered in front of him, Frieda assumed he had been continuing with his self-medication. He got up and tottered unsteadily toward her with open arms.

"You are here. We are both here. Life is all. We must for ever . . ." His words petered out. He sat down abruptly on the nearest chair, still holding his arms out.

"I wish people would stop trying to hug me. I just want a shower and a bed for what's left of the night."

"You must be completely exhausted," said Reuben.

"I don't know what I feel."

"Shock," said Fran Bolton. "It does that."

"First, have something to eat," said Reuben.

"No, thank you."

"An omelette. I make a fine omelette nowadays. With chives. Or there's bread and cheese."

"My poppy seed cake," said Josef, trying to get up but failing. "My borscht in the fridge."

"Nothing."

"Sit," said Josef. "There is much to talk about. Much much."

"There are things to talk about and things to do. But not now. I can't. I'm going to bed."

"Hot water bottle," said Josef. "Tea."

"Could you give Fran anything she needs?"

"Any friend of yours can have anything," said Reuben.

She looked at Fran Bolton. "I'll see you in a few hours."

It felt like more than a few hours. Frieda set the alarm on her phone, then lay on the bed in Reuben's spare room with open eyes. She tried not to think, and then she tried to think of slow, heavy waves, flowing in from a dark sea and breaking silently on the shore, but even through the waves she saw that face staring up at her. Perhaps it had been staring up at her for days, under her floor, as she walked unknowingly back and forward across it. She was sleeping and not sleeping, but when the alarm went off it woke her from some sort of clamorous, chaotic dream. She had slept enough to make her feel dull and fuzzy but not enough to refresh her.

She got up, picked up her shoes and padded out of the room. The house was dark except for a faint glow coming from downstairs. She went into the bathroom and tore a new toothbrush from its wrapping. She brushed her teeth, then washed her face in cold water. She looked at herself in the mirror. Where would that person be tonight? Strange to have no idea.

Still shoeless, she crept down the stairs. Fran Bolton was sitting on the sofa in the front room, leafing through a picture book.

"You didn't sleep," said Frieda.

"I'm working. I'm being paid for sitting here."

Frieda rather liked the sour tone in which she said this. "Not any more. We're going for a walk." She laced up her shoes. They left the house and Frieda eased the front door shut quietly.

"Don't worry," said Fran Bolton. "I don't think you'll wake them."

Frieda set off in the direction of Primrose Hill. "Were they as bad as that?"

"They got quite emotional. They were talking about you."

"That doesn't sound good."

"No, it was interesting."

"I don't want to know."

"And Reuben told me he has cancer."

"Yes."

"Is it serious?"

"I'm not sure yet. He only found out a few days ago. It might be."

Frieda stepped up the pace.

"I can call for a car," Fran Bolton said, struggling to keep up.

"It's good to walk."

"Where are we going?"

"Holborn."

"That's miles."

"Yes."

"What for?" said Bolton. "I need to know."

"There's someone I have to talk to about all of this."

"Are they involved in the case?"

"He was the man who put me in touch with Bruce Stringer. I have to tell him. Before I do anything else, I need to talk to him."

"That sounds like he's involved."

Frieda didn't reply. They reached the park and walked down toward the zoo.

"Josef and Reuben, are they, you know . . . ?"

"A couple? No. I mean, they're friends and Josef lives there most of the time."

"What does Josef do? How do you know him?"

Frieda looked around sharply. "You should watch out for Josef."

"I thought he was your friend."

"He's a good friend. But women meet him and they sort of want to mother him and then . . ."

"I don't want to mother him."

"Well, exactly."

They crossed over the canal into Regent's Park, and as they reached the long central avenue, Frieda pointed to a bench and they sat down.

"We need to get something straight," she said. "I suppose you have to report back to your boss about me."

"You make that sound like a bad thing," said Bolton. "I have to file reports on what I do. You must know that."

"Yes, I know that." Frieda thought for a long time. When she spoke, it was as if she was thinking aloud. "I've always tried to stay clear of power. I don't like telling people what to do and I don't like people telling *me* what to do. Do you know what I mean?"

"I'm in the police, so . . ."

"About a year ago, I was in trouble. I was actually under arrest but a man called Walter Levin appeared and made all the trouble go away. He'd actually done a very dangerous thing to me."

"I don't know what you mean."

"He'd done me a favor. I owed him. I did him a favor in return. I looked into the case of a young woman who had been accused of murdering her family."

"Is that the Hannah Docherty case?"

"Yes."

"I'm sorry."

"So am I. And then I asked him if he could help me find Dean Reeve and he put me in touch with Bruce Stringer and now Bruce Stringer is dead."

"Is this man a policeman?"

"No."

"Does he work for the government?"

"I suppose so, but he's always been a bit vague about who he works for."

"Why?" said Fran Bolton. "Why did he do that favor for you?"

Frieda looked at her and smiled. "That's a good question," she said. "You should be a detective. The answer is, I don't know and I should know. He works with an ex-policeman called Jock Keegan and they have an office and an assistant and someone must pay for it but I don't know who."

She stood up and they walked through the park, which was now becoming busier with the runners and dog-walkers and cyclists. Frieda generally found walking with someone else unsatisfactory. She walked as a way of thinking and also as a way of looking at the world, as if she were a spy. With someone else along, it became different. But Fran Bolton was better than many would have been. She didn't seem to need to give a running commentary on what she was seeing and thinking. When they crossed Euston Road, Frieda felt something of a pang, being so close to her home. Would she ever really go back to it? She was not superstitious, and yet she believed that places, whether buildings or cities, were haunted by their past. Could she ever sit in her living room again, rest her bare feet on the floor, feel that the world was being held at bay?

Going home would have meant turning right, but they turned left and walked past the university buildings, down through Queen Square, and Frieda found herself outside the house that only recently she had spent so much time in. That time seemed a world away now.

"I'm going to have to leave you outside," she said. "I promise that if there's anything at all relevant to the investigation, I'll tell DCI Burge."

"That would be a good idea," said Bolton. "But I think DCI Burge might want to talk to him anyway."

"Good luck with that."

The door opened.

"Hello, Jude," said Frieda.

The spiky-haired, brightly dressed young woman had an unusually somber expression. "I wasn't sure you'd come."

"Of course I was going to come."

Levin and Keegan were sitting in chairs in the front room, facing the door, as if she was arriving for an interview. Both were wearing suits, Levin's dark, pinstriped, rumpled and dusty; Keegan's gray, serviceable, making him look like the police detective he had once been. Levin seemed the same as always, with an air of very slight amusement. Keegan's face was entirely expressionless. Frieda sat opposite them. "It's a terrible thing," she said.

"He knew what he was doing." Keegan's tone was even.

"No, he didn't. He didn't know what he was doing or he wouldn't have been killed. And he was doing it for me. So I wanted to come to you and say how sorry I was."

"All right," said Keegan.

"Did he have family?"

"He had a wife and a son of seven years of age and a daughter of four years of age."

Frieda felt a shock that she hadn't felt before, even when Josef had pulled the planks away and revealed the body. "He shouldn't have been doing this."

"It was his job," said Keegan.

There was a long pause.

"How did you hear?" asked Frieda.

"Does it really matter?" Levin's tone was mild.

"I suppose you always know."

"We do what we can." As he spoke, Levin removed his glasses and took a handkerchief from his pocket and breathed on the lenses and polished them, taking his time. "It must have caused a bit of a stir."

"A stir? Yes. It caused a stir."

Levin replaced his glasses and looked at Frieda with an expression that she found difficult to read. "It must have been a terrible shock. And yet you must feel vindicated. In a way."

"I don't know what you mean."

"I mean about the existence of Dean Reeve. For the past several years you have been claiming that he is alive and a danger to the public and you've been disagreed with and mocked and punished for it. Now your detractors will have to face up to the truth."

Frieda took a deep breath. "Some people expect me to be suffering from post-traumatic stress disorder and they want to hug me and comfort me and I find that oppressive. But, no, I haven't yet got around to feeling vindicated."

"Of course." Levin nodded once or twice. "Of course."

"I assume this whole thing must be upsetting for you. After all, you knew him."

"I didn't really know him. He was more an associate of Keegan's."

"But still . . ."

Levin smiled very slightly. "I probably have an unfortunate manner. We're both shocked, of course." He rubbed his head. "I suppose this is going to be particularly embarrassing for Commissioner Crawford."

"What do you mean?"

"He'll have to accept publicly that you were right and he was wrong."

"A man has been murdered," said Frieda, slowly.

"Exactly. That won't look good for him."

Frieda stood up. "There's a police officer outside. My protection. She'll probably be curious. I find it difficult to tell people what exactly you do."

Levin also stood up. "There's no need to say anything, really."

"I mean, you're not a policeman."

"Yes," he said. "I mean, yes, I'm not a policeman. That's a problem with the English language. You can't answer negative questions yes or no."

"You seem to have a problem answering any kind of questions. I used to think you worked for the Home Office."

"Did you? You should have asked."

"I think I did ask."

"Well, the barriers between departments are breaking down nowadays."

"All you're doing is not giving me an answer."

He looked at her genially. His eyes were cool. "Think of me as an enabler."

"An enabler," repeated Frieda. "Is that a sort of consultant?"

"I try to be more helpful than just consulting."

"Enabling."

"When I can."

"That gets me precisely nowhere. I hope you'll help with the inquiry."

"I'll do anything I can. As a concerned citizen."

"I'll see her out." Keegan held the door open for Frieda.

In the hallway, he started to speak, then stopped and walked with Frieda out onto the pavement where Fran Bolton was waiting. Frieda introduced them to each other.

"I'm a colleague," said Keegan.

"Ex-colleague," said Frieda.

He took out his wallet and extracted a card. He turned it over and wrote a number on the back. "You're probably sick of the sight of me. I'm sure the police will solve all this quickly. But if things get more complicated . . ."

He handed her the card.

"Thank you," said Frieda.

"There'll be a funeral."

"Let me know."

Keegan looked at Bolton. "Keep her safe."

Frieda stopped in front of a newsagent's window. "Already," she said.

"What?"

"That." Frieda pointed to the rack of papers.

As far as she could tell, she was on the front page of every single one of them. Her house was there, her face was there, her name. Lurid headlines. *London House of Horror.* She turned her head away.

As they approached Reuben's house they saw a group of people jostling on the pavement, vans parked along the road. For a brief moment, Frieda thought there must have been an accident, and then she understood that she was the accident, the spectacle they had come to see.

"How did they find out where I was?"

"They always find out," said Fran Bolton. "Sometimes before we do. Is there a back way in?"

"No."

"Don't say anything."

"I wasn't going to."

"Not until we've decided what the line's going to be."

"The line?"

Someone in the small mass of people, who had until now been turned toward Reuben's house, noticed them. It was like the wind blowing across a cornfield: in a ripple, they turned. Faces, cameras were looking at them. The knot of people separated and began to move in their direction. Fran Bolton took her arm and was hissing something but Frieda couldn't make it out. She remembered what she had said to Petra Burge the previous day: that she felt detached, as if she was observing herself. Now she watched herself push through the jostle of journalists. They were calling her name. She saw a woman she recognized, smiling pretty Liz Barron who had taken a hostile interest in Frieda over the years; a man with a beaky nose and hot brown eyes who stepped in front of her and was asking her something; another man, middle-aged and overweight, with a beard that ran in a curly border around the lower half of his face.

"Who was it, Frieda?" someone called.

"How are you feeling?"

A blur of voices. She saw Reuben's face at the window. It wasn't fair to put him through this. They reached the little gate.

"It is true you think Dean Reeve's alive?" It was a loud, carrying voice. "Is this to do with Dean Reeve?"

There was a sudden silence, more shocking than the

shouts had been. Frieda stopped, her hand on the latch of the small iron gate. She could feel the fresh excitement behind her, like an electric shimmer in the air. She heard the babble of sound begin again, louder and more urgent, but none of it made any sense to her, only the repeated name of Dean Reeve, which seemed to be growing in strength.

"Now we'll get no rest," said Fran Bolton, grimly, and they pushed open the front door, then closed it behind them, shutting out the sea of hungry faces.

5

Frieda and Reuben sat in Reuben's kitchen, drinking coffee. The blinds were pulled down. Earlier that morning, a photographer had managed to climb a tree on the other side of the garden wall to take photos of Reuben in his embroidered dressing gown.

"I didn't realize it would be like this," said Frieda. "I shouldn't have come."

"Why?" Reuben raised his eyebrows at her. "Because I've got cancer? I like it that you're here."

Frieda turned on her mobile, saw that there were sixty-three missed calls, turned it off again. How did they have her number? There was a loud bang overhead. A curse from Josef.

"Hangover," said Reuben.

Fran put her head around the door. "The car's on its way to take us to your house. Are you ready?"

"Ready."

Although the rain had stopped, the cobbles were dark and wet. There was a cluster of reporters at the entrance to the mews and camera lights flashed as they drove past. A single unmarked car was parked outside Frieda's house, and a tape stretched across the entrance. A man in green scrubs let them in and handed them plastic overshoes, which they pulled on. Frieda was used to the particular smell of her house: the wood of the floorboards and its beeswax polish, sometimes herbs that stood along the sill of the kitchen window, and also a dry but pleasant smell she had come to associate with old books, charcoal pencils, chess pieces, toast. Now the smell was of astringent chemicals and, underneath that, perhaps there was something else, something that had soaked through into the foundations. She stood for a moment, steadying herself.

The room where she usually sat beside the fire or played through games of chess was harshly lit by the lamp that had been rigged up by the forensic team. There were two people in there, one taking photographs. Frieda looked through the yellow glare to the pit where just yesterday Bruce Stringer had lain. Everything was gone, of course. Even the maggots and flies had gone. It was just a hole. The room was just a room—the rugs removed, the furniture pushed back—but it no longer felt like her room. She turned and went into the kitchen.

"What happened to the cat?" she asked the man in green scrubs.

"Is there a cat?"

"Yes."

"It's not here now."

Frieda went upstairs. Everything looked much the same but she could sense that someone had been in here too. Nothing felt like it belonged to her any more. Quickly, she pulled clothes from drawers and pushed them into a canvas holdall; then a couple of books and some toiletries. She went upstairs to her study in the garret and put her sketchbook and pencils in as well. She didn't know how long she would be away. Living here was a remote memory of a different self. Another life. She imagined Dean Reeve moving softly through her rooms, rifling through her clothes, turning the pages of her sketchbook, bending to stroke her cat. Where was her cat?

"What have you got?" Commissioner Crawford asked Petra Burge.

"It's early days."

"Early days are the important ones."

"The autopsy's being done now, but Ian thought he must have been dead four or five days. The crime-scene guys are certain he was killed elsewhere and put there. I've got people talking to the neighbors and going through CCTV footage."

"What about Reeve?" Crawford's face tightened in a sour grimace as he said the name. "Assuming that Dr. Klein's suspicions are valid. Where are we with him?"

"There are obvious problems with looking for someone who basically disappeared and was presumed dead almost eight years ago. Frieda Klein always believed he was still alive but she never met him, never even saw him. But two associates of Klein actually claim to have met him. Josef Morozov is a Ukrainian builder. I don't quite know what his connection with Klein is."

"Sexual, probably," said Crawford.

"I'm not sure about that. Everything about him seems a bit murky, including his immigration status. He came across Reeve on a building site."

"Knowingly?"

"No. Reeve was working under an alias. And Klein has a sister-in-law. Olivia Klein used to be married to Klein's brother. Olivia met Reeve in a social setting. She was quite vague about it. Got talking in a bar."

Crawford fidgeted irritably. "What's this about? What's Reeve doing?"

"It's all about Frieda Klein. Somehow when they encountered each other, she got under his skin."

"Well, I understand that. She got under mine as well. She's been a bloody irritation from beginning to end. But what does he want? What does he want to do?"

"It's not clear. As yet."

"What about the widow?"

"I talked to Mrs. Stringer this morning."

"And?"

"She's distraught, obviously. She's in a wheelchair. She has MS and apparently he was her caretaker for several years. They have two small children."

"That's all we need."

"She didn't seem to have any real idea about her husband's work. Officers are at his house now, going through things."

"And that's all?"

"We should think about how to deal with the press." Crawford groaned but she persevered. "They could be useful. I wonder if we should get Frieda Klein to do a few interviews."

Crawford muttered something.

"What do you think?"

"You never quite know what she'll say." He winced and leaned forward. "Is she safe?"

"She's under twenty-four-hour protection."

"I mean, that under-the-floor business, it's like he's play-

ing with us. If he were to do something, something else, it
wouldn't look good."

"No, it wouldn't," said Burge.

"I've given you a high-profile case."

"Yes."

"A case like this, it can make a career," said Crawford.
"Or, well, you know."

"I know."

Darkness fell and the wind strengthened, bringing more
rain. On the road outside Reuben's house, the group of
journalists became a huddle, with light glowing from cigarettes and mobile phones. Frieda made scrambled eggs,
Reuben opened a bottle of red wine. PC Kelman, Fran's
replacement, produced a hefty sandwich from his bag and
sat in the hall to eat it. He was a solidly built young man,
who cracked his knuckles when he talked.

All of a sudden, there was a noise.

"What was that?"

"It sounds like shouting," said Frieda, laying down her
fork.

The sound grew louder.

"I recognize that voice." She stood up.

"I don't think you should go out there," said the officer,
as Frieda swept past him in the hall.

She pulled open the door and saw a throng of figures on
the pavement outside Reuben's gate, and an officer trying
to hold them back. Cameras were flashing. Several micro-
phones were held out. In the middle of the crowd stood a
young woman in a red duffel coat and stout black boots,
her head shaved along one side and her eyes fierce: Frieda's
niece, Chloë.

"Leave her alone!" she was yelling. "Go away, all of you." She turned on the man with the beaky nose, whom Frieda had noticed earlier. "Fuck off!" she yelled, into his surprised face.

Frieda saw now that she was holding a box and the box was moving, lurching dangerously. Chloë clutched it as a shape butted through the lid. Her cat, its fur standing up on the back of its neck and its mouth open in a soundless yowl.

Frieda stepped forward and the group swivelled as if with one mind toward her. She put a hand on the cat's head and pushed it back into the box.

"Come on," she said to Chloë.

"Tell us about Dean Reeve!"

"Is it true he's alive?"

"Give us something, Frieda, and then we'll go."

"I have nothing to say. Except that up the road and to the left there's a warm café, and a few doors further on the Ram's Head does quite good food. There's nothing for you here."

She took her niece's arm and pulled her away from the group. Kelman ushered them back into the hall. Chloë looked at the officer suspiciously and he looked suspiciously back at Chloë.

"This is one of the people who're protecting me," said Frieda. "Protecting all of us, in fact."

Chloë gave a grunt.

"And this is my niece," Frieda continued. "Who drifts in and out of my life."

"What she means," said Chloë, "is that I get in touch with Frieda when I'm in trouble. And sometimes she gets in touch with me when *she's* in trouble. And, as you know,

Frieda gets in even worse trouble than I do, which is saying something."

"What sort of trouble?" Kelman asked.

"We don't need to talk about that now," said Frieda, and she bent and lifted the cat from the box. It stood in the hall, its fur bristling and yellow eyes glowing.

6

The following morning, Frieda and Petra stood in the flat that was to be her temporary home. The red-brick mansion itself felt heavy and grim; the furniture was like something from an old lodging house, a couple of battered armchairs, a dark wooden coffee table. On the wall was an engraving of old London and a plate with a scene labeled "Margate 1922." The carpets were dark red, like in the corridors of a corporate hotel. But the light coming in through the large windows in the sitting room was so bright that Frieda was dazzled for a moment. She looked out across Parliament Hill Fields, at the lido and the railway and the running track and, to the right, Parliament Hill itself.

"Nice view," said Petra Burge.

"Impossible for a cat, though."

"Can your friends look after it?"

"What I really want is to be back in my own house."

"When it's safe. You're talking to the journalists at ten tomorrow. Meet me at nine thirty. We'll need to prep you."

"Prep me for what?"

"I've read your file. I've read the cuttings. I know you hate publicity. I know you've been stitched up before. But this is different. We're initiating this, you and me, and we have to make it work for us."

"What does that mean?"

"They're going to write something. That's what they're here for. If you're nonresponsive or bad tempered or sarcastic that will become the story. Remember: there is no such thing as a stupid or offensive question. What there is, is an opportunity for you to put your point across."

"I'll try to remember that."

"Do. You want to create a narrative where you're the sympathetic one, where readers care about you and people will want to help you and try to remember things they may have seen, people they may suspect."

There was absolutely nothing funny about any of this, but even so Frieda couldn't stop herself smiling. "You want me to create a narrative?"

"Yes."

Frieda shook her head. "Sometimes I wish therapy had never been invented."

Josef came around with a cauldron of butternut squash soup and some honey cakes, enough for a large, hungry family. Frieda looked at his anxious brown eyes and ate a cake to please him, though she wasn't hungry. He ate several and drank three mugs of tea. He told her that when he was a boy his mother would make honey cakes every Sunday; the smell would fill the house. He pulled out his phone and showed her the latest photographs of his sons. The eldest, Dima, was tall and quite bulky but the youngest, Alexei, was still small and slight, and his soulful gaze was so like his father's that Frieda gave a laugh of surprise. "You must miss them," she said.

"Sometimes it hurts," he said. "My boys."

"It must."

He laid a broad hand across his chest. "But I carry them here."

DC Yvette Long came around with a bottle of white wine and a look of furious awkwardness on her face.

"Has something happened?" Frieda asked.

"Why does something have to have happened? If it's a bad time, just say so and I'll go away. I know that you mainly meet me when I'm trailing after Karlsson. You can take the bottle of wine anyway." Her words had come out in a flood.

"It *is* a bad time," said Frieda, then felt guilty. "But I'm glad to see you."

"You don't have to say that. I wasn't asking for a compliment."

"Oh, stop it, or I really will tell you to go away." Frieda opened the bottle and poured two glasses.

"You didn't have to open it now," said Yvette.

"Too late," said Frieda, and handed one of the glasses to her. They clinked. "I wish you were on the case," said Frieda. "You and Karlsson."

"There are rules. Emotional involvement and things like that."

"Are you emotionally involved?" asked Frieda, with a smile.

Yvette blushed. Frieda had never met anyone who blushed as often as Yvette.

"I just meant that Karlsson is a friend of yours and I work with Karlsson. And he's on sick leave. And I'm on another case anyway."

Frieda sipped at her drink. So why was Yvette here?

When Yvette spoke it was almost as if she were responding to Frieda's silent question. "I know you're going to talk to the press." She stopped abruptly.

"Yes. Petra Burge thought it might be helpful."

"I've written down a few things."

"Oh?"

"That could be useful. I mean, they might not be. Or you might think they're obvious. Or stupid. But I wrote them down anyway. In case."

"That's kind."

Frieda watched as Yvette searched through her bag, rummaging furiously and finding nothing. She patted her pockets and produced a piece of bent card.

"Here."

She passed over the card; Frieda unbent it. There was a list, in block capitals and marked with bullet points, of the things that she should and shouldn't do.

- WEAR PLAIN CLOTHES.
- TALK SLOWLY AND IN FULL SENTENCES.
- ONLY ANSWER THE QUESTIONS YOU ARE ASKED.
- DRINK WATER BEFORE YOU ANSWER A QUESTION TO GIVE YOURSELF TIME.
- DO NOT WEAR LOTS OF MAKEUP.
- DO NOT WEAR LOTS OF JEWELRY.
- DO NOT SMILE A LOT, OR LAUGH BECAUSE YOU ARE NERVOUS.
- DO NOT WAVE YOUR HANDS ABOUT.
- REMEMBER NOT TO SAY ANYTHING YOU WOULDN'T WANT TO SEE QUOTED.

"Thank you," said Frieda. "I'll try to remember all of that."

"And I was wondering how you were," Yvette said. "After finding that."

"Thoughtful."

"I dreamed about it," said Yvette. "I should be used to crime scenes, but that one stuck with me."

"What did you dream?"

"Just being there," said Yvette. "And seeing that body. Except it was in my own flat instead of yours."

"I'm sorry."

"I've been asked to sit the exams for promotion."

"That's good," said Frieda. "You deserve it."

"I don't know. Sometimes I'm not sure I'm cut out for this."

7

At ten the next morning, Frieda was shown into a room where the journalists were waiting for her, sitting in a row on a long leather sofa. In front of them was a low glass table. On top of it were three cups of coffee and three phones, set to record. When she came in, the press officer in front of her and Petra Burge behind, they all scrambled to their feet and for a brief moment, Frieda recoiled with an instinctive distaste. She saw on all three faces a greedy curiosity. They were looking at her as if she were an object, a specimen. She knew that they were taking in what she was wearing, how she appeared, how she carried herself, her manner, her voice, her expression. They wanted her to display emotion, frailty and damage. She nodded curtly at them all.

"This is Gary Hillier," said the communications officer. "From the *Chronicle*."

Hillier put out his large hand and she took it. He held hers for longer than was necessary and stared at her. His face was jowly; his goatee and round, wire-rimmed glasses seemed inappropriately small, as did his rosebud mouth. He was wearing a sports jacket, and black trousers that were too tight for him; his stomach bulged over the waistband. Nothing about him seemed to fit quite together. But his small blue eyes were shrewd. He started to say something about trauma and shock.

Frieda removed her hand from his and turned to Liz Barron. "We've met before," Frieda said, as the press officer started to introduce her.

"Oh, yes, Frieda and I are old friends," said Liz Barron, brightly. She too took Frieda's hand to shake. Her teeth gleamed; her turquoise jacket glowed. She had a sprinkling of freckles on the bridge of her nose. Frieda remembered crossing the road to avoid her, closing her front door in her face. "I'm still on the *Daily News*. You must be feeling completely dreadful. It's unreal." She shook her head; her glossy hair swung. "Just unreal."

"Unfortunately not," said Frieda. From the corner of her eye she saw Petra Burge frown at her.

Daniel Blackstock, who covered crime for a news agency representing local papers, seemed to be dressed for a different occasion, almost a different profession. He was wearing a checked blue shirt with a white T-shirt underneath and a rough denim work jacket on top. Frieda recognized him as one of the reporters from outside her house, the beaky-nosed man Chloë had yelled at. He wiped his palm down his trousers before shaking her hand and said he was honored to be interviewing her. He seemed nervous, perhaps a bit out of his depth.

They all sat down again. Frieda sat opposite them in a springy black office chair. Petra Burge was seated by the wall and beside the woman from the press office, who was holding her own phone to record what was said.

"Before anything else," said Liz Barron, "can you tell us in your own words how you *felt* when you discovered the body?"

"My feelings were about Bruce Stringer. Later I felt distressed for his family."

"But it was in your house!" said Liz Barron. "In your living room! Under the floor!" With each exclamation she leaned further forward. "You must have been in shock. Perhaps you are traumatized. You know, post-traumatic stress disorder. Like soldiers get after battle. It would make sense."

"I'm not traumatized," said Frieda. "Perhaps I was in shock. A man was killed. That is a shocking thing."

"If it was me, I'd probably be hysterical. Yet you seem so calm and collected now. Almost detached. Is that what you were like at the time?"

"I don't know what I was like at the time."

Liz Barron scribbled something in her notebook. She looked dissatisfied; Frieda could imagine how she was going to describe her.

"Can I ask," said Gary Hillier, "about why this has happened?"

She turned to him with relief. "Yes. That's why I'm here."

"There have been rumors."

"You probably know what I'm about to say." She watched as they leaned forward, waiting. "You have all heard of Dean Reeve and I assume that you know about my connection with him."

They nodded.

"Dean Reeve was thought to be dead, but for a long time now I have known him to be still alive." In as calm a manner as she could manage, she told them everything she knew: how he had murdered his identical twin and thus escaped, how he had reappeared over the years, stalking her, protecting her, avenging her, watching over her. It took her several minutes. She looked at their faces as they listened, avid, perhaps incredulous.

"So he loves you?" said Liz Barron when she came to an end. "You're saying Dean Reeve is in love with you?"

"I'm saying he's obsessed. I'm the one who uncovered him in the first place. Now he wants to have power over me."

"That's a strange way of showing it," said Liz Barron.

"I think he was sending me a message."

"What message?" asked Daniel Blackstock. It was the first time he had spoken. His expression was slightly dazed. He squinted at her.

"Bruce Stringer was trying to find Dean Reeve for me."

"So everyone thought he was dead," said Gary Hillier. "Apart from you."

"He wanted to disappear," she said.

"But now he's back," said Blackstock.

"Yes."

"There are some very serious questions here about the police," said Gary Hillier. He turned to Petra Burge. "Can I ask you for your comments on that, please?"

"You're here to interview Dr. Klein."

"All right," said Hillier. "I'll ask Dr. Klein. Is it true that the police authorities refused to accept that Reeve was still alive?"

"I am not here to criticize the police," said Frieda. "I am here to say what I know. Maybe one of your readers knows something or suspects something."

"I want to get at the real Frieda Klein," said Liz Barron.

Very slowly, Frieda reached for a glass of water, took a sip from it and remembered that she was following Yvette's advice. She needed to stop herself saying something that would be unhelpful.

"I'll do my best to answer any question," she said finally, in a slightly strangled tone.

"Your private life and your public life have a way of getting mixed up, don't they?"

"I don't have a public life," said Frieda.

"Your boyfriend was murdered. Tragically murdered. And you were briefly a suspect. You were actually a fugitive."

"That had nothing to do with Dean Reeve," said Frieda.

"But my readers will want to know about the darkness and violence at the heart of your life."

Frieda glanced around at Petra Burge, who gave a little nod, signaling encouragement or warning. "That's a bit dramatic."

"You've been almost murdered by a schizophrenic, who was then herself murdered, possibly by you."

"Not in fact by me."

"You've been involved in other stabbings and killings."

"If you ask a question, then I'll try to answer it."

"Dean Reeve is a man of violence. Would you say?"

"Yes, I would say that."

"Do you think there is something about you, a beautiful woman attracted to darkness and violence"—at that point Frieda closed her eyes and imagined a newspaper headline—"do you think Dean Reeve somehow finds that fascinating or even attractive? After all, you're a psychiatrist. You're an expert in people's dark sides."

Frieda opened her eyes. "There are psychiatrists who are interested in violence and evil but I'm not one of them. I'm a therapist and I deal with ordinary unhappiness. I don't have any big theory about Dean Reeve. At a certain point in his life, I just got in the way."

Gary Hillier raised his hand. Frieda nodded at him. "What would you say to women about the lessons they should draw from your experiences?"

The interview continued for an hour and Frieda was asked about her childhood, about whether she was single, about whether she wanted children, about her views on depression, about her exercise routine ("I walk," she said). At one point she interrupted a complicated question by Daniel Blackstock to ask if she could say something.

"Is there a problem?" asked Hillier. He was looking at her intently, in a way that Frieda didn't like.

"What we all want, I assume," said Frieda, "is to catch a murderer. I just hope that you'll all say that."

"That goes without saying," said Liz Barron.

"I think the things that go without saying often need saying."

"On that subject," Barron continued, "do you think you have a reputation for being a difficult woman?"

The press officer stood up and coughed and said maybe she should draw proceedings to a close.

"Is it all right if I have a photo with you?" Liz Barron asked.

Frieda was so surprised that she couldn't speak but the press officer said of course, and came over and took Liz Barron's phone, and then Gary Hillier and Daniel Blackstock wanted a photograph as well and then they had a group photograph. Frieda felt as if she were in a strange dream that involved being at a terrible party she couldn't leave. But finally it was over. Once the journalists were gone, Frieda looked across at Petra Burge. "Enough?" she said.

"Just about."

The next morning, the pieces appeared. She glanced at them online, but couldn't bring herself to read them. Liz Barron had called her an "ice queen" and had said she was locked in a "dance of death" with Dean Reeve. She had talked to the psychological profiler Hal Bradshaw, who said that in his extensive experience of Dr. Klein she showed the danger of being a celebrity psychotherapist. Crime-solving was a science, he had said, not an appearance on a talent show. Gary Hillier called her "impressive" and Daniel Blackstock called her "bleak." There were pages of photographs—of her, of Dean Reeve, of her with friends and family, photos that she hadn't even known existed. Where had they got them from? The phone rang so often—how did they all have her number?—that she turned it to silent. Texts pinged onto the screen. Her email inbox filled up with messages. Would she speak on this program, give an interview for that one, write her own account, provide a comment at least for a dozen newspapers. She deleted all the requests but they kept on coming.

She left the flat early with Fran Bolton, walking out on to Hampstead Heath in the cold wind and the rain, then through Primrose Hill and Regent's Park in silence. They arrived at her consulting room and Bolton said she would stay outside. Frieda walked to the window and looked out at the vast building site, where the miniature figures of men in hard hats drove diggers across the cratered space. She collected the files she had wanted, and the telephone numbers of patients she would have to call to cancel their appointments, but she didn't leave at once. Instead, she sat for a while in her red chair, her hands on the armrests, looking across at the empty chair opposite. When would she see patients again? When would she return to her old life, her old self?

8

The police car turned into Saffron Mews, as it did every morning at around eleven. Two female officers got out and let themselves into Frieda's house. One of them picked up the bundle of mail on the mat.

"So, are you going to see him again?"

"I'm waiting for him to get in touch."

"But do you like him?"

They put the mail on the table.

"I don't know what we're meant to be looking for."

"If one of them starts ticking, we'll make a run for it."

"That's not funny. Anyway, it's just the same as every day. Bills and junk and . . ." She stopped and held up an envelope. Frieda's name and the address were written in a large childlike script. "Think we should call someone?"

"This is a letter addressed to you."

Petra picked up a transparent plastic evidence bag and dangled it in front of Frieda.

"Why have you got it?"

"We're checking your mail, obviously, and we want your permission to open it."

"Do you need it?"

"It's a gray area."

"Go ahead."

Petra Burge took latex gloves from her pocket and removed the envelope from the bag. With great concentration she cut the envelope open along the bottom edge and removed a single folded piece of paper. She opened it and smoothed it flat. She read it, then rotated it. Frieda leaned over:

4 Bush Terrace

Dear Frieda,
That's what you get for coming after me.

Daniel Glasher

"Friend of yours?" said Petra.

"No."

"Then who is he?"

"Give me a moment." She took out her phone and rang Josef.

"Frieda?"

"Do you know Daniel Glasher?" There was a pause so long that Frieda thought they'd been cut off. "Hello? Josef?"

"Danny. Yes. I work with him. Not now. Before."

"Was he the one who met Dean Reeve?"

"Yes. I tell you before."

"Have you talked to him recently?"

"He move away. What has happened?"

"I'll tell you when I know." Frieda put the phone back in her pocket. "Dean worked with Josef in Hampstead, a big house that was gutted and rebuilt. This man, Danny Glasher, was there as well. He's an electrician, and he was the one who apparently gave Bruce Stringer helpful information, just before Stringer was murdered."

"Why would this electrician threaten you?"

"He's not threatening me."

"What do you mean?"

"You can even see it in the writing. Look at the 'B' in Bush. Look at it all, the shakiness of it, the trembling. He wrote out the words, but they weren't his. Dean Reeve dictated that letter."

Petra Burge frowned and looked at it more closely. "That doesn't make sense. Why would Reeve show himself like that?"

"Because it doesn't matter."

"And if you're writing a threatening letter, why put an address on it?"

"Because he wants me—or you—to go there."

"You think it's some sort of trap?"

"No."

"I'll find this Bush Terrace and take a team there now."

"Can I come?"

Petra looked at her with disapproval. "This isn't an Open Day."

Bush Terrace was on an estate in Brent that was only forty years old but already looked as if it had been prepared for demolition. Half of the houses were boarded up. The police officers arrived in two cars and a van, blocking off the entrance to the street and approaching the house—armed, helmeted—in a wary formation. Three of the officers carried a heavy steel ram.

Petra Burge rang the bell. There was no reply. She nodded and the officers swung the battering ram, which went right through the flimsy front door. One of them kicked away the splintered wood. They ran inside, boots rattling on the linoleum, then soft on the fitted carpet. Officers disappeared into different rooms and there were shouts of "Clear."

She walked through to the kitchen. The house looked like a slum. The walls were damaged; a broken window had been covered with cardboard but it was neat. The ill-matched cups and plates and glasses had been washed up and neatly arranged on the draining board. The tap was dripping irritatingly. Petra Burge put out her hand to turn it off, then thought better of it.

She felt a hand on her shoulder and looked around. An officer had pulled off his helmet. His face was white. "There's something you should see. It's in the garage."

She was led through the house into the garage that filled half of the ground floor. There was no car. At the back was a chest freezer, open, humming. She walked across to it. It was filled with bulky, heavy-duty plastic sheeting, but through it she could see a face, looking up.

Frieda was in Olivia's kitchen, drinking tea. Chloë had just left after a heated exchange with her mother, but Frieda's friend Sasha was with her, Ethan on her lap, dreamily fiddling with her collar. Sasha had just finished telling Frieda that she and her son were going to be living with her father for the next six months, while she put her life in some kind of order. Fran Bolton was in the living room. Frieda could hear Olivia moving furniture around upstairs. Outside, the hard, cold rain fell; the light was dim as dusk. She longed to be in her little house, beside the fire, just her cat for company.

Her mobile rang and she saw it was Petra. "Hello."

"He's come into the open. We'll get him now."

PART TWO
The Lost Weekend

9

Frieda opened the kitchen door and stepped out into the yard. The day was warm and windless; the cat lay in a pool of sunlight, its tail twitching in its dreams. It hadn't rained for weeks. She turned back to look at the house, which very slowly was beginning to feel like her home once more. Josef had painted every room, accepting only vodka as payment. He had laid a whole new floor in her living room, and she'd bought a richly patterned rug to put over the place where Stringer's corpse had lain.

She heard water running in the bathroom and went back indoors and up the stairs.

"Are you OK?" she called through the door.

"No, I'm fucking not."

"Do you need any help?"

"No."

"Can I come in?"

"If you want."

Frieda pushed the door open. Reuben was bent over the sink, splashing water on his face and then his bald, shockingly white skull. "Were you very sick?" she asked him. She was still taken aback by how much he had changed in the last months. His face was thin and slack; his lovely thick hair, the hair he used to be so proud of, wearing it over his collar like a student, was all gone. He looked smaller and older; his beautiful clothes hung off him.

"Yes."

"Let's go downstairs. I have to go very soon to this meeting, but I'll make you some tea. I've ordered you a cab to take you home."

"I hate bloody tea. Strong black coffee." He glared at her. "And maybe a cigarette."

"When you've just been sick?"

"Exactly."

"All right. I suppose you and Josef will soon be back to your old habits."

He frowned. "I haven't heard from him for days. He's not returning calls. Maybe he thinks I'm infectious."

"He's probably on a job."

Reuben descended the stairs slowly, theatrically, an ill man playing at being an ill man. He raised his eyebrows to Frieda as he passed, and in a flash she remembered him as he'd been when they'd first met—so raffish and handsome and young.

Half an hour later, Frieda arrived at the police station and was shown into a large room whose Venetian blinds were all closed against the sun. She had become familiar with this room, and rooms like it, over the months: the long table, the jug of water, the high metal trolley pushed into one corner with teacups on it, a small pile of plates. Overheated in the winter and in the summer, close and with a smell of air freshener and furniture polish.

Several officers she recognized were already there, pulling out chairs. DC Don Kaminsky was among them, tall and bulky. He looked awkward when he saw her and made a show of being busy, emphatically pushing papers into a folder, intently scrutinizing his phone, making strange grimaces. She saw that Fran Bolton was also there, in the corner. When she met Frieda's eye, she gave a small wave. Frieda took a seat and sat in silence, waiting for what she already knew was to come.

She didn't have to wait long. The door swung open and Petra Burge came into the room, small and thin, dressed in baggy black trousers and a loose-fitting blue T-shirt that made her look like she'd borrowed the clothes from an older sister. Her face was pale, the freckles blotchy. She was followed by several men in suits, who looked grim and serious, and behind them all Commissioner Crawford. He didn't glance at Frieda, or at anyone, but sat at the far end of the table. Someone asked him if he'd like any water but he simply shook his head. Frieda saw his jaw muscles clench and unclench. He seemed broader and pinker than ever, his sparse hair cut to stubble and his cheeks freshly shaved. There was a tiny spot of blood near his ear, where he must have cut himself. He wouldn't like it if he knew that she was pitying him.

When they were all seated, an uneasy silence fell over the room. Petra Burge gazed around the table. She met Frieda's gaze but didn't smile. She started to speak but was immediately interrupted by the sound of the door opening. Frieda looked around and saw Karlsson and Yvette Long walking in. They were both out of breath.

"Are we late?" Karlsson said.

They pulled up chairs and sat beside Frieda.

"I didn't know you were coming," said Frieda.

"Neither did I." Petra didn't seem glad to see them.

"We thought you might need some support." Karlsson poured himself a glass of water.

"It's like coming to watch a bullfight," said Crawford.

"Who's the bull?" asked Karlsson.

"You'll see."

Frieda noticed that the commissioner was speaking more quietly than usual. He seemed tired.

"Are we ready to start?" Petra looked around and the room fell silent. "Six months ago, Bruce Stringer was murdered and his body placed under the floorboards of Dr. Klein's house. Shortly after that, Daniel Patrick Glasher was also found dead. Murdered. We all know this. It seems overwhelmingly likely that the murderer of both was Dean Reeve. Dr. Klein has been saying for some time that Reeve was alive but up until now this was disputed by the authorities."

She swallowed and took a drink from the tumbler of water in front of her. Frieda saw how thin her hands were. Their nails were painted dark blue.

"As you all know, we have been running a major investigation. This has involved several police forces, public appeals, forensic analysis, going door to door, checking CCTV footage."

Now she turned and looked directly at Frieda. "We've had reports of sightings that have remained unconfirmed. There were some CCTV images that were inconclusive."

"We've got nothing," said Crawford.

"The investigation has not progressed the way we hoped," Petra continued. "We're not closing the case."

Frieda nodded at her. "I know that murder cases are

never closed. They just wind down and get gradually forgotten about."

"As I said, we're not closing the case but we're reallocating some of the resources."

"Are you still going to be working on it?"

"I will be available as necessary."

"I'll take that as a no."

"I'm not going to lie to you. There are no leads. We are not hopeful. I'm sorry."

Petra Burge turned back to the glum men and women around the table. "Any questions?" No one spoke. "Right. Commissioner Crawford wants to say something."

Crawford gave a dry cough and ran a finger around the inside of his collar. "In half an hour," he said, "I am giving a press conference. DCI Burge's investigation has been thoroughly professional. But it doesn't look good. There have been questions asked inside and outside the force. There have been insinuations that I resisted the investigation at an earlier stage."

Frieda didn't dare glance across at Karlsson and Yvette. Both of them were all too aware of the truth behind those insinuations. She just hoped Yvette wouldn't say anything, or mutter anything, or give a cough that could be interpreted as sarcasm.

"Criticisms could be made of certain policy judgements," Crawford continued. "And now we have failed to solve this high-profile case. I've always believed that part of the job of being commissioner is to take responsibility. The buck stops here. I am today offering my resignation, which will take effect immediately."

No one said anything. People lowered their eyes. The

man who sat next to Crawford briefly patted him on the shoulder, but lightly, as though he might set off an explosion. The commissioner rose to his feet. "Well," he said. "It's been an honor to serve with you."

A murmur ran around the room. Everyone stood. As he reached the door, Frieda went over to him.

"I suppose you feel vindicated," he said.

"I was going to say that I was sorry."

"Are you?"

"Yes. I don't see why this had to happen."

"Really?" said Crawford, with a sardonic expression. "Maybe you should ask your friend Walter Levin about it."

"Why? What's he got to do with it?"

"How should I know?" said Crawford. "I'm just a simple policeman. Or ex-policeman." He nodded at Karlsson. "Try to stop her being killed, Mal. Right, I've got one last press conference to go to."

Frieda, Karlsson and Yvette watched him leave.

"Wanker," said Yvette.

"Don't." Karlsson frowned reprovingly at her.

"Why not? He's done nothing but fuck you around for years."

"I suspect we might miss him when he's gone."

"I don't know," said Yvette. "Maybe I'm just tired of it all."

"Take your exam first," said Karlsson. "Bank your promotion. Then you can get tired." He turned to Frieda with an expression of concern. "I'm extremely sorry about all of this."

When Frieda got home, the first thing she did was to ring the Warehouse, a therapeutic clinic she worked for sometimes and that referred people to her.

"I'm going to start taking on new patients," she said. "The sooner the better, the more the better. I've been treading water for too long, waiting for something that was never going to happen. Now I want to fill up my life again."

10

Frieda walked back to her house, taking small roads, avoiding the snarl and fumes of traffic. The wind was still strong, carrying drops of rain; litter and branches covered the pavements.

As she turned into the mews, she recognized a familiar figure standing at her door in his old canvas jacket, his hair shaggier than usual, a bag slung over his shoulder and a large battered case at his feet. And then she saw there was someone at his side, a thin shape in a coat that was far too large.

"Josef!" she called, as she came closer.

He turned. His face lit up with relief. He was unshaven and filthy. His jacket was torn. His stout boots were muddy with trailing laces. He looked at her with his pleading brown eyes. The boy beside him had the same large brown eyes. Frieda had seen him before in photographs over the years. She bent toward him. His face was thin and grubby, and his eyes frightened. His coat hung off him. His sneakers were worn out.

"Alexei?"

He nodded.

"You're safe now. Here."

She slid the key into the lock and opened the door, then gestured for Alexei to enter. He looked up at his father inquiringly. Josef put an arm around his shoulders and said something to him in words Frieda didn't understand. His voice had a soft, crooning tone that she had never heard before.

"You went back," she said to Josef, as she shut the door behind them and turned the lights on. "I mean, to Ukraine."

"Yes."

"You can tell me everything in a minute. First, we're going to get Alexei into a bath and I'll make him something to eat. He looks done in."

"Scared, Frieda. Sad."

"Tell him I'm running him a bath. I'll get towels for you both. Have you got clothes in there?" She gestured to the large case.

"Some."

She went up the stairs to run water into the tub that Josef had installed for her, putting out thick white towels, then returned to Josef and his son.

"The bath's ready. I'll make coffee for you and hot chocolate for him."

She watched Josef lead Alexei up the stairs, a large man and a scrawny boy hand in hand.

"Tell me," she said.

They were in her kitchen and Josef was eating toast and marmalade in enormous crunching mouthfuls, washing it back with gulps of strong coffee. He stank of tobacco and sweat and his grimy face was exhausted.

"Vera die," he said, and gave a sudden sob, putting his hand to his eyes for a moment. "My wife gone."

Frieda touched the back of his hand.

"Very quick. From the blue. Her new man call to say." For a moment his face twisted. "I was not good husband, Frieda." His shoulders slumped and his head lowered. "We met when very young. But I did love."

"I know."

"So, of course, I must fetch my sons. They need their father. I tell no one but Stefan. Stefan helped."

Stefan was Josef's Russian friend; Frieda had never liked to think how he earned his money.

"But where's Dima?"

"Dima did not want to come."

"I suppose Ukraine is his home."

Josef nodded. "Family there."

Frieda wanted to ask about the journey, about how he'd got Alexei back to the UK, but they could hear the water running from the bath. Josef pushed the last of the thick slice of toast into his mouth and stood up. "He very shocked, Frieda. No talking, no crying, nothing. Just silent and sad."

"It will take time."

While they were upstairs, she rang Reuben and explained what had happened. "They can stay here," she said.

"Josef's home is with me," said Reuben. "You haven't even got a proper spare room."

"Are you sure that's OK?"

"It'll be good for me." Reuben gave a rueful laugh. "Maybe it will stop me feeling sorry for myself."

She made Alexei scrambled eggs, but he barely touched it. She made him hot chocolate and he sipped at it warily. He'd put on tracksuit trousers that were too short and a long-sleeved red T-shirt that was too large, its sleeves covering his hands. She went into the living room and lifted the cat that was lying neatly curled in an armchair and put it into Alexei's lap. He stroked it very delicately, his head lowered so that she couldn't see his expression.

11

Half an hour later, when Alexei was sleeping in Frieda's bed and Josef was smoking in her backyard, her mobile rang.

"Chloë?"

She heard the sound of breathing, or perhaps it was stifled sobbing. "Chloë? What's up?" She waited. "Talk to me."

"Where am I?"

"What? I don't know. What do you mean? Are you OK?"

"No."

"OK. I'll come now. Tell me where you are."

"Where am I?" Chloë asked again, in a thick voice.

"Listen, Chloë. You're not making sense. Are you in your flat? At Olivia's?"

"I feel bad."

"You don't know where you are?"

There was no answer, just the sound of unsteady breathing.

"Look around you." Frieda spoke very loudly and clearly. "What can you see?"

"See?"

"Yes."

"A tree."

"That's not enough. Stay awake. What else?"

"Church."

"You're near a church. Do you know what it's called?"

"No."

"Can you stand up?"

In answer, Chloë whimpered.

"Can you see anyone?"

"I'm with stones."

"What do you mean, stones?"

"Gravestones."

"So you're near a church?"

"Around the tree. Lots. Pushed together."

Suddenly she knew exactly where Chloë was. "I'm coming," she said. "I'm coming for you."

Gravestones were planted tightly together round the Hardy Tree in St. Pancras churchyard. Underneath them were old bones and above them the spreading branches of an ash. Several months ago, Dean had taken away the sketch that Frieda had been working on of the tree, as a sign that he had been in her house. After the Hannah Docherty case was over, Frieda had gone there once more to think about all that had happened; her friends had joined her. Now it seemed that Chloë was there, befuddled, barely able to speak.

She hailed a cab, but the traffic around King's Cross was slow, so she jumped out early and ran along Camley Street, the canal on one side of her, then into the small churchyard and toward the tree, which was enclosed by an iron fence.

At first, she couldn't see Chloë, but when she walked around to the back she found her, on the other side of the fence. She was sitting propped against an outer gravestone, her legs splayed in front of her, her face pasty and swollen. She had mascara smudged beneath both eyes and her hair was greasy and matted. She was wearing a short gray T-shirt dress and sandals. There was a small canvas bag at her side. As Frieda came closer, she saw that there were scratches on her neck and her bare legs. Chloë's eyes were open but she stared at Frieda with a dazed expression, as if she wasn't really seeing her. Frieda put her hand through the fence and placed it onto Chloë's bare leg; it was cold and clammy.

"Frieda?"

"Yes. Wait. I'm coming to get you."

She hurried around to the gate, but it was padlocked and she had to climb over the spiked fence. She made her way to her niece, took her hands and held them firmly. "Speak to me."

"Mmm?"

Now Frieda took the young woman's shoulders. "Look at me, Chloë. It's Frieda."

"Frieda."

"Yes. Do you hurt anywhere?"

"I don't know."

"What happened to you?"

"I don't feel well."

Frieda smoothed the hair off Chloë's forehead. Her niece didn't smell of alcohol but of sweat, stale and sour. "I'm going to call an ambulance and take you to hospital. Do you understand?"

"Where am I?" Chloë repeated.

"You're near King's Cross."

"Why?"

"I don't know."

"I want to go home."

"You'll be home soon. I'll stay with you. Can you remember what happened?"

"What?"

"It's all right." She sat beside Chloë and put an arm around her. Chloë's head lolled onto her shoulder. "Did someone bring you here? Who were you with?"

"I don't know," said Chloë. Her voice was thick, as though her tongue was too big for her mouth. "My head hurts. I'm thirsty. I feel a bit sick."

12

Frieda stayed with Chloë in the ambulance. She seemed semiconscious. Much of what she said was incoherent, but Frieda recognized her own name. She leaned in. "What?"

"Don't tell Mum."

"I've already phoned her," said Frieda.

Chloë mumbled something and seemed to drift off to sleep. The young paramedic leaned over. She looked at Frieda. "What's her name?"

"Chloë."

"Can you hear me, Chloë?" the paramedic said loudly. No response. She gently slapped Chloë's cheek. "Chloë. Wake up. Talk to me."

Chloë murmured a few words but Frieda couldn't make them out. The paramedic looked at Frieda. "Has she been drinking?"

"I don't think so."

"Do you know what she's taken?"

"I think she should be checked for flunitrazepam."

The paramedic pulled a face. She had fierce, flaming red hair, a face full of freckles and looked barely older than Chloë. "Date rape? We'll see."

Chloë was wheeled straight from the ambulance along a corridor and into a cubicle, Frieda on one side of the trolley, the paramedic and a doctor on the other. On the way Frieda said everything she knew, which wasn't very much. Chloë was stripped and dressed in a hospital gown. The doctor asked Frieda if she wanted to step outside during the examination.

"I think I should stay," she said.

She had seen so much worse, but the sight of her niece's unconscious body being examined, the legs pushed apart, probed, caused a pang of acute distress. It was like the beginnings of a postmortem.

When it was done, the doctor stood upright. "No bruising," he said. "No signs of sexual assault."

"Good," said Frieda. "That's good."

"Does she often get drunk?"

"I smelled her breath. I don't think this is alcohol."

The doctor shone a light into Chloë's eye. "I think you're right." He nodded at a nurse who was hovering on one side. "Let's hydrate her."

He stepped back and looked at Frieda. He had short gray hair, and his face was pale, with dark rings under the eyes. Probably near the end of his shift. "Sometimes we don't fully hydrate them," he said. "We like to leave them with a little bit of a hangover. Teach them a lesson."

"Is that the job of a doctor?"

"You should be here Friday night after Friday night, the same ones coming in time after time."

The nurse called the doctor over. She was inserting a line, but now she moved back and the doctor inspected Chloë's arm. He looked up at Frieda. "What relation is she?"

"She's my niece."

"Is she in any kind of trouble?"

"I don't know of any. Why do you ask?"

"I don't know what she took," said the doctor, "but I know how she took it. Look." He pointed at the pale skin of Chloë's limp left arm. "Three, four puncture marks."

"That's not possible," said Frieda.

"Why?"

"Chloë doesn't inject drugs."

The doctor took his glasses off and rubbed his tired eyes. "If I think of all the times when parents or relatives or friends have stood where you're standing and said that their little boy or little girl wouldn't take drugs."

"So you're saying that Chloë went out on a Monday and suddenly decided to inject herself with a sedative."

"Well, she didn't do it suddenly. As you can see there are at least four puncture marks. So she overdid it a bit."

"That's not Chloë."

He spread his arms. "I'm not the one you need to convince. I'm just the poor sod in A & E who has to pick up the pieces. We've sent the blood off for testing. We'll know soon enough. And don't worry: I'm giving her the full hydration."

"Am I allowed to stay?"

"Haven't you seen the sign on the door? We welcome carers. Except when they're drunk or fighting or shouting, which they often are. Then they're a bit less welcome."

Frieda sat on a chair in the cubicle and stared in front of her. She'd seen Chloë through troubled times but she'd thought that was all in the past. Was it going to start again? But there was no point in thinking about that yet. She just sat there and watched her unconscious niece, the chest rising and falling. She had just got used to the sounds, the voices from the reception desk, the occasional cry from a patient, the clatter of trolleys, the beeping from the monitors, when she heard a familiar anguished voice. She stood up, pulled the curtain aside and was confronted with the tear-streaked face of Chloë's mother, Olivia. She rushed forward and hugged Frieda. Frieda could feel the wetness of her cheek, and was enveloped in the fumes of perfume and white wine.

"It took me so long to get here," said Olivia. "The Tube came to a complete halt. They announced someone was under a train. Why can't they just do it at home and not cause trouble to other people?"

"Shall we talk about Chloë?" said Frieda.

Olivia looked at her daughter and burst into tears. Frieda had to sit Olivia down and fetch her a glass of water. As soon as she could speak, Olivia talked between sobs about her failings as a mother and Chloë's failings as a daughter.

"I love her, of course," she said. "She's all I've got. But she never phones me when things are going well. Whenever the phone goes and Chloë's on the line it's because something's wrong."

"It wasn't Chloë who rang," said Frieda. "It was me."

"That's what I meant."

Gradually the subject shifted from Chloë to a problem Olivia had been having with a man she'd been seeing and from that to some building work that had run into a crisis, and then the curtain was pulled aside by a man holding a clipboard.

"One of you is a doctor," he said. "Is that right?"

"I'm Chloë's aunt," said Frieda. "I'm a doctor as well. Is that relevant?"

"You're the one who said it might be one of the date-rape drugs."

"I said it was something to check for."

"Well, it isn't. And there's no alcohol in her blood. What there is, is phenobarbital."

"What's that?" Olivia's question was halfway to a howl.

"It's used for treating seizures," said Frieda. "But it's a powerful sedative."

"Chloë wouldn't take that." Olivia clutched Frieda's arm.

"I've been saying the same thing."

"You wouldn't believe what they'd take," said the doctor. "They'll inject anything."

"Inject?" said Olivia in horror, and there was a long, painful conversation, with Olivia struggling to talk between gulps and sobs and a handkerchief clutched to her mouth. At the end of it, it was agreed that Chloë would be discharged the following morning.

13

Frieda walked home from the hospital. Josef and Alexei had gone, the only signs that they'd been there a great ring of dirt around the bathtub. She called Reuben, who said they were safely with him and that Alexei had eaten some pasta but had said nothing.

She slept for a few hours, then lay awake in the early light, thinking, trying not to think, of all the events of the day that were going through her mind. In the morning she met Olivia at the hospital, and after a few hours of waiting for the consultant, then for the discharge papers to be signed, they led Chloë out and took a taxi back to Olivia's house. Chloë was still dazed. She looked tired, sad, completely washed out. Even when she was back in what had been her childhood home, she seemed barely to recognize the place.

"I want a bath," she said.

"Frieda?" Olivia had the air of slight panic. "I think it's easier if it's not her mother."

Frieda led Chloë up to the bathroom, undressed her and helped her into the bath. It made her think of Alexei.

"Don't go," said Chloë, in a little voice.

Frieda had no intention of going. She ran the water in

the bath and washed Chloë, as she might have washed a four-year-old girl. Then she pulled out the plug and helped Chloë dry herself. Olivia brought pajamas and together they supported Chloë as she stepped into them; Frieda fastened the buttons of the jacket.

"Can she go to her old room?" asked Frieda.

"I've already made up the bed."

Frieda was expecting the poignancy of a teenage girl's bedroom, with its tattered old posters of stars from ten years ago. Instead there was the poignancy of a teenage girl's bedroom that had been entirely renovated and stripped of every sign that a teenage girl had ever been there. But Chloë didn't seem to notice and at least there was still a bed. Frieda eased her under the duvet and pulled it right up to her chin.

"Would you like some tea?"

"All right."

"Normal tea? Chamomile?"

"All right."

"Which?"

"Either."

She was so different from the normal, angry, assertive young woman that Frieda had known for so long. She made two cups of chamomile tea and took them upstairs. She held one so that Chloë could sip from it.

"Do you want to talk?" said Frieda.

"Tired," said Chloë.

"Do you mind if *I* talk?"

Chloë shook her head slowly.

"I've said this to you before. Whatever is going on in your life—*whatever*—you can come to me. Always."

"I know."

"There are so many things I could say about injecting drugs: you don't know the dose, you don't know the purity, you don't know the needle is safe."

"No," said Chloë, as if it took a great effort.

"I'm not judging you."

"I didn't."

Chloë's eyes filled with tears and Frieda took the mug from her hands, put it on the bedside table, then hugged her niece.

"I'm sorry," Chloë said into her shoulder.

"You don't have to be."

Chloë mumbled something.

"What was that?"

"Your weekend."

"What do you mean my weekend?"

Chloë took a deep breath and seemed to be steeling herself to speak. The words came out one by one. "Sorry. To. Spoil. Your Sunday. And yesterday too. Saturday."

Frieda paused for a moment before replying. She wondered if Chloë was still suffering some cognitive impairment from the barbiturate. "It's not Sunday today, Chloë," she said gently. "It's Tuesday."

Chloë started to sit up and Frieda tried to stop her.

"No," said Chloë. "I don't want to lie down. I need to sit up."

"What happened, Chloë? You can tell me."

"It's all dim. Like it's really far away and long ago. What I remember is it was the end of the week, Friday evening, and I was putting a dress on."

"The gray one?"

"Yes."

"The one I found you in."

"I guess. I think I was going to this bar in Walthamstow. Porter's. I was going to meet a couple of friends."

"Who?"

"Dee and Myla. You've met them." Frieda nodded: not long ago, Chloë had invited them both to her house for an impromptu dinner party she'd decided to throw. "And Klaus said he might join us."

"Klaus?"

"Yes."

"Who's Klaus?"

"Someone I met recently. You know. A guy."

"A guy."

"He's fun," said Chloë, with a hint of her old defiance.

"So did this Klaus join you?"

"I don't know. I can't remember. Maybe. It's a kind of loud blur."

"What else can you remember?"

"Nothing. I don't remember what happened there or anything. And I don't remember leaving. From then on it's like . . . You know when you've had a dream and it's slipped away and you can't get hold of it? The first real memory is seeing your face, the next day."

"Chloë."

"What?"

"It wasn't the next day. It was on Monday."

"Monday. How could it be Monday? That's—that's the whole weekend."

"Yes."

"What happened to me?"

Frieda leaned forward and took Chloë's pale startled face in her hands. "You have to be honest with me. You can spend a weekend injecting drugs and it's like lost time. You can admit that to me. I won't tell anyone."

Chloë's face crinkled up. She suddenly looked terribly young. "Injecting drugs? You know me and needles. I couldn't do that."

"But you went out on Friday," said Frieda. "And we found you on Monday. That's three nights and two whole days. Where were you?"

"Is that possible?"

"You said it's like a dream," said Frieda. "Can you remember anything about it? Anything at all?"

"I don't know," said Chloë, sounding tired again. "It's like in a fog. There's something about a car. I think. Jolting. It makes me feel a bit sick. And there are sounds but I can't see anything. Is that possible?"

"Yes. That's possible." Frieda took out her phone and dialed a number.

"Karlsson?" she said. "You need to get here."

14

Karlsson sat on a wooden chair by the bed. Fat tears were rolling down Chloë's cheeks. She seemed like a little child, thought Frieda. Even her face, rubbed clean of grime and makeup, looked rounder and softer. Frieda saw her lips were chapped and she had grazes on her shoulder.

"I've got a headache," Chloë said.

"I'm sure you have." Karlsson was grave.

"And I feel sick. As if I've been poisoned."

"Which you have been."

"What happened?" Chloë looked from Frieda to Karlsson as if they could magically give her the answer.

"We don't know," said Frieda. "But we're going to find out."

"Someone injected you with a large amount of phenobarbital," said Karlsson.

"It wasn't me," said Chloë. "You do believe me, don't you?"

"Yes." Frieda took her hand and held it for a moment.

"How could they do that? I was in a bar. People would see."

"Presumably they'd slip something into your drink first," said Karlsson. "Rohypnol, maybe."

"There was no trace of that," said Frieda.

"There wouldn't be after three days."

"Why?" Chloë clutched tighter at Frieda's hand. "I wasn't raped. I wasn't robbed. Why did they do it?"

"Sometimes these creeps just like to watch." Karlsson's

expression was grim. "They choose a woman, and they look at her losing control. They have power over her without doing anything at all."

"It was three nights," said Frieda. "Two days."

He nodded.

"What kind of looking is that?"

"I don't know."

"Dee and Myla," Frieda said to Chloë. "I want to talk to them."

"They're on my phone."

Frieda took the canvas bag that had been beside Chloë at the Hardy Tree and opened it. Inside there was a comb, a wallet with a ten-pound note and an Oyster card, and also Chloë's mobile phone. Karlsson took it from her and turned it on.

"Nothing over the missing days," he said. "Until she called you."

"What does that mean?"

Karlsson shrugged. "They took out the SIM card, presumably. A phone can be tracked, even when it's turned off—but not when there's no SIM card. Then the phone's just a lump of useless plastic."

"So whoever did this knows what he's doing."

"Everyone knows that about phones."

"I didn't." Frieda turned to Chloë. "I want to speak to Klaus as well."

"Klaus is nice."

"How well do you know him?"

"I know he's nice."

"Then he won't mind me speaking to him."

"I guess." Chloë closed her eyes. "OK, then. Call him too. I don't care."

"Is there anything else you can remember?"

But no answer came from Chloë except a very faint snore. Karlsson stood up and moved away from the bed; he had a slight limp still although his cast had been removed months ago. Frieda pulled the duvet up higher. She drew the curtains. Then she and Karlsson left the room.

As they went downstairs, they could hear Olivia talking very loudly on the phone, her voice occasionally breaking into a high wail. She was walking agitatedly from kitchen to living room and back, gesturing with her free hand.

"Can we go somewhere private?" asked Karlsson.

Frieda pulled open the door to what Olivia called her study but which was clearly the junk room. It was full of empty wine boxes, old newspapers and magazines, piles of unsorted bank statements, clothes that Olivia didn't want anymore.

"We should call Petra Burge," said Karlsson, as soon as the door was shut.

"Let's say the name out loud. We think Dean took Chloë."

"As you pointed out upstairs, this wasn't just some asshole slipping a drug into Chloë's drink. She went missing for the whole weekend. She wasn't raped. What was it for?"

Frieda's face was bleak. She didn't reply.

"And look at where she was found. Somewhere you know. A graveyard. It's like a predator circling, picking people off."

Frieda put her head into her hands, and spoke through the lattice of her fingers. "So now Dean is targeting someone I love. Someone I've taken care of all her life."

"It could be just to taunt you, now that the investigation has failed."

Frieda raised her head and nodded. Her expression was somber. "I need to talk to Chloë's friends. And this Klaus."

"And we need to find out where she was."

"Thank you."

"What for?"

"For saying 'we.'"

Karlsson's face softened briefly. "She couldn't have been lying by that tree all weekend," he continued.

"She doesn't remember anything—except a car, perhaps."

"Perhaps some memory will return."

"Perhaps."

"I'll talk to Petra."

"They've just spent six months not finding Dean."

"She needs to know."

"You're right."

"Listen, I'm supposed to be going away with my kids for a couple of days."

"Why do you sound like that's a bad thing?"

"I'd like to be around to make sure Chloë's OK, see if you need me."

"Karlsson, your *kids* need you. We'll be fine. And, actually, what could you do?"

"Nothing, probably. But you've got to take care."

"I don't even know what that means."

15

Frieda met Dee and Myla the next day at the café off Shoreditch High Street where Dee worked. It was quite small and filled with bearded young men, and women in round glasses. There was also an enormous dog standing passively in the center of the room.

They were both there when she arrived, sitting at a wooden table near the window drinking herbal tea. Dee was small, with cropped dark hair and a bony, mobile face. Myla was taller, with a secretive air. Frieda remembered her as someone who rarely spoke.

"Can I get you something?" asked Dee.

"It's OK. I know you'll need to get back to work soon."

"What do you want to talk to us about?" asked Myla, abruptly. "Is something wrong?"

"As I said on the phone, it's about Chloë."

Dee leaned forward. "Is she OK?"

"You were with her on Friday night."

"Only for a bit. Why?"

"Someone slipped her a drug," said Frieda.

"On Friday?"

"Yes."

"Shit," said Dee. "Is she all right?"

"She's woozy and sick."

"Has she been examined?" asked Myla. She was staring at Frieda fixedly.

"There were no signs of sexual assault," said Frieda. "Or any assault."

"So what happened?" said Dee. "Where was she?"

"She was left in a churchyard near St. Pancras."

"St. Pancras? That's miles away. How did she get there?"

"You think we were there when it happened?" asked Myla.

"I don't know. I was hoping you could tell me something."

"We should have looked out for her," said Dee.

"Can you tell me what you remember about that night, and the last time you saw her?"

Dee ran her fingers through her hair. "We met at Porter's in Walthamstow. Do you know it?"

"No."

A young man came over and put a plate in front of Myla. "Avocado, black beans and sourdough bread," he said. "Enjoy."

"It was about eight, eight thirty," said Dee. "Right?"

Myla nodded.

"We got there first and then Chloë arrived about fifteen minutes later. She seemed fine. I mean, she can be rather moody."

"I know."

"She was great, chatting away."

"What did she have to drink?"

"I'm not sure."

"Beer," said Myla. "Just a half."

"And she didn't seem drunk or high?"

"No. She said this new man might be joining us. Claude."

"Klaus," said Myla. With concentration, she cut a triangle off the sourdough and pushed some avocado and beans onto it, then lifted it to her mouth.

"Right, Klaus. She said he was nice. She seemed excited."

"Go on."

"Then a few more people arrived we knew and—I don't know. Chloë drifted away."

"Did Klaus arrive?"

"I can't say. When I noticed she wasn't there, I thought she must be with him. It never occurred to me that anything had happened. God, poor Chloë. Is she angry with us?"

"I don't think so."

"What creep would do that?"

"That's the question."

"You think it was this Claude?"

"Klaus," said Myla.

"I have no idea. But the thing is, it's not just that evening Chloë can't remember. She can't remember anything about the entire weekend."

"No memory at all?"

"Just a few very blurry ones. So I want you to think hard about who you saw her talking with."

"Two *days*. Where was she?"

"We don't know."

"This is sick."

"I don't think I'm going to be much help," said Dee, screwing up her face, pressing her fingers into her temples. "I don't think I saw her with anyone in particular. I just realized at some point she wasn't there."

"Myla?"

Myla shook her head from side to side, slowly. "Like Dee said, she was there and then at some point she wasn't."

"That's it?"

"Sorry."

"It can't be helped. Thank you for your time."

"It happened to me once." Myla spoke curtly. Her face was expressionless.

"You had a drug slipped to you in your drink?"

"Yes. They got him in the end. It turned out he'd done it to lots of women. He was the barman. He was there under our noses."

"You never said." Dee was staring at her.

"I can't be sure," said Myla to Frieda, "but I have a vague sense that I did see Chloë talking to a man. I thought it was Klaus. But only because she said someone called Klaus might be coming to meet her. So when she was gone, I didn't give it another thought."

"You can't describe him?"

"Not at all."

"If you do remember anything . . ."

"Of course." Myla prodded the last of her breakfast, her face somber. "A whole lost weekend. It makes no sense."

Dee went back behind the counter. At the door of the café, Frieda turned to Myla. "Were you raped?"

"I was."

"I'm very sorry. Have you talked to anyone about it?"

"Should I?"

"I think so."

Myla held Frieda's gaze. "What about you? Would you, if you were me?"

"Why do you say that?"

"I don't know. You just don't seem the type."

It was lunch hour and Karlsson was told that Petra Burge had gone for a run.

"She does it almost every day," said the officer. "Rain or shine. Even when she's been up all night."

"I'll wait."

Karlsson went outside into the heat of the day. He felt restless, impatient. On an impulse he went into the news-agent across the road and bought a bottle of water, a packet of ten cigarettes—although he'd promised his children he'd given up—a lighter and a newspaper. He sat on a low wall a few yards from the station and lit the cigarette, then opened the paper. He skimmed through the news stories, the sports and business sections, then tried to solve a cross-word puzzle.

Frowning, he stared into the distance. In the glare of the sun, he made out a skinny figure running toward him: black shorts and lime green shirt, thin white legs. He looked at Petra Burge as she came, her stride regular, her head up, moving with an ease that made it look simple. He ran him-self, or had done before he broke his leg, but she was some-thing else. He dropped his cigarette on the ground and stood up.

She stopped beside him, barely out of breath, though there was a sheen of perspiration on her face and her hair was damp. "Trouble?"

"Yes."

She sat on the wall beside him; he held out the bottle of water and she took a swig. "Is it Frieda?"

"Partly."

"Do I have time for a shower?"

"Of course."

"Give me five minutes."

"Why did you come to tell me this? Why didn't Frieda come?"

Karlsson faced Petra Burge across the desk. She seemed angry. She was leaning forward, her fingers gripping the edge, her shoulders tense, her mouth in a tight line. He saw again how thin she was, but not frail. She radiated a kind of nervous energy. He couldn't work out her age. In some ways she looked like a teenager, with her edgy haircut and her skinny jeans. Even though the day was hot, she had changed into a long-sleeved black shirt. But her face had lines in it and he noticed a small tuft of gray at her temple.

"She's a bit occupied," he replied.

"Let me guess. She's out playing detective."

"I think she's talking to some people."

Burge sat back in her chair. "I promised to find Dean Reeve and I failed. I'm no further in solving the case than I was. In fact, I'm further off. It's all gone cold." She pushed a paper across the desk to Karlsson. "Look at this. This is what I was thinking about when I was running."

On the front page were the photos of Frieda, Commissioner Crawford and herself. The journalist clearly laid out the details of the story that had led to Crawford's resignation.

"Look," said Petra Burge, and jabbed her finger at a sentence halfway down the page. "It says here that DCI Burge's reputation has suffered a serious blow."

"We all have cases like this," said Karlsson. "They're the

ones that keep us awake at night. This one's yours. The one that got away."

"I keep trying to work out what I did wrong, what I should have done differently. He's still fucking out there."

"So what will you do with this?"

"You think it's Dean?"

"Everything points to it."

"You reckon he's that brazen? That reckless? Showing us all he's one step ahead."

Karlsson rubbed his face with the tips of his fingers. His leg ached where it had been broken. "Everything with Dean is some sort of a message. That's what Frieda says."

"What Frieda says. Who cares what Frieda says?" Burge rapped her desk angrily. "We just need to find him."

16

Frieda saw two patients, then walked from her consulting room to Islington, where she went down onto the canal path. There were joggers, and children on scooters, dog-walkers, cyclists, all out in the warm weather. The ground was hard underfoot after weeks without rain; the leaves on the trees were limp. Soon it would be autumn. What a year it had been, starting with the darkness and pain of the Hannah Docherty case, straight into the horror of finding Bruce Stringer's body under the floorboards. Then the last six months of a case going cold. And now, when it had felt like it was over, Chloë: Chloë left under the Hardy Tree. It was like a picture she couldn't read.

She remembered Myla's parting question: people talked to Frieda, but whom did she talk to? Perhaps that was what she did: she carried the stories that people gave to her, holding them safely inside herself. So many stories, her little consulting room was full of them; her brain, her body, felt heavy with them. Self-deluding ones, self-protective ones, and also ones that were raw and terrible. But what about her story? Whom did she give that to? She'd had therapy herself, of course, but even then had been very aware of choosing what to say and what to keep secret. Reuben had been her therapist many years ago. She had trusted and admired him—but she hadn't told him every-thing. When people got too close, she pushed them away.

She talked to her patients about the power of speaking, of making words and narratives, but she kept silent, guarded her secret self. No one was having that.

A small girl on a tricycle wove across her path. Frieda lifted her gaze and saw she was near the park: it was time to see whether Chloë's new friend was as nice as her niece seemed to think. She realized that she wanted it to be him. She bit her lip so hard she tasted blood: she wanted Chloë to have been abducted by a creep whom she thought she liked, injected with sedatives, kept for three nights for reasons she could hardly bear to think about. She wanted that, because otherwise it had been Dean.

Klaus laughed a lot. He had laughed, nervously, when Frieda said on the phone that she was Chloë's aunt and needed to talk to him. He laughed when, on meeting at the entrance to Victoria Park, he trod in dog shit and had to spend the next several minutes trying to wipe it off on the bleached grass. And he gave a short, embarrassed laugh when Frieda asked him when he'd last seen Chloë.

"Perhaps you've got the wrong idea." His English, though heavily accented, was impeccable. "Chloë and I met only a week ago. I'm really not sure why you want to talk to me. Your call was a surprise."

Frieda couldn't work out if he was sweet, irritating or even sinister. She glared at him. "You haven't answered my question."

Klaus cast her a baffled look, then shrugged. "I last saw Chloë the night I met her, last Tuesday."

"You haven't seen her since then?"

"No. I have met her once only. Which explains my surprise at your call."

"Have you spoken to her?"

"Yes. A few times. I would like to see her again." They passed a pond where a few ducks bobbed. "Excuse me, I am not a rude person, but I would like to know why you're asking me these questions before I answer any more. Chloë is an adult. She doesn't need protecting."

"Where were you on Friday night?"

"Why?"

"Chloë told me you had arranged to meet her."

"No. We had said perhaps we would meet. That is not the same." He was no longer laughing. "Please, what is this?"

"Did you see her?"

"Why are you asking?"

"Something happened to Chloë."

He stopped. "What happened?"

"Someone slipped a drug into her drink." She stared hard at him as she spoke. "Then they took her somewhere, we don't know where, and they kept her there for the weekend."

"Oh, no."

"So you will understand why I am asking you if you met Chloë on Friday night."

"You can't think that I—that it was me . . ."

"And if you didn't meet her, where you were instead."

"You think I might have done this?"

"And where were you on the weekend?"

"This is nothing to do with me."

"You haven't asked."

"What?"

"If she was sexually abused."

"If she was—oh. No. I mean, was she?"

"Did you meet her?"

"I texted her to say I couldn't make it. My friend came from Berlin. I was with him. Check on her phone."

"The SIM card was removed."

"That explains it."

"What?"

"Why I haven't been able to get hold of her. I wanted her to come and join us on Sunday, before he flew back."

"Can you give me your friend's name and number?"

Klaus gazed at her, color rising in his face, a slow, deep flush. "You want to check my story?"

"Yes."

"You don't believe me?"

"I want to check."

He nodded. "His name is Gustav Brenner and I will give you his mobile." He took his own phone out of the pocket of his jeans and scrolled down before holding it out to her to copy. "Satisfied?"

"Thank you."

"I met Chloë once. I liked her. She was fun. That's all."

"I'll call Gustav."

Chloë was up and dressed, in denim shorts and an over-sized shirt. Her face was a healthier color and her hair was still damp from the shower.

"Jack's coming around in a few minutes," she said.

"I'm glad you're feeling better."

"I am. He was being very sweet on the phone. He said he'd bring lots of different kinds of cheese for me to try." She gave a small laugh. "It's his way of comforting me."

When Jack Dargan had been supervised by Frieda, an awkward and romantic young man, he had, to Frieda's alarm, become involved with Chloë. But that relationship was over, and he was no longer sure he wanted to be a psychotherapist. Instead, he had started working on an artisanal cheese stall on the South Bank and had become something of a cheese zealot, offering soft wedges wrapped in waxed paper as gifts wherever he went. He seemed, thought Frieda, happier than she'd ever known him. "There are worse comforts," she said.

"He's growing a beard."

"Everyone has beards now."

"It's a completely different color from his hair. He looks like a pirate. Not necessarily in a good way." She ran her fingers through her damp hair. "Frieda, there is something I think I remember."

"What?"

"A sound. Not just of the car."

"Yes?"

"Planes."

Frieda tried to hide her disappointment. "It's a good sign that you're beginning to remember. Maybe more will come back."

"No. They were close by. I mean, really, really close. Like they were almost on top of me."

Frieda thought for a moment. "What sort of plane?" she said.

"How should I know? I don't know anything about planes."

"I mean, was it a big plane? Was it a little plane? I'm trying to think whether you were near a flying club or an airport."

Chloë considered for a moment. "It wasn't one of those little two-seaters. They sound like toy planes. It had a heavier sound."

"Was it really big, like a 747?"

"It was big," said Chloë, a bit doubtfully. "But not big-big. I once went to the house of a friend of a friend in Southall and it was right under the Heathrow flight path. There were giant jets going over the roof every minute and the ground shook and there was this deep roaring engine sound. It wasn't as huge as that."

"Were they taking off or landing? Or both?"

"This is like a dream that I've almost completely forgotten. I can't remember things like that."

"Was it a constant sound or a sound that passed overhead?"

"You won't let it go, will you?"

"Compare it to something."

"What do you mean 'compare it to something'? Do you want me to say it sounded like a bee or a motorbike?"

"All right," said Frieda. "Did it sound like a bee or a motorbike?"

"Well, it didn't sound like a bee."

"What about a motorbike?"

Chloë closed her eyes for a few seconds. Then she opened them again, blinking as if the light was too much for her. "It wasn't like a motorbike, really. But you know when someone rides along a street on a motorbike, revving it, showing off?"

"Yes, I do," said Frieda.

"That's probably not much help."

"I don't know. It might be."

On her way out, she met Jack. Chloë was right about his fledgling beard, which was a gingery-brown beside the tawny red of his hair. Today he was wearing a green shirt with the sleeves rolled up to reveal tattoos along both fore-arms, and carrying a brown-paper bag carefully, as though it were breakable. He raised one hand in greeting. It seemed a long time ago that he'd been her acutely self-conscious and adoring student.

"How is she?"

"Better than she was. She's expecting you."

As Frieda walked home, she barely noticed her sur-roundings. She was thinking of airports: Heathrow, Gat-wick, Stansted. She said the names to herself. Strange how they'd kept the names of the little villages they'd obliter-ated. And she thought of Chloë. Chloë was a young woman now, but for Frieda she still contained all the earlier Chloës: the reckless student, the angry teenager. When Frieda looked at her, she even still saw the toddler taking her first steps. Over the years Frieda had cared for her, taught her, even lived with her. And now, because of her niece's con-nection with her, Chloë had been drugged and held cap-tive. When Frieda thought of it, she felt angry and also ashamed. She wanted to say to Dean Reeve: "If you want anyone, come for me."

She remembered the times long ago when she had met Dean Reeve, over in east London, beyond where the Lea River meets the Thames, in Poplar. Suddenly she stopped. She had thought of something.

17

Frieda got out at Pontoon Dock station. She had taken the Docklands Light Railway from Bank through a landscape that was part Hong Kong office buildings, part building site, part industrial wasteland, with just a few fragments of the old East End dotted here and there. She looked across the manicured new park toward the water. She could see the Thames Barrier, like a row of giant scallop shells that had been jammed into the riverbed.

But that wasn't where she needed to go. Frieda turned away from the river and crossed the road, which was shaking with concrete-mixer trucks, one after the other. She turned left, and walked along a chain-link fence, then right into a residential street. This was Silvertown, a strange little enclave trapped between the river and the road on one side, and the vast Royal Victoria Dock circling it on two sides. There were a few older houses that had been missed by the bombs in the Blitz and forgotten by the government and the developers. On the right there was a giant building site, in what looked like the aftermath of a violent civil war. On her left was the new housing development, radiating out in rows.

Frieda walked on until she reached the dockside. When she had first moved to London, many years before, she had sometimes come here. It was a forgotten part of the city, empty warehouses, a defunct dock, bomb sites that nobody had thought of building on. The people who had lived there in the older houses—the dockers, the stevedores and their families—were long gone.

It had all changed. On the water, a wet-suited water-skier was being dragged along on a cable. On the far side was the giant conference center and hotels with names you would find in any city anywhere in the world. Along the dockside were the remnants of cranes, kept as sculptures. There were apartment buildings and waterside cafés and wine bars. Probably on a weekend it would be bustling but now it was almost deserted. And it was quiet.

Chloë had specifically excluded the wide-bodied jets she would have heard if she had been in the shadow of Heathrow. Would Dean have taken her out to Luton or to one of the towns around Stansted? Chloë had been grabbed in Walthamstow, up at the northeast edge of London, so it was possible. Stansted was just a short drive up the M11. But the planes seemed wrong there as well. Big, Chloë had said, but not big-big.

Frieda heard a soft rumbling, growling sound. This was what she had come for. She turned to her right and, almost absurdly, a plane emerged from behind a half-demolished warehouse and passed over her. It was a medium-sized passenger plane and gained height quickly. In a few seconds it was over the river and then it was small and quickly lost in the clouds.

In the newspaper office, a young man wearing a polo shirt, shorts and flip-flops was pushing a trolley between the desks, many of which were abandoned. He stopped at one and handed across a brown A5 envelope.

"A handwritten letter," said Daniel Blackstock. "Don't get many of those nowadays."

The young woman at the facing desk, an intern who was eager to please, gave a small, nervous laugh.

Blackstock slid his finger under the gummed flap and looked inside. "It's a photo," he said, puzzled.

"Is something wrong?" asked the intern, her eyes bright with curiosity.

He held it up so that she could see.

"God! Who's that?" the woman said.

"I don't know." Then he turned the picture around and looked at the back. "Oh, shit."

His editor examined the photograph. "And?" he said.

"That was my reaction," said Blackstock. "But look at the other side."

He turned it. The name "Chloë Klein" was written in large block capitals. "Should I know who she is?"

"Frieda Klein's niece."

"And this is interesting why?"

"I made a couple of calls," said Blackstock. "She went missing for a few days. The police think she might have been taken by the killer."

"Blimey. It *is* interesting." The editor thought for a moment, then shook his head. "We can't run it, though."

"Why not?"

"Because we need to give it to the police."

"It's a scoop."

"It's a scoop we can't use. I'm sorry, Daniel."

"I'll try to get you less interesting stuff in future."

"That's enough."

Daniel Blackstock turned to leave the room, still holding the envelope gingerly. But at the door he stopped. "There's another way. I could give it to Frieda Klein. She can give it to the police."

"Why?"

"A favor. It might come in useful."

The editor hesitated, then nodded. "Go for it."

Frieda walked to one of the cafés. It was a sunny morning so she sat at a table outside. There was no other customer, inside or out. A young woman came out; she was talking on the phone and didn't hurry to complete the call. Finally she was done and looked at Frieda expectantly. She had been speaking in a language that reminded Frieda of when she had heard Josef ringing home to his wife in Kiev, pleading, arguing, justifying. She wondered if this woman was Ukrainian as well but didn't ask. People didn't like it. They thought you might be an immigration official or police in plain clothes. So she just ordered a black coffee, and when it arrived, she took a sip and started to organize her thoughts.

She hated terms like "must have" and "surely" and "probably." Yet she felt almost certain that this was the area where Chloë had been kept during those two lost days. As if in confirmation, another plane flew over and up. A small plane in the heart of London. Where else could it be?

This was where Dean Reeve might have chosen. Frieda knew that people are territorial and that crimes are territorial. Seven years earlier she had visited the house where Dean had lived with another of his victims. Now he was celebrated as a murderer from Poplar. Frieda had heard that he featured in an East End murder tour: a double-decker bus, painted black, drove around sites associated with Jack the Ripper, the Kray brothers, the Richardson gang and Dean Reeve.

She ordered a second coffee and went on thinking, scowling in fierce concentration. Dean Reeve had hovered on the edge of her life, like a blurred image just out of her range of vision, but there had always been a clarity, a purposefulness to his actions. If Frieda did A, Dean responded with B. There had been a cruel logic in the murder of Bruce Stringer and he had told her so himself: *That's what you get for coming after me*. But what was he responding to in taking Chloë, and what was the message? That he could get at her friends and family? She already knew that. He could have done anything to Chloë but he had done nothing.

Only one thing was obvious. The death of Daniel Glasher and its accompanying letter had seemed like an ending, a drawing of a line. Now, somehow and for some reason, the violence had started again. She was being told something. But what was it?

18

Frieda was at her home, taking notes on an upcoming session, when the phone rang. It was Yvette Long.

"What's wrong?" said Frieda.

"Why should anything be wrong? Is this a bad time? I wanted to talk to you about something. In person."

Frieda looked at her watch. "Maybe later. I'm seeing a patient in an hour."

"It won't take long."

"Oh, all right. Are you nearby?"

"I'm about two feet from your front door."

"Why didn't you just ring the bell?"

"I know you value your privacy."

"Don't be ridiculous." She opened the door. Yvette was dressed casually in jeans and a leather jacket. "Do you want to come in?" said Frieda.

"You like walking, don't you?"

"Has something happened?" Frieda asked, as they entered Fitzroy Square.

"I passed," said Yvette.

"Hey," said Frieda. "That's terrific. So you'll be promoted?"

"At some point."

"You should feel proud of yourself."

"Stop," said Yvette, her face flushing. "That's not what I came to tell you."

Frieda took Yvette's arm and directed her toward a bench. They both sat down.

"I thought you liked walking," said Yvette.

"Just tell me what this is about."

"When I heard I'd got through, I didn't feel anything."

"That's not an uncommon reaction."

"Don't diagnose me until I've finished. The last time I felt something was seeing the body in your house and then dreaming about it. It made me feel sick and afraid."

"We all felt that."

"I'm thirty-five years old. It's not too late for me. I don't have to do this. I could leave and become a primary-school teacher. Or I could meet someone and have children. It's not impossible. Admittedly, a bit unlikely but . . ."

"Stop. What are you saying?"

"I'm taking time off."

"To do what?"

"I don't know. Just do nothing except maybe think and sort myself out."

"Where will you go?"

"Just away, somewhere completely different. That's why I wanted to see you." She took a piece of paper from her pocket. "I don't think I've been a good person to you," she said, her voice tremulous. "I think I was all mixed up. I saw you as some mad kind of rival and I also wanted to be a friend and I wanted you to look into my mind and solve all my problems."

"What's on the piece of paper?" Frieda asked.

"That's just my phone number. It's from my other phone, my private one, which I hardly ever use. As I say, I'll be away, maybe walking or hanging out somewhere. But if at some point you need help or you think I could help in some way, someone who's in the police but on your side—I know you've got Karlsson already, so it probably sounds ridiculous—you can call that number and I'll come and do what I can. Not that you'll ever want to."

"Stop putting yourself down," said Frieda, taking the piece of paper. "And thank you. Walk back with me."

"If you want to talk about any of this . . ." Frieda was saying, as they entered Saffron Mews. She paused.

A man was standing at her door, looking up at her windows as if trying to decide if anyone was in. He turned at the sound of their footsteps, took a few paces toward them, then stopped awkwardly. He was dressed in thin gray trousers and a white T-shirt and was carrying a paper bag, holding it slightly away from him, as if it was particularly fragile and he didn't want it to bump against his leg. At first, she didn't recognize him, and then she did.

"Hello," he said. "My name's Daniel Blackstock and—"

"I know who you are. You're a journalist. Not just a journalist. I saw what you wrote about Petra Burge and about Crawford."

"Did I get anything wrong?"

"I don't have anything to say."

"One minute, please."

"Didn't she make herself clear enough?" said Yvette.

"Who are you?" asked Blackstock.

"This is Inspector Yvette Long," said Frieda.

"Actually, I'm not exactly . . ."

"I have something for you. That's all." He sounded angry himself now.

"Something to give me?"

"That's why I'm here. I didn't know whether to give it to the police or to you."

"Then you should probably give it to the police," said Frieda.

"Don't you want to see it?"

Frieda looked at the bag he was holding. "What is it?"

Daniel Blackstock drew out a stiff-backed envelope and handed it to her. "You might want to open it inside."

Frieda ignored him. She lifted the unsealed flap and drew out a glossy A5 photograph. First an inch or so of stone floor slid into view, then the edge of a mattress. On it, first a grubby foot, chipped nail varnish on the toes. Bare legs, one bent and the other straight. The hem of a gray dress. She knew that dress, those legs. She blinked several times to keep her vision clear, then pulled the whole photo into view. Chloë was lying on the mattress, her legs splayed crookedly, her dress up to her thighs so you could see her underwear, one arm folded over her body, the other flung out. That puncture mark, she could see it clearly. Dirty palm. Dirt on her neck, which looked shockingly white in the overexposed shot. And then her niece's face, pale and slightly swollen, the lips parted, the eyes closed. Bluish lids, that ridiculous haircut, which suddenly made her look like a prisoner. For a few seconds that lasted a long time, Frieda stared down at the photo. She knew that Chloë hadn't been raped, but this image was designed to make her look like she'd been fucked over and over and was now lying there, used up and wasted, God knew where.

She showed it to Yvette, who flinched. Then she slid it back into the envelope and turned on Daniel Blackstock. "Where did you get this?"

"It was sent to me."

"Sent? Where?"

"At work. I was there with a colleague when it arrived with the other mail. I just opened it without thinking it was anything special and then—"

"Why you?"

"I honestly don't know. But I guess that's what happens when you write about a case. People see it as a way of getting publicity or recognition or something."

Frieda turned the envelope over and saw it was stamped, and had his name, and the address of his workplace in capital letters.

"Who've you shown this to?" Yvette asked.

"Lindsay Moran, an intern, saw it: her desk is opposite mine. And then I took it to my editor. No one else."

"Why have you brought it to me and not gone straight to the police?"

"We're not all out to screw you over. It obviously has to go to the police, but we thought you should see it first. Even journalists can be decent people. Now she can take it, or is she the bodyguard?" This last he said looking at Yvette.

"No, she's not the bodyguard." Yvette flushed with anger. "I'm a friend."

"I've read about Dr. Klein's friends," said Blackstock.

"I'm not much of a friend."

"What do you mean?"

And Yvette launched into an explanation of her relationship to Frieda and how she'd let her down in the past, and this became an explanation of why she was taking a sabbatical. Blackstock, obviously struggling to make sense of Yvette, said mildly that he would do the same if he could afford to. Frieda tried to stop the conversation.

"Yvette, you don't need to keep explaining yourself."

"I thought you'd approve of me explaining myself."

Frieda turned to Blackstock. "You've dealt fairly with me over this year. Thank you for this."

"It's OK." He hesitated, then added, "Just say you'll think of me if you've got something to say."

"I'll think of you."

"Think of me and then talk to me."

"We'll see."

When Blackstock was gone, Frieda let herself into her house.

"I need to take this to the station," said Yvette. "It's important."

"In a minute," said Frieda. "First, could you take that picture out, put it on the table?"

"What for?"

"Please."

Yvette carefully removed the photo and laid it down. Frieda looked at it. Then she got out her phone and took a picture of it.

"I'm not sure I should be letting you do that," said Yvette.

"I won't tell anyone."

"That's not what I meant."

"I'll show it to Petra Burge now," Frieda said.

"You?"

"Blackstock gave it to me. That makes me some kind of witness."

"And keeps you involved."

"That too."

19

Petra Burge sat in an armchair; it seemed to swallow her small frame. She held the photo by its corners, carefully, and stared at it intently. She turned it over. She looked at the envelope with its block capital letters and its franked stamp.

"It was sent from London."

"Yes."

"Which tells us nothing."

"Almost nothing."

"It was taken when the sun was quite low in the sky. Look at the way the light is falling."

"Evening, then," said Frieda.

"Or morning. We have no way of knowing where this is."

"Maybe somewhere near City Airport."

Petra looked up at her. "Maybe? Where does this come from?"

"Chloë heard planes. Very low, very near. Not great jumbo jets, she doesn't think, and not tiny biplanes. So I thought of City Airport."

Petra shook her head. "There are a dozen other places."

"I went there, and I have a strong sense that it was in that area."

"A strong sense. Is this a sixth sense? Woman's intuition?"

"A working hypothesis that fits the facts."

Petra rearranged herself in the chair. "Even if you're right, this doesn't give us much to go on."

"No."

"But it's shocking."

Frieda glanced again at the image of Chloë lying on that grubby mattress; even looking at her like that seemed an act of defilement. "I've been waiting for a message," said Frieda. "And this is it."

"Was the photograph sent to you?"

"Not directly."

"It wasn't sent to you at all. It was sent to a journalist. If it's a message, what does it say?"

"I don't know. Do you want some whisky?"

Petra smiled. Smiles usually made people seem younger; hers made her look older. "Why not?"

They drank the whisky sitting in the backyard, as the sun sank in the blue-gray sky. At first they didn't say anything. Frieda liked it when people didn't feel the need to speak. She took small, fiery sips and felt something loosen inside her. Anger. Fear.

"The people I love may be in danger simply because I love them," she said at last.

Petra Burge looked at her over the rim of the tumbler.

"So what are we going to do?" Frieda heard herself use that unaccustomed *we* and changed it at once. "How am I going to keep them safe?"

Reuben was lying in bed. It was only just past ten o'clock, and he was never one to go to bed early, but he was tired. No, he was more than tired, he was weary and frail and sad and scared, and his bones felt hollow, his eyes hurt, his chest ached. Nausea occupied every part of his body. He was wearing pajamas, something he never used to do, and now he put his hand on his stomach, under the cotton jacket, and felt how thin he had become, with sharp ribs. This was how it must be to be very old, he thought, but he wasn't old, though when he looked in the mirror he was always taken aback by the change in his appearance. He was ill. Perhaps he was very ill. Perhaps—No, he wouldn't continue that thought. Frieda kept telling him how the treatment he was having was poisoning his whole body in order to destroy the cancer. That was why he felt so bad: it was the cure, not the cancer.

Well, maybe. He closed his eyes and tried not to think about that, and thought instead about all the things he might never do again. Sleep with a woman, drink vodka all night with Josef, wear his dandyish waistcoat at Christmas and sing loudly, give lectures on impotence and male anxiety to a crowded room. Swim—no, he'd never much liked swimming. His thoughts were getting cloudy, sleep tugging him downwards, when he heard his doorbell ring, then the knocker rapped. He waited for Josef to answer, but remembered he had taken Alexei out for a pizza. The bell rang once more. Reuben sat up and swung his legs out of bed. He went down the stairs, making sure his pajama jacket was properly buttoned, and pulled open the front door.

At first he couldn't make out who was standing there in the obscurity of the night, and then he saw. A shape in dark clothes, with a stocking over his face. Or perhaps it was a woman, so perhaps it was her face. And holding something. What? A crowbar, perhaps. He wasn't actually sure he really knew what a crowbar was. It was a word people used. Anyway, holding something designed for hitting. He must look pitiful, standing in his pajamas and staring, his mouth open, air pouring into him, his heart beating too fast. He was all dot and carry one: where had someone used that expression to him? His mother, that was it, many, many years ago. Perhaps it wasn't the cancer that would kill him after all. He thought all of these things and at the same time he was trying to get the door shut, fumbling, his feet sliding across the gritty floor and onto the doormat.

The door wouldn't shut. The figure was still there, in the entrance now. In the hall. Everything was very slow and very silent. His breathing; the breathing of the shape next to him. The arm raised high, the metal bar falling and smashing into his shoulder. Now he was on the floor. He seemed to have time to wait for the pain and he knew it would be bad but it was worse. The first blow was to his face and everything was flashing yellow and blue and he tasted blood, choking on it and spitting it out. The second blow was to the torso and he dimly heard something crack. He was crying now, trying to shift away from the blows but he couldn't move. There was a third blow and a fourth and a fifth until he didn't know where they were striking, lost in a cloud of pain and he wanted to be unconscious or to be dead just so this would stop. Then finally it did stop and everything hurt and everything was wet and there was a terrible smell and still he wasn't unconscious and he could hear himself sobbing and he couldn't see and he couldn't move.

20

It was Alexei who saw him first. He was pushing at the door that Josef had unlocked, but it had stopped against something. He squeezed through the narrow opening and his feet bumped into whatever was on the floor. Josef was saying something from outside but Alexei couldn't make out the words. He bent down in the darkness and put his hand on the soft cloth of Reuben's pajamas, the coldness of an exposed shin, and then something warmer, sticky. He gave a small cry.

Josef pushed the door harder and the shape moved back slightly.

Alexei stood up and felt for the switch. Light flooded the hall. The first thing he saw was his own hand on the switch, red with blood. Then he looked down and saw Reuben's body, still as a corpse, his bald skull shining whitely and his bashed face almost unrecognizable. He couldn't move and he couldn't look away. He stood quite still beside Reuben and at last, for the first time since his mother had died, he started to weep. He wept and he wept and he couldn't stop.

Reuben had a side room in the hospital. When he first woke in it, he didn't know where he was. The strip light flickered above him, the walls were white, the window small and showing only a patch of blue sky. The sounds he could hear might have been inside his own head: an echoing tap of footsteps, small insistent beeps, intermittent cries that reminded him of being a child. He closed his eyes and for a moment everything was blank, and then into that blank memories flowed. A man in a stocking mask; a crowbar cracking against his head, thumping into his body. He remembered staring at the floor on which he lay. Above all, he remembered the horrible silence in which everything had happened.

So he hadn't died, after all. This was a hospital. He opened his eyes and now there was a blurred face. He squinted until it came into focus.

"Frieda," he said. His voice was thick. It hurt to speak. His head hurt and his body ached as if he'd fallen from a great height.

"Reuben."

"Fuck," he managed.

He saw her smile, but her face was terrible.

There were doctors. Nurses. Police officers. There was nothing he could tell them, just a door opening and a figure, faceless. Josef came with vodka in a plastic bottle. Alexei came and stared at him with his huge brown eyes and Reuben tried to smile at him but his face was swollen. Jack brought cheese and the crossword, which together they failed to do. Olivia brought flowers and made a terrific fuss when she was told flowers weren't allowed in the hospital, and Chloë had to lead her away.

After two days, Frieda took him home and he lay in bed, hearing the sounds of the house below him. He felt very weak, like a baby, and sometimes there was a comfort in that: he could just let himself be looked after. But sometimes he would cry, and Josef would soak a flannel in warm water and wipe his forehead with it. At other times he felt sick and Josef would sit by the bed holding a plastic washing-up bowl. When Reuben fell asleep, Josef would lay his large, calloused hand on his friend's naked skull and feel his pulse beating there.

Frieda stood in Reuben's garden with a cup of coffee. She looked at the way the sun fell through the leaves of his apple tree, but what she was really seeing was Reuben's swollen face on the pillow and the way he looked scared and old. Then she became aware of a noise behind her and, turning, she saw Alexei.

"Hello," she said, and smiled at him.

Alexei didn't answer but took a few shuffling steps toward her, a slight figure, with his huge eyes staring at her. He opened his mouth as if he would speak, but no sound came out. She saw how tired he looked and how anxious.

"What is it?" she asked.

Alexei didn't say anything, but slid his small hand into hers, and the two of them stood like that for several minutes, hand in hand in the garden.

"You should go out, Josef," Frieda said.

"No, no. Reuben need me. I stay here with him."

"Alexei needs you too. He's been hanging around here like a small ghost since it happened. He's frightened and lonely. Take him for a walk."

"Really?"

"Really."

So Josef walked with Alexei out onto Primrose Hill and

into the sunshine. As he walked, he talked, even though Alexei didn't reply. He still wasn't entirely used to the relief he felt at speaking his own language. He felt like someone who had been holding his breath under water, suddenly surfacing and breathing air again.

Just now, in his first days back in England, even with everything else that was happening, all the fear and terror of it, the experience of being with Alexei was almost too much for Josef. He felt happy and sad and scared and tender all at once. He felt shy, protective, full of guilt for the past, and anxiety and hope for the future. He thought of Dima, still in Ukraine, and something heavy shifted in his chest. His wife, his ex-wife, was dead. His elder son was far away. His younger son was with him, but mute and mysterious, a code he hadn't yet deciphered.

Alexei was wearing new trainers, new jeans, a new T-shirt. He was tugging at his father's hand, and Josef pointed at the city that felt almost like it was at their feet.

"You see that crane?" He was speaking in their native language, trying to take his son's mind off Reuben's attack. *"You can count them from the left. It's the third."*

Alexei didn't reply but he saw him counting them out.

"Papa worked on that job. It's a big project. We dug down twenty-five meters, thirty meters."

Josef told him about the mass excavators, the bulldozers, the dumper trucks, the cement-mixers, the pile-drivers. Alexei looked up at his father with his mouth open. *"I've driven the bulldozers. I drove a dumper truck. But mostly I work with my hands: drills, electrics."*

He hadn't finished saying what else when Alexei noticed the zoo. He saw it and heard it and then he spoke. *"What animals are there?"*

Josef stopped. His son had spoken at last; he had asked him a question. He knew he shouldn't make too much of it, but a smile was tugging at his mouth. "*All kinds of animals*," he said.

"*Like tigers*?"

Josef paused. "*I'll tell you what*," he said. "*The two of us, we'll go to the zoo. We'll do it soon. We'll make a proper plan.*"

They walked down the stone steps that led to the canal. Alexei slowed. His eyes were bright with a new curiosity and Josef suddenly felt overwhelmed. He had forgotten about this. Now he imagined a future of doing what fathers did, walking in the park, going to the zoo, teaching Alexei to be a craftsman, the way Josef's father had taught Josef. His heart felt swollen, tender as a bruise; he was both happy and sad at once. He looked down at his little son, who seemed so delicate and who had been through so much in his short life and squeezed his hand tighter.

They arrived at Camden Lock, which Josef slightly disapproved of, but Alexei, though he didn't say anything, seemed excited. It had everything. They wandered between the stalls and the smells: roasting meat, bubbling soups, salads, ice cream, multicolored juices. Josef said: "*Later. We'll eat later.*" And then there were the clothes, the leather jackets and the frilly dresses, the Gothic and the Edwardian. Josef felt Alexei's hand slip through his fingers. His son had stopped, staring at a stall of vintage cameras. Then they drifted away again, Alexei darting this way and that, as something caught his eye. Even more exciting, Camden Lock was a building site as well. Alexei pointed at an excavator.

The crowd was thicker now. Josef's mobile rang and he answered.

"Josef?"

"Yes." He watched Alexei out of the corner of his eye. Was his son too thin? Too pale? Was he looking after him properly? He'd make poppy seed cake later, build him up.

"It's Jeannie."

"Jeannie." For a moment, Josef's mind was blank, and then, of course, he remembered. She was pretty, bright, talkative. She had a husband who ignored her and a job she didn't like, and she had been lonely until she met Josef and then, almost alarmingly, she had been happy. But that was all before he had brought his son home. Everything had changed and he had no time for such things now. He was a father—a father who was also the mother—of a son who had been through a war and a death and needed care.

"You haven't called me."

"No."

"Why?"

"I cannot," said Josef, softly.

"What do you mean?"

"I cannot. I am father again."

"What?"

"I am sorry," said Josef.

"But—"

"You are nice," he said. "But this is the end. I wish you fortune."

He ended the call and turned toward the sudden blare of a trumpet from the direction of the canal. Always with the trumpet or the saxophone or even the bagpipes. People threw coins into the open case. Could you really earn enough from that? When he turned back, he couldn't see Alexei. But there was a falafel stall and a coffee stall in the way. The flow of the crowd would bring his son into sight.

It didn't.

Josef sighed. Something must have caught his eye. He walked around the other side of the stall. He still couldn't see him. There was a walkway that led away from the canal toward the high street. But Alexei couldn't possibly have taken that. Unless something had caught his interest. Josef ran along the walkway, looking left and right. He saw a security guard in a yellow high-vis jacket.

"I lose my son," said Josef. He held his hand up. "So high. Hair dark. T-shirt. Jeans."

"I'll keep a look out, mate. He'll just have wandered off."

But Alexei had barely left his side since Josef had arrived to take him to London. He was his anxious shadow, his miniature double. Just in case, Josef ran all the way to the high street. He looked around desperately, as if the boy might suddenly appear. Nothing. He ran back into the market and up some stairs so that he could look down at the crowd. It was so thick that the movement was slow, a sluggish current. There were so many children. Josef saw a dark flash of hair and experienced a moment of hope. But the child was hand in hand with an elderly woman and wore different clothes.

Josef took out his phone. He would give it ten minutes. No. Five minutes had already passed. Five minutes. He ran down the steps toward the canal. Right by the water, a rubbish collector was pushing a trailer along, festooned with shopping bags. The man shook his head. Josef wasn't entirely sure he had made himself understood.

"If you see, tell me. I come back," he said.

He turned left down the canal and approached a couple coming toward him from the east. Had they seen a little boy on his own? They shrugged and said no. He turned and made his way back through the market. Progress was now horribly slow, however much he tried to push himself forward. And always he had to keep looking. On the other side, he turned east up the bridge that led toward Regent's Park. He stopped a woman in running gear, jogging toward her. Laboriously and resentfully she detached her MP3 player from her belt, switched it off and removed one earpiece. Had she seen a boy on his own? She didn't think so. People didn't seem to realize how urgent this was.

He pushed his way back, asking the rubbish collector again, and the security man. He ran back out onto the high street. He was looking in the places he'd already looked. That was it. He took out his phone. He dimly knew that he should call the police but, almost without his thinking about it, his fingers moved a different way.

He called Frieda.

"Stay there," she said.

21

It wasn't that it felt like time was moving slowly. It didn't feel like it existed. Josef was in a fog. He wanted to do anything for his son but he couldn't see or move. He wanted someone to come and make all this go away. He wanted to die. That was all he deserved. His little son, whose hand had been in his just minutes ago. He should have kept hold of that hand. It hurt to breathe; his chest was sore and his throat felt almost closed with terror.

And then from somewhere he heard the lacerating sound of a police siren, the flashing lights, the improbably bright and cheerful blue and yellow colors. The police car came to a halt, then moved out into the wrong side of the road, snaking its way toward him. He held his arm out. He was so scared and guilty and ashamed. It was like he was saying: "It was me. I did it."

The car bumped impudently right up onto the pavement. An interested crowd immediately formed. A young officer stepped from the passenger seat. She looked like a child herself.

"Is me," said Josef. He didn't recognize his own voice.

"How long?" said the officer.

"Fifteen minutes. Less. Please."

She pulled a face at the officer who had come around from the driver's seat.

"He's probably wandered off," she said.

"No," said Josef. "I no think so."

A signal came from the man's radio and he stepped to one side, having a conversation Josef couldn't hear. After just a few moments, he was back.

"The chief said don't . . ." He paused and looked at Josef. " . . . mess around. This is a top priority."

"Do you have a picture?" asked the woman. He did. She showed it to the man, then gave it back to Josef.

"Stand right here," she said. "Show it to anyone who comes."

The two of them walked into the market, separating immediately. Josef just stood there by the empty police car, uselessly clutching his phone with the photo on its screen, surrounded by a crowd that couldn't quite make up its collective mind to disperse. Josef felt a hand on his shoulder. It couldn't be Alexei. He couldn't reach that high. He looked around.

A middle-aged woman was smiling at him. "My kid does that all the time," she said. "He probably doesn't even realize you're looking for him."

Josef just wanted to howl, to hit her, to hit anyone, to lie on the ground like a dog. But he just said: "Yes. Maybe."

Then he said, to everybody and to nobody, "Please. Please help. He is my son."

Another car was approaching, and then another. They were now forming a row. Karlsson got out from the back seat of the second, followed by Frieda. Josef saw her before she saw him.

He had experienced terrible things with Frieda and he knew that Frieda had experienced worse things on her own. But he had never seen her look like this. Her face was like death, but her eyes were terrifyingly alive, looking here, there, sharp as a lash. She caught sight of him and stepped forward toward him. He couldn't speak. He had lost everything. He put his arms around her and started to cry, sobbing and sobbing in a way he hadn't since he was a child. He just couldn't stop himself and he never would be able to. He felt Frieda's hands on his shoulder blades and a reassuring soft pat from them but then she pushed him away. "You can't do this now."

He couldn't stop the tears. He couldn't stop the retching tears.

"Josef!" she said more loudly. And then she slapped him.

A police officer stepped forward.

"Fuck off," said Frieda.

"What?" said the officer, so surprised he couldn't say anything more.

Frieda took the photograph from Josef's hands. "You're no help to Alexei like this."

"My blame," said Josef.

"We can talk about blame later," Frieda said. "But I can tell you it won't be you. What we do now is to think clearly and do what we need to do."

"You do this," said Josef. "You find that boy before. Now find Alexei. You do that, right?"

For a moment Frieda seemed less composed, as if she had been punched unexpectedly.

"We're all going to do what we can. But every minute counts." She looked around at the officer. "I'm sorry I shouted at you." The man started to speak but Frieda interrupted him. "Please take Mr. Morozov to one of the cars. He needs some quiet and some privacy."

Josef tried to protest but Frieda insisted. When he had

gone, she turned to Karlsson. "Now what? Throw a cordon around the area?"

Karlsson was almost as pale and shocked as Frieda. "What area?"

"The market. It's pretty contained."

"It's not contained. There must be thirty exits and thousands of people." He looked at his watch. "Whoever took him would have him in a car by now or on the Tube or they could have walked a mile or more and then got on a bus."

"So what do we do?"

"We look." Karlsson glanced around. Another police car arrived. Officers were running into the market. "How old was he?"

"*Is he*," said Frieda. "We need to keep talking in the present tense. He's eight."

"He's eight. He hardly speaks a word of English. He's in a strange part of a city he doesn't know. Why would he go off with a stranger?"

"Perhaps he was forced. Except this is a crowded public place."

Karlsson thought for a moment. "It was what Dean Reeve used to be good at, persuading little children to get into a car with him," he said. "He used to work with a woman. Children trust women."

Frieda shook her head. "But not here. In the market, in London, with his father ten yards away."

"But he's gone."

"Yes, he's gone."

Frieda knew how this story played out. She had seen it before. For an hour, two hours, there was still hope that it was all a terrible mistake. She had heard of little boys suddenly deciding to play a game of hide and seek and disappearing for hours, maybe even falling asleep under a table somewhere. But was that really credible here in the middle of the busiest market in London? After another hour Frieda saw a group of men carrying some heavy equipment, cylinders, heavy duffel bags from the high street in the direction of the canal.

"He can't have fallen in," said Frieda. "There were thousands of people. The towpath is packed."

"It takes just a second," said Karlsson. "The surface closes over a body very quickly."

Nothing was found. By nine o'clock the story was on the news. Frieda sat beside Josef on Reuben's sofa and the photograph that Josef had shown to the police officer stared out of the screen at them. When, hours later, Frieda said he had to try to sleep Josef looked at her in disbelief.

"He is there in the dark. How can I sleep? How can I sleep ever?"

Frieda had been feeling exactly the same. "There's going to be a press conference tomorrow at ten o'clock. You have to be there."

Josef had a glassy unfocused stare.

"People need to see a grieving parent. They will identify with you and that will help them to remember."

Frieda led him upstairs and got him into his bed. Then she took off her shoes and, still in her clothes, lay on top of the bed beside him and held his hand. Frieda thought that Josef might have slept for an hour or two. She thought of Alexei in the garden with her earlier that day, sliding his hand into hers with trust, and she didn't sleep at all.

22

The next morning Josef sat at the press conference in a tie; he was freshly shaved and washed. He didn't speak. He couldn't. His face was lumpy and his eyes red. Petra Burge read out a statement that Frieda and Karlsson had put out, which represented what Josef would have wanted to say if he had been able to formulate any kind of thoughts or words.

There was a cluster of reporters. Petra spotted Liz Barron, fresh-faced and eager, looking as though she'd just returned from a holiday in the sun, her face tanned and her eyes bright with curiosity.

Reporters asked if there were any leads. Petra said that a blurred image from a CCTV camera under the railway bridge had been recovered. An officer tapped at a laptop and an image appeared on the screen behind them. It was indeed very blurred.

"That," said Petra Burge, "may or may not be Alexei Morozov. And that may or may not be Dean Reeve."

"Do you know which direction they took?"

"No."

"Do you have any witnesses?" This was Gary Hillier, another of the journalists who had interviewed Frieda. He'd shaved off his goatee and now had a very thin mustache, like a line drawn in felt-tip pen above his mouth.

"We're hoping this press conference will encourage people to come forward."

"Do you think," said a man at the back in a carrying voice, "that Dean Reeve is taunting you?"

"I have no comment."

"That he is always one step ahead?"

Afterwards Josef and Frieda were driven back to Reuben's house. Josef went up to his bedroom with a bottle of vodka, his eyes red and dull. Frieda sat with Reuben. Neither of them said anything: what was there to say? They didn't put on the TV or the radio or look online. If anything happened, they would be told. "You can find him," Josef had told Frieda, pathetically. It was true that she had found a boy before. But now she had nothing to go on.

She felt as if she were looking for a finger-hold in an entirely smooth, hard surface. But still she thought and thought, went over everything she knew, and the morning turned to afternoon and they had heard nothing. When her phone rang, it was like being woken from a slow and ghastly dream. She looked at its screen. Karlsson.

"It's seventeen minutes past four," he said. "Or it was, two minutes ago. That's the time Josef rang you. Yesterday. You know what that means?"

"I knew what it meant when they started searching the canal."

"You know what I'm saying. You should prepare Josef. Or start preparing him."

"All right." She broke off the call and walked slowly upstairs.

*

The next morning the sun rose at five forty-five. Jemma Cowan was on the canal at Bow about two minutes later with her little Jack Russell terrier, Seamus. She loved this time of the morning. It was never entirely deserted: there was always the occasional fanatical cyclist. Even today, a runner, shaded against the sun, hooded against the early morning, passed her and ran up the steps.

Seamus snuffled around. He was as enchanted as she was. She sometimes saw cormorants and kingfishers, and other birds she couldn't identify, fish rising and spoiling the clear metallic surface with a slow burp. It was like a country stream, but a country stream in a postapocalyptic landscape, and that was even better. Other people ran and cycled and walked wearing headphones. How could you possibly do that? She loved the unexpected sounds, chirps and barks and screeches. They were as important as the smell of baking bread from the warehouse across the water.

She walked under a low bridge. The curve was so sharp that she had to lower her head and when she emerged on the other side, she saw something that she couldn't quite make sense of. It was a shape on a bench ahead. But why was the shape so small? And why so still? She looked around with a certain unexpected tremor and then she moved closer.

It was a young boy. Dark hair, dirty face, T-shirt, jeans, trainers. It was so strange and out of place that she didn't quite know what to say.

"Are you all right?" Her voice sounded unfamiliar in the stillness. He looked at her solemnly but didn't speak. "Do you know where your mum or dad is?"

The boy looked down at his right hand, which was clenched in a fist. He lifted it up, then slowly pointed the palm at her. There was writing on it, in very small capital letters. She leaned in and read it aloud. "Police," she said. She took out her phone.

23

"Can you tell us anything, Alexei?"

Fran Bolton and Petra Burge were both looking down at the little boy. Alexei was standing in front of them, not speaking, not crying, quite still except he was moving his head, rhythmically, as if he were knocking it against an invisible wall.

"Papa," he said in a whisper.

"He'll be here very, very soon, Alexei," said Petra. "Can you say anything about the person who took you? Big, small? Fat, thin?"

Alexei looked puzzled. Then, after some deliberation, he slowly tapped the top of his right leg.

"What's he doing?" said Fran Bolton.

"There's something in his pocket," said Petra.

She reached into her pocket and took out a pair of nitrile gloves. She knelt in front of Alexei.

"Look," she said to him softly, "I'm putting on these special gloves. Then I'm going to reach into your pocket. Is that OK?"

He nodded, though she couldn't tell if he understood a word she was saying. She pushed her fingers into his trouser pocket. It was tight but she could feel something. She was able to grip it between two fingers and pull it gradually.

It was something wrapped in toilet paper. It weighed almost nothing. She laid it on the table, then carefully pulled the paper aside.

"What is it?" asked Fran Bolton, drawing back instinctively.

It was like a thick, curled up leaf and it gave off a faint, sweetish smell, which made Petra think of damp mushrooms. She turned it over with her finger.

"It's an ear. Part of an ear."

"A pig's?" said Fran Bolton. "Something like that?"

"No, not something like that. Get someone from forensics up here right now."

This time Frieda let Josef cry as much as he wanted. They sat together in the back and Josef leaned on Frieda's shoulder and sobbed and sobbed. When they pulled into the police station car park at Bow, Petra Burge turned around from the passenger seat.

"Can you hear me, Josef?"

Josef lifted his head and she took a tissue from a box in the front seat and passed it to him, then another. He blew his nose and mopped his eyes and his face.

"Josef, as we've told you, Alexei is physically well and, as far as we can see, he's mentally well. Whatever that means after what he's gone through."

"We see him now?" said Josef.

"He hasn't spoken since he was found."

"He speaks no English. And he is quiet always since his mother die."

"All right. Come this way. He's obviously upset."

Josef nodded. For a moment he looked almost frightened; his brown eyes shone with tears. "You too, Frieda?"

"I'll be there in a few minutes. You need a bit of time alone with him."

Josef looked troubled. "Please."

"If you want me to."

"I do want."

As they got out of the car, Petra put a hand on Frieda's arm to detain her. "Two things," she said.

"What?"

"I said Alexei hadn't spoken. That's not quite true. He hasn't spoken except for one thing. He said: 'Frieda Klein.' Whatever they've asked him, that's the only answer he's given. Frieda Klein."

"That's odd," said Frieda slowly. "And the other. You said there were two things."

"There was something in his pocket."

"What was it?" asked Frieda, but before Petra replied, she suddenly knew what she was going to say.

"A human ear, wrapped in toilet paper."

Frieda was going to ask something else and then she realized. "Bruce Stringer's."

"It's a possibility."

"It must be."

"But why?" said Petra.

"Which bit?"

"All of it. You go to the trouble of kidnapping a child, then return him. And you don't just return him. You give him a trophy from a previous murder."

"Trophy," said Frieda, thoughtfully. "I don't think that's right."

"Oh, you don't? Why not?"

"I know there are times when the sexual impulse somehow gets fused with violence. When they commit a crime they need a way of reliving it. Sometimes memory isn't enough. I don't think Dean Reeve is like that. If he was, he might be easier to catch. I think when he does something, he does it for a reason."

"So what's the reason for the ear?"

"It tells us that the person who took Alexei killed Stringer."

"And why do we need to be told that?"

"If we were inside talking to Alexei," said Frieda, "and not outside talking to ourselves, we might find out."

Petra's expression hardened.

"'We.' Sometimes you presume too much."

Alexei was sitting at a table, Don Kaminsky huge but curiously delicate at his side, not speaking and not quite touching him, but solid and close. The boy had a carton of orange juice and a sandwich, but he paid no attention to either. He was wearing unfamiliar clothes. His own had been taken away for examination. His face was blank, wiped clean. He turned and saw Josef and for a moment Josef didn't move, just stared at his son with a look of anguish. Then he crossed the room to where Alexei sat. He knelt beside the chair and opened his arms, speaking crooningly to him in a language nobdy else understood.

He put his arms around his son and, for a moment, Alexei didn't move or react. Then he leaned into his father's shoulder and closed his eyes. Josef was half sobbing and trying not to, and at last a single tear ran down his son's cheek. For several minutes, they stayed like that, Josef stroking the child's soft dark hair and muttering endearments.

When they moved apart, Frieda came forward. She sat

opposite Alexei and didn't speak. He stared at her. His face was pinched with effort.

"Frieda Klein," he said at last. He made it sound foreign and strange.

She pointed at herself.

Alexei frowned, like a pupil called on by the teacher. "This," he said.

It was the first English word she'd ever heard from him; she'd barely heard a Ukrainian one.

"This what?" she asked, aware of the uselessness of the question.

"This," he repeated painfully. "This. Is. Me."

No one spoke, though Josef gave a small gasp. Kaminsky wrote on a pad.

"Look. Somewhere." He obviously didn't understand the words he was saying: he'd learned them by rote. There was a long pause. Somewhere? thought Frieda. What does that mean? "Else," said Alexei. Then, in a gabble of sound: "This is me look somewhere else."

Frieda looked at Josef. "Ask him where those words came from."

Josef and his son had a whispered conversation in their own language and Frieda heard her name being mentioned. Then Josef turned to her. "Man teach him words and say to him: say to Frieda Klein."

"Good," said Frieda to Alexei. "That was good. Thank you."

He gazed at her uncomprehendingly.

"Josef. You need to ask him one question," said Petra Burge. "There'll be others, but this one first. Ask him why he went with the man."

Josef put his arm around his son and they had another whispered conversation. Josef looked suddenly startled.

"What?" said Petra.

"He say the man say in Ukrainian—in very, very bad Ukrainian—'I take you to your mother.'"

"That would do it." Frieda nodded to herself. "Of course."

"So Dean Reeve doesn't know Alexei's mother is dead," said Petra.

"He absolutely knows she's dead."

"Then why would Alexei go with him?"

"Because he's a boy who lost his mother."

Petra gave a comprehending nod. "At least we know the area where Dean Reeve is probably staying."

"No, we don't."

"Why else would he choose this spot?"

"It's where he killed his brother," said Frieda. "He left a memento and he chose a site to make us unequivocally sure that it was him. And, of course, that's the point."

"You're talking in riddles. What are you trying to say?"

"Can we talk somewhere privately?"

"If you want. Don will stay here with you, Mr. Morozov," she said to Josef. Don Kaminsky gave a nod. "Would you like something to drink?"

"Vodka?"

"I was thinking tea or coffee."

"Oh."

For a moment, Frieda thought even Petra Burge would make an exception to a fixed rule because of Josef's mournful brown eyes.

"I'll be back in a few minutes," she said.

She led Frieda along the corridor to an empty interview room and shut the door, gesturing to a chair. "Well?"

"Look somewhere else. You asked what it meant."

"I think," said Petra, slowly, "that I know what you're going to say."

"There are two parts of the message. The first is that the person who took Alexei is Dean."

"Yes. And the second?"

Frieda fixed her gaze on the DCI. "He's telling me he didn't kidnap Chloë or attack Reuben."

Petra nodded slowly. "Why would he bother to do that? Why would he care?"

"I don't know. Out of professional pride, maybe. Sometimes I feel he wants me to know things. That's why what happened to Chloë and Reuben didn't fit. When he killed Stringer and Glasher, it had a logic to it, and it was aimed at me."

"When you talk about Dean Reeve . . ." Petra began.

"What?"

"You sound different. Like you understand each other."

"Don't try to analyze me. Somehow I got tangled with Reeve's life and got into his head. I only want him caught. Nothing else."

"All right. But let's look at all the possibilities."

"What are they?"

Petra thought for a moment. "That Dean is lying," she said, "and that he was responsible for the two other crimes."

"No," said Frieda.

"It's possible. Or second, these could be two unconnected incidents. Your niece could have crossed paths with a pervert."

"She wasn't sexually assaulted."

"That proves nothing. There are people who get off on the control, on just looking."

"And why would he send a photograph to a journalist reporting on the Reeve murders?"

"That's a better point," Petra conceded. "But the attack on Dr. McGill could have been a robbery gone wrong."

"Nothing was stolen."

"That's why I used the phrase 'gone wrong.' And the third possibility is that there's someone else out there."

"Yes. Doing what?"

"Murders attract people, like flies to shit."

"You mean someone is copying Dean?"

"That's the possibility, yes, a copycat. All the roads lead to you."

Frieda stood up and went to the window. She put a hand against it, as if to make sure there really was glass between her and the world. Then she turned back to Petra Burge and said, in a quiet, clear voice, "That's not right. They lead to my friends."

"It's all about you."

"I'm not the one being attacked."

"For the moment."

"You need to protect them. Now."

"Your friends?"

"Yes."

"*All* your friends?"

"You've seen what can happen. Reuben could have died. Chloë . . ." She stopped. The image of her niece lying on a stained mattress, her legs apart, filled her mind.

"How many friends do you have?"

"Chloë and Reuben are already at risk. There's Chloë's

mother, Olivia. I would say my friend Sasha and her little boy, Ethan, but she's living with her father for a few months and miles away, so she's probably safe. There's Josef and his son. And my young friend Jack Dargan."

"And you."

"I can look after myself."

"It doesn't matter. It's not feasible."

"Is it about money?"

"It's about a proper and professional use of limited resources and, yes, it's also about money. It wouldn't have been possible anyway, but now we're cutting our budget by a quarter and that's just the start. We can't do the things we're already doing."

"People are in danger."

"I'm not the one you need to persuade."

"You're not even going to try?"

"Listen, if you're right, and we did get protection for all these people—which isn't possible anyway—then this person can simply pick on someone else, widen the circle of your friends. Protect those six and another group comes under threat. It's just not feasible, whichever way you look at it."

"So that's it."

"Not at all. There is an investigation into the abduction of Chloë, another into the attack on Dr. McGill, and a further one into the abduction of Alexei Morozov. That's how we can protect your friends. We can catch who is doing this."

"I see."

Petra looked at her warily. "What are you going to do?"

"I'm not sure. But something. They're my friends."

*

As Frieda was walking home, her phone rang. She looked at it. It was Paz, the administrator at the Warehouse. She answered the call.

"I've got two new patients for you," Paz said.

"What?"

"You said you were taking new patients again. In fact, you said the more the better."

Frieda paused, almost stunned. It was the worst, most impossible time. But she suddenly felt: if not now, when? If she waited for life to be normal, she would never again practice as a therapist.

"All right," she said. "Put them in touch with me."

"You're welcome," said Paz.

"I'm sorry. Thank you," said Frieda, feeling anything but grateful.

The way stands clear and it was Dean Reeve who made it so. Dean Reeve who came like a ghost in winter and who put a body under her floorboards, so that now the whole world is looking at her.

When the whole world is looking, he can look too. Nobody will see him. He can be as invisible as smoke under a door. Like Dean Reeve himself. The name sends a tingle through him, a small electric nudge of pleasure: they will be linked. Dean Reeve and him.

They won't find Dean Reeve. Nobody ever finds Dean Reeve. But now he can walk in Dean Reeve's path. He can act in his name. No one will know that there are two of them.

Except, of course, Dean Reeve will know. What happened with the boy shows he knows. It's like a duet. Reeve has answered and he will answer back.

24

"This is quite like old times," said Reuben.

His ribs were broken, his face was bruised and thin, there was a purple gash on the back of his bald skull and he walked with a painful limp, but he had put on a fresh shirt that Josef had ironed for him and was wearing his favorite brightly colored waistcoat. He had opened three bottles of red wine and lined them up along the dresser. Josef had poured vodka into shot glasses. He had spent the afternoon preparing a vast Ukrainian meal. Alexei lay in bed, sleeping fitfully; occasionally he would wake and call out for his mother. *Matir, ma.* Josef would run up the stairs, hold his hand and whisper to him, crooning words he had used when Alexei was a baby, then return to the kitchen, which was full of steam, the smell of potato cakes, barley broth with dumplings and a spicy lamb stew.

"We must have candles," said Josef. "Many candles."

"It's still light outside."

"Candles to make special."

So Reuben lit candles along the table he had laid. He felt frail; his body ached. Every so often, he let himself remember the stockinged face at the door, the metal bar thumping into his prone body. But this felt good: the safety of friends gathering, of spicy food cooking on the stove, the sound of Josef's knife cutting through vegetables, wine breathing in bottles, and now candles lit upon the table. Chaos was held at bay for a while.

Chloë arrived straight from the joiner's workshop wearing her work clothes, sawdust in her hair. Jack, bearing blue cheese, tawny hair in peaks. Olivia, with a bottle of wine and already slightly tipsy, a telltale flush in her cheeks, long earrings dangling, lips bright with lipstick, exuberantly hugging everyone. Reuben could tell she was ready to cry.

"Where's Frieda?" she asked.

"I'm sure she'll be here soon," he said.

And she was, coming into the room quietly, so they barely noticed she was among them. She and Josef went upstairs to see Alexei and then they all gathered together in the kitchen. Josef handed around shot glasses of vodka and they drank before taking their places. Alexei came downstairs and sat between Josef and Reuben, his cheeks flushed, his eyes darting now this way and now that. The pots of food lined the table, and Josef presided over them in his apron, anxious and proud.

"This is nice," said Olivia. "So many carbs! But lovely and comforting after everything that's happened." She gave an emotional hiccup and ladled herself some broth with dumplings. "Reuben and Chloë and Alexei." She leaned toward him, earrings swinging, hair falling in small cascades from its knot. "Little darling!"

Alexei stared at her in a kind of fearful surprise.

"I wanted us all to be together," said Frieda, "because there's something I need to say."

"A toast," said Olivia. She held up her glass, voice quavering. "A toast to friendship."

"Not a toast," said Frieda. "I need to say that terrible things have happened and maybe they're not over."

She looked at the faces turned toward her. "I think someone is picking on you because you are my friends."

"Dean Reeve," said Jack. "We know."

"Dean Reeve took Alexei. But he wasn't the one who took Chloë or attacked Reuben. Someone else did that."

"Someone else?" said Jack. "Why?"

"It doesn't matter," said Frieda. "Not now, anyway. What's crucial is that you might be under threat. Each of you."

"And you," said Reuben.

"Maybe. But the fact is that there's someone out there and he may be targeting you all, because you know me."

"It could be a she," said Chloë. "If it's not Dean."

"It could. Whoever it is abducted you, held you for a whole weekend, and attacked Reuben."

Jack ran his hands through his hair. "This isn't good."

"I asked the police if you could be protected. I'm afraid it's not going to happen."

"Does that mean they don't think we're in danger?" asked Olivia.

"It means they don't have the resources."

"I protect my family," said Josef. He banged both fists on the table so that the cutlery jumped. "Friends."

"I'm a woman," said Olivia. "I live all alone."

"I'm coming to that. Josef has a friend called Dritan. He put in new locks for me after I discovered Dean had been in my house."

"How did that work out?" said Jack, but Frieda ignored him.

"He'll go to Olivia's tomorrow, and then here."

"What about Chloë?" asked Jack. "And what about me?"

"I want Chloë to move back in with Olivia."

"I've only just moved out."

"And I was hoping you, Jack, could stay there as well."

"At least you're a man." Olivia took hold of a new bottle by its neck and splashed red wine into her glass.

"Excuse me," said Chloë. "I'm quite good at defending myself, you know. Probably better than Jack."

"Probably," said Jack. The two exchanged glances, a brief flash of their old affection animating them.

"Fine," said Frieda. "We're going to look out for each other."

Josef leaned toward her. "Where are you, Frieda?"

"Come and stay with us," urged Chloë.

"Absolutely not."

"I send my friend," said Josef.

"No. Surely you can see that nobody can live with me."

"What about Karlsson?"

"Karlsson—what about him?"

"He's your friend."

Petra Burge had said that as well.

"That's different."

"Why?"

"It just is."

Karlsson and Frieda sat in his small garden in the mild warmth of the late evening. It was twilight, the sky fading, birds singing invisibly. A time for foxes and bats, for secrets and confessions. There was already the faint outline of the moon on the horizon. A bottle of whisky stood on the table between them, a small jug of water, two tumblers. Frieda poured some for each of them. She added a splash of water to hers. Karlsson did the same.

"The end of a beautiful Sunday," he said.

"When I was little, I hated Sundays," she said.

"How can anyone hate Sundays?"

"It was a day of silences and boredom and nothing to do and going to church and seeing family you didn't want to see."

"At least you grew out of it."

"It's a day when people hide from themselves. When they try to forget what they did on Saturday and pretend that next week isn't going to be the same as last week."

"Is your week going to be the same as last week?"

"No," said Frieda. "I'm starting to see patients again. I've got two new ones tomorrow."

"That sounds like a positive sign."

"I don't think any signs seem positive just at the moment."

"I'm sorry I brought the whole thing up," said Karlsson, looking at his glass ruefully. "But I always quite liked Sunday myself: having brunch, reading the papers, going for walks."

"Speaking of walks, have you heard from Yvette?" Frieda asked.

"She's not really a Facebook sort of person. Nor am I."

Frieda reached into her bag for her wallet to find the little piece of paper she had been carrying around with her. She showed it to Karlsson.

"What's that?"

"Yvette said I should call if I needed help. She would come from wherever she was."

"She'd do that," he said.

"Maybe I could do with her protection. Maybe we all could."

"So you've warned me," he said, with a small smile.

"Yes."

"I'll be vigilant."

"You have two little children." She sensed Karlsson stiffen slightly.

"I have," he said softly. "I'll be vigilant of them as well. You should be too." He smiled without humor. "Beware of strangers," he said.

Frieda laid her glass against her forehead for a moment. "I've put everyone in danger," she said at last. "Everyone who trusts me." She turned to him and he could see her eyes glowing in the half-light.

"Don't think of it like that."

"Those who care about me. Those I care about."

He didn't reply.

25

The following afternoon she sat in her consulting room, in the chair that felt almost like a part of her body, and looked at Morgan Rossiter. He looked back at her. Some patients had trouble meeting her eye, especially at the first session, but not this one. He was dressed in a checked shirt, faded blue jeans and scuffed boots. He looked like a builder but he didn't sound like one. He was a university teacher and he had been referred to her only the previous week.

"Dr. Singh told me that you asked for me personally," said Frieda. "Why?"

"People have been telling me for years that I should talk to someone. Girlfriends, mostly. But I always said that I could never talk to someone I didn't respect."

"Is that an answer to my question?"

"I wouldn't stay in a hotel without checking it in advance. Why wouldn't I do that with a therapist?"

"So why were girlfriends telling you that you needed therapy?"

"I've had problems at work and a relationship broke up and I went to see my doctor and she was about twelve years old and she only gave me about eight minutes."

There was a long pause.

"One important part of therapy," said Frieda, finally, "is why you're doing it. Can we start with that?"

Rossiter answered quickly, as if he had come prepared. "When this relationship broke up—it was me that broke it up, by the way—I wondered if I had a problem with commitment. I keep having these relationships. I'm faithful while I'm in them. Most of the time. But then they get to a certain stage and I end them."

"You also said you were having trouble at work."

"Just the usual."

"You'll have to explain what that means."

He looked down at the carpet. "I'm forty-two, not publishing enough of any merit, just stuff that enables me to keep tenure, not doing what I thought I'd be doing when I was thirty-two. The usual. Blah blah blah."

"And in that situation, you went to your GP and said you wanted therapy and that you wanted it with me, specifically."

"You must have lots of people wanting you as a therapist," said Rossiter. "I thought you'd have a waiting list."

"That's not an answer."

Now he raised his eyes and looked at her once more. "I thought it would be interesting," he said. "The notorious Frieda Klein."

The other new patient was a man in his twenties called Alex Zavou. Six months earlier he had been in a pub just off the Caledonian Road when a fight had started. He had tried to intervene to stop it but a knife had been pulled and a teenage boy had been killed. When he talked about it, his hands trembled and all the color left his face, as if he were still at the scene of the murder.

"I don't really know why I'm here," he said. "I don't see

the point of talking about it. I already went on this short series of . . . you know."

"Cognitive behavioral therapy," said Frieda.

"This man tried to give me strategies and plans and exercises that would stop me going over and over it in my mind." As he said those words, Zavou grabbed his head between his hands. "It didn't do anything at all. And I got the medication. I just keep going over and over whether it would have been better if I hadn't done anything or if I'd done something different. I didn't see the knife. I just remember this boy stumbling against me and looking at me with a really surprised expression, like in a cartoon, his eyes open wide. He just sat down and I saw that the floor was wet with something." He gazed at Frieda almost pleadingly. "I know you're going to say that there's nothing I could have done. The knife cut an artery in his chest. Nothing could have saved him. People keep telling me that. What I want is a drug that will just stop me going over and over it. Or an operation that will cut a bit out of my brain so it's just gone. What I don't need to do is to talk about it over and over."

There was a silence and Frieda let it continue for a long time before she broke it. "As you know," she said finally, "there is no such drug and no such operation and no quick fix because this is life and we're actual people."

"That's not much of a comfort."

"I'm not here to be a comfort and I'm not here to be your friend. Do you have close friends?"

"A couple."

"Do you talk to them about this?"

"A bit."

"That's good. But this is going to be different. I'm going to tell you something. This won't go away. This will never stop being a part of your life, a part of who you are. And that doesn't have to be a bad thing."

"It's easy for you to say that," said Zavou. "Sitting there, you can't imagine what it's like to see what I've seen."

For a moment Frieda thought of what she could have said in response but she stayed silent. That wouldn't be any help.

26

"The trouble," said Olivia, yanking open the fridge door and peering inside, "is that she's never here. What kind of protection is that? There's nothing to eat. How can there be nothing to eat? Where's my bloody quiche gone?"

"I'll have something when I get home," said Frieda.

"There was at least half left. She's eaten it."

"It doesn't matter."

"Oh yes it does. Anyway, at least there's still plenty of wine." Olivia emerged brandishing a bottle that she banged down on the table between them, among the piles of magazines, the unwashed dishes and the unopened bills. "White good?"

"Just half a glass."

"All the more for me."

"I wanted to ask—"

"*And* when she's here she's holed up in her room. Wearing headphones. So she wouldn't hear if anything was happening." Olivia's voice rose. "If, for instance, I was being murdered, she wouldn't hear me screaming. She'd just go on humming along to whatever it is that's destroying her eardrums."

"I can hear now!" came Chloë's voice from above them.

"There you are. She hasn't changed since she was tiny.

Little pig with big ears, that's what your brother used to call her." Olivia poured two large glasses and handed one to Frieda. "Before he fucked off out of our lives, that is, and left me to deal with everything."

Frieda couldn't work out if Olivia had already had something to drink, or if she was just more than usually overwrought. She was wearing a purple jumpsuit and high heels, a chunky gold necklace coiled around her neck several times, hooped earrings, and everything about her seemed slightly awry. The varnish on her fingernails was chipped. Her hair was coming loose.

"Can I—" she began.

"Don't you want to ask me how I am?"

"How are you?"

"Not good. Very, very far from good. For a start, I can't work out how to get into my own house because of all these new locks and security bolts and codes. It's like being in a prison."

"It's for your own safety."

"Right. Because some homicidal maniac is out there. I lie awake all night, thinking I can hear footsteps on the other side of my bedroom door. I don't sleep well at the best of times, but now I don't get a wink. Not a single wink. And then I've got Chloë with me again." She lifted her eyes toward the ceiling and dropped her voice to a theatrical whisper. "She's so bloody judgemental. She thinks I drink too much, she thinks I'm too messy. She criticizes my lifestyle—well, that's being a kettle, or a pot, whichever. She keeps going on about you. Saint Frieda. We shout at each other. It's like having a belligerent teenager back in the house."

"How are things working out with Jack?"

"He's not much help. He leaves early and gets back late. I hardly see him."

"Yes, but—"

"And I'm menopausal, Frieda. *Menopausal.* That means I break out in sweats and I cry all the time and I'm all washed up, Frieda. All washed up," she repeated, with a gloomy relish. "I'll never meet anyone now, will I? Kieran was nice but he left in the end."

"I thought it was you who left him."

"They all leave in the end. This is who I am: the unemployed, middle-aged, divorced, lonely Olivia Klein." Her eyes filled with tears. "I was such a pretty girl," she said, almost dreamily. "I thought it would all be wonderful. Life."

She poured herself another hefty glass of wine.

"I'm sorry about it all."

"Oh, well." Olivia spoke drearily.

"You say you're lonely."

"You've been talking to Chloë."

"No."

"She's been telling you about my dates."

"No, she hasn't."

"It's because I'm scared."

"What do you mean?"

"I don't want to be all alone in this house. So I make sure I have company from time to time. It makes me feel safer."

"You're saying that it makes you feel safer to invite men you don't know very well back here?"

"Don't you go all stern on me. I can see where Chloë gets it from, not that she can talk. It's my life. I can do what I want and I'm not hurting anyone."

"I'm not being stern, Olivia. I just want you to be careful."

"It's like a bad dream." Olivia put out a hand and held on to Frieda's arm.

"I'm sorry. Can you tell me their names?"

"Names?"

"The men you've been dating."

"You can't be serious."

"Just as a precaution." She sounded like a police officer, she thought.

"Oh, God. Oh dear. OK. There's Bobby."

"Bobby who?" asked Frieda.

"I don't know. He told me. It'll come back to me."

"How did you meet him?"

"I met him in a bar." Olivia's cheeks were flushed but she glared defiantly at Frieda.

"What does he do?"

"Something with the Inland Revenue." Olivia snorted. Then she held up a hand. "Astley, that's his last name. Robert Astley."

"How many times have you met him?"

Olivia floated her hands in the air.

"A few. I'm seeing him on Thursday as a matter of fact."

"Any others in the past few weeks?"

"What is this? An interrogation? There was a man called Dick. I don't know his last name either. I only saw him once. He was a bit of a creep, as a matter of fact. And Dominic. I met him on the singles site but it turned out he wasn't single after all. Dominic Gordon, if you want to know. Then Oliver. Ollie. I've only met him twice. He's quite sweet. Younger than me, though he doesn't know that. Or he probably does, actually. Who am I kidding?"

"How did you meet?"

"He came to the door to find out if I was interested in having the house valued and I invited him in for coffee."

"So he's an estate agent?"

"Yes. I suppose so."

"All right."

"You're not really thinking it's any of them?"

"I want you to be careful, Olivia. Don't immediately trust people."

"I'm scared." She gave a dramatically loud sob. "I just want all of this to go away. And what am I going to eat?"

"Shall I make us something?"

"Would you? I can't face it."

"Why don't you go and have a bath and I'll put something simple together?"

She made a rudimentary Greek salad and heated up some rolls she found in the small freezer. Then she set about clearing the kitchen, washing dishes, scouring pans, wiping surfaces, gathering scattered papers and magazines and books and putting them into a pile. Chloë came in while she was doing it. "You shouldn't be clearing up her mess. I'll do it later."

"I don't mind."

"How does she seem to you?"

"Are you worried about her?"

"She's always a bit all over the place," said Chloë. "But does it seem worse than usual?"

"Maybe."

"When I was little, I used to be scared. I never knew what I might find. One day she'd be affectionate, all over

me, then lying in bed crying because some man or other
had broken her heart. Or drunk. Or on a purge and stone-
cold sober and grim with it."

"I know."

"That's why it was so important you were around."

"I'm still around," said Frieda.

"Yeah. But I'm meant to be a grown-up now."

"And you are a grown-up. That doesn't mean you don't
need people any more."

Chloë was rubbing at a small knot of wood on the table.

"It's hard moving back."

"I hope it won't be for long."

"It's all awful, isn't it? The things that have happened."

"Yes. For you especially."

"Me and Alexei and Reuben." Her eyes filled with tears.
"He looks so ill, Frieda."

"It's partly the treatment, of course."

"Do you ever wish things wouldn't change?"

"Is that what you wish?"

"I didn't know it would be this hard."

"Being an adult?"

"I guess. Sometimes I wish I was still doing my A levels
and you were helping me with my bloody chemistry and I
was with Jack."

"You hated school. And chemistry. And there were
good reasons why you and Jack didn't stay together."

"I know."

"And you like what you're doing, don't you?"

"I really do. I don't know why I'm being gloomy. Everything's felt a bit odd since that weekend."

"Your missing weekend?"

"Yes."

She was still rubbing her finger intently into the wood of the table. Frieda couldn't see her expression.

"Have you considered talking to someone?"

"What's there to say? I don't remember anything. How can I talk to someone about not remembering?"

"What we don't know—all the gaps and the silences—can be more powerful than what we believe we do know."

"I'll think about it."

"Do that. It might be helpful. Now, I wanted to ask you something else."

"Go on."

"If I'm right and someone's targeting my family and friends, then it's probably someone who knows one of us, even if only slightly."

Chloë lifted her head at last, and fixed her eyes on Frieda. "That's horrible."

"This might not be relevant, but can you tell me who you've met recently?"

"There's Klaus, of course." She gave a faint smile. "The man you met and questioned."

"It wasn't him who abducted you. He was with his friend from Germany."

"That's good." Chloë nodded several times. She looked young and solemn.

"Are you still seeing him?"

"I think you frightened him off."

"Sorry."

"It doesn't matter, really. He was easily frightened and I'm not in the mood for anything. Not after what happened."

"I can understand that. Is there anyone else that you've met recently? Someone you don't really know about."

Chloë folded her arms across her chest and shivered, though the night was mild. "It feels like I'm accusing someone."

"Who?"

"There's a new guy at work. Scottish. He's called William. William McCollough."

"What's he like?"

"He's older than the rest of us. Good at what he does but keeps himself to himself."

"Right."

"You really think that it's someone one of us knows?"

"It's possible."

"Where's it all going to end?"

Chloë's question was in Frieda's mind as she walked swiftly toward her house, taking the narrow side streets. She thought of Chloë's new work colleague who kept himself to himself. She thought of her new patients, the one with post-traumatic stress disorder, the other with commitment problems. She pictured a crowbar smashing into Reuben as he lay on the floor in his pajamas, of Chloë as she'd found her and as she'd been in that photo the journalist had handed her, lying on a mattress somewhere.

So many people. And they were just the very beginning. Once you started becoming suspicious, the stain spread. *Where's it all going to end?*

She had had the idea of checking up on all her friends' new acquaintances and now she saw that it was impossible, absurd.

She bit her lip, hesitating. She didn't really want to ask Karlsson but she didn't know who else to turn to.

She changed direction and started walking back toward Highbury.

"What are you asking?" Karlsson said, after Frieda stopped talking.

"I'm not sure exactly."

"Maybe because you don't want to say it out loud, so I will. You want to investigate your own friends."

"For their own good."

"So you'll need to hire someone."

"I don't know how to do that."

"I do."

"They'd have to be good at their job."

"Like Bruce Stringer was good at his?"

Frieda flinched but held his gaze. "This isn't about finding Dean. This is nothing to do with Dean, except that he seems to have set someone else off. I'm never going to ask for help with Dean again. Not ever."

Karlsson nodded. He looked tired, Frieda thought, and subdued.

"Are you going to tell them?"

"No."

"Murky waters."

"But will you help me?"

"I always do, don't I?"

All things come to those who wait. His heart is full. He can feel it beating. I am, I am. And I will be. Every morning when he wakes, every evening when he lies in bed and stares into the darkness.

He thinks of the niece on the mattress. Pushing a needle into the soft flesh in her arm. Powerless bodies. Objects. Nothing had gone wrong. There she was, and the place was seething with people. Easy. People should be more careful. Asking for trouble. Well, here comes trouble. Steering her out of the door when she started feeling faint. Catching her as she fell. Heavier than she looks. But car at the ready and in she goes. Hey-ho, and off they go. Playing nice music. Him and her. Frieda Klein's niece in his car. A giant giggle had lodged in his throat. His eyes watered with it.

When he had arrived, everything was ready. He laid her down and then he stood back and looked at her. The noise was so loud he couldn't tell if it was inside or outside his head. His whole body was vibrating.

He thinks of the crowbar hitting Reuben McGill's stomach. The soft thump. The whimpers from the man as he lay on the floor in his stupid pajamas.

At night he lifts the lid of his laptop and looks at what he's got, safely stored on the cloud, floating there. His fingers move across the keys. Her face appears; Dean's. He adds others. Detective Chief In-

spector Malcolm Karlsson. Detective Chief Inspector Petra Burge. Detective Constable Don Kaminsky. Commissioner Crawford. Professor Hal Bradshaw.

And that other one, secretly ticking away. Even Dean Reeve doesn't know about that. Not yet.

27

Dennis Rudkin, private investigator, had his office in Tottenham, above a laundrette and next to a shop selling Italian suits and pointed shoes. Buzzed in over the intercom, Frieda made her way up the unlit stairs and opened the door on to a room that felt threadbare and functional. It was lined with filing cabinets and had a large table by the window on which were two computers, a shredder, two cameras, and multiple piles of papers and folders. On the balding red rug lay a sharp-faced little dog with alert, oversized ears; it didn't bark at her but it followed her movements with its eyes.

At first she couldn't see Rudkin. He was almost invisible behind one of the computers, a meager man, who looked, she thought, a bit like his dog and his room. He was wearing a striped shirt with a white collar and had sparse gray hair and the lined face of a smoker.

"Hello," he said, and shot his hand out between the folders to forcefully grasp hers. It was bony but surprisingly large and strong. "Frieda Klein."

"Yes."

"Take a seat."

Frieda sat.

"Good to meet you. Lots of my clients, I never meet. It's all done by phone or online."

"Before we begin, can I ask you what you call yourself?"

Dennis Rudkin frowned, his face wreathed in deep wrinkles. "I'm a private investigator, is that what you mean?"

"I thought nowadays you might be—I don't know. Consultant in surveillance or something."

"Most people find me online. That's what they'll Google. And they'll find me. But that's not how you found me, is it?"

"No. DCI Karlsson recommended you."

"I'm glad he still remembers me. Now." He rubbed his long hands together. "How can I help you?"

"I'm not sure what kind of things you normally do," said Frieda.

"I do a bit of everything," he said cheerfully. "Not just adultery, if that's what you're thinking, looking through bedroom windows. I hardly do any of that. Most of my work is done from here, sitting at my desk with my computer. In fact, my bread and butter is insurance fraud. That's how I started out. In my old life, I was a claims investigator for an insurance company."

"So why did you leave?"

"I got sick of signing off on claims I knew were false. Everybody lies."

"So you were lying as well."

His eyebrows shot up. He peered at her over his cluttered desk. "And now I'm not. I find out the truth. And tell it. Coffee?" He gestured at the kettle on top of one of the cabinets.

"No, thank you."

"So what do you want to find the truth about?"

Frieda tried to keep the explanation as short as possible, but it took some time. The dog stirred on the rug, curled around on itself, let its tail wag briefly. The sun shone in through the window, showing all the smears on the glass.

When she had finished, Rudkin was silent for a long time.

"You're asking me to investigate your friends' lives."

"Wasn't I being clear?"

"Yes, you were being clear. Do you have their details with you?"

Frieda passed him a piece of paper on which she had written the names and addresses of Chloë, Olivia, Reuben and Jack. Under Chloë's she had written the name of William McCollough; and under Olivia's, all the names of the men she had mentioned she had recently dated. She hadn't included Josef, not yet at least; and she hadn't included Karlsson.

"You're not looking for anything in particular."

"I'm looking for a possible threat."

"You realize that if I don't find anything, it doesn't mean there isn't anything."

"I do."

"It's a shot in the dark."

"Yes."

"And it'll take a bit of time. I'll need help."

"Help?"

"There's someone I use," Rudkin said.

"I'm going to warn my friends in advance," said Frieda. "It seems only fair."

"No, you're not." He stood up and came around his desk, stooping to scratch the dog's pink belly, then took up position in front of the window, his hands behind his back. Frieda saw he was wearing slippers. "What good's a secret investigation if it's not secret? You don't want to betray your friends, so instead you're asking them to betray *theirs*."

"I take your point," said Frieda.

Dennis Rudkin lifted himself onto his toes, then lowered himself once more. Behind him, a double-decker bus drew to a grinding halt and Frieda could see the faces of two young women seated at the front, looking in on them.

"Everyone has secrets," he said.

"I know."

"You don't. You think you know."

"All right, I won't tell them." She hesitated. "There's one other thing."

"Go on."

Frieda drew another sheet of paper from her bag but didn't immediately hand it over. "How discreet are you?" she asked.

"How long do you think I've been doing this for?"

"I don't know."

"Twenty-seven years. How long do you think I would have lasted if I wasn't discreet?"

Frieda handed him the paper. "Alex Zavou," he read. "Morgan Rossiter. Well?"

"I'm a psychotherapist," said Frieda. "These two men are new patients of mine."

"You want me to investigate your patients?"

"Yes."

Rudkin made a little whistling sound between his crooked teeth. "I've got to hand it to you," he said. "You're cold-blooded. You know what you're doing?"

"If it were discovered, I'd be struck off. Quite rightly."

"All right," he said. "Leave it with me."

"Thank you."

"Aren't you going to ask how much I charge?"

"How much do you charge?"

"Forty-five pounds an hour. And there are going to be a lot of hours. And two of us."

"All right."

"Plus VAT."

"Fine."

"You don't care, do you?"

"No."

"Fill this out," said Dennis Rudkin. He crossed to the table and plucked a printed form from the top of one of the piles. He crouched and stroked his dog while Frieda wrote down her contact number, then stood up to shake her hand, even more firmly this time.

"I'll be in touch."

28

Olivia decided she would be safer with Reuben and Josef in Reuben's house. It took careful negotiation. Then Frieda had to help her pack. When she arrived, she saw her sister-in-law surrounded by bags and cases, shoes scattered on the floor, clothes arranged in piles.

"You should think of it like staying with someone for a few days," said Frieda. "Not moving house."

"That's exactly what I was thinking," said Olivia. "I'm not nine years old. This isn't like going somewhere for a sleepover. I'm taking only what I need in order to live a very stripped-down and deprived version of my pathetic apology for a life."

So Frieda ordered a large taxi, the sort designed for a small sports team, and she and the grumbling driver helped Olivia load it up. As they did so, Chloë came out of the house, carrying another of Olivia's bags.

"You'll keep the house tidy," said Olivia.

"And stay alive," Chloë said, rolling her eyes at Frieda. "Jack will be here, most of the time. I won't go anywhere on my own. I won't go and hang around in bars so someone can drop a tab in my drink. I won't let any strange men pick me up." She looked back at Olivia. "You have to remember that too."

"Just let me know if you notice anything," said Frieda.

"Ladies, I'm on a meter, you know." The cab driver's voice was loud and grumpy.

"I know, I know," said Olivia.

"You never said you were moving house."

"Because I'm not moving."

"You ought to have hired a van for all of this."

"Am I paying you for your advice as well?" asked Olivia.

Frieda thought there was going to be an argument or even a fight, but she managed to calm things down between them. Olivia sat in the front seat and Frieda squeezed into the middle, surrounded by cardboard boxes and potted plants. She saw that the pots were spilling soil onto the seats.

They were met by Josef and his son. Alexei had had his hair cut very short, like soft velvet. He looked subdued, forlorn, and kept close to his father, his shadow. And Josef, Frieda saw, couldn't stop himself touching him—laying a broad, calloused hand on his shoulder, on the top of his shorn head—as if to make sure he was real and solid. Alexei had lived through an ugly war, thought Frieda, had lost his mother, and now he was in the middle of this.

She asked after Reuben.

"Sleeping." Josef gave a shake of the head. "He sleeps, he wakes, I give him drink. I make him soup, good soup for the health. He sleeps again."

"What about you?"

"Me?"

"You're looking after Reuben, you're looking after Alexei. Can you manage to work?"

Josef gave a shrug. His anxious brown eyes settled on Alexei. Then he turned back to Frieda and tapped himself on the chest, like a door. "This is my time," he said.

He turned to Olivia, taking in her wildness, and gave a small bow but she scarcely noticed him. She turned to the car and dragged a flowery bag from it, murmuring something to herself. Frieda noticed she had on only one dangling earring; she thought now was not the time to point it out.

They quickly emptied the car, Josef loading himself up so that he almost disappeared beneath the luggage, Olivia watching them. Frieda gave the driver an extra thirty pounds to clean the mud off the seat ("Banditry," said Olivia. "Absolute banditry") while Josef explained that Alexei was moving in with him to free up a bedroom for Olivia.

"That's so good of you," said Frieda, glancing at Olivia.

"When I was his age," said Olivia, "I'd been sent away to school."

"I bring coffee and cake," said Josef. "This your home now. Please."

Olivia looked around the front room, which was dominated by her luggage. "For a start, this needs to be got upstairs."

"Olivia," said Frieda, warningly.

"What?" Olivia opened her eyes very wide, gazing at Frieda and then at Alexei. "Am I supposed to carry all of that myself, then?"

"That's not the point."

"You don't seem to understand how scared I am."

"It's because you're scared that you're here, where you can feel safe."

"Safe?" said Olivia. "What do you mean by safe? My daughter has been kidnapped and God knows what was done to her. Reuben has been attacked in his own home. Now you bring me to the same home. Are we safe or are we just a bigger target?"

Josef came in bearing a tray with mugs of coffee and cake. "Take bags up?" he said.

"Yes," said Olivia, then glanced at Frieda. "Please," she added. "Thank you, Josef. Thank you all." Fat tears started to roll down her cheeks.

Not wanting to leave the house, Josef had started work on Reuben's garden and had enlisted Alexei in the project. He thought it would be good for him.

"And after that?" Frieda asked.

"After?"

"The summer's nearly over, Josef. Alexei needs to go to school."

"What to do?" Josef spread his arms wide in a gesture of despair. "How he go to school, Frieda? I am not—" He stopped, his face wrinkling in the effort of finding the word. "Official. Everything cash. So Alexei not official."

"Have you asked for advice?"

"As soon as I say we are here, we are a problem."

"You can't go on hiding, especially with Alexei."

"Maybe." Josef was dubious. "I think on it." His face brightened. "Gardening is good."

The little strip of lawn had to be dug up, the rubbly earth turned and re-turned, the plants that were already there bagged in their own compost, and then the paving stones lifted and used to make a structure of beds that would be filled with soil. It was heavy work but Alexei, who was scrawny but surprisingly strong, did it without any protest, as if he were used to laboring and expected it. It was hot, and he took off his T-shirt and silently, patiently struck the fork into the baked ground. Olivia took tall glasses of elderflower cordial out to him, filled with clinking ice, and he drained them silently before settling back to his toil.

Josef watched him for a while and then, satisfied, decided he could leave them to go to the hardware shop on Camden Road, then to the market to buy food for tonight's supper. He would make casserole, he said, meaty and full of herbs and spices. It was winter food, really, but it would reward Alexei for their hard work, it would comfort Olivia and strengthen Reuben. It would fill the house with good smells, the smells of home.

29

Dennis Rudkin looked down at his notes, sniffed and rubbed his nose. "Did I give you the warning?" he said.

"You told me that everyone has secrets," said Frieda.

"When a husband contacts me and asks me if his wife is lying I always start by saying I can tell him that for nothing. She's lying. Everybody lies. Everybody is hiding something from everyone else."

"I know that," said Frieda. "I'm a psychotherapist."

"And you think your patients tell you the truth?"

Frieda had a sudden uneasy feeling. "Have you found out something?"

"I haven't got on to them yet," he said. "I'm picking the low-hanging fruit first. I just wanted to see if you really had an appetite for this."

"We've already discussed it, haven't we?"

"People sometimes feel different once I start finding things out. I haven't moved out of my office much for this. It's mostly been done on the computer. A few phone calls."

"Is that usual?"

"Depends." He put his glasses back on and glanced at the notes.

"Your niece Chloë. Works as a carpenter in Walthamstow."

"I know."

Rudkin ignored her and went on reading: "Rents a bedroom in a three-bedroom flat nearby. Landlord, name of Gerry Travis William, a well-known shark."

"Oh dear."

"Flatmates all seem OK. Some drug consumption. Do you want to know about that?"

Mutely, Frieda shook her head.

"Thing is, this means little or nothing—they're young women and there are lots of people who come to the flat, sometimes stay there for varying lengths of time, and it's impossible to investigate all of them. You understand what I'm saying?"

"That this is a waste of time?"

"Not quite. It's partial, that's all." He scratched his head. "I'll inevitably turn up lots of things that appear suspicious— but they might not be relevant to what you're wanting. They might just muddy the picture."

"I understand."

"OK. At your niece's work. This may interest you. A new person has joined the team. Know anything about him?"

"Chloë mentioned him and I told you his name. William McCollough."

"That's the one. So, how much do you want to know?"

"I'm looking for someone I should be frightened of."

Rudkin rifled through several pages of the book.

"It seems like you've got a lot," said Frieda.

"Not so much. Also lives in Walthamstow, near his work. Brought up in care in Dundee. And elsewhere. He gave evidence in an inquiry. I mean an inquiry into one of the homes."

"Sexual abuse?"

"No charges were brought. But, yes, that was the remit of the inquiry."

"That's probably not relevant."

"But he works with your niece."

"Yes."

"Who was kidnapped."

"This McCollough was a victim, wasn't he? If he was giving evidence to an inquiry."

"Perpetrators usually start as victims."

"Does he have a criminal record?"

"A bit of theft, a bit of drugs."

"Any violence?" asked Frieda. "Any sexual offenses?"

"No. At least, no convictions."

"That's all I was asking for. Any of them recent?"

"The last was five years ago. Six, in fact." He closed his notebook. "So this is just the start."

"Thank you, Mr. Rudkin."

"Dennis, please. If you want to continue, we're going to spend a lot of time together."

"All right, Dennis. I want to continue."

30

That night, Frieda lay in bed and thought about what she had learned. Rudkin had been right: almost all perpetrators have been victims. But that didn't mean that all victims became perpetrators. Or anything like it. Nevertheless. Had William McCollough told his employers about his criminal convictions? Was he even obliged to tell them? If there was anything that was important to Frieda, it was that people like McCollough could be saved and given a second chance, a third chance and a fourth chance. But what if anything happened to Chloë? Should she warn her? And if she did, what could Chloë do with that warning, if it wasn't to get McCollough fired?

At last, she got out of bed and started to dress. She wasn't going to get any more sleep that night. She sat in her kitchen for a while with a large mug of tea, thinking of the two households, Reuben's where Olivia, Josef and Alexei were living, and then Jack and Chloë in Olivia's house in Islington. Almost everyone she cared for was in those two houses. Except Sasha. And Karlsson. She pushed away the thought of Karlsson. She thought of Alexei, with his father's anxious eyes. She thought of Reuben with his naked vulnerable skull and his shrunken body and the cancer inside him. Was he asleep now, or was he lying awake in the dark, waiting to hear footsteps?

She stood up and went to the living room, where she pulled up the photograph of Chloë on the grubby mattress in some bare dank room. She stared at it for a long time, looking for a clue. The broken pane of glass, the cracked plaster on the walls, the wedged shadow that lay across the floor: was that cast by the person taking the photograph or something else? Somewhere abandoned, but near the slide of the widening Thames, where planes flew low overhead. She had the feeling that she was simply waiting for the next thing to happen, reacting to what this person—who wasn't Dean but was copying Dean, following in Dean's footsteps—was doing. She had to act. The need of it was like a tight coil inside her, like a band around her forehead.

When it was at last light, the silvery sky of early morning, she went and had a shower, then pulled on clothes, tying her damp hair back tight. She made herself a mug of strong coffee that she drank in four large swallows, and ate half a grapefruit. Then she walked to Holborn.

At the front door, before she even pressed the bell, she saw Walter Levin coming down the street toward her. He was walking briskly, swinging his battered briefcase. There was a jaunty air to him.

She stepped in front of him.

"What a nice surprise."

"Is it?"

"It's always good to see you. Are you coming in?"

"I can talk to you here."

Frieda looked at him, with his thick glasses, his frayed tie and expensive shirt, the dusty brogues whatever the weather. "You're good at arranging things, aren't you?"

"I like helping people, if that's what you mean."

"It's not what I mean. You used me to get rid of Commissioner Crawford, didn't you? You knew he didn't like me, so you used me as a weapon against him."

Levin smiled faintly. "Don't be modest, Frieda. I think you're an effective weapon without anybody else's help. As for Crawford." He made a dismissive gesture. "He had enemies and failed in his job. You can do one or the other but not both."

"I should have realized."

Levin looked at her. "I'm surprised," he said.

"Why?"

"I thought you'd be angrier."

"You'll never know what I am."

"No doubt. Well, if there's nothing I can do for you . . ." He let the sentence trail away.

"There is one thing. It's why I'm here."

"Yes?"

"I have a friend who wants to become a British citizen. He has a young son, as well. He's never dared to do anything about it. His name is . . ."

"Josef Morozov. From Ukraine."

"Yes."

"Leave it with me."

"That's not what I was asking."

"Yes, you were."

She didn't immediately go to her consulting rooms. Her first patient had canceled because he had the flu; the next— Alex Zavou, the one suffering severe post-traumatic stress, whose details she had given to the private investigator— was not until half past ten. She had three hours. She took the photo of Chloë out of her bag and stared at it again, as though, if she concentrated hard enough, it would yield up its secret. Then she walked to the Underground station, took a train, then the Overground to the landscape of scooped and cratered fields of clay, tall cranes and empty warehouses, across whose cracked facades ran faded lettering telling of their past: old mills and paint factories, back in their glory days.

Once again, she got out at Pontoon Dock and walked toward Silvertown. She didn't know what she was expecting to find. Nothing had changed since she'd come here last. Yet she felt sure that this small area, between the river and the docks, with planes rumbling overhead, was where Chloë had been taken. She stood on the road, the crumbling warehouse behind her, the incongruous row of Victorian semis in front. Where was private, where was accessible, where could someone hide a drugged young woman for a whole weekend and not fear discovery? Whoever had taken her would have to have driven her, surely. Frieda turned to look in all directions: toward the broad flow of the river, where the great cranes stood on the horizon among the gleaming buildings; toward the housing development, not yet finished; the old and crumbling factories; the raw new bungalows waiting for their occupants. She realized that she had seen barely anybody, on foot or in a car: for all the development going on, this was still a deserted landscape.

She squinted up into the bright sky, at the warehouse that stood behind the chain-link fence. It had scaffolding up one side; the lower windows were boarded up against intruders but the upper ones were not and in some the glass was smashed. She tried to imagine all the empty rooms, the scuttling of mice and rats. Perhaps there were people in there, secret inhabitants. Was that where Chloë had been?

Alex Zavou was late for his session and when he did arrive, he almost ran into Frieda's room, out of breath and slightly frantic. "I could hardly bring myself to leave the house," he said, before he even sat down.

"But you did. You're here and that's good."

"It's like I've got into a habit of panic. As if it's not about anything any more, it's just inside me, this panic."

"The habit of panic—that's interesting," said Frieda. "We'll come back to that."

"I'm just stuck. On a loop."

"You're here to get unstuck," said Frieda. And she thought of how she'd asked a private investigator to look into his life. "As we talked about at the last session, it's going to be one step at a time. I'm going to ask you to tell your story to me again, with every detail you can remember. I might stop you with questions."

"Right." He swallowed hard. "Off I go."

People are stupid. They're like sheep, following each other, bleating. They don't know what to think until they're told. They think they're being good when they're only being obedient. In love when it's just the blind cravings of their bodies. They think they're free, but they're just part of a system. Ants in an anthill.

But Dean Reeve isn't stupid. Frieda Klein isn't stupid. He isn't stupid. They belong to a different tribe.

Crazy times when the world comes right like this. Crazy good times. His times. He pushes his hands into his pockets and squeezes them into fists; he squeezes his eyes into slits, then opens them again. His throat is thick with excitement.

31

"You're a fast worker," said Frieda.

She was in Rudkin's office once more. The only thing that was different from the last two times was that his dog was awake and was nosing its way around the room, snuffling into corners.

"You asked for preliminary reports and these are preliminary reports," said Dennis Rudkin. "Not to demystify my job, but most of this was just me sitting at my screen. Obvious stuff."

"What did you find?"

"OK. Your sister-in-law and her new friends."

Frieda shifted uneasily in her chair; the dog came over and pushed against her leg.

"Yes?"

"It's a bit of a tangle," said Rudkin. "But you probably knew that."

"In what way?"

"They're all married, for a start."

"*All* of them?"

"First off, Robert Astley."

"The tax inspector?"

"Married for a second time. Three girls, aged eleven to seventeen. And he's not strictly a tax inspector."

"What is he, then?"

"An ex–tax inspector. Unemployed now. Had a gambling problem, I gather. Not good for a tax inspector."

"Oh."

"And Oliver Volkov isn't an estate agent either."

"I half expected that. He was going door to door. That was how he and Olivia met. What is he?"

"Difficult to say. This and that. Does some painting and decorating, some gardening. He was in prison for nine months."

"What for?"

"Aggravated assault."

"That doesn't sound good," said Frieda.

"The other two look pretty straightforward. Speeding fines, parking tickets, that kind of thing. Nothing else that leaps out."

"Do any of them live near City Airport?"

Rudkin leafed through the pages he was holding.

"Not that I can see," he said. "Dominic Gordon lives in Beckton, that's pretty close."

"Yes."

"But a friend of Jack Dargan does."

"Who?"

"Does the name Tom Sylvester ring any bells?"

"No."

"He and Jack have communicated a lot on Facebook in the last few weeks. I gather they were at school together, lost touch, and then Mr. Sylvester reconnected with him. Very eager to meet up. Which they duly did. Reading between the lines, I think your friend was bullied by him at school and Sylvester wanted to apologize, make amends, you know the kind of thing."

"I do." Frieda thought of Jack with his self-consciousness, his awkwardness, his bouts of excruciating self-doubt.

"Tom Sylvester is only twenty-seven, but he works in the City and has obviously made enough money to buy himself a three-bedroom house near East India Docks."

"Anything else about him?"

"Not really."

"What does that mean? Just tell me what you know."

"Both his parents and his younger sister died in a road accident five years ago. Hit by a bus. He was in the car and escaped with minor injuries."

"How awful." She paused, tentatively patted the dog's head. "But not suspicious."

"When you do my job," said Rudkin, "everything's suspicious."

"And Reuben."

"You'll be relieved to hear I've found nothing to concern you there. Though of course that might be because he's gravely ill and has been largely housebound."

Frieda nodded. But that hadn't stopped him being savagely beaten up. She waited a few seconds, then asked, "And my clients?"

"You'll have to wait for the next installment."

"I've been reading about therapy," said Morgan Rossiter.

"Why?" said Frieda.

"I thought you'd be pleased. It's like doing my homework. Being a keen student."

"I'm not sure that's a good idea."

"Why not?"

"It's a distraction. You ought to be thinking about what's important to you."

"Don't you want to hear what I was reading about?"

"You can talk about anything you want to talk about."

"I was reading about this thing called 'transference.'"

Frieda's heart sank. She knew what was coming, but she didn't speak.

"It's about how patients have this habit of falling in love with their analyst. Does that really happen?"

Rossiter was looking at her with an amused, challenging expression.

"I think it's true of all authority figures," said Frieda. "Teachers, doctors, bosses. People can become fascinated by them or interested or even obsessed. The point is to talk about it."

Rossiter continued to smile. "Do you ever find it a problem?"

Frieda looked at Rossiter. She was expecting him to mention counter-transference: where the therapist has strong feelings for the patient. Just now, Frieda was thinking about a different kind of problem in the relationship: when the therapist starts to feel a strong dislike of the patient. One of the difficult lessons to remember was that even this was a kind of evidence, something to be used. "When Dr. Singh referred you to me, he said that, even before you asked for me personally, you had insisted on being analyzed by a woman."

"Is that a problem?"

"Like everything else in this room, it's something to talk about."

"I just thought I'd be more comfortable talking to a woman."

Frieda thought for a moment. "Tell me about your mother," she said finally.

Rossiter's easy smile faded. "Tell you what about her?"

"Describe her to me."

Now Rossiter's whole demeanor had altered. His eyes flickered from side to side. "I don't know what you're trying to get at," he said. "But there's nothing strange in any way at all about my relationship with my mother." Frieda didn't speak. She just waited. "It's not even interesting, if that's what you think." Again Frieda didn't speak. "I told you right from the start that the problem was my relationships with women, moving from one to another. If you think that you're tracing this all back in some cheap sub-Freudian way to some problem with my mother, then . . ." He paused.

"Then what?" said Frieda.

"Then . . . It's just that that's not what I'm here for."

So, Frieda thought. It was clear what they needed to talk about.

As Rossiter left, he passed through the waiting room. Another man was sitting in a chair.

"I guess it's your turn," said Rossiter.

"There's several minutes," he said.

The two men looked at each other awkwardly, as if they had a connection they didn't know what to do with.

"We're probably not meant to discuss it," said Zavou.

"So many rules," said Rossiter, and continued on his way.

32

The next time Dennis Rudkin phoned Frieda, he said he was going to be in town and that he could come to her house. She felt a sort of horror at the idea that she couldn't define. Frieda had always had a rule that she would never see any patient in her house. It would encourage a personal curiosity that would be inappropriate. Even that rule she had broken, when Sasha moved from being a patient to being a friend. But the idea of Rudkin seeing where she lived, seeing her possessions, her private space, seemed intolerable. She didn't even want to suggest meeting anywhere that she normally went. She had her suspicions that he would have investigated her own past, either as a method of investigating others or else out of simple curiosity. She didn't want to provide him with anything else. So she suggested a nearby pub, the Duke of Rutland, that she had never been to.

"Is that your local?" Rudkin had said over the phone.

"Well, it's local," she had replied.

When Frieda arrived at the pub, Rudkin was sitting in the corner with a pint of bitter, a glass of Scotch and an open packet of crisps. Frieda asked for a tumbler of tap water and bought herself a spicy tomato juice, then joined him. "I was planning to buy you a drink," she said.

"You're paying for this anyway," said Rudkin, cheerfully, and took a gulp of his beer. He pulled a small black notebook from his pocket and laid it on the table. "You've got mixed feelings about me, haven't you?"

"I've got mixed feelings about myself. You're doing what I'd be doing if I was capable of it."

"And yet you won't have me in your house."

"I won't have you in my house because you're good at your job. You already probably know more about me than I'd want you to know."

"I like to get a sense of who I'm working for," said Rudkin.

"Most of what you need to find out about me is online. Unfortunately."

Rudkin picked up his black notebook and leafed through it. Then he put it back on the table. "So which one would you like to hear about first?"

"I think I'll leave that up to you."

"All right, I'll put it another way. Do you have particular suspicions about either of them?"

"Look, it's a bit late to be saying this, especially to you, but these two men are my patients. Just tell me anything that seems relevant and nothing else." She repeated the last two words for emphasis: "Nothing else."

"All right," said Rudkin. "I'll start with Alex Zavou, your have-a-go hero. He's got form."

"You mean a criminal record?"

"No. But he's someone . . ." He paused. "I'm trying to remember the expression from the Bible. Alex Zavou isn't someone who has a habit of walking by on the other side."

"You mean he's a Good Samaritan?"

"Well, it's a long time since I was at Sunday school, but as far as I remember the Good Samaritan didn't take on the robbers himself. He just helped afterwards."

"What exactly did Zavou do?"

"Two years ago he got involved in a bit of a tussle in a pub in Walthamstow. Apparently someone disrespected a friend of his. There were bottles involved, serious damage was done. Several people were arrested."

"Was he charged?"

"No charges were brought." Rudkin smiled at Frieda. "But as you know—from personal experience—just because no charges were brought, it doesn't mean that serious violence didn't take place."

"Anything else?"

"A few months after that, there was another club and another row. Apparently it was over a girl who was with a friend of Zavou's. Words were exchanged, punches were thrown, several people—your Mr. Zavou included—ended up in A & E. Again, no charges were brought. But Zavou is someone who feels the need to get involved."

"It may just show that he has a sense of justice."

"I have no opinion about that. All I'd say is that it was just a matter of time before someone in one of his scuffles pulled a knife."

"But it wasn't him."

"No. He just uses his fists. And whatever comes to hand. Still, he doesn't seem like a bad lad. But the record shows that he's drawn to violence. Or that violence happens when he's around." Rudkin smiled again. "I suppose that's something you can talk to him about."

Every mention of the fact that Alex Zavou was a patient of hers made her feel slightly nauseous, but she didn't respond.

"What about Rossiter?"

Rudkin picked up his notebook and flicked through a

series of pages, then put it down again. "Ten years ago, Rossiter was at university in Cardiff. A young woman called Delith Talling went to the police and said that she had been sexually assaulted by Rossiter after a party. When I say sexually assaulted, I mean raped."

"What happened?"

"Rossiter said she had consented. The young lady had been drinking heavily and passed out. It never went to court."

Frieda didn't speak for a long time. She took a long drink of water. She felt as if she needed to wash her mouth out. "Anything else about the case?" she said finally.

"As always, it was his word against hers. She was very drunk and he had excellent character references."

"Is that it?"

"There's one other thing."

"What?"

"He'd done it before. I mean, allegedly."

"What had he done?"

"Six months earlier, he'd done it to someone else. Or, rather, was accused of doing it to someone else."

"What happened? Did that case come to court?"

"She didn't even report it to the police. But she came forward while the second case was under way. The prosecution were hoping to call her as a witness. To establish a pattern. But Rossiter's lawyer got the earlier woman's testimony excluded, arguing it was prejudicial. Without that witness, the prosecutors decided that the case couldn't proceed. Rossiter's lawyer was a woman, by the way."

"What's that got to do with anything?"

"I suppose it seemed ironic."

Frieda forced herself to stay calm. There was no point in

having a discussion about Rossiter's lawyer being a woman. "I'm sorry to snap at you," she said. "I suppose you're used to people getting angry with you when you deliver disturbing news."

Rudkin reached into an inside pocket of his jacket. He took out an envelope and slid it across the table. "While we're on the subject of disturbing news," he said.

Frieda picked up the envelope. It had her name on it. She recognized Rudkin's handwriting. "Is this something I should be worried about?"

"It's my bill."

"Good," said Frieda. As she talked she tore the envelope open, then took a checkbook from her pocket and started filling one in. "You've done a good job. I wish I could say that you've laid my fears to rest."

"You're welcome."

"I'm half curious about how you got all this and mainly think I shouldn't know."

"It's just about contacts and access and knowing who to ask."

"It can't be that easy."

"I didn't say it was. Is there anyone else?"

Frieda found the idea almost comic. "I think you'd better stop while I've still got some illusions intact."

"You don't look like someone with many illusions."

33

Jack had cooked spaghetti. "Do you want some?" he asked hopefully. "I made enough for an army."

"I'd love some," said Frieda, not because she was hungry but to see the look of pleasure on his face.

"I need to branch out," said Jack. "I can make a few pasta dishes and I'm quite good at risotto. But it's a limited repertoire." He spooned pasta into a serving dish and poured over the sauce.

"How's the cheese stall?"

"I'm better with people who buy cheese than I was with patients who needed help."

"Give it time. You may come back to it. How's living here?"

"A bit weird. Chloë's back in her old room, I'm in the spare. It won't be for long, though, will it?"

"I hope not. Is there anything else you want to tell me about?"

Jack was lifting pasta onto two plates.

"That's plenty," said Frieda.

"Are you asking as an analyst or as a friend?"

"I'm asking as someone who is concerned for you."

"You're wondering whether there's someone new in my life."

"That would be one thing to discuss."

"Do you mean Chloë?"

"Is Chloë back in your life?"

"She's never been out of it—but not in the way you mean, no."

"Anyone else?"

"People are always coming and going in people's lives."

"Just at the moment I'm interested in the people who are coming."

"All right. A person I knew from school got back in touch with me."

"Oh?" She tried to keep her voice neutral.

"I hadn't seen him in years—a decade or more. And I'd tried not to think about him, either."

"Why?"

"For about two years he made my life a misery."

"He bullied you?"

"He was good at it too. He didn't just bully me himself, he got everyone else to bully me as well. It was almost impressive."

"Did you tell anyone about it?"

"Not even when I was in therapy. Or not properly. I couldn't somehow. So I was a bit surprised when he suddenly got back in touch."

"Did you see him?"

"A few times. He looks exactly the same except older— round-faced, rosy-cheeked. All the teachers loved him—he seemed so straightforward. It was odd. He wanted me to forgive him. I think he'd been having counseling and he'd decided to go around to all the people he'd injured."

"And did you?"

"What?"

"Forgive him."

"He's been through his own trauma. A few years ago his parents and sister were killed in a car crash. He said it made him look at his whole life from a different perspective. Maybe we're all damaged in our way."

"Maybe. Are you going to keep in touch?"

"I don't know. To tell the truth, now that I'm through being angry with him, I realize I still don't actually like him. Suffering doesn't necessarily make someone nicer."

"No."

"But it made me remember everything I've tried to push away. For the first time in months, I started to think about the value of therapy rather than its downsides."

"You should think about both. Always."

Frieda had considered canceling her next session with Morgan Rossiter, but in the end she didn't. She was troubled by the idea of him simply being out there in the world, being a teacher, interacting with young women. Rudkin had found out about those two cases when he was at university. Was there anything significant that he hadn't discovered? What had Rossiter done after he had left university? Or was that all behind him? There was something to be said for seeing him, for continuing to see him. If there's a wasp in the room, you'd rather know where it is.

When he arrived for the next session, he simply sat down and started talking. At first Frieda could barely concentrate on what he was saying. She just saw his lips moving, saw the crinkle of a smile around his eyes. He was sprawled in his chair, as if he was occupying as much space as possible, dominating it. His legs were spread.

"I'm sorry," said Frieda. "I'm going to have to stop you there."

There was a pause.

"Go on," said Rossiter, almost as if it was he who was conducting the session and she had to seek permission to speak. In another context Frieda might have discussed this with a patient. Therapy sessions could become a battle for territory with the patient trying to seize control. She wasn't concerned with that today.

"The point of these early sessions is to make an assessment—"

"I'm sorry, is there a problem?"

"Please. Let me finish. The point of these early sessions is to make an assessment, to see whether this is the right setting for you, whether I am the right therapist. I've decided that I'm not the right therapist for you."

"Why?" said Rossiter. "What's wrong?"

"I'll write to Dr. Singh and I'll make some recommendations."

"What do you mean you'll write to Dr. Singh? If something's not working, can't we just talk about it and fix it?"

Frieda could hardly bear even to look at him. At the same time she felt shamefully compromised by what she knew about him. She worried about the consequences of setting him loose, but she couldn't think of an alternative. She had a dim feeling that people should be warned about this man, yet whom should she warn and in what terms and on what authority? But she had to say something.

"I strongly feel that you should be in therapy," she said. "But I was struck by what you said in our last session about wanting a woman therapist and about specifically wanting me. I am absolutely certain that you should see a male therapist."

Rossiter clenched both hands on the arms of his chair so that the veins stood out. "I asked for you," he said.

"You don't get to do that. This isn't a supermarket."

"But what if it's important to me to have a female therapist? What if I think you're the only person who can help me?"

"Then that's something you should talk about," said Frieda. "With a male therapist. Obviously you won't be charged for this session."

"Well, obviously, since this isn't going to be much use to me as therapy."

Morgan Rossiter continued to sit there. What if he wouldn't leave? When he spoke again, it was in a softer tone. "I was probably too eager to impress you," he said. "You know, to make Frieda Klein interested in me. I don't suppose you could give me another chance."

Suddenly Frieda thought about those two young women from Morgan Rossiter's student days. Where were they now? Were they free of him? Free of what he had done to them?

"When you see your new therapist," Frieda said slowly, "you should talk about your difficulty in hearing what someone is saying to you and acting on it."

Rossiter stood up. "I don't need a fucking therapist," he said, and stormed out of the room, slamming the door.

And then it was the easiest thing in the world. Easier than the first time. Easier than the niece. Easier than Reuben McGill. It was what he'd been telling himself: you have to learn to improvise, be in a state of readiness and wait for the perfect moment.

It came when he wasn't expecting it, but he was prepared.

When they are angry, people want to talk. They want to tell their side of the story. Soon enough they were in the man's room. He didn't even have to ask. He had put on his friendly face, sympathetic and interested. A smile was growing and growing and he could feel it pull at his mouth. He put his hand over his mouth and pretended to cough, to hide his exultation.

And there was still that other one. Ticking.

34

Karlsson sat in the kitchen of Crawford, once the commissioner, now retired early from the Met, his career overshadowed by its ending. He didn't know why he was in the little house in Hammersmith and he felt ill at ease.

Crawford was making coffee in an enormous machine that took up most of the counter, steaming, hissing, gurgling. He looked as if he was doing battle with it. His face was redder than ever; his eyes seemed smaller. His stomach bulged over his trousers. It was strange to see him in casual clothes, in his own home. He seemed too large for the small room and the small house.

"How've you been?" asked Karlsson.

Crawford pulled a handle violently. Coffee started to drip into a cup. "I blame you, Mal."

"What for?"

"You brought her into my life. If it hadn't been for that, I'd still be doing the job I'm good at, the politicians wouldn't be getting their hands all over our work, everything would be all right."

Karlsson couldn't think of what to say in reply.

"It was down to me as well," said Crawford. "I know I fucked up." He handed Karlsson the coffee. "Don't look so glum. I know she's a special friend of yours."

"Just a friend."

"Whatever you say."

"You wanted to see me."

"I wanted to ask a favor." He brought his own coffee to the table, dropped in several sugar cubes and stirred vigorously, then took a small sip. "You know Hal Bradshaw."

Karlsson did indeed know Hal Bradshaw, psychologist, criminal profiler, used by the Met. He popped up every time the media wanted a quote on a particularly nasty crime, and he had crossed swords with Frieda on multiple occasions. What was more, Dean Reeve had once set fire to his house. "I do," was all he said.

"He's doing some series on TV. Forget the title—*Crimes in Mind* or something. I've agreed to be interviewed."

"Oh?"

"Yes. But I'm having cold feet. I wanted to ask you—as an old friend—if you think it's a bad idea."

Karlsson tried to keep his surprise off his face. Crawford had tried to fire him. He'd treated Frieda with hostility that had become almost pathological by the end. Was the man so friendless that he thought of Karlsson as his friend?

"I suppose you need to establish what areas the interview will cover."

"It's about various cases I was involved in over the years. Can I trust Hal, do you think?"

"Well, everyone has their own agenda."

"Obviously."

"And he hates Frieda."

A little smile came over Crawford's broad, florid face.

"I'd be careful," Karlsson said softly. "He might be using you."

*

It was the smell.

Sofie Kyriakos was taking a baking course, and when she was at home in her top floor flat in Dalston, she spent most of the time in her tiny kitchen, making the starter and then the leaven, kneading dough, watching it rise into a soft pillow. Gradually, beneath the yeasty, crusty, doughy aroma, she noticed something else—a rotting, rubbishy smell with a touch of sweetness to it that was even worse. Had a rat died somewhere? She had heard of that. A rat would eat poison and become ill and crawl into a recess under the floorboards or behind paneling and die and rot and there was nothing for it but to wait until the smell went away. But this was too strong.

She went out onto the public landing. There were three other flats on this level and three more on the floor below. The smell was even worse there. She knocked on one of the doors. No answer. She knocked on the other two with the same result. Everyone was at work or away. She didn't know any of the other tenants. People came and went and the flats were sublet and friends stayed. She saw names on the envelopes piled up inside the street door, but most of those were of tenants who were long gone.

After another day of it, she couldn't take any more. She met the man in flat three who said it must be the drains. Sofie said, no, this wasn't drains. She tried to call the landlord and emailed him and messaged him. But he lived out of London somewhere. He only got in touch when a tenant was late with the rent, and then only with a solicitor's letter. So she called Hackney Council and couldn't even get an actual human being to answer the phone. In the end she called the police. Had she checked all the tenants? Had she called the health department? Couldn't it just be the plumbing?

Finally two young police officers arrived. They seemed bored and irritated as she met them downstairs and told them that it was at the top, up three flights of stairs. Finally they arrived, breathing heavily, outside her door.

"There," said Sofie. "Can you smell it?"

They could. They looked at each other, then things started to happen quickly. They made a series of calls on their radios. Sofie began to edge away. One of the officers noticed her and told her to stay where she was.

"On their way," the other said.

They started to question Sofie without any significant result. She couldn't tell them when she had last seen the tenant because she didn't know who it was. She didn't even know if it was a man or a woman. Had she heard anything? She was always hearing things but she couldn't tell what flat any particular noise came from.

The officers went downstairs and then she heard a thumping and rumbling of boots coming up and then the landing filled with men in uniform, so many Sofie couldn't count them. A heavily built gray-haired man approached her. "You the neighbor who called?"

"Yes."

"Stay here. But you'd better stand back."

Two officers came forward, carrying a long metal battering ram. The corridor was too narrow for it and they couldn't get the right angle against the door. There was much muttering and some raised voices.

"Just hit it sideways," said the gray-haired man.

Four men, two on each side, took hold of the ram and swung it. It took several attempts before there was a splintering sound and the door swung inward. There was a wave of hot air from inside that Sofie could feel from several yards away. Two officers stepped inside and she heard gasping and swearing. One of them, pale-faced, sweating, appeared at the door and addressed the gray-haired man. "You'll want to see this, Sarge."

"Can I go?" said Sofie.

"Not for the moment," he said, and went inside.

Another of the officers emerged. He walked toward Sofie and leaned against the wall, taking deep, slow breaths.

"What is it?" Sofie asked, but he just raised his hand. He didn't seem able to speak.

After a few minutes, the gray-haired sergeant came back out. "Fucking hell," he said. "We need to call this in."

"What is it?" Sofie asked again.

The sergeant looked at her as if seeing her for the first time. "There's a body in there. It's in a bit of a state. All the gas was left on, all the heaters." He paused. "So you didn't know him?"

"No."

"Frieda Klein," said the sergeant.

"What?"

"Do you know someone called Frieda Klein?"

35

Petra Burge hated waiting. The traffic was bad, the sun shone through the car's window; she felt hot and in a fury of impatience. At the traffic lights she told her driver she would walk the rest of the way, then opened the door and almost ran along the busy road, dodging other pedestrians. At last she reached the mouth of the cobbled mews, where she slowed to catch her breath and order her thoughts. Frieda knew that she was coming, but she didn't know why.

When Frieda opened the door, Petra saw how dark her eyes were and how pale her face was, in spite of the long hot weeks they'd had. Petra's own face was splashed with summer freckles from the hours she spent running, through parks and along canals, mile after mile until her body ached and her mind was calmer.

"Come in," Frieda said. "Can I offer you anything? Tea?"

"Just water."

They went into the kitchen. Petra watched her as she ran the water till it was cold, filled a tumbler, dropped in an ice cube, then wiped her hands on a tea towel before handing it over. There was a pot of basil on the windowsill, a vase of yellow roses on the table. She was wearing a gray shirt with the sleeves rolled up and cotton trousers; her hair was gathered in a loose coil at the back of her head and she

seemed cool, self-possessed. Everything she did was so ordered and yet her life was filled with violence and disorder.

They both sat. Frieda looked at her and nodded.

"Do you know a man called Morgan Rossiter?" She
thought she saw Frieda flinch, very slightly. There was a
tightening in her expression.

"He used to be a patient."

"But isn't any longer?"

"I wasn't the right person for him. Why?"

"He's dead."

"What?" said Frieda.

"He was murdered. His body was found last night. You
might ask why I've come to you about this." She waited but
Frieda didn't speak. "Your name was found."

"I was his therapist," said Frieda, in a low voice.

"Is it common for people to paint the name of their
therapist on the wall?"

Frieda put one hand to her throat; the silence in the
room seemed to thicken. "A message," she said at last.

"Of some kind."

"Can you tell if he wrote my name himself?"

"We're working on that but I think we can assume that
he didn't."

"So whoever killed him did it."

The two women looked at each other across the table,
then Frieda stood up abruptly. "Can we walk?" she said.

"Walk?"

"Yes. I have to walk."

"Where?"

"Anywhere."

"All right."

They left the house together. Frieda strode in an apparently random direction, turning left and right on small streets until they were in a large square. They went into the public garden at its center. At the far end, two men were playing tennis; Frieda walked over to a bench in the shade of a tall plane tree and sat down. "Someone abducted my niece," she said. "They held her for an entire weekend. They took photos of her lying unconscious on a mattress and sent it to me. Someone went to Reuben's house and beat him up so badly it still hurts him to walk—and don't forget this is a man who has cancer and is very ill and frail. It could have killed him. This someone has now killed a man who was my patient."

Petra nodded.

"I had just told him I could no longer be his therapist."

"Why?"

"We were incompatible," Frieda said shortly. "It's not uncommon."

"I see. There's nothing else you can tell me?"

Frieda turned her face away. Petra saw her hands clench and unclench in her lap. "I don't think so," she said.

"Right."

"I think—" She stopped.

"Yes?"

"This isn't Dean Reeve. He already sent his message via Alexei. But it's also not Dean because it feels out of control, frantic. Karlsson once told me that Dean likes to fish. He sits by the water hour after hour, waiting for a fish to bite, and never gets frustrated. He's a very patient man, very controlled. The person who is doing this is not patient, not patient at all. He's in a hurry. On a binge. Or she, or they. Three people in three weeks, and the third has died. Because of me." She turned to Petra. "And who will be next? Olivia?"

"You?"

"I'm his audience." When she spoke again, her voice was so low Petra had to strain to catch it. "Perhaps if I wasn't here to watch him, he would stop."

The public gardens were quiet in the heat, only the sound of the tennis ball, hit back and forwards, the occasional call of one of the men, a bird overhead. A plane was unspooling its vapor trail in the flat blue sky.

"That's one possibility," said Petra, emphatic.

"What's the other?"

"If this person is a copycat, as we believe, then Dean is his audience, not you."

"Meanwhile we do what?" asked Frieda. "Just keep on waiting until this person gets another chance."

"I have a suggestion. Which you won't like."

"What?"

"We go public on all of this."

Frieda's instinct was to say no but she had no other idea to offer, so she let Petra continue.

"Last time, we set up three journalists to interview you. Now we should go wider: TV, radio, newspapers, whatever. We'll make the link between you and the violent attacks and now this death, and you'll also make yourself available to be interviewed."

"All right," said Frieda. Her voice was dull.

"I knew you'd hate the idea."

"I do hate it, but that doesn't mean I disagree."

"I'll set it up."

Frieda gave a sigh and rubbed her hand against her forehead. "I need to talk to Chloë. Even if we don't mention her by name, it will soon be public knowledge, won't it?"

"It would be hard to keep it secret."

"I'll call her now."

Frieda watched Petra walk away through the gardens, a small wiry figure, light on her feet, slightly bowlegged, looking both younger and older than her years. A curious woman. Should she have told her about Rudkin and what he'd discovered about Morgan Rossiter? She almost had.

She called Chloë and, after a small silence, Chloë said that of course she agreed, if Frieda thought it was necessary. Frieda ended the call. The sun poured down through the limp green leaves. She knew whom she needed to talk to.

There's a song he can't get out of his head. An earworm. Horrible name. Now he can't stop imagining a worm softly winding its way down the ear and into his head. "It was on a Monday morning that I beheld my darling, she looked so neat and charming in every fine degree." Something like that. "Dashing away with the smoothing iron." Day after day. He couldn't stop humming it. "In every fine degree." He didn't know all the words.

He doesn't need sleep and now he doesn't want food either. He pushes it away. Piles of mashed potato. Slabs of meat. He can't put it into his body. He feels hollow, light on his feet; his head is clear.

36

Frieda poured whisky into two tumblers. She set a small jug of water between them and gestured to Karlsson to add what he wanted. The cat came into the room and wound itself around her legs, asking to be stroked. The last light was gone and now the room was dim, shutters closed, a standard lamp throwing a soft pool of yellow.

Karlsson raised his glass, took a small sip, felt it burn in his mouth and throat. He had rarely seen Frieda look so bleak. Her face was all angles and shadows; her dark eyes glowed. "Tell me," he said.

Frieda was visibly making up her mind. "I'm talking to you as a friend," she said at last.

"Why does that make me feel nervous?"

"You know I hired that private investigator."

"Rudkin."

"I asked him to look into the people who had recently come into the lives of Olivia, Chloë, Reuben and Jack."

"That sounds reasonable."

"I didn't ask about Josef, and that might have been a mistake. It's hard to know where to stop."

"I can imagine."

Frieda put a hand to her throat, a gesture she had only recently started making. "It was probably illogical. I had a sense that whoever was doing these things is somehow among us, in our lives, and I had to do something." She leaned forward as she spoke.

"Did Rudkin find anything useful?"

"I don't know if it's useful. He certainly found things out."

"Such as?"

"Such as Chloë works with a man who was abused as a child and has been on the wrong side of the law. Olivia's got lots of friends who are creeps and who are pretending to be single when they're married, or pretending to be employed when they're not. Jack's met up with a young man who bullied him very badly when they were at school, who's very rich from deals in the City and whose parents were killed in a road accident a few years ago."

"So you know things you shouldn't."

"I've spied on my friends."

"For their own good."

Frieda made a grimace of disgust, then poured more whisky into his tumbler. "But that's not what I want to tell you about."

"I'm listening."

"I asked him to investigate two of my patients. They are both new. Were." She waited to see if Karlsson would speak. His expression didn't alter. "I don't need to tell you that's not allowed. It's also wrong. I mean morally wrong. Rudkin found that one of them had some secrets in his past: serious sexual assaults. Though he was never charged. Knowing that, I couldn't keep him on as my patient so I told him I wasn't the right therapist for him. He was very angry."

"I see."

"And then yesterday his body was found."

Karlsson stared at her. "Morgan Rossiter was your patient?"

"Yes. And my name was written on the wall of his flat."

"My God, Frieda."

"I know."

"I'm not sure where to start."

"Then let me start: should I tell Petra Burge about hiring Rudkin?"

Karlsson was silent for a long time, one minute, two minutes. Frieda could hear the traffic rumbling along Euston Road. "No," he said finally.

"Don't just tell me what you think I want to hear."

He shook his head. "I'll tell you what would happen. It would get leaked to the papers by someone, your career would be finished, and it wouldn't even help the case. The police will find out about his past in five minutes."

"I don't need to be told I'm right."

"You know, Frieda, I'd stand by you if you were wrong. God knows I've done it in the past. This time you were probably right, in a messy sort of way. You need to think about what's happening next. By the way, what *is* happening next?"

"We're going public. Tomorrow morning there'll be wall-to-wall coverage. Petra Burge thinks it might help."

Karlsson nodded. "That makes sense."

"No more hiding." She glanced around the room. "No more privacy."

"Are you dreading it?"

"That's irrelevant. Someone must know something."

Karlsson stood up. "One thing," he said.

"What?"

"Did you have me investigated too?"

For the first time that evening, Frieda smiled. "No."

"Why?"

"You think I should have done?"

"I'm your friend too."

"You are indeed."

37

Everything was different: there had been attacks, but now someone had died. Morgan Rossiter's face was in every newspaper, on the TV news. A middle-class young man brutally slaughtered, an apparently motiveless murder. None of the stories mentioned Frieda but she knew that was about to change.

All through that morning of interviews, she felt it was happening to someone else, not Frieda Klein but a stranger who was impersonating Frieda Klein. The same questions and the same answers, sentences on a loop, till by the end she couldn't remember if she had repeated them or missed them out: performing what was real.

She sat in TV studios in the brightness and the heat and told her story; she had it down to a few minutes, a neat chronology of disorder. She heard her calm voice. She did the same for radio. Always a glass of water poured out for her, a spongy microphone just a few inches away from her mouth. Petra Burge was with her. She was being interviewed too—Frieda noted that she spoke well, with authority but was never pompous—and also a woman from the communications department, who held Frieda's elbow as she led her into cars and out of them. They didn't give Chloë's name. She was identified only as a close relative. But they did name Reuben. Morgan Rossiter was at the center of everything: a young man had been killed simply because he was Frieda Klein's patient.

Then they were in a press conference, a room full of reporters and flashing cameras. She saw faces she had seen before. Liz Barron, of course, in the front row, fresh as a daisy and her eyes gleaming; would she never go away? Daniel Blackstock, whom she'd last seen when he'd handed over that photo of Chloë and she'd snapped at him. Gary Hillier from the *Chronicle*, who was dressed in a black suit as if he had just come from a funeral. Others, faces she had encountered over the years. Out of the corner of her gaze, she saw one she hadn't been expecting. Walter Levin, quizzical and twinkling and sinister: what was he doing here? Her mood lifted a bit when she saw that Karlsson had also come. He was standing at the back, leaning against the wall, and when their eyes met he didn't smile but gave her a small nod.

Petra spoke, first and briefly about the case against Dean Reeve, then about a new and concerning spate of attacks and now a murder, all of which seemed to have been prompted by friendship or acquaintance with Dr. Frieda Klein and pointed to a copycat. Here she gestured to Frieda, at her left. Frieda felt all the eyes in the room settle on her. She sat quite still, her hands on the table in front of her. Petra said that although Dean Reeve couldn't be ruled out as a suspect, the police were working on the hypothesis that this was the work of someone else. She talked about the police investigation and appealed to the public to come forward if they could cast any light. She turned to Frieda and asked her to say a few words.

Frieda looked at the sea of faces.

"Someone must know something," she said. She

stopped. The room became very silent, but she didn't know what to add. Gary Hillier, near the front, was staring at her as though she were a complicated knot that had to be untied. She felt Petra's hand on her forearm and continued: "This person, who has attacked a very ill man, slipped drugs into the drink of a young woman and then abducted her, and now killed someone, apparently because he had come into contact with me, is disturbed and very dangerous. They must be stopped, not just because of what they have done up to now, but what they might do in the future."

There were questions, a buzz of raised voices, people asking about Morgan Rossiter and her relationship to him. Liz Barron asked Frieda how she felt, about her emotional state—but Frieda didn't answer. Nor did she answer the person at the far end of the room about whether she was cursed. There were several questions for Petra about the failure of the police investigation.

"Are you scared?" someone shouted, as the communications woman called the meeting to a close.

"Yes," Frieda replied. She couldn't see who had spoken. There were too many people. "Of course I am. Wouldn't you be?"

PART THREE
The Body Behind the Door

38

"Are you scared?" asked Daniel Blackstock.

"Yes. Of course I am. Wouldn't you be?"

She looked in his direction but he didn't think she was actually looking at him. Perhaps he could get a one-to-one in a few days' time. After all, she owed him a favor.

Then it was over and she was gone, a woman at her elbow steering her from the room, Petra Burge following. Daniel Blackstock stood up and shouldered his canvas bag. On his way out, he bumped into Liz Barron.

"What do you make of all of this?" she said. Her eyes gleamed. Even her hair looked brighter than usual.

"Awful," he said shortly.

"Of course, but—"

He didn't wait to hear the end of the sentence. The woman was a pest and she couldn't write properly either, yet she was one of the *Daily News*'s star reporters. Life wasn't fair.

A fellow crime reporter slapped his back in a comradely fashion. "You interviewed her once, didn't you? Maybe you'll be next."

Daniel Blackstock went out onto the street, into the hot blue morning. At the café opposite, he bought a takeaway coffee that he drank as he slowly made his way through the traffic. He decided to walk all the way to Bank, to allow his thoughts to settle, and as he did so he composed the story in his head. It would certainly be on the front page tomorrow, and then an inside spread, presumably by him as well because he was becoming the Frieda Klein expert. Perhaps he could syndicate it. The foreign press were starting to show interest. He would be busy.

The first paragraph was the most important. Nothing sensationalist—he didn't want to write like Liz Barron, an adjective or two in front of every noun. "Somber": that was how he would describe Frieda Klein as she sat on the platform. And scared, yes, she had said she was scared. Of course she was—how could she not be?—and yet she hadn't seemed it. He reached the entrance of Bank where he drank the rest of his coffee, then tossed the empty cup into the bin before going down the escalators.

He was so familiar with this route that he could recite the names in his sleep. Shadwell, Limehouse, Westferry, Poplar, Blackwall, East India . . . He knew how quickly London unravelled into a landscape of crumbling warehouses and vast, half-finished building sites. He got off at West Silvertown, just a few minutes from home—and just a few minutes from that other place, too: his secret place.

He heard the screeching of a horn, again and again. He looked around. It was like he had been woken up. He was in the middle of North Woolwich Road, a white van halted just a few meters from him, a man leaning out of the window, shouting, swearing. Blackstock didn't trouble to reply but continued across the road.

Almost as soon as he reached the pavement, his phone rang. He looked at it. It was his editor from the paper. Or one of his editors. There were so many of them and they kept changing. But they all had one thing in common: they could tell him what to do and he had to do it. This was Brian.

"Where the hell are you?"

"I've been at the press conference."

"What press conference?"

"The Frieda Klein case."

"Is it still going on?"

"No."

"So where are you?"

"I'm on my way home to write it up."

"Going home? What century are you in? What about the other stories you're working on? Are they going to write themselves?"

Daniel Blackstock listened with a kind of fascination to the other Daniel Blackstock, the one other people saw, the public one, the pretend one, the unreal one, as he mumbled on the phone and said that he was progressing with the other stories and that he was really sorry he wasn't in the office but he could make progress on them at home and he would be in early tomorrow. Daniel Blackstock didn't like the Daniel Blackstock he was listening to. It would be horrible to really be like that.

When the phone call was finished, he let out a breath. If they only knew who he was, what he could do, what he had done. The familiar streets looked different to him today, clearer colors, more sharply in focus. He could picture the room, his secret place.

A plane passed over his head, soaring up from City Airport. He felt as if it was welcoming him home.

*

"Was everything all right?"

Daniel Blackstock looked across the table at his wife. All right? What did she mean? Oh, yes, the meal. She had been talking about her day and he hadn't been paying attention. It was as if the radio had been left on in the next room. He had murmured something occasionally and nodded but this was something that needed some sort of an answer. He looked down at his plate, at the remains of his meal. He could hardly remember eating it. The bone of a lamb chop, some mashed potato, greens. What could you say about something like that?

"Fine."

He looked across at his wife. Lee Blackstock, née Bass. When she came home she always changed from her work clothes into something she considered suitable for leisure. This evening she was wearing a flowery shirt and a light blue cardigan. She noticed him looking at her and a pink color appeared on her pale face. Pale face, dull hair, pale eyes. "How was your day?" she said.

"Fine."

"What did you do?"

"Do you want me to go through it detail by detail?"

"I'm just interested."

"I went to the Frieda Klein press conference."

"Oh," said Lee. "Frieda Klein."

"What does that mean? 'Oh. Frieda Klein,'" he said, imitating her.

"It doesn't mean anything."

"You must have meant something or why did you say it?"

"It's just that it's a case you're interested in, that's all."

"I'm not 'interested' in it. It's my job."

"I just want to know about your work."

She reminded him of a yapping little dog that was snapping at his ankles. He wanted to kick her away. He wanted to shut her up. Looking at her eager face, he knew it was unfair, but it was impossible for her to understand. It was impossible for anyone to understand. He barely understood it himself. There was so much happening in his head. He needed to get things straight. He stood up. "I've got to work," he said.

"But we're eating."

"This is urgent."

"I thought . . ." she began, and stopped when she saw the expression on his face.

"You want to know about my work?" he said. "Then I'll tell you. They're looking at every office, every paper clip, every job. This is the sort of story that could make someone famous and I've got it. And I need some space."

"I just want to help."

"Right now you can help by leaving me alone and not bothering me with questions."

He got up and left his wife sitting at the table with the half-finished supper. He walked up the stairs to his little office at the back. He had kept the room as simple as possible. His computer sat on the desk under the window, which looked out on the small, concreted yard and beyond that the wall and the house in the next street. Only one window was visible, the frosted glass of what must be a bathroom. Sometimes he saw a blurry shape moving behind it.

Apart from the desk, the only items of furniture were an office chair and a brown veneer filing cabinet. There were no pictures on the wall. Once, Lee had asked whether she couldn't put some up. She had never asked again. There was nothing on the desk apart from the computer. Nothing was allowed to be there that wasn't being used. Not even a pen. Files were put back in the cabinet, pens and spare ink cartridges in the drawer.

He sat in the chair and stared at the blank screen of his computer without seeing it. What he was really seeing was the picture in his mind of a young woman, unconscious, lying on the floor. He had been careful not to leave any trace on her but he remembered the smell of her and the warmth. He had pressed his face against the soft fold under her jawline. There was nothing sexual about it. Nothing at all. She had been completely in his power. He could have undressed her, done what he liked. He hadn't even been tempted. That would have been pitiful. He wasn't going down that road—not even now, when it would have been so easy.

Next he saw a middle-aged man, helpless under his blows. That had been unsatisfactory. It was important but it had been rushed and anxious. There was too much that could have gone wrong. He could have been seen. Even so, it had brought him close to her. Daniel Blackstock had read about the man in the papers: he was a friend of Frieda's. A father figure. Probably more than a father figure.

They were both becoming fuzzy in his mind, although he had the photograph of the niece, which was something. But Morgan Rossiter was clear. As soon as Daniel Blackstock thought of him, he was back there in his flat. He could see the look of puzzlement that came with the first blow and then the fading of the light in his eyes as they went from the windows into a man's soul to just stuff, blobs of slime. I did that, Daniel Blackstock thought, I really did that. I made that change in the world.

And the other one—but that was unfinished business.

Another face came into his mind. Frieda Klein's. When he had first met her, met her properly, close up and face to face, he had felt his pulse race so that he could barely think, let alone ask coherent questions. Somehow he had managed it. Now, looking back, he remembered in fragments and flashes: the way she talked, low and clear, with the faintest trace of an accent he couldn't place. Her smooth, long-fingered hands; her sharp cheekbones; a wisp of hair across her face, which she had swept away; she had bitten her lower lip, perhaps out of impatience. Above all, he remembered her eyes, dark and bright, and how occasionally they would settle on him with an attention that made him think she must know. She must know.

Behind it all there was another, dimmer, figure. Daniel Blackstock only knew Dean Reeve's face from one picture, the image they always used in the newspapers. It must be an old passport photo. Dean Reeve stares straight at you. There's no smile. Smiles aren't allowed in passport pictures. But, as with Frieda, Daniel Blackstock had the sense that they were looking at him, understanding him. Except in this case he wanted to be seen and understood. That he had been one of the first journalists on the scene when Bruce Stringer's body was found felt like fate. Once he had learned what had actually happened inside Frieda Klein's house he almost wanted to laugh and applaud. It was so clever and so funny. What a way to send a message. By contrast, his own messages were scrawled notes. But he was learning.

Suddenly the office felt stuffy and constricting. He

needed to get out. He walked down the stairs and put his jacket on. As he opened the front door, his wife emerged from the sitting room. "Where are you going?"

"I'm going out to get some milk."

"Shall I come with you?"

"I can get milk on my own."

Outside he felt free. He walked past the place but didn't go in, though he could feel it tugging at him, like a magnet. Then he went northwards to the Victoria Dock and looked across the water. Suddenly it all felt right. He had researched Dean Reeve's life. If he crossed the bridge it would be just a short walk into Canning Town to where Dean Reeve had lived when he was living in our world. He was one of the few who would understand the way Daniel Blackstock was feeling now. He closed his eyes and played over and over again that moment when the life had gone from Morgan Rossiter, like a light fading. Everything else—the research, the spying on Frieda and her friends, the kidnapping, the assault—all that had been trivial and scrappy. Now he had taken the step into a new world. It was like what they said about losing your virginity. Except that losing his virginity hadn't been much of a deal for Daniel Blackstock: a fumbling when he was fifteen years old, and the world hadn't changed at all. But it was different now. He had joined the club: people who have killed. Dean Reeve might already know about him. He would probably be amused and flattered. And this was only the beginning.

Daniel Blackstock looked around him. A group of people were sitting at a table outside the coffee shop. One was showing the others something on her phone and they

were all laughing. If they noticed him at all, he would probably seem insignificant. If only they knew. That was a part
of his power, to be able to do what he had done and not feel
the need to tell anyone. He could put up with his treatment
at work, the disrespect. None of that mattered to him. He
knew who he was.

He looked in the direction of where Dean Reeve had
lived. He could almost feel it on his face, like sunshine.
With reluctance, he turned away and walked slowly back to
his house.

"Did you get the milk?"

"I forgot."

"It's all right. We've got a full carton."

"Were you trying to catch me out?"

Lee's face went very pale. "Why would I do that?"

"Never mind."

He walked back up to his office. He had an article to
write but he didn't begin it right away. He needed to think.
That hadn't been very good. He had been caught out telling a stupid, completely unnecessary lie. Or would Lee believe that he'd gone out to get the milk and forgotten it? He
was going to have to think seriously about his wife. Was
she going to be a liability? Was it possible that she had noticed anything strange about him? He felt different. Did he
look different?

At least there was no reason to think anyone would dis-
cover that room with the mattress on the floor. And he had
nothing to worry about in his office. There was nothing in
his files apart from the notes and cuttings and press re-
leases that any journalist would have. His computer was a
different matter. So he protected it with a password. It had

been long before but now he made it longer. It was twenty-two characters long. It consisted of the maiden names of his two grandmothers, the postcode of the house he had lived in at college and finally, most important, the date on which he was going to kill Frieda Klein.

39

The next day, the paper wanted him to write about the planned garden bridge over the Thames (the case for and the case against) and also do a quick telephone interview with a local entrepreneur who had made his fortune from scrap metal and had now set up a charity. Daniel Blackstock, standing in his little office and staring out of the window at the concrete yard, had difficulty controlling his voice.

"Don't you think," he said, "that it's more important to follow up the Frieda Klein story?"

"Is there something new?"

"This is the only story that matters at the moment."

"What have you got that all the other papers haven't?"

"That's why I need time. I've covered this from the start."

"I was thinking of getting Suzie to do a feature on it. Woman's angle."

Blackstock could feel the rage in his chest, thick as sludge. His eyes burned. The yard looked white in the glare of the day; the sky shimmered an electric blue. "I know everything there is to know about Frieda Klein," he said. "I've been there from the start. I'm the one who should write about it. And if I get something fresh, then the paper can syndicate it all over the world."

There was a silence. Money always did the trick.

"I'll give you till after the weekend."

*

"Where are you off to?"

"Work. Or had you forgotten I worked? Paid the bills, put food on the table."

"I work too," Lee said timidly.

Blackstock looked at his wife. She worked in a residential care home. She came back, especially after a night shift, smelling different, something sweet and sharp. When he thought of what she did—the physical stuff, the bodily stuff—it made him shudder. The pay was pitiful. He didn't tell people at work what she did: he said she was a teacher.

"Right. See you."

"Do you know when . . ."

But he'd left, stepping out into the warmth of the morning and feeling his spirits lift. He glanced at his mobile: he just had time to pay a quick visit to his secret room, the one where he felt most fully himself, and then he would have a look at Frieda.

There were still a few photographers in Saffron Mews, but they told him that Frieda Klein had left earlier in the morning, striding past them without so much as lifting her head for a photograph. Blackstock thought for a moment, then turned away. He went instead to where he knew her consulting rooms were, in the mansion block less than ten minutes' walk from her house. It stood overlooking a cratered building site.

He bought himself a large cup of coffee from the store on the corner and shook in three sugars. His whole body was pulsing with anticipation and excitement and he felt he needed energy. He had been here just a few days ago, watching like this; that was when he had seen Rossiter go into the building and then he had seen him come out again, his face blazing with rage, and he had known, just *known*, that he was one of Frieda's and ripe for the picking. He kept seeing Morgan Rossiter's face as he toppled, as he died, and seeing his own figure as well, standing over him. It was like replaying a film, over and over.

He sat on a bench across the road from the building, where he could keep an eye on the exit. He knew that each morning she came here, but had assumed that after Rossiter's death she would be taking time off. He chuckled softly to himself: typical Frieda Klein, if she'd gone back to work straightaway. Not like his wife. When Lee had a cold, she'd take to her bed with a pile of tissues and lots of magazines.

He drank his coffee. A few feet away a man in shabby clothes was playing his violin, its case open for coins. Daniel Blackstock's phone rang and he looked at the screen. It was work, so he didn't answer. They'd given him till after the weekend. Fifteen minutes later, it rang once more. This time it was Lee. He pushed it back into his pocket. At just before midday he saw a familiar figure: short, scrawny, ginger-haired, flat-chested, wearing sneakers, as if she was a teenager not an adult. The detective. Petra Burge. He was about to shrink out of sight when he remembered: he had a right to be here. He was a reporter, a Frieda Klein reporter. However much he followed her, it wouldn't be suspicious. He sat up straighter, waiting for her to notice him but she didn't look around, just pushed her way through the doors and out of sight.

"The public are eager to help," said Petra.

"That's good, isn't it?"

Frieda was sitting in her red armchair, and Petra was opposite her, where patients usually sat. Between them was a low table and a box of tissues; on the wall was a drawing, on the windowsill a flowering plant. It was cool and quiet in this room, a haven from the hot roar of Oxford Street just minutes away and the heaving building site just outside the window.

"Hundreds and thousands of them. We can't keep up. So far, it's simply taking up a lot of time. By the way, Professor Hal Bradshaw contacted me. He thought I could use his expertise."

Frieda could feel that Petra was observing her reaction. "Why are you telling me?"

"I know you two have a history."

"How did you respond to his offer?"

"I thanked him politely. He's going to be presenting a big television series about twenty-first-century killers, including Dean Reeve and all the latest developments. I thought I should warn you."

"Thank you."

"They'll want to interview you."

"I think I'm done with all of that."

"He's contacting people who know you."

Frieda's heart sank. She stood up and crossed to the window. "When I first came here, there were houses. I saw the wrecking ball demolish them all. It happened so quickly—one day they were there and the next gone, just rubble on the ground. Then the work was stopped for a while and kids moved in and made it into a kind of playground for themselves. They had games of football out there. Teenagers went there to smoke or take drugs or just lose themselves for a while. Lovers came. Lonely people.

There were lots of foxes at night. And now it's all started up again, the digging and the building. That's London. It changes all the time."

"After I've gone through everything with you once more, I'm going to talk to Chloë, at length."

"She says she's being badgered by the press. Her name got out, after all."

"It usually does."

"So why are you wanting to interview her again?"

"I have to start somewhere."

"Why with her?"

"There's a theory that the first crime someone commits is the impulsive one. After that, they get more planned. So the first crime can reveal more."

"A theory," said Frieda. She wrinkled her brow.

Petra nodded. "It's certainly true that with serial murders, for instance, the first body tends to be nearest to the perpetrator's home."

"It sounds a bit dubious to me."

"Nevertheless, when I leave here I'm going to Walthamstow to talk to your niece."

"But she doesn't remember anything more than last time you talked to her."

"She met this person. She might know him, or know people who know him. It's not going to help her or any of you to be protective. We have to investigate everybody, everything."

Frieda looked at her broodingly. "You're right, of course."

"But?"

"I can't help feeling there's something I'm missing. Something I'm not seeing."

"That's something I can relate to." Petra looked around her. "So this is where you see your patients."

"Yes."

"And transform their neurotic misery into common un-happiness."

"What?"

"I said—"

"I know what you said. You've been reading Freud."

"Perhaps," said Petra, defensively.

"Because of me?"

Petra shrugged. "I thought it might help me in my inquiries."

"Has it?"

"Not exactly. But it's interesting."

"What is?"

"How strange everyone is, even to themselves, how mysterious."

On her way out, Petra saw one of the journalists who had interviewed Frieda hanging around on the other side of the road, presumably waiting for her to come out. What was his name? Daniel something. He was always at the press conferences. He'd done a pretty good job, accurate at least. Shortish, with a pigeon chest, beaky nose. He always wore his trousers pulled too high up his waist. She ignored him.

40

At eleven o'clock that evening, when Frieda was reading a book in her living room, there was a banging at her door. She lifted the cat off her lap and went to answer.

"Are you all right?" Chloë didn't look all right. Her cheeks were blotchy and her expression desolate as she tumbled over the threshold. "How did you get here?"

"Don't worry. I got a cab, and there are two police officers at the entrance of the mews, in case you didn't know."

"I did. Come and sit down. Here." Frieda gestured to a chair on one side of the hearth, where every winter evening a fire burned. "Is there anything in particular? I know Petra Burge was coming to interview you."

"It's not that." Chloë made an impatient gesture, running her hand through her hair. "It's not as if I don't go over it in my head all the time."

Frieda nodded. "So if not that, what?"

"It's William. You remember I told you about him. William McCollough. He's the new guy at the workshop."

"I remember," said Frieda. She also remembered what Rudkin had found out about him: that he had been in care, had been abused as a child, had a criminal record for theft and drugs.

"I told her about him. Not just him. Everyone I worked with, of course. But he's the one they're interested in. A couple of detectives came back a few hours later and then he went off in their car with them."

"That doesn't necessarily mean anything."

"He was staring at me as he went, as if I'd betrayed him."

"You just answered the questions you were asked, which is what you have to do."

"You don't think it could have been him?"

"I don't know."

"He's sweet. A bit odd. He's got long gray hair in a ponytail and he won't meet your eye and he mumbles when he talks. I feel sorry for him."

"The police have to investigate everyone."

"I know. But they're not investigating my other workmates. Anyway, that's not all."

"Go on."

"I stayed late. We were all a bit upset and Robbie—he's one of the guys, we dated for a bit but now we're just friends—he went and got some beers and we sat around talking. I told them everything that had happened." She looked at Frieda, her face smudged and anxious. "It was good. They were great about it. I don't know why I hadn't been able to say anything before."

"And that's why you're upset now?"

"Sorry. I keep getting sidetracked. Suddenly a journalist turned up. Why had William McCollough been taken in for questioning? Did we have suspicions?"

Frieda didn't reply.

"How the hell did she even know?"

"Police officers leak information like that."

"She was all smiley and friendly and unbelievably persistent."

"Let me guess. Liz Barron."

"Do you know her?"

"We've met." She thought of Liz Barron's fresh and shining face, her implacable girlishness.

"She was saying all these things about Will. How he'd been abused as a child. How he'd been a drug addict and been in prison for theft. It was horrible. She was pretending to be sympathetic, but all the time she was insinuating that if you've been abused as a child, then you're going to be an abuser as an adult. That's not true, is it?"

"It probably isn't," said Frieda. "But it can be."

"It'll be in all the papers now, won't it?"

"I think it will."

"This is because of me. I don't believe it was Will. I just don't. I think I'd know."

"I thought you said you were the Frieda Klein expert."

"What?"

Daniel Blackstock was bleary with sleep: he'd been woken by his phone ringing and he saw that, although it was getting light outside, it was not yet six. He sat up in bed. Lee was working nights for the rest of the week so he was alone in the house: that was good.

"I've just spoken to the night editor. You said you knew everything there was to know about Frieda Klein," his editor said.

"Yes."

"So how come Liz Barron's got a scoop and you've got nothing?"

"What's the scoop?"

"Does the name William McCollough ring any bells?"

"William McCollough?"

"A joiner who works with the niece. Creepy-looking

guy. He was taken in for questioning yesterday afternoon. It looks like they might have found their man. Why does Liz Barron know about this and not you?"

Daniel Blackstock's brain was working slowly. He got out of bed and opened the curtains, blinking in the onrush of light. He had never even heard of McCollough. "I'll go and read what she says and get back to you," he said.

"I want something online by nine. Then we'll talk."

He sat in his small bare study and turned on his computer. Liz Barron's article occupied the entire front page of the *Daily News*, under a photo of McCollough, who looked seedy and furtive, his long hair in a ponytail and his eyes half closed. There was a double-page spread as well, with more pictures of McCollough, and also a photo he'd seen many times before of Frieda Klein and a smaller one of her niece, Chloë Klein. He paused, looking at both women. He felt an intimacy with them, a connection. He remembered the day he had handed Frieda the envelope, their fingers touching, her eyes looking into his.

What to do? There would be a great media clamor now. McCollough suited the part all right: he was just the kind of person the public wanted to be a killer, a damaged loner. Then it would die down. He had to find a way of using this. He was thinking more clearly now. He'd had an idea, a good idea. He could feel that he was getting better at this.

William McCollough's doorbell was ringing. His phone was ringing. He pulled back the curtain and looked out of the window. A small crowd was on the pavement, staring up. Lights flashed at him, and he jolted back. He sat on his bed and put his face into his hands. He tried to block out the sound of the world, but the phone went on ringing, ringing, ringing and they wouldn't go away and he was filled with shame and fear. He would never be free of the past. However far he went, however much time passed, even when he was old, even when he was dying, it would follow him.

Frieda sat in Petra Burge's office. Her face was white with fury. "You say he's not a suspect."

Petra leaned her face on her hand and fiddled with a pen on her desk. She looked drab with tiredness. "I'm saying that William McCollough has not been charged."

"So how did they get hold of him? Have you seen all the papers, everything that's being written about him?"

"Of course."

"He's being hounded. Who told Liz Barron?"

"I don't know. I'm trying to find out. We've released a statement to the media saying he isn't under suspicion."

"But they're not going away."

"No." Petra sat back in her chair and pushed her fingers through her ginger hair. "You know how it is. He's got a history. He looks a bit strange."

"He was in care. He was abused. Because of that, his life is being wrecked all over again."

"I'm sorry. You can be sure I'll find out who leaked the story."

"And then what? Give McCollough his life back?"

Frieda left the station, walking rapidly in her angry distress, barely aware of which direction she was going. She had paused at a road, waiting for a gap in the traffic, when there was a voice behind her.

"Dr. Klein?"

She turned to see the journalist who had interviewed her and, more to the point, had handed her that photograph of Chloë. "It's Daniel Blackstock, isn't it?"

"Yes." He took a step toward her. "You've got a good memory."

"I don't want to talk to any of you," she said.

His face puckered. "Because of what's happening with William McCollough?"

"How can you all do this?"

"Look at me," he said. "I'm here, not there, which is where my paper wants me to be. Believe me, I'm disgusted by it. That's not what I'm like. I've always treated you fairly, haven't I?"

Frieda looked at him. "You have," she said grudgingly. "I know you're not all the same. But I'm angry."

"So am I. No wonder people don't trust us."

She half turned away.

"I could do something to make amends," he said. "You said, that time outside your house, that if you were going to talk to anyone it would be me."

He was reminding her that she owed him a favor. She studied him. His face was earnest; his brown eyes gazed back at her.

"What are you suggesting?"

"You could give me a quote about how appalled you are. And I was wondering . . ." He stopped, licked his lips.

"Yes?"

"You might not like this idea but I think it could be very powerful."

"Go on."

"I could perhaps interview your niece."

"Chloë?"

"She knows William McCollough. An interview with her, one of the victims, would do more good than a thousand statements from the police."

"I'm not sure it's a good idea. I don't want Chloë dragged into the spotlight. She's been through quite enough already."

"So has McCollough." The unspoken, *because of you*, hung in the air between them.

Frieda frowned. He watched her intently. "I'll talk to Chloë," she said eventually.

"You have my word that I'd be very unintrusive. And she and you could see the copy before it was published. I know it's only a London paper but I promise it would be picked up by everyone, like that." He snapped his fingers in front of her face. "And it might make a huge difference."

"We'll see."

"Here's my card." He pulled his wallet out of his trouser pocket, took out a card and handed it to her. "Call me any time. But, for McCollough's sake, don't wait too long."

41

Frieda sat at her kitchen table; opposite her was Chloë, who looked as if she had turned up for work somewhere smart and discreet. Gone were the heavy boots and the oversized man's shirt, the exaggerated eyeliner, the stud in her nose and in her eyebrow. When she arrived, she had taken off her jacket to reveal a blue blouse that Frieda recognized as her own, one she hadn't been able to find for months. She wore a cotton skirt, unobtrusive leather sandals. Her face, bare of makeup and piercings, seemed defenseless and young.

"You're sure about this?" Frieda asked. "It's not too late to pull out."

"I want to." Chloë's expression was fierce. "I *need* to. You would if you were me."

"You don't need to tell him anything you don't want to."

"I know that. You've told me a hundred times."

"And you mustn't say anything about the sound of planes."

"I know."

"And I'm going to be here throughout."

"You've told me that as well. It's OK. He'll ask me things. I'll answer them. I've not got anything to hide. Nothing to be ashamed of." Her voice wavered. She looked momentarily lost. "And then I'll talk about what's happening to Will."

"Good."

"What's he like?"

"Who?"

"Daniel Blackstock. He sounded OK on the phone."

Frieda hesitated. She thought of him handing over that photo of Chloë; that was a good, unexpected thing to do. And then she thought of his hot brown eyes as he'd asked if he could interview her niece. But of course he was a journalist on a newspaper that was fighting for survival. His life must feel precarious, and this interview must be like his trump card. "I don't know him," she said. "But he's behaved well over all of this and he seems reliable."

"Do I look all right?"

Frieda smiled. "You look fine."

"No, I don't. I hate these clothes."

"Why did you put them on, then?"

"To appear frail and vulnerable, I suppose. Or at least respectable. I shouldn't have done. Hang on a minute."

She disappeared. Frieda heard her feet going up the stairs. When she reappeared she was wearing an old black T-shirt of Frieda's over the skirt and had put on Frieda's heavy walking boots; her legs were white above them, a bruise along one shin. She'd heavily lined her eyes.

"There," she said. "That's better. This is more like me."

"He's not going to take photos."

"I know. It's about wanting to be myself. Not pretending."

Frieda nodded. "That's good, then. Have you thought any more about talking to someone?"

"I'll think about it," said Chloë, "when all this is over."

"It never is over. You'll never get to a time that's magically right. If you need to talk to someone, you should do it now."

"Shouldn't he be here?"

"In about five minutes. I've said he can have half an hour with you."

Chloë's face took on a sarcastic expression that reassured Frieda. "You're like my press agent. You'll make sure I don't get asked awkward questions about my private life."

"I'll only be present if you want me to be."

"God, no. You've bloody got to stay, but—" Chloë didn't get to finish her sentence because at that moment the doorbell rang.

Daniel Blackstock took Frieda's chair directly opposite Chloë. Frieda sat to one side, like an onlooker. There had been a delay in beginning the interview. Frieda had offered him tea, assuming he would be eager to get on with the interview. But Blackstock said, yes, he would love some. So Frieda went to the kitchen and made a mug of tea with a teabag. He wanted sugar as well and she had to search through a cupboard to find it.

He seemed nervous, she thought. He had obviously dressed smartly for the occasion, in a gray shirt done up to the top button so it appeared to be throttling him and a jacket that was too warm for the day. His face, newly shaved, was smoothly pink. He kept licking his dry lips.

"I want to say, right from the beginning, that I appreciate you letting me come here. I also want to say that when I have written the article I'll show it to you both before I file it."

"That would be great," said Chloë. She smiled encouragingly at him and sat up straighter in her chair. Her hands were clasped together in her lap.

"That's unusual, isn't it?" said Frieda.

"I don't see this as normal journalism," said Blackstock. "The real point of doing this, as far as I'm concerned, is if it can be of some help. But don't tell my editor." He took his phone from his pocket and laid it on the table. "You don't mind if I record this, do you?"

Chloë didn't. Her face, though pale, was composed.

"First of all," said Daniel Blackstock, with a nervous cough, "and tell me if you find the question too disturbing, can I just talk you through the terrible thing that happened to you?"

"The trouble is," said Chloë, "that I barely remember anything. That's what's horrible. There are these lost days and I don't know what happened to me."

"It must feel like a nightmare," said Blackstock.

"It does. What kind of creep would do that?"

"So, you remember being in the bar with your friends, and then—what? Waking up somewhere?"

"In a churchyard. Yes. Inside railings that surrounded a tree. But even that's a blurred, distant memory, like a smudge in my brain."

"Smudge in your brain," said Blackstock. He wrote something on his pad. "So you were out of it for . . ." He seemed to be calculating. " . . . nearly sixty hours!"

"He injected me," said Chloë, matter-of-factly. She held out her bare forearm. "Several times. You can still see the faint marks."

He leaned forward. "You must feel violated."

"Must I?"

Frieda smiled to herself at Chloë's answer. She was doing well.

"Well, when you think of how you were kept, how you were displayed."

Blackstock looked at Chloë, at her eyes flashing in surprise, her lips parting slightly, breathing more quickly.

"What do you mean? Nobody knows how I was displayed. I don't know myself."

He assumed an expression of puzzlement. "Didn't they show you the photograph?"

"Hang on," said Frieda, sharply.

"Oh, I'm sorry," said Daniel Blackstock. "I just thought—but I see I was wrong."

"What photograph?" said Chloë. There was a silence. He waited. "What photograph, Frieda?"

"A picture was sent to Mr. Blackstock. He gave it to me and I gave it to the police."

"Why didn't you show it to me?"

"I thought it would upset you."

"I can't believe you didn't tell me about it."

"It was a decision I had to make."

"I want to see it."

"I have a copy," said Blackstock. "But Dr. Klein may not think it's right for you to see it."

Blackstock looked at Chloë as Chloë stared in dismay at Frieda. He could hardly breathe. He felt shivers running down his back, his arms and his legs. His heart was racing. How could it not be visible to them?

"Show it to me," said Chloë.

"If that's what you want," said Frieda, slowly.

"It's what I want."

Frieda nodded at Blackstock and he reached into his

shoulder bag, took out a copy of the photograph and handed it to Chloë. His hand was perfectly still, as if he felt nothing, but Chloë's trembled so fiercely she had to put the picture on the table before she could see it properly.

"Tell me how you feel." Daniel Blackstock spoke gently.

When Chloë looked up, her eyes were full of tears. She was panting, as if after an intense effort. "He was there," she said. "Taking that picture, staring at me, putting it on record."

And now he felt he was back in that room with her, standing over her. He remembered the feel of her, the smell of her, the texture of her hair, her body.

"And?" he prompted.

"I feel . . . I don't know. He could have killed me. He could have . . . done things to me. But he just took those pictures and let me go."

"What do you want now, Chloë?"

"I want to know what happened. I want the person who did this caught so he can't do it to anyone else."

Daniel Blackstock nodded.

"I don't feel damaged," said Chloë. Her voice was suddenly loud. "I don't feel ashamed or humiliated or traumatized. I feel angry. Very angry."

He wrote on his pad. "So, at the moment the media seems to have focused on your colleague from work. William McCollough."

"The bastards," said Chloë. "Almost the whole point of me doing this interview is so that I can say, completely clearly, that Will McCollough had absolutely nothing to do with this."

"I'm really glad to hear you say that and say it so passionately. And I'm sure you're right. So what can I put in this article that will convince skeptical readers that your friend is innocent?"

Chloë banged her fist on the table. "Because he just bloody could not have done it."

"Why? I'm not asking for myself."

Chloë became almost agitated. "I can list the reasons. He shares a flat, he doesn't have a car and can't drive. How the fuck would he kidnap me and drive me across London, keep me prisoner and then dump me?"

"How do you mean 'drive you across London'? How do you know that?"

"Why do you ask?"

"Do you have any idea where you were held?" said Blackstock. "That could be very useful for the article. It might jog people's memory."

Chloë glanced across at Frieda, who minutely shook her head. "I don't know," she said. "I can't remember."

"Nothing?"

"It's just a blur. But where was I?"

"You were saying why William McCollough couldn't have committed these crimes."

"The police haven't charged him. They let him go. They say that he isn't under suspicion."

Daniel Blackstock looked doubtful. "I've been a crime reporter for ten years now, and you can't always take what the police say at face value, you know. William McCollough has a history of mental disturbance."

Chloë put her head in her hands for a moment, then lifted it. "That's what I can't bear. He's been through so much and he's survived it. I didn't know about his past before, no one did. He's very private. Now, because of me, everyone knows about him and he's going through all of this."

Daniel Blackstock turned to Frieda. "What's your opinion?"

"This isn't about me," said Frieda. "I'm here to support Chloë."

"I'm just asking about William McCollough. Do you agree with what Chloë has just said?"

"Yes."

"If that's right, then why did the police pick on him?"

"Because they have a theory."

"What theory?"

Frieda thought for a moment. Was she going to do this? Yes, she decided. Yes, she was. "It's a profiling idea that's become a bit of a cliché. The idea is that the first crime is, in a way, the real one, the impulsive one. So it's much more likely to be close to home. Later crimes are a form of distraction."

"Do you disagree with the rule?"

"Rules can be useful, but not when people use them as a prop to save them the trouble of thinking."

"Can I quote you on that?"

"If you like. The attack on Chloë was premeditated and highly organized. I don't mean by that that the attacker is a person of any particular capacity."

"Don't you have to be pretty capable and smart to bring something like that off?" asked Daniel Blackstock.

Frieda shook her head. "Acts like that are a sign of weakness, not strength. Of course, what happened to Chloë and Reuben and, above all, to my patient is terrible. But there's something basically pathetic about it."

Daniel Blackstock was writing again but at this point his pen slipped off the notebook and fell to the floor. He bent and picked it up. There was sweat on his back now, a broad dark arrow on his shirt. "That's interesting," he said.

"It's not interesting, it's obvious. Dean Reeve is someone who defines himself emotionally through violence. It's like a crossed wire. That's bad enough. But these crimes are something different. It's someone who's trying to copy Dean Reeve, as if that will fill some sort of gap, compensate for some sort of inadequacy."

"An inadequacy that involves killing people," said Daniel Blackstock.

"Yes. As if causing pain was a sign of being important."

"Hey," said Chloë. "I thought this interview was with me."

Just over an hour later Chloë and Frieda were in William McCollough's kitchen. On the way, Frieda had bought a bottle of whisky. McCollough opened it and poured them all some. They clinked glasses and she saw his hands were trembling slightly. He was wearing canvas trousers, ripped on one leg, and a baggy T-shirt that couldn't disguise how thin he was—even thinner than he looked in those awful photographs of him all the papers had carried, almost cadaverous. His long, graying hair was drawn back from his face. She saw his teeth were nicotine-stained and slightly crooked.

"I don't know which journalists are worse," he said, in the throaty voice of a smoker. "The ones who threaten me or the ones who say they want me to tell my side of the story."

"I'm extremely sorry you got dragged into this," said Frieda.

"I just did an interview," added Chloë. She reached out and rubbed him on the back with an oddly maternal gesture. The older man looked at her and blinked. "We did it to clear your name."

"I hope you got well paid."

"We didn't get paid at all. We just did it to help."

McCollough took a gulp of his drink. "You think it'll do any good?"

"People have short memories," said Frieda.

"But the internet has a long one. From now on, when someone mentions my name, I'll be the one who was picked up by the police on suspicion of murder and kidnapping." He took another sip. "And maybe someone will say, 'He didn't actually do it in the end,' and then someone else will say, 'Yeah, but wasn't there something funny about him? Wasn't he the one who was involved in some kind of sexual-abuse thing?' And then people won't be able to remember whether I was the one who was abused or whether I was the abuser, or maybe it was a bit of both. Anyway, the police must have known something, eh?"

"Surely it will fade," said Chloë, urgently. "Surely. Once they find who really did it."

His face softened slightly as he looked at her. "Sometimes I reckon if I didn't have a ponytail this wouldn't have happened. Maybe I'll cut it off."

"That's a good idea," she said. "Really short hair would be good on you."

"Do you want to do it?"

"Me?" asked Chloë.

"Why not?"

"OK." Chloë grinned. "As you say, why not?"

Now people, housemates and friends, were starting to

arrive. The doorbell rang; they drifted into the kitchen, greeted William casually, pulled beer from their backpacks, cigarettes. He looked a bit dazed, almost hunted, as they filled the room, and Frieda realized that it must have been Chloë who had organized this, a gathering of supporters, while outside the journalists still waited. The idea was typically generous but perhaps not entirely wise. Soon it became a blur of tattoos and beards and piercings that made her feel old and far from home. She stood up. "If you need any help, just get in touch. Chloë can always tell you where to find me."

McCollough stood up as well and shook her hand. She smelled tobacco and whisky on him. He had light gray watery eyes and he gazed into her face. "I thought I'd escaped," he said. "But no one escapes in the end."

"I'm so sorry."

He shrugged. "You've done what you could. You've done more than anyone else, you and Chloë."

"Scissors," said Chloë. "Comb."

42

Frieda received a text from Daniel Blackstock at seven the next morning: "I've emailed you the article. Get back to me soonest." She read the article quickly. She usually hated any publicity but this felt different. It was serving a purpose. And she had to admit that it was a solid piece of work, well structured, accurate. Even so, she flinched at some of his language. Chloë was a "vivacious" young woman who was very brave. Frieda herself was a "celebrity psychologist." Frieda wrote back that she was a psychotherapist, not a psychologist, but otherwise he could go ahead.

But there was something wrong. She sat very still and waited to remember, not straining for the memory but ready for it to come to her. And then she had it.

It was still early, so Frieda drank coffee and went through her notes for the sessions in the afternoon. At half past eight she phoned Petra Burge.

"You've got quite a nerve."

"What?"

"I've read Blackstock's interview with your niece. So our investigative theory is a cliché, is it?"

"Did he send you the piece?"

"No, he didn't. He put it up on the paper's website for all to see."

"That was quick."

"The quickness isn't the issue."

"We need to talk," said Frieda.

"Talk? Who do you think you are?"

"This is important."

"We're talking now."

"These things are better face to face." Frieda thought for a moment. "In front of the Imperial War Museum." She glanced at her watch. "I can get there in half an hour."

There was silence on the line.

"All right," said Petra, eventually.

As Frieda approached the museum, she could see Petra was already there, wearing jeans, sneakers and a black bomber jacket. When she noticed Frieda, there was no smile of greeting.

"So?" she said.

"Is it all right if we walk? I think better when I walk."

"If you reckon you'll be safe from me because of being in a public place, then you're wrong. I don't know whether to punch you or to arrest you for interfering with a police inquiry."

"Please," said Frieda. "Shall we go this way?"

They set off through the park, away from the museum. It was a sunny morning and there were children running around on the grass kicking a ball.

"Any reason for meeting here?" said Petra.

"A hundred and fifty years ago this was marshland—streams and mud—and then it was drained and banked."

"I'm sorry I asked."

"It's a strange area. It was outside the old city. So it attracted people who didn't fit in, vagrants, circus performers, prostitutes, criminals."

"I know that. I grew up along here, just off the Elephant and Castle."

"There used to be preachers here. Women who had visions. Demonstrations. Anything that wasn't allowed inside the city walls."

They walked in silence for a few minutes.

"So you're not here to apologize," said Petra.

"I gave that interview for a reason."

"And was it necessary to disrespect the people who're trying to protect you?"

"You know I didn't agree with your idea of picking on William McCollough."

"We didn't pick on him. We interviewed him."

"And someone leaked his name to the media."

"What was it you said exactly? Something about using rules as a way of avoiding having to think? If you had complaints to make about the investigation you go to me about it, or a senior officer. You don't sound off to the media."

They had reached Elephant and Castle, which was a vast building site. They took a circuitous route through.

"I suppose it's changed since you lived here," said Frieda.

"The problem isn't what they're knocking down. It's what they're keeping. If it were up to me, I'd flatten the whole lot and start again."

They turned right down the New Kent Road, and Petra continued, "When I was fifteen, I ran with a gang in the flats along there. I was on the edge really. But I got this." She pulled the collar of her jacket back to show the scar that ran from her ear down her neck.

"A knife?" said Frieda.

"A broken bottle."

"You were lucky. It just missed the carotid artery."

Petra shook her head. "It didn't miss. I was in hospital for two months. My best friend died. Ellie. She was a few months younger than me, only fourteen, a hell-raiser. I realized I had to get out. I went back to school and from then on I made sure I was the best at whatever I set out to do. But I took one lesson away from that time. You don't turn against your own."

"I've never believed in unconditional group loyalty," said Frieda.

"I know. I've read the paper. So you believe you know better than everyone else."

"I wasn't going to stay quiet while you set a mob on William McCollough and ruined his life."

"He was an obvious suspect. He was close to Chloë. He had the opportunity, he had the record. We had to talk to him. You know that."

"It wasn't him."

"I am not saying it is him. We simply took him in for questioning and then we let him go."

Frieda stopped and looked at a building across the street. "Look up there." She pointed at the painted façade of the building. "Neckinger Mills."

"I can read."

"Does the name mean anything to you?"

"I used to have friends on the Neckinger Estate. And I know Neckinger Street."

"Do you know the Neckinger River?"

"No. Is there such a thing? Where is it?"

"We're standing on it. That's why the Mills were there. They were tanning works. They used to treat the hides with water and dog shit. Tons and tons of it. Can you imagine the smell?"

"What happened to the river?"

"Dirtied, clogged up, buried. And forgotten. But it's still there somewhere. This was an area for things that London needed but didn't want to look at or think about or smell. It's a useful reminder."

They crossed over Jamaica Road.

"This was Jacob's Island," said Frieda. "It used to be so dangerous that the police wouldn't even go there. I'm talking about a century and a half ago. And now it's somewhere you and I couldn't afford to live."

"Would you prefer it the way it was? People starving to death in the streets."

"It's not one or the other."

They walked through warehouses converted into flats.

"When I was a kid," said Petra, "I used to come here on a Sunday morning. These were empty and falling down. We used to go inside, wander around, break a few windows."

They emerged from the shade of an alley and suddenly and improbably were on the river facing Tower Bridge and the rows of gleaming City buildings on the far side. The two women turned and walked along the river until they got to the inlet of St. Saviour's Dock. It was low tide and there was nothing but mud.

"That's all that's left of the Neckinger," said Frieda. "Not that there was ever much of it."

"Typical of this bloody area. It can't even produce a proper river." Petra turned to Frieda. "So did you bring me on this walk to tell me that William McCollough is innocent, which you've already told me and already told the press? Without any real evidence, incidentally."

"No," said Frieda, staring down at the mud, waiting to hear herself say the words out loud and make it real. "It's not that. There's someone you should take a look at."

"Is it another one of your friends?"

"No. It's not one of my friends. It's the writer of the article. Daniel Blackstock."

"You're joking."

"No."

"Daniel Blackstock."

"Yes."

"Who's been covering the story since the word go."

"Yes."

Petra stared at her. Then her eyes narrowed and she started to laugh—a loud, uninhibited laugh that crinkled her small face and made her narrow shoulders shake. "Why?" she managed at last. She held up her hand—small and thin, bitten nails. "Don't tell me. Your gut instinct."

"Not only that. Yesterday, when he was asking Chloë about what she remembered before she was abducted, he mentioned her having been in a bar. But how would he know that? No one does, do they?"

"No," said Petra slowly. Her laughter was all gone now. She seemed suddenly older, tired. "I don't think they do."

"And he was the one who gave me the photo. He could have sent it to himself at the newspaper. That would fit."

"Fit with what?"

"And he showed her the picture when he was interviewing her. I watched him watching her. I think he's getting off on all this—doing the crimes and then controlling how they're covered in the media. From his point of view, he's writing the story he's starring in."

"How you jump to conclusions." Petra sounded almost admiring. "One remark and you've worked out everything."

"It makes sense. He's got the perfect excuse to be anywhere I am."

"Or he could simply be a journalist who's covering the story. Because he's a crime reporter, you know."

"Will you check him out?"

Petra nodded. "I will. But don't get your hopes up."

43

Daniel Blackstock tried to keep his face steady. There was a tic at the corner of his left eye; his tongue felt thick. He knew he was blinking too much, but he couldn't stop himself. He had to appear composed and friendly.

"Of course I want to help in any way I can," he said to Petra Burge, who sat across from him. "But I don't think I know anything that you don't. I would always pass on information." He aimed for a tone of aggrieved innocence. His face felt rubbery with the smile he gave; his voice sounded strange in his ears. "After all, I gave that photograph to Dr. Klein when it was in my best interests to give it to my editor."

Her face was unyielding and he couldn't tell what impression he was making. There was sweat under his armpits and down his back; sweat on his forehead.

"Just a few questions, Mr. Blackstock," she said. He didn't like the way she looked at him, as though he was a specimen in a laboratory.

"Ask away." Too cheerful, he thought; too loud.

"Just for the record, I would like to know where you were and what you were doing over the weekend that Chloë Klein was abducted."

"*Me?* What I was doing?" He let himself stare for several seconds.

"It's a simple question."

"You can't think I had anything to do with this?" He paused but Petra Burge didn't say anything, just waited. "Well, I was at home, with my wife. On Friday night we had a takeaway and watched TV together. She'll confirm this." She will, he thought. Oh, yes. "As far as I remember, we went to the shops on Saturday. We had a walk along by the river, had coffee by the Thames Barrier. I wrote a piece for the paper on a spate of robberies in the area. That's about it."

"Where do you live?"

"Between West Silvertown and Pontoon Dock. Kilkenny Road, number seventeen."

"And your wife's name."

"Lee Blackstock." He was feeling steadier now. His face wasn't jumping and twitching. His voice sounded quite normal. He had to protest a bit, he thought. "But why are you asking me all these questions? I'm just a reporter doing my job."

"Where were you on Monday, August the twenty-second?"

Daniel Blackstock could almost feel his brain working, cogs moving. That would be the date Reuben was attacked. Best not to be too sure. An innocent person wouldn't have prepared an alibi. "I don't know," he said.

"That was the date of a further attack."

"I'd have to look at my diary. I imagine I was at home with Lee. We lead a quiet life," he added. "Just the two of us."

"All right. You have a look and let me know. Have you ever met Dr. McGill?"

"No." He thought of asking who he was, but didn't: after all, he was the journalist who knew everything about

Frieda Klein. Of course he would know who Reuben Mc-Gill was.

"What about last Wednesday?"

Morgan Rossiter. For a moment, he let himself remember that face looking at him, the eyes bright with shock, then dimming.

He rubbed his face. His fingers were rough against his skin, which felt papery and frail. Attack is the best defense, he thought. "I know what happened on that evening and I can't think why you're asking me this. It's ridiculous." He lifted his hands, curled them into fists, let them drop with a muted bang onto the table. "I gave Frieda Klein that photograph. I haven't run with the mob picking on that William McCollough. In fact, I did an interview with the niece about her experience to help him out."

"Mr. Blackstock—"

A thought struck him, cold and hard. "Who put you up to asking me these questions?"

"That's not how it works."

"Was it Dr. Klein by any chance?"

"Why would she do that?"

"I don't know. But I very much hope you're not letting your professional judgement be contaminated."

"One more thing. How did you know that Chloë Klein was at a bar when she was abducted?"

"What?"

His thoughts were snagging; he had to think straight.

"You said in the interview that Chloë Klein had been taken from a bar. How did you know that?"

"How?" He took a breath that tore at the tightness in his chest. "I'll tell you how. One of your lot told me."

"A police officer?"

"That's right."

"I see. Who was this police officer?"

"You don't expect me to tell you that."

"I certainly do."

"Then you're going to be disappointed."

He could see a slight tightening in Petra Burge's jaw and that was all. He waited.

"This is a murder inquiry," she said at last. "It's a very serious matter to withhold information from the police."

"I don't reveal my sources. That's part of the job."

"Very noble," she said drily. "But this isn't going to go away."

"Do you have any more questions or can I get back to my work?"

"You can go. For the time being. You'll find out what you were doing on those dates?"

"Of course."

"And you should think if there's anyone else who can corroborate what you say—apart from your wife, that is."

"I'll let you know."

What had happened? Daniel Blackstock poured extra sugar into his tea. His hands were trembling so much that the liquid spilled over the brim of the paper cup. His legs felt shaky as well. He needed to sit down somewhere. He needed to think. Had it just been that remark about the bar? How could he have been so stupid? It was Frieda Klein. It must be. He thought of her eyes looking through him.

His head was hurting and the bright sunlight made his eyes ache. He had felt invisible, but now he was in full view.

*

Petra Burge called Frieda.

"So?"

"I've talked to him."

"And?"

"And now I've let him go."

"Why?"

"Because I've got no reason to keep him."

"That's it?"

"No. We'll check up on him. But there is no evidence against him."

"What about him knowing about the bar?"

"He said it was a police source."

"That's rubbish."

"It could have been. Liz Barron's been getting information through leaks too."

"Did he say who?"

"He says he never reveals his sources."

"Very convenient."

"Would you inform on your patients?"

That made Frieda hesitate for a moment. "If they were breaking the law, yes. Did he have an alibi?"

"Not really—which doesn't mean anything, of course. On the days when Chloë was missing he was at home with his wife, having a quiet weekend—shopping, watching TV, taking a walk by the Thames Barrier."

"Thames Barrier?"

"Yes."

"Which side?"

"What do you mean 'which side'?"

"North or south of the river?"

"How can that possibly matter? Anyway, I don't know. He lives in Silvertown, so it was probably the north side."

Frieda felt her breath catch. "Silvertown."

"Yes."

"Near City Airport."

"There is no proof that your niece was kept near there."

"It's him. I know it is. It's Daniel Blackstock."

44

Jack walked up the road toward Olivia's house. He had worked late at the cheese stall and was looking forward to a bath to wash off the day, then a meal. The house would be his—Chloë was at Reuben's, having dinner with Frieda and Olivia. He relished the thought of an evening alone, sitting with a beer in front of the TV. He was planning a risotto and had the ingredients in his backpack: red onions, dried mushrooms, Parmesan and even a small jar of truffle sauce that someone at the market had given him in return for a circle of soft cheese.

He slid the key into the lock. It took a knack to turn it, easing it out slightly and jiggling it. He pushed the door open and stepped into the hall. It was still dusk, but only just, the last glimmers of light picking out Chloë's boots, the picture on the wall.

There was a sound behind him—later, he couldn't remember what this was: a breath, a cough, a whisper. He swung around in the doorway and saw a shape step into view, a shape in dark clothes, with a stocking over the face. In the seconds before he moved, thoughts rushed in a thick stream through Jack's mind: that there was something glinting in the figure's right hand, that he'd not be making that risotto now, that perhaps he was going to die, that maybe Chloë would push the door against his body when she returned from Reuben's, that there was a smell of rosemary in the air that must be coming from the bush outside the front door.

Jack always said that he was a coward. He shrank from any kind of violence or confrontation. But before he had time to know what he was doing, he found himself charging at the figure and there was a hoarse yell coming from him. And then came a dark flash, a feeling that later would turn into pain but for now was more a series of colors in his brain, reds and purples. A crunching sound. He knew, as he thudded to the floor, that his nose was broken. Then he heard a shattering. His jar of sauce, he thought. The door shut and they were in the small dark hall. He could see some pointed shoes belonging to Olivia just a few inches away, but dimly. And there was a smell of truffles, potent, unpleasant. A boot kicked his cheek. He could hear the gasp of his breathing, and above him the figure was breathing heavily as well, as though this was hard work. He was laboring over Jack, bringing a metal bar down on his legs, his back.

Then, abruptly, he stopped. He leaned down. Jack couldn't see any more, not even when he opened his eyes, but he could feel the person fumbling in his pockets, fingers probing. He could smell him, sweat and something fragrant, like perfume. His mobile was being pulled out. Silence and then he heard a ping as a text was sent.

Then there was a voice in his ear, a whisper in the darkness.

"Left or right-handed?"

Jack groaned.

"Left or right-handed?"

"Left," he managed to say.

With a horrible delicacy, the figure took his left hand and laid it out, palm down on the dusty floor. There was a pause. Then pain crashed through him: from the hand up the arm, flooding the entire body, the brain, the whole self, nowhere to hide. Again. Again. A boot stamping on his hand. There was nothing left but pain and the animal sounds he was making.

The boot stopped. The heavy breathing above him lessened. There was a sound he couldn't make out, slightly squeaky. Then it too ceased. A door opened. A door closed. Jack was alone again.

Frieda was with Olivia, who was crying and lamenting her life, between gulps of wine. It was half past nine. Through the window she saw Josef and Reuben in the garden, sitting on the bench together in the warmth of the night. A cigarette end glowed. Whenever Olivia stopped crying, she could hear their low voices: what an unlikely friendship it was, she thought: a Bohemian psychotherapist from north London and a Ukrainian builder. From upstairs came the tinny sounds of a computer game, bouncy repetitive music and guns firing, bombs exploding: Chloë and Alexei were up there together.

A message pinged onto her mobile and she glanced at it. It was from Jack. *Your friend needs your help.*

Jack lay in the hall. His only wish was to lose consciousness but, stubbornly, his mind refused to let go. Pain came in waves, drawing him under and spitting him out. He put his tongue on his lip and tasted blood. His phone was ringing and ringing but he didn't know where it was and he couldn't get to it. He tried to move and for a few seconds slithered uselessly on the floor, getting nowhere.

There was a scratching sound. A key in the lock. The person was coming back, he thought, to finish the job. At least the pain would be done with. But then there was a low voice calling his name and a cool hand on his forehead and now at last he could let go because he was safe. Frieda had come.

45

Don Kaminsky pressed the button on the recording machine. Daniel Blackstock smiled. He felt better this time. In control. This was happening on his terms now.

"I can't believe you're still using cassette tapes," he said.

Petra stated the time and the date and the names of those present.

"I used to use them for interviews," he continued. "But that was years ago. You probably still use fax machines."

"You do not have to say anything," said Petra, "but it may harm your defense if you do not mention when questioned something which you later rely on in court. Anything you do say may be given in evidence."

There was a pause.

"Could you say that again?" said Blackstock.

"Are you serious?"

"I've heard those words so often on TV. It's like the Lord's Prayer. You hear it over and over again, but you don't really take in the meaning. 'Thy kingdom come.' What does that mean? How can a kingdom come? Is he telling the kingdom to come? So I want to hear what the words really say."

Petra repeated the caution with exaggerated care.

"Defense?" he said. "I don't need a defense."

"You are also entitled to a lawyer. If you don't have one, we can get you one."

"I know all about that. I wrote an article about it. Entitled to a defense. That's a load of rubbish. Are you talking about anything more than a quick phone call to a duty solicitor with better things to do?"

"People are usually more nervous than this," said Petra. "In an interview room with a tape going. Except for criminals."

"And journalists," said Daniel Blackstock. "You forget that this is my job."

"You were more nervous last time. Now you almost seem to be enjoying it."

"I'm not enjoying it and I don't need a solicitor. I'm happy to answer any question you put to me. Just tell me what you want to know."

"Where were you last night?"

"At what time?"

Petra thought of the text that had been sent to Jack. "Between eight and ten," she said.

Blackstock considered for a moment. "I was at home with my wife and then I was in the hospital."

"Hospital?" said Petra. "What for?"

Now Blackstock put his hands on the table. His right hand was heavily bandaged.

"Have you had an accident?" asked Petra.

"Well, obviously."

"Do you mind telling me what happened?"

"I was cutting a linoleum tile with a Stanley knife. My hand slipped and I cut across my other hand. It was bleeding everywhere. I went into the hospital and they had to stitch it up."

"What time did this happen?"

"Why does it matter?"

"There was an incident last night."

"What sort of incident?"

"I'd like you to answer my questions first."

Daniel Blackstock paused. "You're asking things the wrong way around. You need to tell me what you're accusing me of and then I can defend myself, if I've got a defense."

"All right," she said. "Last night a man called Jack Dargan was assaulted at a house in Islington. The man was wearing a mask. In the course of the attack, the assailant sent a text using Dargan's phone."

"Why would he do that?"

"The attack wasn't done as part of a robbery. It was done as some sort of a statement or a message."

"Who did he send the text to?"

"To Frieda Klein."

"Oh." He whistled. "I see. That must have been a bit of a shock."

"Does that interest you?"

"As a journalist, of course it does. I've been covering the Frieda Klein story from the start. But you can't seriously think I could do something like that."

"The text message was timed at nine thirty-two. So if you can show us where you were at that time, you can go home."

Blackstock stayed silent for a while. "This is all crazy. I don't even know why you suspect me of this. But if you want to play this game, I'll go along with it. That must have been about the time that I cut myself and went into the hospital."

"Can you give me exact times for that?"

"You know, I don't think I can. When I'm living my normal life I don't keep a constant record of timings."

"But I suppose there are ways of checking."

"When it happened, I was trying to stop the bleeding and my wife dialed 1 1 1 and asked for help. They probably keep a record."

"They definitely keep a record."

"She talked to them and described what was happening. They said the best thing would be if we got to A & E. So my wife drove me to St. Jude's."

"What time did you get in?"

"I don't know. Half an hour, forty minutes after it happened." He made an angry gesture. "Look, what do you want me to do? Do you want me to rip off my bandages and show you my wound? I'll do it, if you want."

"Whoever assaulted Jack Dargan could have been injured."

"Was it a knife fight?" said Blackwood, angrily. "You can check the wound and you'll see it's been gouged with a knife by someone who's terrible at doing DIY."

"How did you get to the hospital?"

"My wife drove me."

"And how long were you there?"

"We got back just after midnight."

"You know that when I say we're going to check this we really are going to check it."

"Check anything you want," said Daniel Blackstock. "And if you need any more information, just get in touch."

Petra nodded at Don Kaminsky, who leaned forward and switched off the tape.

"All right," she said. "We're done."

*

Frieda didn't speak at first, but Petra found the narrowing of her eyes alarming enough.

"You must be wrong," she said at last. "You've missed something."

"I know what you must feel," said Petra. "But I didn't."

"You'd better come in," said Frieda.

"I need to get somewhere."

"Just five minutes. There are things I have to say."

Petra stepped inside and Frieda led her through to the kitchen.

"Drink?" said Frieda.

"No, thank you. Tell me."

They sat down facing each other across Frieda's table, where Petra felt as if she was back in the interview room except now she was the one being interrogated.

"Have you properly checked the alibi? Was the injury really serious?"

"Of course. I've heard the 1 1 1 call his wife made. It was timed at nine thirty-eight. It was made from their home. He was logged in at the St. Jude's A & E department just after ten twenty. I talked to the consultant on duty. The wound was severe, bleeding copiously. The consultant said they should really have called an ambulance. He said that Blackstock was lucky he didn't hit an artery or sever a tendon."

Frieda drummed her fingers insistently on the table. "It seems too convenient to me."

"Of course it's convenient. It's an alibi. If an alibi doesn't cover the time of the crime then it's not called an alibi."

"But why just at that particular moment of that particular evening does he happen to be somewhere where he was recorded? Why wasn't he just sitting at home with his wife the way he normally would be?"

"All right, Frieda. If Blackstock had been sitting at home, like he normally does, with no witness except his wife, would you have believed him then? That would have been called 'not having an alibi.'"

"The obvious answer is that he got the injury when he was attacking Jack and then . . ." She paused.

"And then what?" said Petra. "It may be obvious, but what? Phone your wife and get her to call it in? And then somehow get across London with a disabling wound that was bleeding so heavily he needed multiple stitches and meet up with his wife on the way? Anyway, I talked to Jack Dargan. There was no meaningful struggle. No sign of a knife. Your friend said there was no possible way that the attacker could have been injured at the scene, let alone suffered a major laceration. And there was no blood at the scene except Dargan's."

Frieda frowned at Petra and Petra frowned back.

"What?" said Petra. "Give me something and we'll look into it."

"You've looked at him," said Frieda. "The way he wants to worm his way into the case, the way he's enjoying it all. Doesn't that strike you as suspicious?"

"He's a journalist. That's what he's paid to do. You may not like it, I may not like it, but we've got to live with it."

"I told you I was suspicious of him. At that time I didn't even know he lived in Silvertown, just where Chloë was held, right by City Airport."

"You can't be certain about that."

"Chloë heard the small planes taking off."

"It's still just an assumption. There are other small airfields around London. There's one just beyond Chigwell. You could drive to that in twenty minutes up the M11."

"I know that airfield. That's just a tiny flying club. If Chloë had heard one of those little two-seater planes, she would have said so."

"So you're both experts on small planes now, are you? Your whole theory depends on the evidence of a young woman who was drugged, blindfolded, semiconscious, in a state of trauma. And you're setting it against an alibi that you may not like but which is backed up by completely solid evidence. We know the accident was called in at nine thirty-eight. We know he was at the hospital, badly injured, at just after ten twenty. When we're training, we're told over and over again about the investigations that were derailed because the detective in charge had a theory and just wouldn't give it up."

Petra looked at Frieda who was still frowning and biting her lip. She seemed to be in pain. "I'm going to give your friends protection," she said more gently.

Frieda nodded. "My new plan is for everyone to move into Reuben's house for the time being."

"Sounds like a good idea."

Frieda stared past her, out of the window. "You should search his house," she said.

"We cannot search his house. We don't have probable cause."

"So what is your plan?"

"My plan is to start again."

46

Karlsson almost burst into Frieda's house. "Look," he said, and threw a newspaper down.

"At what?" said Frieda.

He angrily leafed through it, then laid it open on the center pages. There was a large headline: "MY LIFE AS A SUSPECT." Below there was a portrait of Daniel Blackstock looking somberly into the camera.

"I'm not really interested," said Frieda, scowling.

Karlsson picked up the newspaper again and started reading from the article: " 'The floundering police investigation took a new desperate turn as they turned on the press. It was a case of blaming the messenger.' Little shit."

"Karlsson, it's not worth bothering about."

"Hang on, Frieda, you'll want to hear this bit: 'I was taken into a police interrogation room and faced the remorseless questioning of Detective Inspector Petra Burge. The police seem to be wondering why the press know so much more about the case than they do. Perhaps, I tried to explain, it's because we're doing our job.' Bastard."

"I really would rather you didn't read the whole piece out to me."

Karlsson shook his head and folded the newspaper so that it was more manageable, then stood up and limped rapidly around the room as he read from it.

"Here," he said.

"You're going to fall over. You don't want to break your leg all over again."

"Just one more extract. This was the one that really got to me. Wait, let me find it. Yes, here it is." Karlsson gave a preparatory cough. "'I consulted the expert profiler Professor Hal Bradshaw. What did he think was behind these crimes? "In recent years, Frieda Klein has deliberately turned herself into a celebrity. She has inserted herself into criminal investigations. The damage this has done to serious police procedures is a matter for the authorities to deal with and I wouldn't presume to comment on it . . ."'" Karlsson stopped reading for a moment and shook the paper. "Then why are you commenting, you fucking idiot?"

"Why don't you sit down?"

"Hang on. '"My interest as a psychologist is in the impulse that turns a person who should be a doctor and a healer into a celebrity and an attention-seeker. The result has been not just to put herself into danger. That is her own affair. Some people like to bungee-jump, some people like to jump off mountains with parachutes, some like to get involved with criminal investigations. But she's also putting other people at risk, innocent lives. I'm not saying that psychologists cannot be of use in criminal investigation. In my upcoming TV series, *Crimes of the Mind,* I'll be showing how the skills of an expert can tackle unsolved crimes. Frieda Klein has always wanted fans. Well, they say you should beware what you ask for."'" Karlsson threw the newspaper onto the table. "You don't think someone could arrange for Dean Reeve to attend to Hal Bradshaw?"

"Don't," said Frieda. She left the room and went into the kitchen.

"Is it too early for a drink?" Karlsson shouted after her. "Yes, it is."

A few minutes later she returned with two mugs of coffee.

"I don't know how you can bear it," he said. "Having your name out there like that for people to kick around. I probably didn't help much by coming and reading it aloud to you. I was probably scratching at a sore point, but I felt you needed to know what frauds like Hal Bradshaw are up to."

Frieda looked down into her coffee. "I don't care about that. It's just something outside. It's like the weather." She took a sip of her coffee. "But he's right."

"In what possible way?"

"I've put people in danger. It may not be what I planned or what I wanted, but I have to take responsibility for that."

"Frieda, that's not true. The number-one rule is that the perpetrators are to blame, never the victims."

She looked up at him. "Yes, that's a useful story I can tell myself. And meanwhile we're just sitting here waiting to see what whoever it is out there decides to do next."

"There is a police inquiry proceeding."

"Yes." Frieda nodded. "A police inquiry is proceeding."

Alex Zavou looked down at the floor, then at Frieda, then back down at the floor. He was biting his lip. Frieda recognized the signs. "If there's something you need to say," she said, "then this is a safe space."

A safe space. Frieda had always hoped that her consulting room was a place of escape for her patients, a place of refuge. Now it felt like that for her. Just at the moment, she felt as if her consulting room was a hole in the ground. She wanted to stay there, hiding, and never come out. Meanwhile, she waited for Zavou to speak. Sometimes the silence could last many minutes. At certain times it had lasted almost the whole session. Silence could be a kind of therapy.

"I promised myself," Zavou began stumblingly, "that if I was going to do this, I was going to be completely honest. I wasn't going to hold anything back." He stopped, as if he were waiting for something from Frieda. Approval, maybe. But she didn't speak, so he continued: "I think I made it look as if this incident, the fight, the violence, was something completely new in my life. It wasn't. That's all."

Frieda suddenly felt a terrible flushing of shame. She already knew what Zavou was going to tell her and she was going to have to put on a performance, to pretend. At that moment she felt she had brought a terrible corruption with her into her consulting room.

"Tell me about it." Her tone was as neutral as she could manage.

"I've got into fights before," he said. "I don't start them, but I don't hang back. It's hard to put into words, but I've always had the feeling that you don't back down. If you go in, you go in. I'm not so bad if someone insults me or knocks into me or spills my drink, you know, all those stupid things that start fights. But if they do something to someone I'm with, I feel I've got to stand up for them. I've just got to. So . . ." He stopped.

Frieda felt a moment of relief. It was out in the open. Now they could talk about it. "So?" she said.

"I'm not the person you thought I was. You thought I was an innocent who had just wandered into the situation and tried to rescue it and didn't manage to. Now maybe you reckon I was the one who started it, or that I made it worse, escalated it."

"When you didn't tell me," said Frieda, "what was it you were worried about?"

"That you'd think I was involved. That I wasn't an innocent victim."

"The one thing you need to believe is that you can say anything to me. I won't say I'm not here to judge you, because we all judge each other with everything we say, but you don't need to present me with a nice neat version of yourself. We don't go through life with clean hands. There are gray blurry areas everywhere. The people I worry about are the ones whose stories are too neat, where the pieces fit together too easily."

Afterwards, when Frieda was writing up her notes, she stopped at that exchange. *Where the pieces fit together too easily.* She had said something like that to Petra Burge about Daniel Blackstock. Petra had had an answer, but the feeling hadn't gone away. He had had a perfect alibi. That was the problem. Normal people didn't have perfect alibis.

47

She walked swiftly from her consulting rooms to St. Dunstan's in Clerkenwell. She had been there the previous night with Jack, traveling with him in the ambulance, accompanying him as far as the operating theater. He had been heavily sedated by then, pumped full of morphine, but he had managed to say something to her before they wheeled him away.

"I lied to him," he had croaked.

"What about?"

"He asked me if I was right- or left-handed. I said I was left-handed." Frieda looked at his heavily bandaged left hand. "I'm not."

She had smiled at him and watched his eyes close on her, then leaned down and kissed him on the forehead. "I'll see you on the other side," she'd said.

Now, as she walked back to the hospital through the summer drizzle, she made several phone calls. The first was to Reuben.

"It's me."

"Thank God."

"Are you OK?"

"Never mind me. How's Jack?"

They were talking fast, as if they had no time for ordinary conversation any more, only for the important things.

She could picture him, bald and thin, sitting in his study, and outside the thin rain falling on his lawn. "I'm on my way there now."

"Let me know."

"Of course. How are things there?"

"Oh, you know. I'm being sick. Josef is baking cakes and cooking stew as if the smell of Ukrainian cooking can save the world. Alexei is barely speaking but he is playing computer games at full volume. Olivia is drinking her way through my wine cellar and crying."

"It sounds crowded."

"You can say that again."

"Any chance of it being even more crowded?"

There was a brief silence.

"Chloë. She can't be alone."

"She's at my house most of the time anyway."

"Reuben—"

"You don't need to say anything."

"All right. I'll ask Josef to collect whatever she needs later. She shouldn't go back there at all. Oh, and, Reuben, two police officers will be parked outside your house, day and night. They might be there already."

As she approached St. Dunstan's, she saw a familiar figure standing outside the revolving doors.

"Chloë. I thought you were at work."

"I had to come." Chloë lifted her tear-stained face to Frieda.

Frieda took her hand. "Let's go and see him together."

"I've already tried. It's no good."

"What do you mean?"

"They won't let me in. It's not visiting hours."

"Oh, really," said Frieda, grimly. "We'll see about that."

The door of Jack's ward on the third floor was firmly closed. They both rubbed alcohol gel into their hands, then Frieda knocked loudly. Through the strips of glass she could see nurses passing to and fro. A porter approached from behind, pushing a trolley. He punched in the security code and pushed the double doors open. Frieda walked in behind him, beckoning Chloë to follow.

"Excuse me." A nurse stood in front of them, blocking their way.

"We're here to visit Jack Dargan. He's in bed seventeen."

"It's not visiting hours."

"We need to see him."

The nurse looked at the watch hanging on her apron. "You can come back in two and a half hours. Then you can see him."

"No."

"Excuse me?"

"No."

"Frieda," said Chloë, in an urgent whisper. "Don't make a fuss."

"A fuss?" Frieda gave her niece a stern look. "It's quite simple. We're not going anywhere until we've seen him."

Beside her, Chloë gave a nervous giggle.

"I'll call hospital security."

"Do that," said Frieda.

"What is it, Theresa?" asked a woman in a nurse's uniform that was white not blue. "Is there a problem?"

"I've told them it's not visiting hours. They won't go away."

"Won't go away?"

"Our friend Jack Dargan was attacked and injured last night. He has no family to visit him so we are here to see him and reassure him. I'm sure you'll agree that it makes no sense to turn us away."

"The rules . . ."

"If your rules say I shouldn't be allowed in, they deserve to be broken."

The second nurse looked at her, at Chloë who had stopped giggling at last, at Theresa. She sighed. "Go on, then," she said.

When Chloë saw Jack, she started crying. He was propped up in bed with his hand in a large cast that was supported by a hoist. He had stitches running across his forehead and one eye was closed; around it the skin was violently bruised and swollen. His nose was swollen and purple. He had a drip attached to his uninjured arm and was hooked up to a machine that beeped continuously.

Jack tried to smile at them, but his face was too sore and battered. His one good eye looked at them and a single tear ran down his cheek. "Hello," he said, in a thick, slurred voice. "I thought I heard you."

"You don't need to talk," said Frieda. "Are you thirsty?"

He nodded. Frieda picked up the beaker of water from the side table and put the bendy straw into his mouth.

"Does it hurt?" asked Chloë.

"Drugs. Lots of drugs."

"Was it terrifying? Well, you don't need to answer that. I can see it was, of course. I'm just saying stupid things because I don't know what to say. Your poor hand. And your poor face. I hardly recognize you. God, it must have been so scary. You probably thought you were going to die."

"Is there anything you need?" asked Frieda.

Jack shook his head.

"Frieda told me you said you were left-handed. That was amazing. Just amazing. I couldn't have been so quick while someone was attacking me."

"Listen, Jack," said Frieda. "I'll come back later. We'll all be here as much as you want until you leave the hospital. If there's anything you need, tell us. When you leave, you'll come to Reuben's as well. That seems safest. But I need to ask you something first. Is there anything else you remember?"

"Smell."

"You remember his smell?"

"Sweat."

"That's good. Everything helps."

He gazed at them helplessly out of his one eye. Even his red hair had a desperate air.

"You did well," said Frieda.

"Darling," said Daniel Blackstock, tenderly, standing behind his wife as she made their dinner, massaging the back of her neck with the hand that wasn't injured. "How can I help?"

"Help?" Lee Blackstock looked alarmed at the thought.

"Yes. You work so hard and you look after me as well and I don't show you often enough how grateful I am to you."

Lee Blackstock twisted her head to look at him. His expression was warm. She smiled at him and let him go on massaging her neck, even though he was pressing rather too hard.

"I've only got the mashed potatoes left to do."

"My favorite!"

"Is your hand hurting a lot?"

"It's nothing."

"Daniel." Her tone was wary.

"Yes."

"I'll always help you. You know that." She stopped but he didn't say anything, just continued to dig his fingers into her flesh. "I just wondered if you wanted to tell me—" She faltered and came to a stop.

"Is this about yesterday?"

She nodded.

"Do you trust me, Lee?"

"Of course I do."

"I'm working very hard, day and night, to make sure we have enough money and are secure. You do understand that?"

"I only wondered. If you don't want to tell me, that's all right."

"Things are going well for me just now."

"That's good, Daniel. I'm glad. You deserve it."

"I've got chances and I need to take them."

"Of course."

"People want to interview me. I might be on the radio. You wouldn't want to get in the way of all that."

"No!"

"Good. I know you trust me, and you know that I trust you. I'm right to trust you, aren't I?"

"Yes."

"Because we're partners. Everything we do, we do for each other. Right?"

"Oh, yes."

"Then we don't need to say anything else."

When Frieda opened Reuben's front door she heard loud shouts and a scream, a wail from Olivia, a sound like slapping. She rushed toward the living room and at first couldn't make out what she was seeing.

They were all crouched on the floor in a ragged circle, leaning in, hands flailing.

"What's going on?" she asked, raising her voice above the hubbub.

"That was mine!" cried Reuben, not looking up, slapping down a card. He was wearing a new dressing gown, a full-length Moroccan tunic in stripes of yellow and purple, and his face was flushed.

"Cards," said Frieda. "This is about a card game?"

"Racing Demon!" shouted Chloë. "Join in."

"Not just now."

She looked at them all, with their packs of cards and their wildly animated faces. Even Alexei was playing, though it seemed to Frieda from where she stood that he had no idea of the rules.

Frieda thought of the family she had grown up with: a father who had killed himself, a mother who had never wanted children and had said so even on her deathbed, brothers who resented and disapproved of her and whom she never saw. Blood ties. This was her real family, ramshackle and rowdy, here in this hot, noisy room.

48

At six thirty the next morning Frieda was in Silvertown. The day was already warm and muggy, the sky low and gray. She hoped that later it would rain, clear some of the dust and grit from the roads and water the parched earth. Daniel Blackstock lived on a modern estate, dwarfed by the crumbling old warehouses on one side and the tower blocks on the other. His house was on a cul-de-sac, with a small neat front garden and a space for their red Honda. The curtains were closed.

She positioned herself by a skip where she could see his door but wouldn't be seen, and waited. It wasn't Daniel Blackstock she had come here for, it was his wife, who had called 111, and who had driven her husband to St. Jude's Hospital. At twenty past seven, the curtains in an upstairs window were opened. Ten minutes later, the ones downstairs were as well. She could make out a shape moving about the room.

At just after eight, the front door opened and Daniel Blackstock appeared. He patted his jacket, obviously checking if he had his keys on him, before closing the door and stepping briskly onto the pavement. So he wasn't using the car today. He was carrying a briefcase that he swung as he walked and even from where she stood he looked brisk and jaunty. She watched him until he disappeared from view. Then she went to the little house with its sparse, well-tended garden and pressed the buzzer. She heard the tinkle of music inside.

"Yes?"

The woman who stood in front of her was still in a dressing gown. She was quite short and solid, with a round face and brown hair cut in a severe fringe. She had a smudge of dirt on her cheek.

"Lee Blackstock?"

"What do you want?" the woman said. Her voice was high-pitched and girlish. Then her expression changed from one of anxious inquiry to fearful recognition.

"I'm Frieda Klein."

"I know. I've seen your photo." She stopped. "Daniel's not here."

"It's you I came to see. Can I come in?"

Her eyes darted from Frieda to over her shoulder. She clutched the neck of her dressing gown. "Why?"

"I'd like to ask you about something."

"I don't understand. It's Daniel you need to talk to."

"It's a very simple matter."

"I'm not dressed."

"That's all right."

Frieda stepped into the house.

"I haven't cleared up yet," Lee Blackstock said apologetically, and she showed Frieda into the kitchen.

But the place was spotless, just a plate and a mug on the table. The only splash of color and life in the germless room came from a huge bouquet of flowers on the side. Frieda watched as Lee brushed away a few invisible crumbs, ran her hands down her dressing gown, tied it tighter. She seemed nervous.

"I wanted to ask you about the night before last."

"What do you mean?"

"Your husband had a nasty accident."

"Yes, he did."

"Can you tell me about it?"

"Why?" The question seemed to make her bolder. "What's it got to do with you?"

"Rather a lot, I think."

"You'll have to ask Daniel, not me. I'm not very good with words."

"You don't need to be good with words and you don't need to be scared," said Frieda. She saw the woman flinch, a flush spread over her face and down her neck. "I just want the truth."

"I've got nothing to hide." Again, Lee Blackstock ran her palms up and down her dressing gown. Then she took a seat at the small, bare table and folded her hands together to stop them trembling. "I'll tell Daniel you've been here, you know."

"Of course you will. Could you tell me what happened? Just as you remember it?"

Lee Blackstock looked away from Frieda. She took a deep breath and when she spoke it was in a monotone.

"We were here together. We had eaten supper. I was in the living room watching a quiz show on the TV. Daniel was in the back room and he was cutting a linoleum tile. I heard him shout and went to see what was wrong. The Stanley knife had slipped and he had cut his hand. There was lots of blood. I called 1 1 1. They said to come to the hospital. I drove him there and he got it seen to. Then we drove home." Now she looked back at Frieda. "That's all."

"What time did he cut himself?"

"Half past nine," she said promptly.

"You called 1 1 1 at once?"

"Yes."

"And you drove to the hospital at once?"

"I bandaged him up first and cleared up the blood. Then I drove him."

"What time did you get there?"

"About a quarter past ten."

"Was he in pain?"

The question seemed to throw her. "He must have been."

"How did you react?"

"Me?"

"Yes."

"I told you. I rang 1 1 1 and drove him to St. Jude's."

"I mean, were you very shocked?"

"Oh. Yes. I was shocked."

"Did you ask any of your neighbors to help?"

"No."

"Did anyone see you?"

"See me?"

"Both of you."

"I don't know."

"You obviously reacted calmly." Frieda stood up. "Do you work?"

"I'm a care assistant at an old people's home."

"That's a good thing to do."

"You think?" Lee Blackstock looked at her doubtfully.

"I do."

"It doesn't pay much."

"So-called woman's work never pays well—that doesn't mean it's not important. I imagine you work nights a lot."

"Yes."

"It must be tiring."

"It is. Though Daniel says I'm just—" She stopped.

"Yes?"

"Nothing."

"How long have you been married?"

"Thirteen years. I was very young, a high-school graduate. I met him when I was only fifteen." For a moment, her eyes shone. "It was love at first sight," she said.

So she was in her late twenties or early thirties. She seemed much older, almost middle-aged.

"And you don't have children."

"No. Not yet."

"Those are lovely flowers. Did Daniel give them to you?"

"Yes."

"Is it your birthday or an anniversary?"

"No. He just gave them to me." An expression of satisfaction crossed Lee Blackstock's face. Frieda watched her curiously. Then the flush returned and she looked lumpy and awkward in her stained dressing gown. "I still don't understand why you're here."

"I needed to get a clear picture of what happened."

"It's funny, isn't it?"

"What?"

"He's out finding out things about you, and you're here finding out things about him."

"Yes," said Frieda. "Funny."

*

Daniel Blackstock stood in Saffron Mews, looking at Frieda Klein's narrow house with the blue door, and whistling softly through his teeth. The shutters were closed. He wondered where she was, what she was doing. But he'd find out.

49

Frieda walked back down to the main road. She was starting to cross it to reach the station when she saw a taxi approaching. An idea occurred to her and she hailed it.

"St. Jude's Hospital," she said to the driver, as she got in. "How long will it take?"

The driver sniffed. "About ten minutes. Depends on the traffic. Are you in a hurry?"

"No hurry."

When the taxi left her outside St. Jude's, she looked briefly at the main entrance. It was an established fact that Daniel and Lee Blackstock had arrived there at around ten twenty in the evening. A serious cut in his hand had been stitched up. Would it be useful to talk to the doctor who had treated Blackstock? Was it worth finding out what his behavior had been like? The condition of the wound? The extent of the bleeding? But it was totally impractical. She looked at her watch. The doctor who had treated Blackstock would almost certainly not be working now. If they happened to be there, they wouldn't be happy about being questioned by a stranger, even if she was a doctor. Perhaps at some future time, Petra Burge could arrange for them to be questioned, but what was likely to be learned, really?

She turned away. There was nothing for her there. But

it didn't matter. That wasn't why she had come. Daniel
Blackstock had been here at around ten twenty. Jack had
been attacked in Islington shortly after nine thirty. She
was going to walk from one to the other. She closed her
eyes as she always did at the beginning of a walk like this,
going over the different possible routes in her mind. This
one had its difficulties. It was obstructed by large roads, by
a gas works and a bus depot and a network of warehouses.
Beyond that was the River Lea, snaking its way through
Canning Town and Bow. She knew the river crossing at
Twelvetrees Crescent because she had once worked at
St. Andrew's Hospital just beyond it. She heard a sound
behind her and looked around. A plane was rising up from
City Airport. It was like a reminder.

She set off on a route that had been designed to frustrate
a walker, with rumbling big roads and dead ends and residential streets curling back on themselves. At one point
Frieda even had to take her phone out to check her position.
Finally she was able to wind her way through the industrial
estate and reach the River Lea. On a normal day she would
have turned right onto the towpath and made her way up
through the Olympic Park toward home. But today was different. He couldn't have come along the towpath, not late at
night and in a hurry. She needed a feel for the route he could
have taken.

She crossed the river and took the underpass beneath
the big road. She walked through the streets of Bow and
past the west side of Victoria Park toward Haggerston. The
city was gradually becoming more familiar and she could
walk without checking the route. She could now start to
think.

The alibi. His seriously injured hand was part of that

alibi, which meant it hadn't been an accident. He had done it himself then, though it was hard to deliberately slice through your own hand with a Stanley knife.

And then the emergency call made from their home, their joint arrival at the hospital, the text sent from Jack's phone. That was to taunt her but it was also a crucial part of the plan. The time of the emergency call would be no use if Jack had been imprecise about the time of the attack.

Frieda looked around. She had been walking without thinking and for a moment she wasn't sure exactly where she was. She was in Hoxton. It felt like another world from Newham, a world of coffee shops and young men with trim beards and bicycles.

Something else had been nagging at her and she hadn't quite been able to pin it down. It was to do with the timing. When she had talked to Lee Blackstock, she had concentrated on the length of time it had taken to get to the hospital. It felt too long. As the taxi driver said, it was just a ten-minute drive. And this was a man who had supposedly cut himself so badly that his wife had rung an emergency line. But that wasn't necessarily impossible or even implausible. People acted strangely in crisis. They could have been trying to bandage the cut themselves and only gone to hospital when they hadn't been able to staunch the bleeding. Sometimes things go more slowly rather than more quickly during an emergency. It becomes harder to make decisions, harder to do the things you normally do. No, that wouldn't necessarily have been grounds for suspicion.

What struck Frieda now was the time of the two calls. The text from Jack's phone to Frieda was timed at nine thirty-two. The call from Lee Blackstock to the emergency service was timed at nine thirty-eight. If it had been the other way around, Frieda would have found their story much harder to disbelieve. She told herself the narrative of what must have happened. Daniel Blackstock had to attack Jack, then send the text, then phone his wife—presumably on a pay-as-you go phone that wouldn't reveal his location. Then, at some point, he would have sliced open his hand. They couldn't just have prearranged a time for Lee to make the phone call. Jack might not have been at home. There might have been someone with him. He would have had to let her know as soon as he had carried out the attack. If the text to her had come after Lee's phone call, Frieda would have been forced to believe that the attack had been carried out by someone else.

Now she was standing outside Olivia's house. She looked at her watch. It had taken her an hour and a half to walk. Blackstock hadn't walked. How had he got to St. Jude's? There was no station close to the hospital. The journey would involve long walks and changes. No, she thought. Going by train or bus would be hopelessly slow and he would have been seen by multiple people. There was CCTV. Even a bike would take too long. A car, she thought. He went by car. During the day there was the risk of being caught in traffic, but by nine thirty, there would be no problem driving through east London. He wouldn't have taken a taxi or an Uber. They keep records, they leave traces. He would have used his own car, parked somewhere near Olivia's, walked the last couple of hundred yards. Then he would have driven back, met Lee somewhere near the hospital. She could have walked there, to a prearranged spot.

This scenario didn't just depend on Daniel Blackstock. It depended on his wife as well. Frieda went through it over and over again. There was no way around it. She couldn't have been a simple dupe. He would have to have told Lee some story, perhaps the real story or perhaps a fiction. And whatever the story, he would have to trust her. She would need to make the phone call, meet him. She would have been present when he inflicted the wound on his own hand. Frieda knew what such an injury was like, the sight of the blood, the smell of it. And then she would have had to go with Daniel to the hospital and talk to doctors and nurses. Could the awkward, anxious woman she had just talked to have managed all that? Frieda thought of that bunch of flowers in the kitchen. She thought of the flicker of satisfaction that had crossed Lee Blackstock's face when she had mentioned them. Who knew what people could do?

"Frieda Klein came to see me," said Lee Blackstock, as soon as her husband stepped through the door.

"Here?"

"Yes. She came in and we talked. Was that right?"

"What did she want?"

"She wanted to ask about your accident."

"And what did you say?" Daniel Blackstock stepped closer to her. She could smell his breath and see the prickles of sweat on his forehead.

"I said you'd cut yourself and we'd gone to hospital together."

"And she believed you?"

"I think so."

"Good."

"She's good-looking, isn't she?"

With a visible effort, he took his wife's hand in his uninjured one. "You don't need to worry about other women," he said.

"Daniel."

"Yes."

"It's all right, isn't it?"

"What?"

"Just—there's nothing to worry about, is there?"

"Nothing in the whole world."

50

"This feels like a meeting," said Reuben.

Frieda looked around his living room. Josef was beside Olivia on the sofa. Reuben was in his special armchair. Chloë came in with mugs of tea on a tray. She handed them around.

"It is a sort of meeting," said Frieda.

"Anyone want biscuits?" asked Chloë.

"Can I just speak for a moment?" said Frieda.

Chloë pulled a face and sat down.

And so Frieda described in detail her suspicions about Daniel Blackstock. They listened in utter silence, apart from Olivia who gasped and occasionally made a small moan, and Josef who banged one fist slowly on his knee. When she finished, there was a stunned pause and then a sudden babble of sound and movement. She looked from face to face, waiting.

"You're sure about this?" said Reuben.

"I'm sure."

"He interviewed me." Chloë's voice was hard and flat. "He pretended to be friendly and sympathetic. He asked me questions about what happened, how I felt."

"I know."

"He showed me that photograph. And you're saying he was the one who took it, who drugged me and grabbed me and kept me locked up and unconscious?"

"Yes."

"I feel sick."

Josef was standing with his arms folded by the door. His face was dark. Frieda wondered why he wasn't saying anything.

"He's playing with us," Reuben said to Frieda.

Olivia bent forward and put her face into her hands, her hair falling forward.

"So?" said Chloë. "Why aren't you making this speech to the police? Isn't this the point where they go and arrest him and we can all go home and carry on with our lives?"

"I've told them about Daniel Blackstock. I couldn't do any more."

"If you believe it, why don't they?" asked Chloë.

"It's not just a matter of believing it. First, they don't entirely believe it. And second, even if they believed what I believe, that wouldn't be enough. They need to be able to show that he did it. At the moment, he's showing them he didn't. He has an alibi. It's a fake alibi but it might be enough."

"So what are we supposed to do?" Chloë continued. "Just sit here and wait for him to do something else? I mean, Jack's unable to attend this meeting because he's in a fucking hospital bed."

Olivia murmured something unintelligible.

"And Reuben has been attacked and one of your patients has been murdered. And someone who worked with me has been hauled in by the police and had his life ruined.

And it all began with a body that was actually found under the floor in your own house and you're saying these other attacks don't have anything to do with that?"

"No, I'm not saying they don't have anything to do with it. I'm saying they're not done by the same person."

"What does that even mean?" asked Chloë.

"I think that the murder of Bruce Stringer set him off."

"Set him off?" said Olivia.

"Inspired him."

"So he's a sort of fan?" said Chloë.

"That's one way of putting it."

"Of you or of Dean Reeve?" asked Reuben.

"I think it's like when someone sees a work of art and wants to copy it."

"But they're never quite as good as the original," said Reuben.

Frieda shook her head. "Violence is violence. It doesn't matter why someone is doing it. If you're the victim, that is."

"So what do we do?" said Olivia.

"I know what to do," said Josef. It was the first time he had spoken.

"What?" said Frieda.

He simply looked back at her without speaking.

"No," she said.

"I talk to a friend. He talk to a friend. We say nothing more here. Say nothing again."

"No," repeated Frieda.

"I get," said Josef. "You all know nothing. You can deny."

"No, really, Josef," said Frieda, horror-struck. "This is real denial. You do nothing, do you understand?"

"You say you sure," said Josef. "You say you know what he

did. You see what he do to Chloë. Do to Jack. Do to Reuben."

"Frieda is going to give you a lecture," said Reuben. "She's going to say that without law we are nothing. Or what would life be like if we did things like that? Or what if she's wrong?"

"I wasn't going to say that."

"Then what were you going to say?"

"I don't know." Her face was set, her eyes dark. "Just that we don't do that. It's not much of an answer. It's probably not as good as what you said I was going to say. But it's all I've got. We can't do that." She looked at them in a kind of anguish. "Do you agree?"

"So what we do?" said Josef. "We just wait for him."

"No. You stay together. You watch out for each other. You do not go out alone and you do not leave just one person in the house alone. You do not go anywhere without the police knowing where you're going—and they will be outside keeping watch day and night. And maybe they'll find something, some evidence against him."

Daniel came to bed late that night. His skin was hot and he was breathing more heavily than usual.

Lying beside him, Lee went over and over it. In her mind it was like the first time her husband had kissed her. She remembered that first kiss so vividly that she could smell it and taste it. She had waited and waited, and then there was the sudden closeness and his mouth on hers, the warmth of his tongue, his hand on her breast. She had felt a warm spasm through her, so that the pleasure of it was almost like a sickness.

It had been like that. She was almost out of breath by the

time she got to the recreation ground. The walk had taken a bit longer than Daniel had said. She stayed away from the leisure center. Daniel had said there would be cameras.

She waited five minutes, ten. Could something have gone wrong? Then the car appeared and turned into the side road where she was waiting. She got in beside him. His eyes were shining with energy and excitement.

"You made the call?"

She nodded.

"You'll need to drive," he said.

"Sorry, I forgot."

She got out of the car again and moved around to the driver's side. He spread the bath towel on his lap. This was going to be messy. She opened the glove compartment and took out the Stanley knife. She had scrubbed it and scrubbed it. She looked at it.

"We need to hurry," he said. He looked at her. She was still breathing heavily from the quick walking, almost running. "Can you do this?"

His hand rested on the towel. She held the knife tightly and put the blade against the back of his left hand. It had to be his left hand. She pushed and felt the slight give of the flesh. She lifted the knife. Even in the glow of a streetlight, she could see a small dark bubble on the skin. She took the hand and raised it to her mouth and dabbed the dark bubble with her tongue. It tasted of salt and iron.

"That's not enough," said her husband. "That's not nearly enough."

She gently moved the hand back down onto the towel. "Ready?" she said.

"Just get on with it."

She pushed and pulled and he leaned his head back and she heard a low whimper, a tearing groan.

That was the sound she heard as she lay in the dark beside him. She could play it to herself in her head, over and over again.

51

The phone rang. It was Karlsson.

"Switch the TV on," he said. "You won't like it but you'd better do it."

"We're in the middle of supper," said Frieda.

"Just do it."

Frieda looked around the table. "Karlsson says I need to see something on the TV. It's probably about me so you can stay here and carry on with the meal."

"Miss you on TV?" said Chloë.

"It's probably nothing," said Frieda.

"Grab your glasses, everyone," said Reuben. "Josef, get the other red from the shelf."

There was a bustle of clinking glasses as Reuben, Josef, Olivia, Chloë and Alexei followed Frieda through to the living room. They squeezed together on the sofa and on the rug as Josef switched on the TV. A man with a sun-tanned face was holding a green bottle.

"So how much do we think this could fetch at auction?" he said to the woman next to him.

"I don't think this is it," said Frieda.

Josef changed the channel. A young woman in a yellow apron was kneading some dough.

"It's really important," she said panting slightly, "to have the right starter."

"That's absolutely true," said Olivia. "Do you think your friend Karlsson thinks we should be making our own bread?"

"He's not going to bloody ring us up to tell us to watch a cooking program," said Chloë.

Josef changed the channel again.

"This is the one," said Frieda, immediately.

A man was walking along the side of a river. Frieda saw that it was the Thames. When she saw the Thames Barrier behind him, she knew, with a sinking feeling, what was coming. The man was dressed in a blue suit with a burnt-orange shirt and no tie. He wore glasses with dark frames that ran only along the top of the lenses. When Frieda had last met him, he had been clean-shaven, but now he sported a modish beard, neatly trimmed.

"London is a city of ghosts," he was saying. "Full of secrets."

"Who is this?" Olivia asked.

"Hal Bradshaw," said Reuben. "The TV profiler."

"He hates Frieda," said Chloë.

"That can't be true," said Olivia.

"He think she burn his house down."

"What?"

"Quiet," said Frieda. "I need to hear this."

"For me London is like the mind," Bradshaw said, "full of hidden people, hidden places, hidden rivers."

"What rubbish," Olivia said.

"It's not exactly rubbish," said Frieda.

"Did you really burn his house down?"

"Quiet," said Frieda, then hissed at her sister-in-law, "Of course I didn't."

"Some of us," said Bradshaw, looking earnestly into the

camera, "try to use our professional skills to uncover those secrets, to right those wrongs, to track down the guilty, to protect the innocent. But our profession comes with responsibilities. In the wrong hands, it can wreak havoc. It can destroy lives. In this week's program I want to tell one man's story of what happens when the precious tools of the crime profiler fall into the wrong hands."

"Wanker," said Chloë.

The image then cut to another man walking along the Thames Path. It was Daniel Blackstock. He stopped and leaned on the railings, looking out across the river as Hal Bradshaw's voiceover identified him and told the story of how a dogged crime reporter had become the suspect in a series of alleged offenses.

"Daniel Blackstock," Bradshaw concluded, "is a valuable witness. A distinguished crime reporter and then— briefly and absurdly—a suspect, he has seen the legal process from both sides." Bradshaw walked into the frame and shook Blackstock's hand. The two of them began to stroll away from the camera. Another cut, and the two of them were seen from the front, as they strolled along.

"Daniel," said Bradshaw, "if I can begin with a personal question. How are you, after all you've been through?"

Blackstock's expression turned somber. "Devastated, of course. I'm a reporter. But I'm not just a reporter. I genuinely wanted to help the inquiry. When I was sent some evidence, I didn't print it. I went straight to . . ." He paused.

"Straight to who?" said Bradshaw. They had stopped walking and he laid a gentle hand on Blackstock's shoulder.

"I went straight to Dr. Frieda Klein."

"Maybe you should explain to us who Frieda Klein is."

"I'm not sure if I need to say too much because she's a bit of a celebrity, these days. She's a psychoanalyst who got involved in the Dean Reeve kidnapping and murder case a few years ago. Since then, Reeve has apparently had a strange relationship to her."

"Strange indeed," said Bradshaw. "But—I may not be remembering this rightly—hasn't she had legal problems of her own?"

"Oh, for fuck's sake," Chloë shouted at the screen.

"She's a difficult woman," said Blackstock. "I believe she's been arrested a few times. And she was even on the run from the police at one point."

"And this was the woman who set the police on you," said Bradshaw. He pulled his jacket tighter around him and looked up at the sky. "It's getting cold. What say we go and get a coffee?"

The scene changed to Bradshaw and Blackstock in a café with a waitress placing large mugs in front of them.

"Do you feel angry about what happened to you?" asked Bradshaw. "Do you feel damaged by the experience? Being arrested, being under suspicion, is a terrible thing."

Blackstock looked thoughtful. "I wasn't traumatized, because I knew I was innocent. The only anger I felt was that time was being wasted while the real criminal was out there at large."

"Not everyone would be so forgiving about what a person like Frieda Klein can do," said Bradshaw.

"Can't you sue them?" asked Reuben.

"No," said Josef. "I go see him."

"Stop it," said Frieda. "Nobody's going to do anything. But I need to hear this."

"I know," said Olivia. "It's rather exciting hearing you being talked about on TV."

"Shut up, Mum," said Chloë.

"It's just that I haven't known anybody famous before . . ."

"Please," said Frieda.

"Enough of this," Bradshaw was saying. "We both have skills in this area. You're an experienced crime reporter. For years, I've tried to show that psychological profiling is a crucial tool in the solving of crime."

"How's that going?" shouted Chloë.

"Sssh," hissed Frieda.

"Sadly," Bradshaw continued, "it's not been helped by amateurs and attention-seekers. But let's talk about our own views on this tragic case. My own sense is that Frieda Klein is reaping the whirlwind of her own celebrity. It's clear that the person who has assaulted friends and colleagues of hers is delivering a message to her. I think it's significant that the one death has been of a Frieda Klein patient. It's as if the murderer is telling Dr. Klein that she's in danger of forgetting her true responsibilities."

"But what about the murderer himself? Or herself?" said Blackstock. "Have you developed a profile?"

"I'm still forming my ideas," said Bradshaw. "But my preliminary thoughts are that the police should be looking for a white man in early middle age, strongly built, educated. He owns a car or a van. He is resident in London."

"That's quite a large category."

"As I said, it's early days. But what about you, Daniel? With all your experience in reporting crime, who is it that you think you're looking for?"

Blackstock paused before answering. "I've been doing

this job for more than ten years. I've written about rapes
and kidnappings and assaults and a few murders. What I've
found is that when someone is finally caught, it's a bit dis-
appointing. They're just an ordinary person. But I think
this case is different."

"How do you mean?"

"I think you're right that these crimes are a message. I
just don't think they're a message to Frieda Klein. I think
they're a message to someone else."

"To whom?"

"I don't know."

"To Dean Reeve?"

"You're the profiling expert, not me. But that sounds
like an interesting possibility."

"It's my experience that these crimes usually escalate.
Do you think it's possible that, with this murder, this particular spree may be over?"

Now Blackstock spoke slowly and he looked from the
camera to Bradshaw and back to the camera, as if he wasn't
sure which to address. Frieda suddenly had the feeling that
he was speaking to her personally. But was it her or could it
be someone else?

"I've got an odd feeling about these crimes. That was
why it felt so strange when I was in custody. I think that
this perpetrator, whoever he is, isn't doing what people
think he's doing. I think he's one step ahead."

"What does that mean?" asked Bradshaw.

"I don't know. But we'll all find out."

Bradshaw turned to the camera. "That was Daniel
Blackstock," he said, "reporter and innocent victim. Until
next time, good night."

Frieda leaned forward and switched off the television.

She looked around at Reuben and Josef and Olivia and Chloë. "What?"

"You should report him to the General Medical Council," said Reuben.

"I'm not reporting anyone to anything."

There was an immediate babble of voices but Frieda paid them no attention, lost in her own thoughts.

"Hey," said a voice beside her. It was Reuben. "I'm sorry you're having to go through this."

Frieda looked at her old friend and supervisor. "That doesn't matter. I was interested in what Daniel Blackstock was saying. It felt like he was talking to me."

Reuben laughed. "When people start thinking that their television is talking to them personally, that's generally the moment when they need to stop seeing a psychoanalyst and start seeing a psychiatrist."

Frieda shook her head. "There was something there," she said.

When Frieda was led into Petra Burge's office, the detective was on the phone but she saw Frieda and waved her into a chair. Apparently the person at the other end of the line was doing most of the talking. After several minutes the call ended.

"Fuck," said Petra.

"New case?"

"New budget."

"I'm sorry."

"I know you've got your own problems. I thought I'd be seeing you in here."

"Did you see the TV?"

"I did."

"So what did you think?"

"I didn't think much of it. But basically I'd rather Hal Bradshaw was fucking around making TV programs than fucking around on police inquiries."

"But what did you think of the program?"

"Look," said Petra, "I know it's worse for you. The police were attacked in general, but you were attacked in person. I'm sorry."

"I don't care about that. If I were Hal Bradshaw, I'd hate me too. None of that matters."

"Then why are you here?"

"I thought it was interesting."

"In what way?"

Frieda got up. There was a watercooler in the corner of the office. She walked across, filled two plastic glasses and brought them back.

"One of the things I've learned from my job," she said, "is that when people are asked a question, they answer it. They may not think they're answering, but they are. They may think they're lying, but a lie is still revealing."

"So what lie did Daniel Blackstock tell?"

"I don't think he even lied. Bradshaw asked him about the killer and he said that he thought the killer wasn't doing what people think he's doing and that he's one step ahead. I thought that was a strange thing to say. It's somehow weirdly vague and weirdly specific at the same time."

"I can see the vague bit. What's the specific bit?"

"I think we've been looking at things the wrong way around," said Frieda. "We've been waiting for him to do something. What if he's already done it?"

"Done what?"

"That's the problem. I can't see what it would be."

"There's another minor problem, of course, which is that it can't be Daniel Blackstock. You may remember he has an alibi."

"Yes, I wanted you to talk about that."

Frieda looked around. Petra had a map of central London on her wall. Frieda walked over to it and described how she had walked from the hospital in Poplar to Olivia's house in Islington, how Blackstock could have managed it with a car, but that it would have needed the help of his wife.

"Convinced?" she said, when she had finished.

"All right, it's not physically impossible. But would it work? Would he do that to himself?"

"I think he would have needed her to do it for him," said Frieda.

"Possibilities aren't evidence."

"But you realize that this is urgent. Last night I think Daniel Blackstock was telling us—telling me in particular—that he's already done something. We can't just wait."

"Yes, we can."

"In particular, you can't. You have to bring them in. Both of them. Put them under pressure. Her especially."

"Under pressure?" said Petra. "What is this? Guantánamo Bay? We can ask them questions and they can refuse and that's that."

"No," said Frieda, shaking her head. "There's something happening out there. You have to act now."

There was a long pause.

"I'm not convinced Daniel Blackstock is a suspect," said Petra. "And, to be honest, I'm not convinced he was talking specifically to you via the television."

"Petra, you have to bring him in."

"I don't think they'll crack in twenty-four hours."

"I thought it was ninety-six hours in a murder case."

"In very specific circumstances, which we don't have."

"But will you do it?"

Petra drummed her fingers restlessly on the desk. "I'll consider it."

52

"*Déjà vu*," said Daniel Blackstock. His nose was red from the sun, his cheeks pink. He smiled at Petra, smiled at Don Kaminsky, settled back in his chair, put his hands behind his head. Maybe he wasn't so calm, after all, thought Petra. There were circles of sweat under his arms. She read him his rights again.

"Got you." He sat up straight and took a notebook out of his jacket pocket and a pencil. "All right with you two if I make notes?"

"It's all going to be on tape." Petra gestured at the machine, which was silently whirring.

"For my next story. Part two, as it were."

"You are also entitled to a lawyer. If you don't have one, we can get you one."

"I do believe you're using the exact same words as last time." He wrote busily.

"Would you like a lawyer?"

Daniel Blackstock bounced his pencil on his notebook a few times.

"Maybe I would," he said at last. "I've been a crime reporter too long to have much faith in the police."

"Very well. Shall we get one for you?"

"Do that."

"Right. In the meantime, we'll go and talk to your wife." She looked at his expression; it didn't alter. But he jiggled his right knee. He seemed an odd mixture of nervous and cocky.

"No comment," said Lee Blackstock. She sat very straight in her chair, her hands folded in her lap. She was wearing a pale blue shirt-dress and her hair was slightly greasy so that it lay flat on her head, the fringe almost in her eyes, making her blink. Her lips were pale and dry and she licked them repeatedly. She spoke dully, like a schoolgirl repeating a lesson learned by rote, each word separated from the next, and did not meet Petra's gaze but looked slightly to one side.

"You do understand, Mrs. Blackstock, that the charge of conspiring with another to pervert the course of justice is a serious one, which can carry a long prison sentence."

"No comment."

"We are interested in the night that your husband injured his hand. Do you remember that night?"

"No comment."

"It's a simple enough question, surely." Lee Blackstock continued staring just past her. "Was he at home with you that evening, when he cut his hand?"

"No comment."

"On August the twenty-ninth, at about half past nine in the evening, you called 1 1 1 and reported the accident." Lee didn't say anything. Petra saw her unfold her hands and wipe the palms on her dress. "Was your husband with you when you made that call?" She waited a few seconds. "Or did you make the call, then drive to meet him at a pre-arranged place?" She thought of what Frieda had said yesterday. "Lee, did you perhaps inflict that wound yourself, to give your husband an alibi?"

"No comment," said Lee Blackstock. Her voice was hoarse. She coughed, putting up a hand to her mouth.

"I know that it is very painful to give evidence against a partner," said Petra, softly. "Very hard. But you need to tell us, Lee. If your husband has done something bad, you mustn't shield him. That would be very wrong and you'd be getting yourself into big trouble."

The silence in the room was thick. Petra could hear the cassette machine running; beside her Don Kaminsky shifted in his seat. She watched Lee's face intently.

"This is about a series of brutal attacks," she said. "And a murder. Someone has been killed. So if there's anything you know, you can tell me. It's not too late."

Lee looked down into her lap; now Petra could see only the crooked parting in her hair.

"No comment," she said.

The duty solicitor, Simon Neaves, was a man in late middle age, with receding gray hair and pouches under his eyes. Everything about him seemed worn, from his suit to his battered leather briefcase to his air of frayed tiredness.

"We are interested in your alibi for the evening of August the twenty-ninth," said Petra, after she and Don Kaminsky had resumed their seats, turned on the tape and read Blackstock his rights once more. "I know you gave us an account of that evening before." She picked up her file and pulled out his statement. "Yes. Here we are. I'd just like to go through it again."

Simon Neaves nodded at Daniel Blackstock. Daniel Blackstock nodded at Petra.

"I'm not going to say anything different," he said genially. "I was cutting linoleum tiles. My hand slipped. The Stanley knife cut my hand. My wife called 1 1 1. Then she drove me to the hospital and I was stitched up. I'm sure you've had all this corroborated by the hospital."

"What time did the accident occur?"

"About nine thirty."

"And when did you get to the hospital?"

"Sometime around ten fifteen. I'm sure the hospital records will give you the exact time."

"So at exactly the time that someone was attacking Mr. Dargan, you conveniently have a verifiable alibi."

"Exactly," said Simon Neaves. "Which makes it rather strange that Mr. Blackstock is here."

"There is no evidence at all that you were in your house at the time of the accident. We only have your wife's word for it."

"My hand—" began Blackstock, then stopped with a visible effort.

"Your wound could have been inflicted anywhere. Outside the hospital, for instance."

Blackstock's face flushed. He leaned forward, but the solicitor laid a hand on his shoulder briefly and he sat back again, straightened his shoulders. "No comment," he said.

"You could have driven from Islington, met your wife and driven to the hospital. And that would make sense," continued Petra, "of the unrealistic neatness of the timing, and of the fact that your alibi was established after we had taken you in for questioning. Almost as if you attacked Mr. Dargan to prove that you *hadn't* attacked either him or anyone else."

"Are you going to ask a question?" Blackstock made the words sound derisory.

"We are talking to your wife, of course, to see if she wants to change her story. And we are checking CCTV." She watched his face carefully. He looked hot. His brown eyes were sharp. "But in the meantime, I want to ask you about other times and dates. Can you tell me where you were on August the twenty-second?"

"No."

"As you probably know, this was the night that Reuben McGill was attacked and badly injured in his own home. Do you have an alibi for that evening as well?"

"No comment."

"Where were you over the weekend of August the thirteenth and fourteenth?"

"How do I know? Probably with my wife, watching telly and—" He broke into a strange smile. "I don't know. Domestic tasks. Like cutting linoleum tiles."

Petra rang Frieda.

"Well?"

"I don't know, Frieda. He's a smug bastard, but so are lots of people. I haven't got anything on him."

"What about her?"

"The only thing she has said, apart from confirming her name, is 'no comment.' It's like she's zoned out and isn't even hearing what I'm asking."

"You've got twenty-four hours?"

"About fifteen now."

"You can't hold them for longer?"

"I need just cause."

"Can't you bend the—"

"No."

There was a pause.

"Can I come and talk to them?"

"You?"

"I think that maybe Daniel Blackstock wants me as his audience so he might give something away."

"I don't know."

"Please," said Frieda, not in a pleading tone but in a firm one, almost a command.

There was a pause. Petra thought about the failed Bruce Stringer investigation, the series of attacks on Frieda's friends, the death of Morgan Rossiter. She thought of Daniel Blackstock sitting in the interview room with his sunburned nose and his hot brown eyes, his strange mixture of agitation and excitement. She thought of his notebook, the story he would write if they released him without charge again, and her stomach tightened

"OK. Why not? They're both taking a break."

She ended the call.

"Hello Frieda."

She didn't reply but sat opposite him, Petra to one side. Their eyes met and, with a sickening lurch, she felt his excitement. Why, when he was in a police interview room, his wife next door, did he seem so full of restless anticipation?

"You couldn't keep away?" asked Daniel. He had a notebook open on the table in front of him and now he looked at her intently, then jotted down a few words. "Gray shirt," he said. "Hair tied back severely. Readers like to know things like that." He wrote again. "Looks tired, pale, under strain. You do, you know."

"Do you really think," said Frieda, "that you have killed a man, injured two others, abducted a young woman and left no trace?"

Daniel glanced left at Simon Neaves, raised his eyebrows, and smiled. "No comment," he said.

"Your alibi is fraudulent."

"No comment."

"You've got your wife to cover for you, I think you got her to inflict the injury on you."

"No comment."

"What kind of husband would do that?"

"No comment."

"I met your wife. Do you think she'll stick to her story, once she knows the trouble she's in?"

"You have nothing," said Daniel Blackstock. "The famous Frieda Klein, and you have nothing. How does it make you feel?"

"Who are you trying to impress, Daniel? Me?" Frieda stared into his hungry face. "Dean Reeve?"

"Nothing," repeated Daniel Blackstock.

"It's over," said Frieda. "Even if you walk out of here this time, there's nothing left for you. You will be charged, you will be sent to prison, and when you're there, in the empty days, in the years stretching ahead, do you think anyone will remember your name?"

He gazed at her, then leaned forward. "Nothing," he said.

"My client has nothing to say and we are going to take a break." Simon Neaves put a hand under Blackstock's elbow as if to raise him from the chair.

"No. You'll be just another pathetic little man who's locked behind bars. You have no legacy."

Daniel stood up. "You have no idea," he said. "No idea at all."

Lee's face was heavy, like dough. Her eyes were cloudy, resting on Frieda but with no sense of actually seeing her.

"I know you're loyal. But sometimes there are things that are even more important than loyalty," said Frieda, softly. She was conscious of Petra in the room with her, watchful by the door. "Sometimes to support your husband is to do something very wrong, Lee." She waited a few seconds. "You don't need to be his accessory. You can be your own person. That would be very brave." Another pause. "He didn't cut his hand in your home, did he?"

Lee said, in a low, muffled voice, "No comment."

"You did it for him, didn't you? Near the hospital?"

The woman made no answer. Behind her, Frieda heard the door open.

"This doesn't need to continue, Lee," said Frieda, not turning, trying to hold her attention. "You can stop it now. It's not too late."

"I think it is *this* that isn't going to continue," said a voice. Frieda looked around to see a tall woman in the doorway, with gray hair and a long, angry face. "DCI Burge, a word. And you too, Dr. Klein," she said to Frieda.

They went to the door.

"Who—"

"As of yesterday, I'm the acting commissioner. And I'm not terrifically happy." She switched her attention to Petra. "We've had enough of rule-bending, rule-breaking. Do you understand the scrutiny we're under at the moment?"

"That's not a reason—"

"I understand you've asked for an extension."

"Yes."

"On what grounds?"

Petra held her gaze. "I believe Daniel Blackstock murdered Morgan Rossiter, abducted Chloë Klein, attacked Reuben McGill and Jack Dargan."

"I know what you believe. Why do you believe it? What evidence do you have?"

"His alibi is shaky and—"

"What evidence, DCI Burge?"

"He did it," said Frieda.

The woman turned to scrutinize her. Her eyes were sharp and clear. She gave a sigh. "I know what you've been through, Dr. Klein. But you have to understand, we have rules for a reason. And we can't have a private citizen interviewing a suspect."

"Then let Petra do it. Just give her extra time. He did it."

"No."

"He's dangerous."

"There's feeling and there's evidence. There's belief, and there's proof. Give me evidence, and we can hold him. Otherwise, he and his wife must be released."

"He's done something else," said Frieda, abruptly.

"What do you mean?"

"I don't know."

"You must see that doesn't help me."

"You can't just let him go."

"I can't not let him go. But," her face eased slightly, "we are going to put him under surveillance." She held up her hand to stop them speaking. "That's all I can do."

*

Frieda walked to Reuben's house. It was early evening and she had rung in advance to say that Daniel and Lee Blackstock had both been released without charge.

Reuben came to the door. He had put on an old summer suit that hung off him, and was wearing new frameless glasses. He gave Frieda a light hug and beckoned her through into the garden. There was a tray of glasses on the table and a bottle of white wine.

"Sit," he said, gesturing to a chair.

She sat, took off her jacket and her sandals, shut her eyes briefly. She heard the splash of wine in glasses. The garden smelled of mown grass. "They've released them both," she said. "Not enough evidence."

"Have a drink."

He passed her a glass and raised his own to her.

"You look smart," she said.

"You mean I'm not in pajamas."

"Well, maybe."

"There's comfort in shuffling around being an invalid, but it wears a bit thin. Today I did some work on a paper I'm writing. And made phone calls to people I've been avoiding."

"That's good."

"It's something at least."

"So where is everyone?"

"Everyone?"

"You've got five people living in your house, remember."

"Four until Jack's out of hospital. Lucky that Josef fitted the new boiler last year."

"Do you mind?"

"I'm assuming it's not for long."

"Reuben—" She stopped. He looked at her for a moment and put a finger to his lips.

"To answer your question, Josef and Alexei are making a meal. Josef seems to have given up being a builder and is turning into a bloody chef. He and Olivia battle it out in the kitchen: she keeps giving him handy hints that he doesn't appreciate—and eating his ingredients before he has time to use them. She's in the bath at the moment, though. I think Chloë's gone to see Jack."

"Chloë's here," said a voice, and they turned to see her coming through the kitchen door. "How did it go, Frieda?"

"They released him."

Her face crumpled. "Oh. I thought—I hoped—" Tears welled in her eyes. She scowled ferociously and rubbed them away with the heel of one hand. "Shit," she said. "Shit. We're like prisoners here and he's free."

"Does the prisoner want some wine?" asked Reuben.

She took the glass he handed her and took a large gulp. Her hand was trembling. "What are we going to do?"

"The police have him under surveillance."

"So we're just going to wait? All of us here together? Wait till he does something again?"

She was asking Frieda what Frieda had asked Petra. There was no answer.

"And another fucking thing," she said.

"What's that?"

"William."

"What about him?"

"He's being tormented."

"The press are still harassing him?"

"No. There's a gang of teenagers who are making his

life hell." Tears stood in her eyes again. "He's scared to go out. They call him horrible names and barge into him and push him about and jeer. It's foul."

"Has he called the police?"

"What do you think? He's just cowering in his room."

"OK." Frieda was thinking hard. She could get Petra on to it—but it wasn't going to be a top priority with Petra just at the moment. And she had no faith in the local police to deal with it. Reluctantly, she decided to ask Karlsson if he could help.

But then she had an idea.

"Wait here a minute," she said, and went into the house to find her bag. In the wallet was the slip of paper on which Yvette had written her mobile number. Frieda remembered her expression as she'd pressed it into her hand, telling her to ring if she ever needed help: awkward, eager, intense. She would ask Yvette to deal with William McCollough's persecutors: she would do it at once and efficiently, and she would be glad to be asked. It would make her feel needed.

She dialed the number and got only silence. She frowned, checked the number, and dialed once more. Again, there was no message, just a silence.

Odd, she thought. She walked back into the garden, deep in thought.

"What is it?" asked Chloë, seeing her troubled expression.

"I'm trying to get hold of Yvette."

"She'll ring back."

"I'm getting nothing."

She rang Karlsson's number but it went straight to voicemail. She stared at Chloë and Reuben, gripped by a sick, cold feeling.

"What?" Reuben was saying. "What is it?"

Her mobile rang and it was Karlsson.

"Frieda? Are you OK?"

"Have you talked to Yvette recently?"

"Yvette? No. She's on indefinite leave."

"She hasn't been in touch at all?"

"No. Why?"

"I'm trying to get hold of her. Her phone's dead."

"And?" Karlsson was cautious.

"I'll phone you back."

53

"No," said Petra.

"Just hear me out."

"No."

"All you need to do is search Yvette's flat. Just to check."

"Frieda . . . Actually, I think I'm going to go back to calling you Dr. Klein. Do I come into the middle of one of your therapy sessions and tell you how to do your job?"

"Daniel Blackstock's done something and Yvette is missing."

"Yvette Long is on a much-needed sabbatical."

"She hasn't returned my calls."

There was a pause.

"You're ringing me because she didn't return one call?"

"I have called many times. It doesn't go to voicemail. There's just silence."

"What are you? Thirteen years old and waiting for your boyfriend to call? I talked to Yvette and she was exhausted, finished. She's escaping for a while. Let her have that."

Frieda started to say something and then she realized that the line was dead. She looked at her phone angrily as if it were slightly responsible for what had happened. Then she dialed another number.

"Can you come and pick me up?" she said.

"She said no, didn't she?"

"Who?"

"Don't play games."

"I don't have time for games."

"All right, all right."

"You know what I'm going to say," said Karlsson.

He and Frieda were sitting in his car.

"The last time I saw Yvette, she said that if I needed anything, just to call. I called and there was no reply."

"No reply. For how long? A week? A month?"

"Her phone is dead. I'm concerned."

Karlsson thought for a moment. "And what Petra said to you is that the simple explanation is that she's away and doesn't want to be contacted."

"She said something like that."

"I'll bet she did. Sometimes it feels like you're working your way through the Met, officer by officer, driving them to despair. In the end I'll be the last one standing, the last one who'll do your bidding. And, by the way, Petra is right."

"Then no harm will have been done."

"By what?"

"By searching her flat."

Karlsson turned around sharply, looking really troubled for the first time. "Is there something you know? Something you're not telling me?"

"I know something's wrong."

"How were you planning to get into her flat?"

"I suppose we could break a window or something like that."

"And if anybody sees you? Us, I should say."

"We could say we smelled gas. Or saw an intruder."

Karlsson started the car and began to drive. He shook his head. "Smelled gas? Where do you get these ideas from? You sound like a burglar. A really incompetent burglar."

"This is Yvette we're talking about," said Frieda, unsmiling.

"Yes. Yvette, who said she wanted to get her head straightened out by escaping from everything, by getting away from the pressure of the job."

"We'll see."

The traffic up Seven Sisters Road was agonizingly slow.

"I should have taken the Tube," said Frieda, almost to herself.

"I'm sorry that the taxi service isn't to your liking."

The journey took twenty minutes more—in silence—before Karlsson turned off the main road into a residential street, made a couple of turns and then parked. The two of them got out.

"I've never been in her house before," said Frieda.

"She's a private person."

Karlsson opened the garden gate of a small terraced house and led Frieda down the steps to the basement. The window and the door were both heavily barred. "This is Tottenham," he said. "Your breaking-and-entering plan was never going to work in this area."

"So what do we do?"

Karlsson took a key ring from his pocket with two keys on it. He shook it so they tinkled. "Yvette gave me a spare set, in case of emergencies."

"Why didn't you say?"

"I wanted to hear your plan. Such as it was. Careful what you touch when you're inside," he added. "I don't know why I'm even bothering to say that. As if you'd pay attention."

He turned a key in the lock and pushed the door open. The two of them stepped inside together and Frieda took a breath and felt an immediate sense of relief. She had been dreading that horribly familiar sour-sweet smell, the one from under the floorboards. But there was none of that, just the slightly stuffy, dank smell of a home that hasn't been lived in for a while, where the doors and windows have been closed in hot weather. Karlsson gestured Frieda inside and she stepped through the door, straight into a small living room. She walked quickly through the tiny flat. Bedroom, bathroom, miniature paved patio at the back. She wanted to see if there was anything obvious. There wasn't.

"No sign of a struggle," said Karlsson.

She couldn't tell at first if he was being mocking, then decided he wasn't. He cared about Yvette. She knew that. She looked around more carefully.

"Is this owned or rented?" she asked.

"Yvette owns it," said Karlsson. "Well, sort of. She has a mortgage."

In the kitchen everything was stowed away. When Frieda opened a cupboard she found a neat pile of plates, four wine glasses, four tumblers. In the living room there was a small flat-screen television and DVD player against the wall facing the front door. A large pot stood next to them on the floor, with the blackened dead remains of a plant in it. There was a low glass coffee table with an armchair on one side. On the other, against the left wall, there was a matching sofa. There was one picture, just above the sofa, a photograph of a fox—startlingly red—sitting on a frozen lake.

"It feels rented," said Frieda. "Or as if she's just moved in."

"She moved in three years ago," said Karlsson. "Maybe four."

"It doesn't feel like a place where someone has been happy."

"Remember what I said about Yvette being a private person? I cannot convey how distressed she would be about the idea of us being here and you making judgements about her life based on how it all looked."

"How well do you know this flat?"

"I've been here once, literally once, and that was when she moved in. I drove some things over for her."

"So you don't know the flat well."

"As I said, I've been here just the once."

"And you wouldn't be able to tell if there was anything unusual or out of place?"

"No. Although it's obvious that there isn't anything unusual here."

"There is one thing."

"What?"

Frieda pointed at the dead plant.

"What's so unusual about that?"

"If you go on holiday, you get someone to water your plants."

"You should see my place."

"I have seen your place. Many times."

"Then you know that it's full of dead or dying plants. I keep buying them and I try everything. I overwater them and underwater them. I feed them, I starve them. And still they die."

"It doesn't seem like a worrying detail to you?"

"It looks to me like it may have been dead for a long time."

The two of them walked together into the bathroom. Frieda opened the cabinet.

"Everything's here," she said.

"What?"

"Toothpaste, toothbrush, perfume, face cream, face wipes, shampoo, deodorant, Tampax, makeup, dental floss, indigestion tablets."

"That's a logical error."

"What kind of logical error?"

"You can't see the things that aren't there. The things she took with her. Her new toothpaste and toothbrush, her favorite perfume, and so on and so on."

"You may be right."

They walked back into the kitchen. Frieda opened the fridge while Karlsson opened cupboard doors. "Are we going to confess to Yvette about this?" he said.

"'Confess' isn't the right word."

"How would you feel if Yvette and I were to do this to your house when you were away?"

"I think I'm beyond caring what people do to my house."

"I don't believe you."

"Look," said Frieda, holding up a small plastic carton of low-fat milk. "Do you leave milk in the fridge when you go on holiday?"

"Yes," said Karlsson. "Milk and almost anything perishable you can think of. I usually come back to find my fridge has turned into some kind of zoo of mold. It's part of . . ." And then he paused. "I'm not sure I want to show you what I've found."

"What do you mean?"

Karlsson held up a passport. He opened it. "Before you say anything, yes, this is Yvette's. But it changes nothing. I always assumed she was going somewhere in Britain. Wales or Scotland or the Peak District. Somewhere with lots of remote walks."

"The plant. The milk. The passport. Doesn't that add up to something?"

"I don't know. Maybe it adds up to someone who is distracted and a bit down, and left in a hurry. I've always trusted your instincts. Well, except when I haven't. But, honestly, if you've been looking for some kind of smoking gun, this doesn't amount to one."

Frieda felt dissatisfied but she didn't reply. They went into the bedroom and Frieda opened drawers, picking up items of clothing.

"I feel I shouldn't be seeing this," said Karlsson. "For God's sake, fold them so they're the way Yvette left them."

After another half hour of searching, Karlsson called a halt. "You're looking in the places you've already looked. It's time to go."

Frieda surveyed Yvette's living room. The idea of leaving was unbearable. "There's something," she said. "You know how when you have a local anesthetic and you can't feel the pain but somehow it's still there somewhere? That's what I'm feeling."

"We're done here. There's nothing."

"You're right." Frieda spoke reluctantly. "And thank you. Thank you. Thank you for bringing me here and for not saying, 'I told you so.'"

"I don't do that, do I? I'm tempted, of course. But I don't do it."

*

Back in the car, Karlsson switched on the engine once more.

"Are you all right?"

She shook her head slowly. "Switch off the car," she said.

"What?"

"Please."

"We've done this, haven't we? Can't we go home?"

Frieda's face was set hard in an expression Karlsson recognized. "There's something wrong with Yvette's living room," she said.

"It could do with a few more pictures," said Karlsson. "More of a personal touch."

"It's the television," said Frieda, speaking slowly, as if she wasn't aware of her surroundings, as if she were somewhere else. "You remember the layout?"

"Of course I remember it. We've just left."

"The television is against the back wall. The sofa is against the left-hand wall, and the armchair is facing it on the other side of that little glass table. Right?"

"Yes, that's right. So what's the problem?"

"How do you watch the television?"

"What do you mean how?"

"I mean where from?"

Karlsson shrugged with an expression of puzzlement and slight irritation. "You sit on the chair. Or on the sofa."

"But they're both at a ninety-degree angle to the screen."

"So you rotate your head slightly."

"You could do it once but that's not the way you would set up your furniture."

"I cannot believe we're having a serious discussion about the arrangement of Yvette's furniture, but perhaps when she wanted to watch TV, she moved one of her items of furniture."

"You mean she dragged a heavy sofa across the room to watch the news?"

"Or an armchair."

"We need to go back inside."

"Oh, please, Frieda."

"Just for two minutes. One minute."

He took a deep breath. "I'm counting to ten," he said. "In my head. Right. I've done. Now I'm calm again and we can go back into Yvette's flat for two minutes."

"Thank you, Karlsson."

"You're welcome, Frieda."

But he didn't speak again as they got out of the car and he locked it, then fumbled for the keys and unlocked Yvette's front door. As soon as she stepped into the room she fell to her knees and examined the carpet.

"There," she said immediately. "I can't believe I was so stupid."

Karlsson looked where she was pointing. There was a small depression in the carpet, circular, two inches or so across.

"All right," he said. "So the sofa or the chair was there. I was right."

"No," said Frieda. "You were wrong. It was the sofa, by the way. Pull it back into position."

"Yes, ma'am," he said sarcastically.

He laid his hands on the sofa and pulled it out. Almost immediately he stepped back.

"Oh, fuck," he said. "Oh, fucking fuck."

Frieda stepped forward and they both looked at the words written in broad strokes on the wall: "Frieda Klein."

54

Things happened quickly after that, although at the same time it all seemed in slow motion: Karlsson calling the police, calling Petra, making sure Frieda didn't touch anything. Frieda wasn't about to touch anything, or even move. She stood quite still in the glare of her thoughts, staring at the daubed words, reaching back to the time she'd last seen Yvette and calculating the weeks and days it had been since that time, at her house, when Yvette had emotionally pressed her phone number into Frieda's hand, then Daniel Blackstock had arrived with that terrible photograph of Chloë. Yes, he and Yvette had met, she thought, and Yvette had talked of her vulnerable state and of her sabbatical. Then almost immediately after had come the attacks, on Reuben, fatally on Morgan Rossiter, on Jack. Two weeks, Frieda thought, counting back. Two weeks and three days. So little time, and yet such a long time if that was when Yvette had gone.

Gone. But was she dead? She heard Karlsson speaking calmly, precisely, to someone on his mobile, giving instructions. Underneath his calm she heard something else. Horror. She forced herself to think. If Yvette was dead, why wasn't her body here, beside the painted letters? She remembered Daniel Blackstock in the police station, that look of triumph in his eyes. All this time, she thought, all this time, at every meeting they had had, every contact, he had been thinking of Yvette, his great secret. "You have no idea," he had said.

She wasn't dead, she was being kept by him. She was sure—she had to be sure. Where? She thought of Chloë in that room, pictured the way the light fell on the grubby mattress. She closed her eyes and concentrated, shutting out every other sound or thought, feeling as if a sharp point was screwing its way into her brain, so that at length it would reach some dark, hidden place and she would find the answer. What was she missing? What had she always missed?

There was a hammering at the door and Karlsson went to open it. Light flooded in and hurt her eyes. People were coming in, men and women with stern faces, for it was one of theirs now, nothing else like it, and Karlsson, taking her by the elbow, was leading her out.

"Karlsson," she said.

But there was Petra, small and wiry, her eyes glittering in her bony face. "You were right," she said to Frieda. "What has he done?"

Then she walked past and away out of Frieda's sight. More cars were arriving. The bright day felt like a dream.

"I think she's alive," said Frieda to Karlsson. "He's got her somewhere."

He looked at her but didn't speak.

Petra came out again, pulled off the gloves, bent down to remove her plastic shoes. "Right," she said. "This is it. Follow me to the station at once. We'll haul them both in, grill them, call a press conference, the works."

"No." Frieda put a hand on her arm, stopping her as she was about to stride away.

"What are you talking about?" said Petra, fiercely. "This is what you've been asking for."

"Don't you see? If he's got her, we need him free to go to her. He can lead us to her."

"No." Petra shook off her hand. "We're going to bring him in."

"If he's brought in, who's going to give her water, food? It's very hot. She'll die in days. You mustn't."

"This is my call," said Petra.

"No." They all turned. The acting commissioner stood on the pavement, tall and imposing, dressed in a charcoal-gray suit in spite of the heat, her face stern. "I agree with Dr. Klein."

Petra looked at the two of them, her eyes flickering with anger at being overruled.

"Is he under surveillance?" asked the commissioner.

"Of course," said Petra.

"Make sure he doesn't know."

"Yes."

"He mustn't be aware of the search either."

"Which means it's got to be limited, small-scale."

"We'll risk that for the moment."

"There's his wife," said Frieda. "We need her to be watched as well."

The commissioner nodded at Petra. "See to it. Call me in one hour and give me an update."

She turned on her heel. Petra looked at Frieda. "You'd better be sure about this."

The sun shone bright and hot through the window of Petra's office. Frieda stood by the large map on the wall and put her finger on an intersection of roads. "There," she said. "This is where he lives. Nearby there's a wasteland ready for development, a vast abandoned warehouse, floor upon floor of empty rooms. I've often wondered if that was where Chloë was held."

"This is assuming that Yvette is being held where your niece was held, and that it was near an airport, and this airport was City Airport."

"Yes."

"She could be anywhere. Not even in London."

"I know."

"She could be dead."

"Yes."

"All right," said Petra. "We'll begin our search there."

Daniel Blackstock couldn't stop smiling. Even when he tried to keep his lips firm, he couldn't; they twitched open and he smiled and smiled. Sweat trickled down his face. The sun pricked his skin. He walked along the street slowly, stopping in front of shop windows, bending to tie his laces. He wasn't stupid: that man in jeans and a scruffy T-shirt, and before he came, the young woman wearing head-phones. Both trying to be casual. There was an ice cream van and he bought a single scoop in a cone and sat on the bench near the small green to eat it. He took his time. Later, he would write that piece he'd promised his editor on being arrested a second time. Everybody wanted a bit of his story. His phone rang constantly and messages pinged onto his screen, invitations to write, to talk, to give his opinion, share his pain.

He took another lick of the softening ice cream. Behind him was the river; in front, the old warehouses, the broken windows glinting in the sun. He let himself remember the faces of those two women, Frieda Klein and Petra Burge, as they'd looked at him across the table, one with sharp, pale eyes and one with dark, intense ones. They hated him, but hate was close to love. Dean Reeve knew that. After so many years of being invisible, of people who weren't as clever as him ordering him about, Daniel Blackstock was now visible.

He took another lick of the ice cream, then another. When it was finished he ate the cone, slowly, though, nibbling his way down to the point, like he used to do when he was a boy. He licked his fingers and wiped his forehead with a crumpled tissue. Then he stood up and walked home in a zigzag route. Give them some exercise. Tease them with hope.

Lee Blackstock was sitting at the table in the spotless kitchen and crying. She kept trying to stop, blowing her nose and dabbing her face with a handkerchief, but then she'd remember being in the police station and what they'd said to her, and the tears would start again.

When she heard his key turn in the lock she jumped to her feet and busied herself at the stove, so that her back was to him when he entered.

"Apple crumble and custard," she said. "Is that all right?"

"Whatever."

"You used to say it was your favorite."

"Is that all you can think of?"

"Of course not."

Of course it wasn't. She thought of being in one of those police vans and getting out, her head covered with a coat so no one could see her face, of standing in the dock and people staring at her. Tears filled her eyes again. She stirred custard power into the hot sweetened milk and watched it thicken.

Daniel came over and put his uninjured hand on her shoulder and she turned. "Your eyes are all pink." He sounded irritated. "You've been crying."

"I was scared."

"What did you say to them?"

"I told you. Nothing."

"Not even to her?"

Lee Blackstock knew whom he meant: Frieda Klein, with those eyes that looked at her, looked into her, could see everything she most wanted to hide; whose expression was a terrible mixture of knowledge and pity.

"No. I wouldn't, Daniel. I just said 'no comment.'"

His hand was still on her shoulder, heavy and hot through the cotton of her shirt. "That's right. Good girl."

"But—" She stopped.

"What?"

"What have you done?"

She watched his face darken and was filled with fear.

"If I've done anything," he said, "it's for us. And if I have, you know what you are, don't you?"

"What?"

"An accessory."

"I just did what you told me. That's all."

"An accessory," he repeated, as if he could taste the word in his mouth. "That's a serious business."

It was what they'd said to her at the station. And they'd said that it wasn't too late: she could tell them what she knew. She lifted her eyes to his and he took his hand from her shoulder at last and tucked her hair, damp from sweat and weeping, behind her ears. "There now," he said. "You just do what I tell you and everything will be fine. You and me together, eh? You and me against the world."

She nodded. "Yes," she whispered. "You and me."

There were ten men, none in uniform. Karlsson was in charge. He separated them into pairs and he told them to be discreet: Daniel Blackstock's house was just a few hundred feet away. Although it wasn't visible, the estate was, and the road that circled through it.

The warehouse where they were to start was like a ruined city that towered over the building sites around it, serried ranks of vast buildings joined together into a wall of red brick, hundreds of windows, dozens of entrances. Karlsson stared up at its crumbling mass and frowned. He needed a hundred men, not ten, and even then they wouldn't be able to do an exhaustive search. He tried to do a rough calculation of how many rooms there were but gave up. He could see the length of the building but not the width.

There was a main door, boarded and heavily chained. Before reaching it, there was the fence that circled the entire thing, with a padlocked metal gate. But Karlsson didn't need to use the key that Feldman's Security had given him. It was simple to get in through one of the many gaps in the wooden boards and walk across the caked wasteland of yellow-brown mud and thick weeds. Now he did use the key, but he could see that several of the tall windows on this section of the building were smashed and he imagined many others would be as well. Anyone could get in here, kids, couples looking for privacy and shelter, homeless people, the curious, the mad, the lonely and sad.

Once inside, in the tall atrium that led to the storerooms,

it was clear that people had come here. Scraps of litter stirred in the wind that blew through the open door. There were cigarette ends, a few needles, a sodden newspaper, an old shoe, the ammonia smell of piss. In one corner there was an ashy circle from a fire someone had built. Karlsson looked up at the steel girders, the wormy wooden rafters. Beetles must live here, spiders and bats and thick-tailed rats. Birds must build their nests. But was Yvette here? He wanted to call out, his voice echoing through all the empty spaces, to tell her they were here, they were coming, she was safe. Clumsy, tactless, honorable Yvette, who blushed easily and spoke abruptly and walked heavily through life.

"There are ten floors in this section alone," he said to the officers. "Two floors for each pair. I'll take the top."

He climbed the metal stairs. Some of the steps were missing. There was a thin banister, whose rust stained his hand. It was dim, but at each landing light fell in slabs through the windows that looked out at the shining sweep of the Thames, the Barrier glinting in the distance. His leg ached as he climbed. He could hear the men beneath him, their footsteps and low voices, and then he couldn't, just the sound of water dripping, an old building creaking, a rustle somewhere, so many secret things stirring behind the walls.

On the tenth floor, several of the wide boards were missing, others rotten, and he could see through gaps to the rooms beneath. He made his way carefully. Dust balls rolled across the floor. There was a dead bird in one room, and a long table in another. He looked out of the window at the railway line and the rows of neat modern houses, each with their patch of lawn.

"Where are you?" he said, and his voice sounded unfamiliar in that high, empty room, the voice of a stranger.

No one had found anything: no sign that Yvette, or Chloë, had ever been there.

"What next?" asked one of the men, a young officer with eyes that were large and distressed behind his spectacles.

"We've covered about a fifth of this building. We'll take it staircase by staircase. When we're done, we move to the other buildings."

"What are the parameters of our search, sir?" asked another.

It was a good question, and Karlsson couldn't answer it. They were searching for a woman who might be anywhere, and who might be dead. Even there, in this inch of the great map of London, there were thousands of buildings: factories, warehouses, houses, flats, shacks, huts, containers, crannies. For a brief moment, he let helplessness wash over him, then steeled himself. "Let's just think about this building."

55

At first Frieda had thought of going over to Silvertown, just to be there, to walk around, to drink it in, maybe to feel something. But she knew it would just have been a gesture. All she could do was wait, and she had always been terrible at waiting. She had to do something, anything, rather than think of Yvette somewhere in this city, alive or dead. Alive. She was sure she must be alive. She remembered Daniel Blackstock's expression. It would be more interesting for him. It would give him more power. But there was no point in dwelling on it. That was unproductive. She should leave the police to do their work. She looked at her watch, then thought: What does it matter what the time is?

She should do something else. Work was out of the question. She could tidy the house, except that she had been compulsively doing that in the previous few months, trying to eliminate anything that Dean Reeve might have touched. She had already cleaned and scoured and scraped. She looked at the coffee table. Rays of light were coming from the front window, forming a pool on the flecked brown surface. Frieda walked to the kitchen and half filled a tumbler with water. She returned and placed it in the pool of light, moving it this way and that until the shadow fell on the table surface just right. She rummaged through a drawer and found two pencils, hard and soft, and a drawing pad. She sat at the table, laid the pad and the pencils in front of her and stared at the glass, emptying her mind of everything except the light and the shadow. Then, after a full minute, she picked up the hard pencil and traced the first line. As always, she had to ignore the ache of disappointment that came as she started to draw. Before, in that moment of thought, the drawing could have been anything, but now it was already limited by the frailty of her fingers. It was already starting to fail.

She changed to the softer pencil and was trying to capture something of the soft gray shadow created by the water and the swirling refracted shades in the water itself when she was interrupted by a ring at the door. She almost ran to answer it. Josef was standing there.

"Oh, it's you," she said.

"No happy to see me?"

"I'm waiting for news," she said.

Josef stepped inside and saw the glass on the table and the sketchbook. "I think maybe you out looking," he said.

"Looking for what?"

"You know. For her. For Yvette."

"How can I look? Where? This isn't a game of hide and seek."

"We do this. You have the instinct."

"Josef, I do not have the instinct. I'm not a witch. Anyway, the police are doing their job. The phone will probably ring in five minutes and they'll have found Yvette and we can all go back to our lives."

"You want me going?"

"No, it's fine. You'll probably do less harm here than anywhere else."

Josef frowned. "Do harm?"

"Sorry. I'm in a bad mood. It's not your fault."

"The punching bag," said Josef.

"In a way."

"The post that the cat scratches."

"All right, that's enough."

"I get us a drink."

"Tea," said Frieda.

Josef went into the kitchen and Frieda heard the sound of cupboards opening, water running. When Josef came through with two mugs, she hadn't moved.

"Continue," he said.

"What?"

"The drawing," he said.

Frieda took the mug and sipped at the scalding tea. It almost hurt her mouth, but it felt good. It was keeping her alert. She picked up the pencil and tried to continue but the spell had been broken. "Aren't you working on Reuben's garden?" she said.

"Tomorrow."

Frieda resumed her drawing. With the hard pencil, she tried to capture a patch of shadow with some delicate cross-hatching. She didn't feel happy with it. Maybe it would look better from a distance. She glanced up. Josef was examining her wall, rubbing his fingers along it.

"Is there a problem?" she said.

"Is old," he said. "The plaster. Get wavy and then crack. Strip away, re-plaster, beautiful."

"Is it cracked now?"

"Soon. Few years it start to crack."

"Good. I can live with it for a few years. And when it starts to crack, I can live with it for a few years more."

"The wiring," said Josef. "When you do the rewiring?"

"Josef. Please, I—"

She was interrupted by the doorbell ringing. As soon as she opened the door and saw Karlsson's face, she knew it wasn't good news.

"We haven't found her," said Karlsson.

"Then what are you doing here?"

"Thank you, Frieda. It's good to see you too. I have to meet Petra and the acting commissioner and then I'll go back. I've got twenty minutes, enough to let you know the news, or lack of news, and pick up a sandwich."

"You can eat something here," said Frieda.

Karlsson's face fell when he saw the contents of the fridge.

"I can go around the corner and get something," said Frieda.

"Don't worry. I don't need much."

Karlsson made himself a sandwich with cheese and a tomato. It didn't look particularly appetizing but he consumed it in a few bites, almost desperately. He took a gulp of water from the glass on the table, then noticed Frieda's drawing.

"Sorry. It's your still life."

"It doesn't matter. Tell me about your morning."

"There is that abandoned warehouse. Redevelopment is supposedly under way but I couldn't see any sign of it. We've been over it and we didn't find anything."

"Did you find any signs that someone's been there?"

"What's a sign? It's been abandoned for years, and people get inside one way or another. It could be kids playing there or down-and-outs looking for somewhere to sleep or thieves looking for some scrap metal. Basically there's crap everywhere but nothing that seemed relevant."

"So you can definitely eliminate that place as some-where where Yvette is being held?"

"You sound like a lawyer."

"It's an important question."

Karlsson thought for a moment. "I've got two answers. The first is, no, we can't definitely eliminate it. It's bloody enormous, like a town not a single building, and there aren't many of us. There are hundreds and hundreds of little rooms. I'm sure there are little storage spaces we didn't check, cellars, gaps between the walls. We'll keep looking but I don't think she's there. It's like a building site, sur-rounded by wires and gates and CCTV cameras. A couple of teenagers could get in. Blackstock could get in on his own. I just can't imagine him trying it with Yvette, con-scious or unconscious."

Frieda flinched, even at the mention of the name. "So what's your plan?"

"The plan is for me to go to this meeting, then get back to supervising the team. We'll look in the other warehouses, in the old factories, anywhere deserted, and then we'll keep looking. Probably we'll take another day or so and then we'll have to change strategy."

"What does that mean?"

"Stop the secrecy. Announce that a policewoman has been kidnapped, go to the media, put her photograph ev-erywhere."

"You know what you're risking?" said Frieda.

"Is it more of a risk than this? Another day of being held captive somewhere, in conditions we can't imagine. If we put her photo out there, somebody might have seen some-thing or heard something or suspect something. Just be-cause it's the traditional strategy doesn't make it wrong."

*

When Karlsson was gone, she and Josef looked at each other.

"What?" said Frieda.

"I wait for you to do something. Or say something."

"All right, Josef, so what have we got?"

"I the one who ask you that first."

"The photograph," Frieda said.

"What?"

Frieda took out her phone and placed it on the table. She sat down and drew up another chair next to her for Josef to sit on. She clicked through to the photograph of Chloë, drugged, captive, splayed on the mattress. "There," she said.

"What is this?" said Josef, drawing back, his face horrified.

Frieda explained about the picture, how she had got it, how she had copied it before handing it to Petra Burge.

Josef groaned and put his head into his hands. "Is terrible. Terrible. Young Chloë."

"Don't think about that," said Frieda. "That's not what's important. Is there anything in that picture that can help us?"

Josef lifted his head. "Like help how?"

Frieda stared at the picture so hard that it almost hurt. "I had a hope that we might be able to see what direction the light is coming from and that might give us some clue about where it is." She looked around at Josef. He was frowning.

"I no think so," he said.

"Don't be so stupid," said Frieda.

"What?"

"I'm talking to me, not you. The direction of the light source wouldn't tell us anything useful and there's no obvious light source in the picture anyway. It just looks gray and blank. There's just a mattress and a blurry gray background." Frieda enlarged the image and then enlarged it again, as far as it would go, and the image became grainier and grainer. "I was hoping we'd see some sort of maker's name on the mattress," she said. "And that it would turn out to be very rare."

"No name," said Josef.

Frieda used her finger to move the image around. "So what are we looking at? A mattress like any other mattress. And behind it an out-of-focus background, which is probably a bit of floor and wall. What we'd like is a window with a glimpse of a famous landmark outside. What we've got is a blurry gray background with a couple of little blurry white patches, which look like rough licks of paint."

"Is plasterboard," said Josef. "Gypsum."

"So what's that?"

"Is board for the room." He got up and rapped his knuckles on the wall and shook his head. "No. Is brick here." He reached up and rapped on the ceiling. There was a hollow sound. "Is the plasterboard. Cover everything, keep out the fire. Is flat, easy. Then you put on the paint, the wallpaper."

"I hope you're going to tell me that you're an expert on gypsum plasterboard, that you can tell me exactly what kind it is."

Josef shook his head. "No. The plasterboard is the plasterboard."

"Could the plasterboard be in a building like the one Karlsson has been searching?"

"Is possible."

"Josef, you've got to help me out here. Before, that photograph told us nothing that Daniel Blackstock didn't want to tell us. Now we've found one thing. That's our finger hold."

Josef made a helpless gesture. "Frieda, I want to help. I want to find Yvette. But every job I do, every room has the plasterboard, on the walls, on the ceiling, on the floor."

There was a long pause as Josef and Frieda stared at each other. "We can do better than this," she said finally. "When this huge building has been turned into offices or luxury flats and they are being offered for sale, at that point there will be no visible plasterboard. Right?"

"Then is covered."

"Right. And Karlsson said that the building he was searching was still littered with stuff from kids messing around. In a project like that, what would you have to do before putting up plasterboard?"

"Much," said Josef. "Big, big clear-out. The structure engineering, the plumbing, the electrics. The plasterboard near the end."

"Good," said Frieda. "That's very good. So you're not going to have new plasterboard in an old abandoned shed or cellar or lock-up or abandoned warehouse. You put up the plasterboard at a fairly late stage, just before the decoration, right?"

Josef gave a shrug. "Is possible."

"I think they're looking in the wrong place," said Frieda.

"So what you do?"

"We're going to Silvertown."

56

First, she called Petra.

"There's no news," said Petra. "I'll let you know if I hear anything."

"I think they're looking in the wrong place."

"Where should they be looking? Tell me."

The question wasn't hostile: Frieda could hear from Petra's voice that she was in a state of hyper-alertness. She could picture her tense, narrow shoulders, her thin face and her pale eyes.

"I don't know," she said. "But there's something . . ." She let the sentence trail away. She had nothing except Josef's knowledge of plasterboard.

"If you have anything, anything at all, give it to me."

"I will. Is he under surveillance right now?"

"Yes."

"Are you sure he hasn't given them the slip?"

"I came off the phone to the officers a minute ago."

"Blackstock's been in custody, then under surveillance for nearly three days now."

"Yes."

"So if Yvette is alive she's been alone, probably without water."

"Probably."

*

As they walked toward Josef's van, Frieda made another call. "Chloë?"

"Yes. Has anything happened?"

"Where are you?"

"I'm at work. What's up? Has—"

"I want you to go to Silvertown."

"Silvertown? Near City Airport?"

"Now. I'll explain when I see you."

"All right," said Chloë. She sounded wary, perhaps scared. "But it might take a bit of time. I'll get the Tube to Tottenham Hale, then take the Overground. Give me an hour at least, probably longer."

"Take a cab."

"What's going on, Frieda?"

"Call when you're nearly there."

"They're watching both of us," said Daniel Blackstock "You understand?"

Lee stared at him.

"I said, do you understand?"

"Yes." The word was more like a sob. "But I don't know what's happening. Everything's so awful. What's happening?"

Daniel looked at his wife. Her skin was clammy and she had pouches under her eyes. Her hair was greasy. He saw that there was eczema on her wrists and the inside of her elbows. He could feel his heart jumping and his blood coursing through him and his skin twitching, as if thousands of insects were crawling across it. He forced himself to be still and calm. He took one of her hands, which was large and soft and lay in his without moving.

"Lee," he said, trying to make his voice tender, though

she was so heavy and inert and he wanted to hit her, shake her, push her away from him. "Lee, my love."

"Yes?"

"You know I said how it was you and me against the world?"

She nodded.

"That's how it's always been, hasn't it? You're my partner. We protect each other, right?"

After a long pause, she nodded again. He put a hand under her chin. "I can trust you, can't I?"

"Yes," she whispered. A fat tear trickled down her cheek and onto his hand.

"And you've already crossed a line, you know that." A pause. He said again, louder, "You know that. Don't you?"

Another nod.

"So they're watching both of us. But me much more than you." He took his hand from her chin and stroked her face gently. "So I'm going to tell you what to do." He smiled at her, a vein ticking in his neck. "And then you're going to do it."

"I'm outside the station," said Chloë.

"We're nearly there."

"I don't have enough money for the cab driver and he's getting rather cross."

"I'll pay him as soon as we arrive. I can see you now."

Chloë was standing beside the minicab, dressed in baggy canvas shorts and a singlet. Josef pulled over and Frieda got out and paid the driver, who counted the money suspiciously before driving off.

"This is where he lives, isn't it?" asked Chloë, as she and Frieda waited for Josef to park his van.

"Near here."

"And this is the area where you think I was kept?"

"Yes."

"So why is it so urgent for me to be here?"

"To help find Yvette."

"How can I?" Chloë's voice rose almost to a shout. "What do you think I can do? I know what you want: you want me to think myself back into that room and to remember something. Do you think I haven't tried? Do you think I don't try and remember every day?"

"Perhaps you try to remember and at the same time try not to," said Frieda.

"It's a blank, Frieda." Chloë clutched at her hair. "I can't magically put myself back there."

"I thought that being here, in the place where it happened, might help."

"What—that I might *sense* something? *Feel* it?" Chloë wrinkled her nose.

"That's right."

"This is insane." Chloë stared helplessly around her, at the people, the buildings, the cars and vans and motorbikes going past in the dusty heat of the day. Three bedraggled pigeons landed by her feet and started pecking at something on the pavement. "What am I supposed to do?"

Josef came toward them. "Where we go?" he asked.

Frieda looked at the two of them, then pointed. "Those huge buildings over there," she said. "That's where the police are looking. They'll probably go into the old factory after that. But I believe Yvette is being held in a newer building. Some new development, perhaps, but one that's not quite finished." She heard her words: there was so little to go on.

"Perhaps," said Josef.

"It must be standing empty, and it can't be a place where anyone is actually working at the moment. Maybe a project that's been abandoned—God knows there are enough of those around."

She opened up her *A–Z* and put her finger on a grid of roads. A plane flew overhead, coming to land and so close they could almost feel its heat.

"We're here." She drew her finger in a circle. "And this is the area we are going to search. OK?"

"Why?" asked Chloë.

"What do you mean?"

"Why there? Why that particular circle? Why not there?" She jabbed angrily. "Or there? Why not a larger circle?"

"Because this is where Daniel Blackstock lives." Frieda put a finger on his road. "I am treating his house as the center of the circle. And the circle is this big because that is the amount of ground we can reasonably cover today."

"That's it? That's all you've got?"

Lee Blackstock left the house. The Stanley knife was in her shoulder bag: it was the one she had stabbed over and over again into her husband's hand. She remembered how the blood had bubbled up on his skin, but the feeling of excitement had gone. She was cold in spite of the heat and felt slightly queasy. Her eyes ached in the sun's glare.

She walked slowly down the road, not looking around. There would be someone following her, Daniel had said, but just one person and it would be child's play to lose them. He'd told her what to do, staring at her in the hot, impatient way that made her skin prickle.

First, into the shops. She bought a tin of tuna in the first.

She would make a tuna bake for supper, although it seemed impossible that they would sit down and eat a meal together. She walked into the newsagent's, picked up magazines and put them back, then out again. Then she started walking toward the Thames Barrier Park, still quite slow, her neck aching with the effort of not looking back. Giant cranes hung above her, unmoving. The Thames was sluggish, like something in a bad dream. The grass was parched, the leaves dark and limp on the trees.

Daniel had said that as she turned the corner by the entrance there would be a gap in the privet hedge that fringed the park that she could slip through and, sure enough, there it was. She went through it, stumbling in her haste, and now she was in the sunken garden, among the shrubs. There were lines of lavender bushes and other herbs, and the dry fragrance made her fear she would start coughing. She could hear footsteps passing by and she scarcely dared to breathe. She began to walk along the hidden path in the direction she had come from, fast now and almost at a jog, her bag bumping uncomfortably on her shoulder. In a few minutes she was back on the main road, among the crowds. She went into the first shop she came across. It was a DIY store, and she walked through aisles of paints, her breath coming in rasps that hurt her chest.

Standing by the tool section, she took out the map that Daniel had given her and worked out her route to the point he had marked with a cross. When she'd memorized it she put it back into her bag, wiped her sweating palms down her skirt and stepped back out into the busy street.

57

"I tell you," said Chloë, angry so that she wouldn't be distressed, "I'm feeling nothing, I'm sensing nothing. I don't think I've ever been here before but that means nothing either. I don't know what you expect from me."

They were standing on a small road that looped around a central patch of lawn with one tree planted at its center. All the houses were brand new, some with curtains at their windows and cars in the parking spaces, though with muddy, rutted earth where gardens would be, others clearly not yet completed. The day was still hot but the sun was getting lower in the sky.

"Is not here," said Josef. "Look." He pointed at a house several doors down, where two men in hard hats were perched on the roof. "People come and go. Is not possible."

"You're right." Frieda pulled out the *A–Z* once more. "So we've been here." Her finger described their route. "Now we'll go this way. OK?"

"What's the point?" said Chloë. "I'm just trailing after you. I don't know what you expect from me."

Frieda looked intently at her niece. Then she took out her phone. "Look at the photograph again."

"I don't need to. I see it whenever I close my eyes."

"Please."

Josef walked away and stood with his back to Chloë, pretending to be absorbed in the pitch of the roofs.

Chloë wrinkled her face in a grimace. "All right."

Frieda handed across her phone. Chloë gazed at the image of herself lying spread-eagled on the stained mattress. She stared at it for a long time, quite expressionless, then handed it back.

"It's like looking at a stranger," she said. "I can almost feel that mattress under me. Or feel myself trying to open my eyes but the lids are so heavy I can't. And a smell."

"Yes?"

"I don't know. That's it."

"All right. You tried."

As they walked, her mobile rang. She pulled it from her pocket and saw that Petra was calling.

"Yes?"

"I thought you should know. We've lost sight of Lee Blackstock."

"How the hell could you let that happen?"

"I'm as angry as you are."

Frieda paused. She didn't know what to say.

"What about Daniel? Have you lost him as well?"

"He's going on long circular walks."

"He knows he's being watched."

"Maybe."

"He knows."

The moment had come at last and he had planned what to do. But just as he was readying himself, his mobile rang. He saw the name on the screen: Suzie Harriman, the journalist from the press agency who was always being given the stories that should belong to him. His chest tightened and he was about to cut off the call, then changed his mind.

"Suzie," he said.

"Daniel." Her voice was breathy. "I'm so glad I've got hold of you. I'm writing a story about domestic violence and of course with all your expertise you're the very person who can help me to—"

"No."

"What?"

"I am never going to help you again." He had a feeling of freedom and exaltation. "Because you're a shallow, ignorant cunt. Flashing your tits around the office. I wouldn't fuck you if I was paid to do it."

He stopped and waited but there was silence. She'd ended the call.

For a moment, anger burned in him and the world seemed to sway. He took several deep breaths. That hadn't felt as good as it should have done. But he mustn't let himself be diverted: he had a task.

He walked at a steady pace. He knew they were behind him, but a fair way off, and probably bored because of all the fruitless walks he'd led them on over the past days. The Docklands Light Railway was on his right and he could see a small red train clattering toward him. Between him and it were expanses of wasteland, the slabs of paving split through and grown over by brambles and nettles and head-high weeds; the old rotting buildings where litter was piled high, smashed-up hulks of rusting cars, heaps of tires, a remnant of a London bus turned on its side. He'd walked there many times, watching the gulls peck at the heaps of rubbish.

He turned the corner. This was his chance. He took his

mobile from his canvas bag and dropped it into the ditch, then took a deep breath, feeling it rip through his chest, and scrambled over the fence into the neglected area. He felt pain shoot through him as he landed, one knee giving way, a whimper coming from him. But he ran, bent low, to the shed where dozens of fridges with ripped-off doors and beaten-up washing machines were stacked. He'd gone over this as he lay in bed at night, open-eyed beside Lee, or when he walked the streets, followed by the officers on his tail. He knew every move, so he didn't have to think. Through the long shed, at a run, a foot kicking something soft—he didn't want to think what that might have been—out the other end where the walls had given way. Now he wasn't visible from the road. Past the great mountain of half-crushed cars and vans, seeing without seeing their ripped seats and smashed windows, the plants growing out of their innards. Down the steep incline and along the row of trees. He looked back, half expecting to see them just behind him, but there was no one. He ran toward the line of disused factories, their shadow falling over him so that he was suddenly cold in spite of the sweat pouring down his face.

For a moment, beside a pile of coal, he stopped to catch his breath. Again, he glanced back and saw no one. Ahead was Pontoon Dock station. He took a baseball cap and a blue top from the bag and put them on. He took the pay-as-you-go phone from the bag as well and put it into his pocket. He'd thought of everything—even a new Oyster card, bought with cash. Although soon, of course, none of that would matter.

Then he went up the bank and through the undergrowth and came to the station. He straightened himself. He slid his hands into his pockets. He even tried to whistle but his mouth was quivering and his lips were so dry he couldn't manage it. The train arrived, he climbed on and pressed his face against the window.

Lee had been walking more and more slowly. She had a raw blister on the heel of one foot and sweat had gathered under her breasts and in the small of her back. Now she stopped, for this was the place. This was the place and this was the time. Soon it would all be over. Once she had tried to kill a rabbit with myxomatosis that was dragging itself along the road outside their house. She had picked up a brick and stood over it, but it had looked at her with its bleeding blind eyes and she hadn't been able to do it.

She sat down on a low wall, put her arms around herself and closed her eyes. She stayed like that for several minutes, rocking herself slightly. Then she opened her eyes and put her hand into the bag to touch the Stanley knife and the longer one, the one that would do the damage. This was really going to happen.

Frieda and Josef had done this once before, walking around a maze of interconnecting streets in search of a lost boy. They were silent, both of them looking, pondering, alert for some kind of sign. Chloë lagged behind them, her feet hot in their boots, not looking outwards at the rows of new houses and the building sites and the fences with large signs telling people to keep out, but inward. She was thinking of the photograph of herself lying on the mattress with her legs apart and her dress up to her thighs, and she was trying to put herself back in that room.

They had come to a crossroads with houses radiating

out in all directions: small, square, red-brick and identical, each with a garage and a tiny front garden.

"Which way?" asked Josef.

Frieda gazed around her. Her face was blank, her eyes dark. She pointed left. "That way."

It was quite deserted. The sounds of the world—the cars on the main road, the plane rumbling high above her—seemed very far off, like a dream, of normal life. The door was fastened with a large lock that Daniel must have fixed on and padlocked, but Lee had the key. She took it out of her bag, her hand trembling and her fingers thick so that she dropped it and had to grope for it on the gritty earth. At last she unlocked the door and gave a small push. It swung open and she stepped inside.

The oppressive heat, the musty smell of a house closed up and unaired, of raw brick dust and sawdust, and something else: another smell. What was it? Fear clogged her throat: what would she find when she went up the stairs to the room on the right?

"This is possible," said Josef.

There was a plane high above it, spooling out its vapor trail in the flat blue of the sky.

"You think so?"

"These houses just left alone," said Josef. "Nobody come here."

"How can you tell?"

"Builders leave marks," said Josef. "No trucks come here. No scaffolding. Nothing."

They were standing at the end of a cul-de-sac, looking at a development of houses that were brand new, yet at the same time seemed neglected and abandoned. They stood in their individual plots of churned-up baked mud, their windows uncurtained and blank, their parking spaces unfilled.

"Many sites like this," said Josef. "We need many houses. Here are houses. But building companies . . ." And he made a dismissive gesture with his hand.

"They go bankrupt?"

"That is it."

"Let's look."

Josef nonchalantly smashed through the door of the first with his foot.

"Cheapest wood," he said contemptuously. "Like plywood."

Frieda put a hand on Chloë's arm. "All right?"

Chloë's face was chalky. She bit her lower lip. "I think . . ." she began.

"What?"

"The smell."

Josef gave a loud sniff. "Many houses smell like this. Cheap bricks and cheap wood, is it."

"You remember?" asked Frieda, urgently.

"Maybe. Yes. Yes, I do."

"Good. Well done. Now we need to search all these houses. Quickly."

Lee went up the stairs like an invalid, one foot on the step, then drawing the other foot up beside it. There wasn't a sound save for the faint tap of her shoes and her labored breathing. She stood outside the door on the left, listened and heard nothing. She pressed it with her fingers and it eased open an inch. The smell was stronger here, as if something was decaying. The light was dim: Daniel must have covered the window.

She pushed the door open further and she stepped inside.

"This is not good," said Josef, after the third house. He looked up the road. "There are many houses, Frieda."

"It's one of these. It must be. We have to separate. Is that all right with you, Chloë?"

Chloë nodded. Her lips were bloodless. "Yes," she said.

Frieda looked at Josef, who was staring ahead, his hand shielding his eyes. "What?"

"Look." He pointed. "The house up there."

"Yes?"

To Frieda it looked just the same as every other house.

"The upstairs window. You see?"

"It looks different," said Frieda slowly. "It's not glinting."

"Is covered. Someone puts something over it."

And now they were running down the road, the three of them together.

58

"Call Petra," Frieda said.

"I don't have the number."

Frieda handed her phone to Chloë. "You'll find it there. Stay outside for them."

They stood in front of the house. To Frieda it looked the same as its neighbors, but Josef shook his head. "Lock is different," he said. "Is changed."

"Can you get in?" said Frieda.

Josef gave something like a laugh and raised his foot and kicked at the door, then once more and there was a crack and the door swung inward. He ran up the stairs, Frieda close behind him. He turned at the top of the stairs and ran toward the front of the house. The door was shut. They both looked at it. Frieda moved to open it. Josef held her back and pointed to himself. Frieda shook her head. She turned the handle as softly as she could and pushed the door inward. It was dark. Josef stepped forward and moved his hand inside, feeling for the light switch. There was a click and the room was illuminated. Frieda pushed past Josef. There was a shape on the far side, against the wall, and it took her a moment to make sense of it.

"Ambulance," she said to Josef. "Now."

She stepped toward the shape, a hooded figure, seated

on the floor, back against the wall. Frieda tried to take it all in. Something around the neck, some sort of ligature. Hands tied together with wire. Blue T-shirt with dark patches, oozing blood. On the body's right side, high up above the breast, a knife-handle protruding, the blade sunk deep into the flesh.

Frieda knelt down and pulled the hood off and saw what she was expecting to see, though so thin it was barely recognizable: Yvette's pale, sweaty, dirty face, spotted in sores, eyes staring wide and huge in their sunken sockets. Her mouth was covered with masking tape. She gave a groan that seemed to come from somewhere deep inside. Frieda put her hand to Yvette's cheek and stroked it. There was a smell of the filthy, emaciated body decaying. Mortal flesh.

"Yvette. I'm here. Listen to me. I'm going to pull the tape off. It will hurt, just for a moment."

Frieda knew that she had to do this but she also knew that Yvette was bleeding. She didn't know how seriously. The wrong movement could do even more damage. She put her left hand against Yvette's forehead, holding it firmly against the wall. With her right hand she tried to get some purchase on the tape. With her thumbnail she managed to ease a corner of it away until she could grip it between her thumb and forefinger. She pulled it sharply away.

"Take it slowly," said Frieda. "Just stay calm. I'm here. We're all here. You're safe."

Yvette opened her mouth, but the wire around her neck was so tight that she couldn't speak.

Frieda looked around at Josef. "Have you got anything to cut this?"

Josef reached into his jacket and took out what looked like a large penknife. He unfolded it, so that it became a pair of miniature clippers. His hands were rough and reddened with work, but he reached around behind Yvette's head with extraordinary delicacy. There was a sharp sound and he was able to peel the wire away from her neck. She immediately began to cough.

"I can't see," said Yvette, her voice sounding scratchy.

"It's the light," said Frieda. "You've been in the dark so long. Just wait a moment. Your eyes need to get used to it."

Yvette took several deep breaths before she spoke next, and it seemed to take a great effort. "She's here."

"What? Who's here?"

"She was saying things and hitting me." It came out on a broken sob. "Hitting and hitting."

Frieda saw the spreading bloodstains on Yvette's shirt. There was also blood dripping from her forearm, as if she had raised her arms to ward off the blow. Frieda knew—knew from her own experience—that being stabbed felt like being punched. Frieda turned to Josef.

"I go check," he said, and left the room.

Frieda looked more carefully at Yvette's injuries. There was no spurting, no pulsing of any of the wounds. That was something. She leaned in close again.

"Yvette, can you see me yet?"

Yvette nodded slightly, as though the movement hurt her shrunken neck. Her face was smeared and dirty, her hair matted.

"I'm here. Josef is here. You're safe."

"No," said Yvette, in a sort of sob. "No."

"You are." Frieda talked to Yvette in a soothing tone, as if she were a child scared of the dark. "You're safe. But you've been hurt. You're bleeding. I'm going to check you to see how things are, all right? It's important that you stay where you are, keep sitting up, and people will be here to help you any minute."

Josef came back into the room.

"Back door is open. Yard behind go into street behind. That where they park car. Bring Yvette in. Bring Chloë in."

"We'll talk about that later," said Frieda. "That knife thing of yours, does it have scissors?"

"Little ones. Small."

"Yvette. How are you feeling?"

"Tired. Really tired."

Now Frieda spoke in a louder, more urgent tone: "That's fine, but what you're going to do now is to keep talking to us. It's important that you stay alert. Do you understand?" Yvette gave a murmur. "No, Yvette, you've got to say that in words. I know it's hard, but you've got to say the words: I understand."

"I understand." Yvette's eyes stared. Her tongue was thick in her mouth. How long was it since she had had any water?

"And now I'm going to cut your shirt off, so that I can look at you properly. Is that all right? Say yes if that's all right."

"Yes."

Yvette sounded as if she were about to go to sleep. She mustn't go to sleep. Frieda took the tool from Josef. First she cut the wire holding Yvette's hands together and they fell limply to her sides. Then she cut right through the middle of the T-shirt from the bottom up to the neck. She carefully pulled the two sides of the shirt aside, making sure not to touch or move the knife. Blood had dripped down onto the light blue bra, but there were no wounds underneath on Yvette's breasts. It was as if Lee Blackstock had avoided them out of some kind of compunction, some hesitation. Frieda could see three wounds in the stomach. They were bleeding, so much that the blood was pooling in Yvette's lap. Even so, it was a good sign. The knife hadn't hit an artery or a major vein. It was difficult to tell, but it didn't look as if these stomach wounds were deep. Frieda imagined Lee jabbing at Yvette's body, as if working up the resolve to really plunge the knife in. She must have been disturbed by the sounds from the street. If not, she would have done it again and again and they would have found Yvette dead.

"It's looking all right," said Frieda. "Can you hear me? Say yes if you can hear me."

"Am I going to die?" said Yvette, in a slow, dreamy tone.

"No, you're not going to die. Don't even say that."

She turned her attention to the knife handle, projecting obscenely from Yvette's body. Josef followed her gaze.

"I pull it out?" he said.

"No, no. Don't even touch it. You might do more damage. It could be pressing against an artery. You've got to think of it like . . ." She looked at Yvette. She didn't want to frighten her. "It might be stopping something worse happening. It needs to stay where it is."

"What?" said Yvette, sounding far away.

"We've been checking you over," said Frieda. "You're injured but so far as we can see the wounds are not serious."

"How you feel?" asked Josef.

"Are you here too?" said Yvette. "Always together. Frieda and Josef. Josef and Frieda. I used to think you'd be a couple."

"Stop this," said Josef, hastily. "Rest now. Don't speak."

"No," said Frieda. "She needs to keep talking."

"She's wrong in the head."

"I was going away. On the train. Walking on my own."

"Where were you going?" asked Frieda.

"To Scotland. There was a ring at the door. He was there. I saw his face. So I knew then. And I knew he'd kill me. I knew I was going to die."

"But you aren't."

"I've not been a good person, Frieda. Not been a good friend."

Frieda heard the sound of a siren and then a blue light flashing in the window, voices. She shouted to Josef. "Show them up."

He clattered down the stairs. Frieda took Yvette's hands in hers. "Darling Yvette. We all just do what we can."

Frieda could feel and hear the heavy footsteps on the stairs. The house was shaking with them. And then the room seemed full of people in green uniforms. A tall, strongly built woman crouched beside Yvette.

"Serious blood loss," said Frieda. "And you can see we've left the weapon in place. She's been held captive. She's severely dehydrated and malnourished."

"All right," said the woman. "Stand away."

Frieda stepped back until she felt the wall. Suddenly Yvette looked small and lost beneath the paramedics leaning over her, talking to each other in loud voices. Frieda watched with concern as they connected her to two separate drips, which they suspended above her.

"Dying?" said Josef, close by, murmuring into Frieda's ear. "But she is strong and fighting, I think."

"Sometimes being strong and fighting is no help," said

Frieda. Josef's expression changed but Frieda shook her head and made an attempt at a smile. "But I don't think she's dying."

Frieda heard a muffled sob beside her. Chloë had come inside with the paramedics.

"I told you to stay outside," she said, but not angrily.

"I couldn't. I had to see where . . . Is this it?"

"Yes. This is it."

Chloë looked at the scene in front of her. "What did they . . ."

And then she started to cry. Frieda folded her into her arms.

Now the room was even more crowded, blue uniforms as well as green. Frieda suddenly felt almost faint in this blur of sound and vision.

"You found her," said a voice beside her.

Frieda looked around and saw Petra. "You need to find the Blackstocks. Both of them."

Lee fumbled for her phone. "They're here," she said.

"What do you mean?" said her husband.

"I saw them on the street. Frieda. That friend of hers. And the niece. Chloë."

"Where are you?"

"I got out. I had to get out."

"Course you did. Are you safe?"

"I think so."

"Did you do it?"

"I think so."

"What do you mean?"

"It was hard. Harder than I thought. I did what I could. There was blood everywhere. I got it on me."

"Good girl."

"But it's all gone wrong. They're here. They know about you. And me." She gave a small moan. "We're finished."

"It had to end this way. But we're not finished."

"How can I find you?"

"Not now. I've got to do something first."

"What?"

"It's better that you don't know anything."

"But what do I do? Where do I go?"

"You'll be fine," said Daniel. He sounded indifferent. "Just don't go anywhere you normally go. Get yourself something to eat. See a film."

"A film!" She was bewildered. Panic rose in her, like a filthy tide.

"Enjoy yourself."

"Daniel, I'm frightened."

"There's nothing to be frightened of. You'll be fine. We'll be fine."

"When will I see you?"

"I'll find you. When I'm done."

59

Daniel had always known that this time would come. He was in the endgame, but he could still win. After that, they could do what they liked and it wouldn't matter. He would be justified.

So Lee had done it. Who would have thought it? She had been the weak link in his plans, but she'd held together in the end, and now she'd outlived her usefulness. He wondered what would happen to her, when they would find her, but idly, for it seemed now that his old world and his old self were dissolving away, and all that remained was what was here and now. This was his moment—like standing in a spotlight, with darkness all around its bright circle. He, Daniel Blackstock.

He had got off the train at Bank and taken the Underground to the Angel, Islington. When Lee had called he had been sitting by the canal, near the tunnel. On one side of him a man with a long straggly beard, wearing a combat jacket, was fishing with fanatical patience. On the other, a man wearing eye shadow and a purple cape was smoking a joint and singing to himself dreamily.

People walked past in groups or singly. Runners plugged into their earphones; cyclists; dog-walkers. A boat chugged by. The two women and three men on a deck were drinking wine and dancing to music he couldn't hear. The sun was low in the sky. Soon it would be twilight. Soon it would be night.

Daniel stood up and brushed himself down. He put his phone back in his pocket. He threw his baseball cap into the water. He opened the canvas bag and made sure everything was there: Yvette Long's police ID; a length of coiled rope; several screwdrivers; a knife. He had spent long enough in Saffron Mews to know which buildings would give access to her yard. He needed only to wave Yvette's ID in people's faces and they'd let him through. And if the place was already crawling with police, he would improvise, like he had all the way. Look at what he'd done, how he'd come through, quick-witted and always thinking on his feet, making the plot up as he went along. He had written story after story about the crime that he himself had committed. He had been its director and its star and its publicist. He had snatched Chloë from under the nose of her friends. He'd taken Yvette Long, who was a police officer, and all those people whose job it was to find out such a thing hadn't even noticed she was missing. He had wiped that smile off Reuben McGill's face. He'd done for Morgan Rossiter for good, like snuffing out a candle. He'd stamped on young Jack's hand until he had heard the bones crack and, at the same time, made himself an alibi that had foxed them all. No, not foxed her, but that was all. He let himself remember the way she looked at him with her dark eyes; looked into him, looked through him.

But I am not nothing, he thought. Look at me. Look. Here I am. No escape for her. No escape from me.

He lifted himself up onto the balls of his feet, then down again. He flexed his shoulders. His heart was beating loudly but quite steadily; his breathing seemed normal. He wiped his palms down his shorts and started to walk. Like a soldier walks: one two, one two, arms swinging, feet slapping on the hot ground, chin up, eyes ahead, looking for danger and seeing none. Past the homeless men and women, past the Canada geese with their outstretched necks, through Camden Lock and the thick throng of drinkers, glistening with summer excitement.

He didn't stop. If someone was in his way he barged them aside, spilling their beer, making them shout out crossly. Some looked curiously at the small man, who was smiling as he pushed into them, whose eyes were fixed ahead on nothing, and who walked like an automaton.

Far from him, Lee Blackstock sat huddled in the thick undergrowth. She hadn't moved since she had talked to Daniel on the phone. Perhaps, she thought, she would sit there all night and darkness would come and the stars would shine above her, and all the time she could watch the river ripple past in the distance. But then it would be morning again and what would she do? What would she ever do?

The grass scratched against her bare legs and she looked down and saw blood. On her calf. On her left forearm. Perhaps there was some on her face. She licked the tips of her fingers and rubbed her cheeks and forehead. She felt hollow with hunger but nauseous as well. Maybe this was what morning sickness was like, but she would never have a baby now. It was all she had ever wanted: her own baby to hold and look after; to love and be loved. But Daniel had always said—she squeezed her eyes shut. She didn't want to think of Daniel. Or of that woman on the floor and what it had felt like stabbing and hacking at her flesh and blood everywhere and the eyes staring up at her.

She rubbed at the patch of blood on her leg but it was sticky and wouldn't come off. She scratched it away but now the blood was under her nails. She needed to wash, to change out of her clothes, to sleep. But where could she go? Not home. It wasn't home any more: just a little box where she and Daniel had lived. The police would be there now. They'd be trampling across her clean floor, looking at everything, opening drawers, putting hands among her underwear, her little bits and pieces.

She looked at the phone lying in her lap. He wouldn't call again. He didn't care. He had never cared, and she had always known that really. Now he was gone and here she was, just her, alone among the shrubs and weeds and darkness growing around her. She pulled her legs up and put her arms around them; she put her head on her knees. She waited, but waited for nothing.

There was a sound above her and she looked up: a police helicopter was hovering. Was it searching for her? She held her breath and remained quite still, not a movement, though her limbs were quivering with terror and her chest was sharp with pain. At last it moved on, drawing the light with it. She let out her breath.

She looked at her phone: it was past nine o'clock. She could call someone, beg for help, weep and confess and ask what she should do. Who could she call? Perhaps the woman at the residential home who came from Turkey. She couldn't speak much English but she seemed friendly. But Lee didn't even have her number.

She had no one. She had nothing. She was no one, nothing, never. She was over.

Lee Blackstock stood up. She put her phone in her bag and walked down the slope toward the river. The helicopter was far off now, like a toy. Still holding her bag, she walked into the Thames.

Nobody had ever taught her to swim. The water was cold, and then it wasn't so cold any more and it closed over her heavy, sad body, and for a while the body tried to save itself. But soon the struggle was over and what had been Lee Blackstock was carried east with the outgoing tide.

Daniel Blackstock kept walking: around the corner and past the floating Chinese restaurant; under the bridge. The day was dimming. Ahead he could see the aviary of London Zoo, and large birds circling under its vaulted netting. He turned off the canal and was now on the edge of Regent's Park. Cars, buses, bikes. He stepped into the road and heard horns blaring. He saw the sun on the horizon, like a dark yolk. He heard someone laughing. A fresh wind was blowing and it cooled the sweat on his face and made him feel strong and ready. The world was rushing into him.

Screwdriver. Rope. Knife. He saw her face before him. Cool face, watching eyes. How dare she look at him like that? Who was she, after all, but the woman he was going to kill?

He was quite near her house now, just a mile or so away. The little house in the cobbled mews, with herbs in a pot and a tortoiseshell cat. He imagined her when she realized he had come for her.

Left, right, left right. "Left, left, you had a good home and you left. Right, right, it serves you jolly well right." No stopping now. Traffic roaring, the hot fumes of exhaust on his legs, and then a curved road where there was silence. He could see the Post Office Tower. Great cranes against the sky.

Just a few minutes away. He put his shoulders back and felt a tear trickle down his cheek.

There was a van parked on the road in front of him, and as he approached, the door opened. A figure got out, but because the sun was behind it, Daniel couldn't see the face. Just a cutout blocking his path.

"Daniel," said the figure.

"What?" said Daniel, and then he understood.

"I knew you'd find me," he said. "We're together now."

But before he had finished speaking, everything went black.

60

"I don't agree," said Frieda.

"Why doesn't that surprise me?" said Petra Burge. "You might as well have 'I don't agree' printed on a card and just hand it to me after everything I say."

"If your team hadn't let Blackstock get away, we wouldn't even be having this conversation."

Karlsson stopped pacing up and down Frieda's kitchen and sat down at the table with the two women. Frieda looked at him with an expression that, even after all these years, he found unsettling.

"I hope you're not going to tell me to calm down," she said.

"My leg's only just recovering. I'm not risking another injury." He gave her a small smile, but his expression was somber. Frieda knew that he was thinking of Yvette, in hospital a few streets away. "But look, Frieda, one thing we know is that Blackstock has nothing to lose. It's almost certain that he'll try to get at you. It's Petra's duty to make sure that doesn't happen. You will be guarded both inside your house and out until further notice. End of."

"But if you're right—and you probably are—when he sees policemen standing outside my door, he'll just bide his time."

"Whereas your plan is what?" said Karlsson. "If you're not guarded, you can draw him out and then we can catch him in the act. Is that it?"

"Before the act."

"You know that plans have a way of going awry."

"He's out there. They're both out there."

"What is it you want?" said Petra, sharply. "Do you think you'll prove something by gambling with your own life? If he got to you and you pressed your panic button or whatever you've got in mind, and we arrived just too late, would that be worth it, sacrificing your life for someone like him? We'll get Daniel and Lee Blackstock the old-fashioned way, by looking and waiting and making inquiries, and it's not very glamorous but it'll work in the end."

"He's not that clever," said Karlsson.

"You don't have to be that clever to kill people," said Frieda. "It's not hard. Blackstock's a pathetic mediocrity, but he killed Morgan Rossiter and he attacked Reuben and Jack. And he kidnapped a police officer and almost killed her. What else is he going to do?"

Suddenly there was a rattling sound. It was Frieda's phone vibrating on the counter next to the cooker. She got up and went over to it.

"Who is it?" said Karlsson.

"It's a number I don't recognize."

Karlsson turned to Petra. "Have you got her phone under surveillance?"

"Not yet."

Frieda looked at them both inquiringly. The phone stopped ringing. "Well, that solves that problem," she said.

"I think you should call the number back," said Petra, picking up the phone. "I'm putting it on speaker, if that's all right." She took her own mobile from her pocket. "I'm going to record it."

"It's probably just someone trying to sell me double-glazing," said Frieda.

"Let's see, then."

Petra put the phone back on the table, in front of Frieda. She placed her mobile beside it. Then she pressed the return-call button on Frieda's phone. All of them leaned forward. Frieda felt they were like three participants in a séance. There was a click from her phone but no other sound. Petra nodded urgently at Frieda.

"Is someone there?" asked Frieda. She was almost angry to feel a tremor in her voice.

"Is that Frieda Klein?" The voice spoke slowly and de-liberately. There was a slight slurring in the speech, but she recognized the speaker immediately.

"Daniel?"

"I've got a message for you. I . . ."

"Where are you?"

There was a pause.

"I've got a message . . ."

"How do I know this is really you? Tell me something about where you are."

Another pause.

"I've got a message for you, Frieda."

Frieda was starting to speak again but Karlsson shook his head and put his finger over his lips.

"I send you flowers. Is that any way to behave?"

Petra, with a puzzled expression, was mouthing a ques-tion. Karlsson took an unopened letter from a pile on the table.

"You send people after me and I send them back to you."

Karlsson was writing on the envelope and then held it up. He had written one word: "Reading." Frieda nodded.

"But I won't send Daniel Blackstock back to you."

He was saying each word separately and slowly. Frieda wondered if he was trying to communicate something. Probably he was just drugged or scared. As she listened, Frieda tried to get some sense of the space in which Daniel Blackstock was. Big or small? Hard surfaces or soft? Any exterior noises? She couldn't make out anything.

"Daniel is a child who has been bothering the grown-ups and we know what happens to bad children."

Frieda gestured despairingly at Karlsson.

"Bruce Stringer told me about his wife. Christine Stringer. Tell Christine that he cried when he told me about her and he cried about his children and then he pleaded for his life. Frieda Klein, Frieda Klein. How could you?"

There was another pause. There was a coughing, snuffling sound.

"I like your house. I like its smell. I like its feel. I'm sorry if I damaged it but I needed to return your property."

Now there was something like a sob in his voice and a groan.

"Where are you?" said Frieda, urgently. "Are you with Dean Reeve? Tell me."

When Daniel Blackstock spoke, the words came even more slowly, as if each one was an effort.

"Frieda Klein, I once told you that it wasn't your time. Why do you not listen? Frieda. Stop fighting. Stop trying. We are all just leaves on a tree and it's nearly September and autumn is coming."

"Stop," said Frieda. "Just let him go. He's got nothing to do with this."

"Frieda, please, I . . ." And now, suddenly, Daniel Black-stock's tone was entirely different, as if for three words it was really him speaking, but then the line went dead. The three of them stared at the phone.

"What the hell was that?" asked Petra.

"I think you can call off the protection," said Frieda.

"That could have been a deception. To make us drop our guard."

"Did it sound like that to you?"

"We still need to find him."

"Daniel Blackstock has been found," said Frieda.

"What was that about 'bad children'?"

"I think that he is going to be punished."

"Like Bruce Stringer?"

"I think worse than Bruce Stringer."

"Punished for what?"

"For barging in where he wasn't wanted." Frieda stood up.

"What are you doing?" Karlsson asked.

"I'm going for a walk."

"I would offer to come along."

"I know. But you need to go to Yvette."

"Can I come?" asked Petra.

"If you want."

"I do."

The two women walked through the streets together. For a long time, they were silent and the shadow of the long day lay over them. At last Petra spoke. "You did well."

Frieda glanced around but didn't reply.

"But it's strange, isn't it, that this should feel like an ending?"

"What do you mean?"

"We met nearly six months ago, when a body was found under your floorboards."

"Yes."

"Then we were looking for Dean Reeve. We found Daniel Blackstock—or you did. But we haven't found Dean Reeve."

"No, we haven't."

"He's still out there."

Frieda nodded. "Yes," she said very softly, looking straight ahead. "He is."

61

He sat by her bed, under the sour glow of the strip lighting. Sometimes he watched her face and sometimes he watched the monitors above her: the line that zigzagged across the screen, sometimes rising in a series of steep peaks and sometimes almost leveling out. There were tubes everywhere, attached to different parts of her body. It would have been hard to hold her hand if that was what he had wanted to do, but he didn't want that. It seemed presumptuous to touch her as she lay unconscious when he'd never touched her before, except for a pat on the shoulder, a grasp of her hand as he helped her through some high entrance or over a wall.

He thought of all that they had done together over the years, the cases they had solved and the ones where they had failed. He thought of her grumpy, clumsy, stalwart presence; her heavy boots and her scowl and the way she blushed. Now she was both Yvette and a stranger. It wasn't just that she was so thin that her face was startlingly changed, all the features enormous, almost cartoonish. It was that without her anxious, self-conscious expression she had become someone he didn't know. Her eyes were closed, her mouth slightly open; her chest rose and fell with her shallow breathing.

Nurses came in and out of the room, but quietly. They

bent over Yvette, looked at the monitors and her charts, checked the little bags that were dripping their contents into her veins, left again. A consultant came in with his junior doctor and they spoke in hushed whispers, then departed. Shortly after Karlsson had arrived, the acting commissioner had paid a visit. She had said little but she had stood at the side of the bed and looked at Yvette for several minutes, her face tight.

At just past three in the morning, Frieda arrived. She pulled up a chair and sat on the other side of Yvette and gazed steadily at her. An hour or so later, Josef came with Reuben and Chloë and Jack. Frieda heard them in the corridor, explaining why they needed to be let in, and then the door opened and they filed into the little room and stood awkwardly at the foot of the bed. Josef, whose stubble was almost a beard and whose face was grimy, pulled a small bottle from his jacket's inner pocket, took a swig, then passed it to Jack, who did the same. Frieda saw that Jack was wearing striped orange and green pajama trousers under his coat and his hair stood up in wild peaks. His left hand was huge in its cast. Chloë had on an old coverall and her face, devoid of makeup, looked bruised with tiredness. In fact, Reuben was the brightest of any of the ramshackle group whose lives Daniel Blackstock had tried to destroy.

"Is she going to be OK?" asked Chloë, in a piercing whisper. "Will she pull through?"

"Don't talk as if she isn't here," said Frieda. "She can probably hear us." She looked back at the figure in the bed. "We're all here," she said. "Waiting for you."

"Come back to us," said Karlsson. His voice was gravelly with fatigue.

*

An hour later Yvette opened her eyes. At first she couldn't see anything, just a harsh light that made her eyes hurt. Then she saw shapes. She wanted to ask who they were but she couldn't form the words. She didn't know where she was, who she was. She tried to remember, but it was like hauling a heavy weight out of a well and it was easier to let it go again. She closed her eyes.

"Yvette."

She knew that voice. She didn't open her eyes but she smiled, though her mouth hurt.

"Yvette," said Karlsson. "My dear friend."

"Friend?" That was her voice, a croak.

"Yes. Of course."

She opened her eyes. She could see him now, her boss and the man she loved, who would never love her. And that was Frieda on the other side. Of course. The two of them. But he had called her his friend. At the foot of her bed were other people. She made a huge effort to focus and saw they were most of that group she had always wanted to join. Frieda's gang.

"Am I dying?"

"No." Frieda took her hand between her own and held it. "Living."

And now Yvette remembered, like a wash of darkness, and with the memory, her body felt the pain and dread again. That knife hacking at her, and the clear understanding that her life hadn't been what she had hoped for and now it was finished.

"Is it all over?" she asked.

"It's all over," said Karlsson. "You've come through."

*

Dawn came softly, grayly. The hospital became once more a place of bustling activity; they could hear the gathering noise of the streets outside. Olivia and Alexei arrived, Olivia haggard and Alexei gazing at everything with his dark eyes. They left Yvette and Karlsson, went down the stairs together and out through the revolving doors into the new day.

"I think," said Jack, blinking in the pale light, "that it's time for a very large breakfast. There must be places near here that open early. I'm starving."

"Then a fry-up for all," said Josef, brightening. "Many eggs." He put an arm round Chloë. "You good?"

"I think so. I feel a bit dazed. Breakfast would be nice."

"Frieda?" Reuben looked questioningly at her.

Frieda shook her head. "Not me. I need to walk."

"Can't you have breakfast first? Or coffee at least?"

"I need to walk," she repeated.

"OK. Call us if you want to join us later."

"Of course."

But they knew that she wouldn't.

Frieda watched them as they walked away from her: Jack in his loudly striped pajamas, his hair wild, Olivia in a brave red dress, Reuben in his summer suit with his bald skull gleaming, Chloë with her stout boots and cropped hair, and Josef bulky beside her with his arm around her shoulders, his other hand in Alexei's, his son tiny beside him.

When they were out of sight, she turned and walked in the opposite direction, and only then did she let all the thoughts and all the feelings that she had been holding at bay close in on her.

She walked fast, turning off the main road and down the smaller streets where the day for most people was just beginning. Behind her lay the urban wastelands of Silvertown, the Thames Barrier and the crumbling warehouses, the little house in a deserted cul-de-sac where Chloë and then Yvette had been held. To her left were the gleaming skyscrapers, all the corporate headquarters of global enterprises where men and women in suits were already sitting behind computer screens. She walked on, past shops whose metal shutters were being lifted, past enclaves of terraced houses that had survived the Blitz and modern apartment blocks, large empty churches and small parks. A road-sweeper came toward her, pushing his trolley hung about with bags; she saw that he had attached photographs of his family to the handle.

Her friends had survived, although at a cost: Reuben had been savagely beaten, Jack had been attacked and his hand broken, Chloë had been abducted, drugged and photographed, Yvette had been within minutes of death. Other people hadn't survived. Morgan Rossiter hadn't; Bruce Stringer; Daniel Blackstock himself. So many people had died because of Dean, and because of her. She saw all their faces in her dreams; they were her ghosts and they would always haunt her.

She halted. There was a bike attached to the railings, painted white and garlanded with dead flowers and wreaths: it was one of the ghost bikes marking the death of its owner.

Josef had ordered the full English breakfast: fried eggs, two rashers of streaky bacon, a large pink sausage, fried bread, fried tomatoes and mushrooms. He squirted tomato ketchup onto his plate and added a dollop of mustard, then stirred three sugars into his coffee.

"Are you really going to eat that?" asked Chloë, cradling a mug of herbal tea.

Josef looked puzzled. He speared a mushroom and a chunk of sausage on his fork, dipped it in egg yolk and put it into his mouth. "Is good," he said. "Food comforts."

"A Bloody Mary would comfort," said Olivia, "but I don't think they do that here."

They had all gathered. Karlsson had left Yvette for an hour or so and now sat eating a Danish pastry and drinking coffee between Reuben and a puffy-faced Olivia. Alexei sat close to his father, staring around him with brown, anxious eyes.

They were like survivors after a terrible accident, thought Karlsson, glancing around the table. They didn't need to talk, but occasionally they'd touch each other on the shoulder or hand, say a few words, smile. Chloë spread marmalade on Jack's toast for him. Josef munched his way through the pile of food in front of him, occasionally wiping his hand across his mouth.

But Frieda wasn't here. Frieda, who was the center of this unlikely group of friends, yet always stood outside it.

62

Her feet had taken her at last to Waterloo Bridge. She stopped in the middle and looked down the river, the city reflected in its brown waters, the lights of the building breaking up in the eddies and swirls.

She had stood here long ago with Sandy and he had asked her if she would ever live somewhere else: Manhattan, Berlin. She'd told him that you can only have one city, and London was hers. But Sandy's body had been found near here, pulled by the current. She thought of him, how he had loved her and how she had left him; how he had died. She thought of poor mad Hannah Docherty in her hospital for the criminally insane. Of the stubborn, obsessive Jim Fearby, who had never given up in his pursuit of the truth and who had been murdered because of it. And there were others, a family of ghosts. So many people she had not been able to save.

She stood there for a long time, looking down at the great river and thinking with such fierce concentration that she didn't notice how the crowds of people walking over the bridge were thickening, the sun rising higher in the late-summer sky.

We are leaves on a tree . . . . Autumn is coming.

In spite of the warmth, she shivered. Autumn was coming. Darkness was coming. The end was coming.

*

At last she turned and walked to the Embankment. Not far from here, her house was waiting for her. In her mind, she went into the cobbled mews, pushed at the blue door and entered. She stood for a moment in the hall, smelling the familiar odor of beeswax polish and books. Then into the living room where a chess table was laid out for a game, a tortoiseshell cat curled in the armchair, and where in the winter the fire always burned. To the kitchen, with its yellow roses on the table and a pot of basil on the windowsill. Upstairs, past her bedroom and the bathroom with its great bath that Josef had installed for her, up the next narrow flight, into her garret study. In her mind, she saw the sketchbook opened at a page, the soft-leaded pencils in a mug, the skylight from which she could see the city laid out around her.

Her city. Her home.

But she walked in another direction, through the narrow streets of Soho, and knocked at the familiar door.

Levin took off his glasses and polished them on his yellow tie. He blinked at her and smiled the smile that never quite reached his eyes.

"I heard the news," he said. "Well done."

She fixed her dark eyes on him. "I want you to do something for me."

"What?"

"Make me disappear."

It started with *Monday*.
But it doesn't end with *Sunday*.

Read **SUNDAY SILENCE**, the new novel in the series that Louise Penny calls "fabulous, unsettling, and riveting"—and brace yourself for the breathtaking series finale in summer 2018.

Lover of London, gifted psychologist, frequent police consultant—Frieda Klein is many things. And now she's a person of interest in a murder case. A body has been discovered in the most unlikely and horrifying of places: beneath the floorboards of Frieda's house.

The corpse is only months old, but the chief suspect appears to have died more than seven years ago. Except as Frieda knows all too well, he's alive and well and living in secret. And it seems he's inspired a copycat . . .

As the days pass and the body count rises, Frieda finds herself caught in a fatal tug-of-war between two killers: one who won't let her go, and another who can't let her live.

Crackling with suspense and packed with emotion, *SUNDAY SILENCE* is a psychological thriller perfect for fans of Elizabeth George and Paula Hawkins.

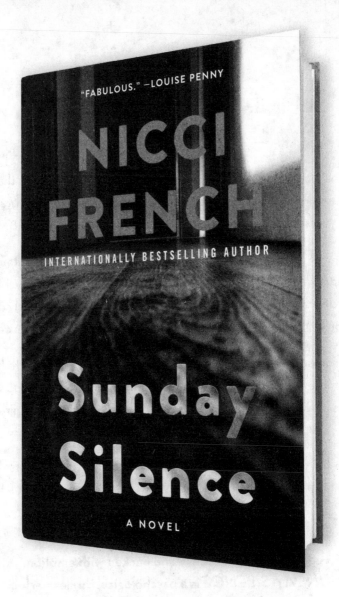

"FABULOUS." —LOUISE PENNY

NICCI FRENCH

INTERNATIONALLY BESTSELLING AUTHOR

Sunday Silence

A NOVEL

ON SALE JANUARY 9, 2018